"A true page-turner, a novel that offers a million-mile-a-minute action and suspense. Definitely, a must have with constant thrills and chills."

—HEATHER GRAHAM,
#1 *New York Times* Bestselling Author

Fran screamed.

She thought of her son. She thought of his teenage years, just around the corner, which he'd have to face without any parents if she died.

Fran couldn't let that happen.

Reaching behind her, she felt along the shelves, her hands clasping around a five-pound can of tomato paste. The flashlight came on again, less than five feet away from her. Fran threw the can as hard as she could. She didn't wait to find out if she'd hit the killer. She was already running away from him, climbing on the desk, seeking out the window to the alley.

Her fingers met cool glass. She found the latch, tried to turn it.

Painted over. Wouldn't budge.

Frantic, she reached around, found the phone, and cracked it hard against the window.

Glass shattered. The window was small, and shards jutted from the pane, but Fran forced her upper body into the hole. Her hair snagged, but she pushed forward as glass cut her palms and elbows. Then her hands touched the brick on the outside of the building, and she was dragging her hips out, thinking that she'd actually made it, and her fear transformed into a crazy, almost hysterical sense of relief.

That's when the killer grabbed her ankle.

—from *AFRAID*

Please turn to the back of this book for a preview of Jack Kilborn's next terrifying novel, *Trapped*.

AFRAID

JACK KILBORN

GRAND CENTRAL
PUBLISHING

NEW YORK   BOSTON

Copyright © 2009 by Jack Kilborn
Excerpt from *Trapped* copyright © 2010 by Jack Kilborn
All rights reserved. Except as permitted under the U.S. Copyright Act of 1976, no part of this publication may be reproduced, distributed, or transmitted in any form or by any means, or stored in a database or retrieval system, without the prior written permission of the publisher.

Cover art and design by Dale Fiorello
Book design by Giorgetta Bell McRee

Grand Central Publishing
Hachette Book Group
237 Park Avenue
New York, NY 10017
Visit our Web site at www.HachetteBookGroup.com

Grand Central Publishing is a division of Hachette Book Group, Inc. The Grand Central Publishing name and logo is a trademark of Hachette Book Group, Inc.

Printed in the United States of America

First printing: April 2009

10 9 8 7 6 5 4 3 2 1

This book is dedicated to four very smart publishing folks.

Miriam Goderich, for making me do it.
Jane Dystel, for never giving up on it.
Jaime Levine and Vicki Mellor, for seeing its potential.

For their help, support, and suggestions, thanks to fellow writers Raymond Benson, Blake Crouch, Barry Eisler, Henry Perez, Marcus Sakey, James Rollins, and especially JA Konrath—without whom this book couldn't have been written.

For inventing the horrific thriller genre, thanks to Stephen King, Dean Koontz, and David Morrell.

Special thanks to my wife, Maria Kilborn, for her years of encouragement and enthusiasm.

Courage is resistance to fear, mastery of fear—
not absence of fear.
—MARK TWAIN

There is no decent place to stand in a massacre.
—LEONARD COHEN

AFRAID

The hunter's moon, a shade of orange so dark it appeared to be filled with blood, hung fat and low over the mirror surface of Big Lake McDonald. Sal Morton took in a lungful of crisp Wisconsin air, shifted on his seat cushion, and cast his Lucky 13 lure over the stern. The night of fishing had been uneventful; a few small bass earlier in the evening, half a dozen northern pike—none bigger than a pickle—and then, nothing. The zip of his baitcaster unspooling and the plop of the bait hitting the water were the only sounds he'd heard for the last hour.

Until the helicopter exploded.

It was already over the water before Sal noticed it. Black, without any lights, silhouetted by the moon. And quiet. Twenty years ago Sal had taken his wife, Maggie, on a helicopter ride at the Dells, both of them forced to ride with their hands clamped over their ears to muffle the sound. This one made a fraction of that noise. It hummed, like a refrigerator.

The chopper came over the lake on the east side, low enough that its downdraft produced large eddies and waves. So close to the water Sal wondered if its wake might overturn his twelve-foot aluminum boat. He ducked as it passed over him, knocking off his Packers baseball cap, scattering lures, lifting several empty Schmidt beer cans and tossing them overboard.

Sal dropped his pole next to his feet and gripped the sides of the boat, moving his body against the pitch and yaw. When capsizing ceased to be a fear, Sal squinted at the helicopter for a tag, a marking, some sort of ID, but it lacked both writing and numbers. It might as well have been a black ghost.

Three heartbeats later the helicopter had crossed the thousand-yard expanse of lake and dipped down over the tree line on the opposite shore. What was a helicopter doing in Safe Haven? Especially at night? Why was it flying so low? And why did it appear to have landed near his house?

Then came the explosion.

He felt it a moment after he saw it. A vibration in his feet, as if someone had hit the bow with a bat. Then a soft warm breeze on his face, carrying mingling scents of burning wood and gasoline. The cloud of flames and smoke went up at least fifty feet.

After watching for a moment, Sal retrieved his pole and reeled in his lure, then pulled the starter cord on his 7.5 horsepower Evinrude. The motor didn't turn over. The second and third yank yielded similar results. Sal swore and began to play with the choke, wondering if Maggie was scared by the crash, hoping she was all right.

Maggie Morton awoke to what she thought was thunder. Storms in upper Wisconsin could be as mean as anywhere on earth, and in the twenty-six years they'd owned this house she and Sal had to replace several cracked windows and half the roof due to weather damage.

She opened her eyes, listened for the dual accompaniment of wind and rain. Strangely, she heard neither.

Maggie squinted at the red blur next to the bed, groped

for her glasses, pushed them on her face. The blur focused and became the time: 10:46.

"Sal?" she called. She repeated it, louder, in case he was downstairs.

No answer. Sal usually fished until midnight, so his absence didn't alarm her. She considered flipping on the light, but investigating the noise that woke her held much less appeal than the soft down pillow and the warm flannel sheets tucked under her chin. Maggie removed her glasses, returned them to the nightstand, and went back to sleep.

The sound of the front door opening roused her some-time later.

"Sal?"

She listened to the footfalls below her, the wooden floors creaking. First in the hallway, and then into the kitchen.

"Sal!" Louder this time. After thirty-five years of mar-riage, her husband's ears were just two of many body parts that seemed to be petering out on him. Maggie had talked to him about getting a hearing aid, but whenever she brought up the topic he smiled broadly and pretended not to hear her, and they both wound up giggling. Funny when they were in the same room. Not funny when they were on different floors and Maggie needed his attention.

"Sal!"

No answer.

Maggie considered banging on the floor and wondered what the point would be. She knew the man downstairs was Sal. Who else could it be?

Right?

Their lake house was the last one on Gold Star Road, and their nearest neighbors, the Kinsels, resided over half a mile down the shore and had left for the season. The solitude was one of the reasons the Mortons bought this property. Unless she went to town to shop, Maggie would often go days without seeing another human being, not counting her husband. The thought of someone else being in their home was ridiculous.

Reassured by that thought, Maggie closed her eyes.

She opened them a moment later, when the sound of the microwave carried up the stairs. Then came the muffled machine-gun report of popcorn popping. Sal shouldn't be eating at this hour. The doctor had warned him about that, and how it aggravated his acid reflux disease, which in turn aggravated Maggie with his constant tossing and turning all night.

She sighed, annoyed, and sat up in bed.

"Sal! The doctor said no late-night snacks!"

No answer. Maggie wondered if Sal indeed had a hearing problem, or if he simply used that as an excuse for not listening to her. This time she did swing a foot off the bed and stomp on the floor, three times, with her heel.

She waited for his response.

Got none.

Maggie did it again and followed it up with yelling, "Sal!" as loud as she could.

Ten seconds passed.

Ten more.

Then she heard the downstairs toilet flush.

Anger coursed through Maggie. Her husband had obviously heard her and was ignoring her. That wasn't like Sal at all.

Then, almost like a blush, a wave of doubt overtook her. What if the person downstairs wasn't Sal?

It has to be, she told herself. She hadn't heard any boats coming up to the dock or cars pulling onto their property. Besides, Maggie was a city girl, born and raised in Chicago. Twenty-some years in the Northwoods hadn't broken her of the habit of locking doors before going to sleep.

The anger returned. Sal was deliberately ignoring her. When he came upstairs, she was going to give him a lecture to end all lectures. Or perhaps she'd ignore *him* for a while. Turnabout was fair play.

Comforted by the thought, she closed her eyes. The familiar sound of Sal's outboard motor drifted in through the window, getting closer. That Evinrude was older than Sal was. Why he didn't buy a newer, faster motor was beyond her understanding. One of the reasons she hated going out on the lake with him was because it stalled all the time and—

Maggie jackknifed to a sitting position, panic spiking through her body. *If Sal is still out on the boat, then who is in the house?*

She fumbled for her glasses, then picked up the phone next to her clock. No dial tone. She pressed buttons, but the phone just wouldn't work.

Maggie's breath became shallow, almost a pant. Sal's boat drew closer, but he was still several minutes away from docking. And even when he got home, what then? Sal was an old man. What could he do against an intruder?

She held her breath, trying to listen to noises from downstairs. Maggie did hear something, but the sound wasn't coming from the lower level. It was coming from the hallway right outside her bedroom.

The sound of someone chewing popcorn.

Maggie wondered what she should do. Say something? Maybe this was all some sort of mistake, some confused tourist who had walked into the wrong house. Or perhaps this was a robber, looking for money or drugs. Give him what he wanted, and he'd leave. No need for anyone to get hurt.

"Who's there?"

More munching. Closer. He was practically in the room. She could smell the popcorn now, the butter and salt, and the odor made her stomach do flip-flops.

"My . . . medication is in the bathroom cabinet. And my purse is on the chair by the door. Take it."

The ruffling of a paper bag, and more chewing. Open-mouthed chewing. Loud, like someone smacking gum. Why wouldn't he say anything?

"What do you want?"

No answer.

Maggie was shivering now. The tourist scenario was gone from her head, the robber scenario fading fast. A new scenario entered Maggie's mind. The scenario of campfire stories and horror movies. The boogeyman, hiding under the bed. The escaped lunatic, searching for someone to hurt, to kill.

Maggie needed to get out of there, to get away. She could run to the car, or meet Sal on the dock and get into his boat, or even hide out in the woods. She could hurry to the guest bedroom, lock the door, open up the window, climb down—

Chewing, right next to the bed. Maggie gasped, pulling the flannel sheets to her chest. She squinted into the darkness, could barely make out the dark figure of a man standing a few feet away.

The bag rustled. Something touched Maggie's face and she gasped. A tiny pat on her cheek. It happened again, on her forehead, making her flinch. Again, and she swatted out with her hand, finding the object on the pillow.

Popcorn. He was throwing popcorn at her.

Maggie's voice came out in a whisper. "What . . . what are you going to do?"

The springs creaked as he sat on the edge of the bed.

"Everything," he said.

General Alton Tope had barely poured a finger of twenty-five-year-old Glenfarcas into his crystal rocks glass when his pager went off. He unclipped the device from his belt and squinted at the display. The number *6735* appeared. Following procedure, he mentally added the four digits of today's date, coming up with *6762* and frowning at the unfamiliar code. What the hell was a 6762?

General Tope headed for his bedroom, the scotch forgotten. He made sure the blinds were drawn, sat down at his desktop, and punched in his password. A military virus detection program automatically ran, deemed his equipment secure, and allowed him to log into USAVOIP—the U.S. Army Voice Over Internet Protocol. He snugged on the headphones, noted the attached microphone smelled faintly of cigarette smoke, and automatically reached for the pack of Winstons next to the monitor. He punched in another password and listened to the phone ring through the foam speakers hugging his ears.

"Good evening, General," came the same soothing voice that always answered. "Please speak the alert code."

General Tope sometimes imagined a buxom young

blonde owned the voice. But the likely culprit was probably computer-generated, programmed by some overweight civilian geek with posters of Wonder Woman in his bedroom.

"Six-seven-six-two," he said, shaking out a cigarette and hanging it in the corner of his mouth. The lighter was in the same place he always left it, in a paper-clip container next to the mouse. A plastic disposable. He'd had the same one for over three years; Tope smoked only during these encrypted calls, and they didn't come often.

"We have a Fallen Angel, General," the voice said. "Highest Priority."

General Tope drew deeply, filling his lungs with heat. When he answered, he tried not to exhale.

"What type of unit?"

As the computer on the other end of the conversation processed his question, Tope closed his eyes, waiting the twelve seconds for the nicotine in his lungs to hit his bloodstream and activate the pleasure receptors in his brain. Four seconds prior to that happening, the reply came.

"Red-ops."

General Tope coughed so hard that spittle flecked his monitor.

"Repeat."

"Red-ops."

General Tope disconnected from USAVOIP, sucked in more smoke, and clicked on the icon to connect him to the White House.

• • •

Big Lake and Little Lake McDonald formed a horseshoe around the small town of Safe Haven—a sixty-thousand-acre horseshoe that effectively acted like a peninsula, cutting off the town from the rest of northern Wisconsin. Safe Haven had a single road coming in and out. For years there had been talks of widening the road and adding some attractions. The lucrative tourist trade enjoyed by neighboring towns never reached Safe Haven, partly because it was so secluded, but mostly because the 907 full-time residents preferred it that way. At town meetings, the value of the U.S. dollar was always outvoted by the value of privacy, so the road stayed narrow and the town stayed isolated, even at the cost of economic depression.

Sal was one of those residents, and the seclusion, along with the decent fishing, was the main reason he and Maggie bought property here. They enjoyed the solitude. No neighbors to exchange fake pleasantries with. No strangers to worry about. No excitement, no crime, and no surprises. Sal had spent the first half of his life hustling in the big city. Retirement in isolation was his reward to himself.

It was October, and the snowbirds had all gone back to California or Florida or wherever they lived during the cold months, which left only a handful of people still on this part of the lake.

When the screaming began, Sal knew of only one person within shouting distance.

He adjusted the touchy throttle on the Evinrude and squinted toward home, still several hundred yards away.

Another scream. A terrible scream. The scream of someone in horrible, agonizing pain.

Sound did strange things over water. It echoed, amplified, reverberated, and made it damn near impossible to pinpoint its location. But when Sal heard that second scream he knew whose it was and where it was coming from.

Maggie.

The realization made his stomach roll. He pushed the engine as hard as it would go, beelining toward home.

What could make Maggie scream like that? Had she fallen, broken something? Burned herself? Appendicitis? A toothache?

Or was it something to do with that helicopter?

As the screaming continued, Sal felt his stomach go from sour to ulcerous. He had to get home. Had to make sure she was safe. Had to—

The motor chugged twice, then died.

"Goddammit! Goddamn hunk of junk!"

Sal lifted the large red tank by the handle and found it still half full. He reached for the fuel hose, squeezed the bulb, discovered it firm. The motor was getting gas. He pulled the starter cord four times, and each time it failed to turn the engine over.

Then Maggie's screams changed. They went from incoherent and bestial to forming words.

"STOP STOP STOP GOD STOP STOP!"

Sal touched his chest. The pain in his gut had shot up into his heart. Who was Maggie yelling at? What was happening to her? He stuck the oars in the locks, turned around on his seat, and began to row.

"NO NO NO NO STOP NO!"

Sal had to get home. He hadn't rowed in years, maybe decades. When the Evinrude refused to work, Sal would pop the cover and futz around until it started again. Sometimes it took an hour. Sometimes he had to flag down another boat and get a tow back to his dock. But rowing—never. That was for young men or those without patience. But he had to get to Maggie and had to get to her *now*.

"PLEASE PLEASE GOD PLEASE GOD!"

Sal's chest and arms screamed at him. His lungs were two burning bags, unable to get enough air. His back and his knees pleaded with him to stop, to rest. But Sal kept rowing. He glanced painfully over his shoulder, saw he was less than fifty yards away.

"KILL ME! KILL ME! KILL ME!"

Sweet Jesus, Maggie, what is happening? Sal's arms shook, and he could barely lift the oars out of the water, but he kept the rhythm, kept the pace.

Stroke.

Stroke.

Stroke.

Stroke.

Each stroke closer to home, closer to the woman he loved.

I'm coming, honey. I'm coming.

Sal hadn't thought anything could be more terrifying than his wife's screams. But he was wrong. It was much more terrifying when the screams stopped.

Sal put his entire body into one final stroke, and momentum took him to his pier. He fumbled with the line, hooked it to a cleat on the dock, and then pulled himself out of the boat.

"Maggie!" His shout came out more like a wheeze.

On wobbly knees, Sal shuffled up to shore, toward his house. The door was open wide. Maggie would never leave it like that. Someone was in their house. Someone doing something terrible to his wife. He looked around for a weapon. On the porch, next to the tables, he saw the two-by-four. He used it to club fish before he filleted them. Sal picked it up, reassured by its weight. Then he went into the house.

The living room and kitchen were empty. He smelled burned popcorn, and something else. Something he'd smelled before, but never so strongly.

Blood.

"Maggie! Where are you!"

No answer. He went up the stairs as quickly as his old legs could carry him, up to the bedroom.

Something was sprawled out on the bed.

". . . kill . . . me . . ." it said.

Sal couldn't understand what he was seeing. It didn't look human. When he realized what had been done, that the thing on the bed was what remained of his wife, the board fell from his hand and hit the floor with a dull thud. He was barely aware when someone came up behind him and pressed a blade to his throat.

"You must be Sal," the man whispered. "We need to talk."

Ashburn County Sheriff Arnold "Ace" Streng had just settled down in his easy chair for a cup of microwave chili and a marathon of *MythBusters* on the Discov-

ery Channel when his cell phone rang. He set the chili on
the TV table next to his chair and squinted through his
reading glasses at the number. His phone blinked FIRE-
HOUSE 4.

Safe Haven.

Streng sighed. Safe Haven required a forty-minute
drive, and it probably wouldn't be anything more than a
cat in a tree or some campers annoying the residents with
their fireworks. He hit the *accept* button.

"This is Streng."

The line disconnected. Streng brought the phone closer,
saw he had two black bars indicating reception. It flickered
to one bar, then back to two. Good enough. The fault was
probably on the other end. Why anyone in this county vol-
untarily used cell phones was beyond Streng's comprehen-
sion. A typical three-minute conversation usually involved
being dropped eight or nine times. Streng often joked that
instead of cells he was going to give his deputies tin cans
tied together with string.

The phone rang again. Streng craned his neck so the
phone was a precious two inches higher up, that much
closer to the satellite signal.

"This is Streng."

"Sheriff, it's Josh VanCamp from the Safe Haven fire
station. We have, um, a situation here."

Josh was a good kid, tall and strong like his late father.
Kid was probably a misnomer—Josh had to be over thirty.
But Streng was nearing seventy, and that meant he consid-
ered almost everyone a kid.

"Is this an emergency, Josh? I've got my old carcass
parked for the evening."

"It is, Sheriff. There's been a . . . helicopter crash."

Streng didn't know of anyone in the county who owned a helicopter. He looked longingly at his chili. The cheddar cheese he'd crumbled on top had melted perfectly.

"A helicopter? You're sure?"

"I'm standing at the wreckage site. And there's been some . . . *fatalities*."

Streng sat forward in his chair. "People are dead?"

"Two."

"Did you call for an ambulance?"

"Uh, no. They're dead, that's for sure."

"Where are you at, Josh?"

"Off the big lake, on Gold Star Road, two and a half miles down. I brought the tanker. Fire's under control. We'll keep the lights on so you can find it."

"Gold Star, you said?"

Streng hadn't been down Gold Star in a while. The last time was to visit his cousin Sal Morton. They'd caught some walleye, tilted a few back, and promised to do it again real soon. That had been two months ago. Streng had planned to call him, see how things were going, maybe set up a date to get on the lake once more before it got too cold. They'd been close friends since childhood, and it was wrong they didn't try harder to stay in touch.

"Yes, Sheriff. Should I call the staties?"

Streng considered it. The state police were the ones who dealt with highway accidents, but Gold Star was a private road. They wouldn't want jurisdiction any more than he did.

"No, this is ours. I'll be there in half an hour. Anyone with you?"

"Erwin."

"Tell him not to touch anything. Same goes for you."

Streng hung up, then pulled himself out of the recliner. He dipped his spoon into the chili, blew on it, and took a single bite. Delicious. Then he put the cup into the fridge, strapped on his sidearm, and went out to his Jeep Wrangler, reminding himself that he only had three more weeks until retirement. Then it would be someone else's job to take care of these late-night calls, and he'd be able to enjoy a little chili in peace.

Erwin Luggs made up for his deficiencies in the brainpower department by being helpful, dependable, and an all-around nice guy. He didn't have the strong jaw and athletic build of his buddy Josh, but his oversized frame and an abundance of hair accentuated his friendly demeanor. The ladies thought of him as a big, cuddly teddy bear. One particular lady, Jessie Lee Sloan, liked him so much that she had agreed to be his wife, and their wedding was set for next month.

The wedding troubled Erwin, because it was costing a lot more than he originally thought. He had the part-time-fireman gig and taught gym at the junior high nine months out of the year, but Jessie Lee had just added a string quartet to the growing list of wedding expenses. Even without totaling up the final numbers, Erwin knew he'd need at least two more jobs to cover all the bills.

But all thoughts of money, and the wedding, and Jessie Lee, vanished as he stared into the cockpit of that chopper.

"Don't look at it," Josh told him.

"I can't help it. Never saw nothing like that before. You?"

Josh was staring past the wreck, into the dark of the forest surrounding them. He shook his head and spat.

Erwin asked, "Which head belongs to which, you think?"

"Coroner will figure it out."

"Must have been the helicopter blades, right?"

Josh didn't answer. Erwin stepped away from the wreck, but his eyes didn't leave it. Their fire truck—a three-thousand-gallon tanker parked a few yards away on the sand road—had its emergency lights on, teasing the crash site with alternating flashes of red and blue. Erwin and Josh each held flashlights, but even with those and a full moon they couldn't see everything at once—the trees were too thick.

When they arrived, the fire had mostly gone out by itself. A few of the nearby pines had been scorched, but the rain from two days ago prevented anything major from starting. Debris littered an area of about twenty yards in every direction, though it was hard to see because their flashlights weren't powerful enough. The smoking shards of metal were out of place in the woods, making it look like an eerie alien planet. Erwin didn't like it.

He backed up until he could no longer see the corpses in detail. A twig snapped, to his right. Erwin startled, focusing his light into the woods next to him, wondering what deer or coon was curious enough to come and see the wreckage. As his beam played across the trees he saw a brief glint of two eyes, which quickly vanished.

Erwin looked over at Josh. His partner had approached the cockpit and was peering in reverently. Erwin glanced back to the woods. The eyes couldn't have belonged to a deer, because these were side by side. A bear? Maybe, if the bear was standing up. But Erwin knew bears, and the whole forest shuffled when a bear moved past. Erwin craned his neck forward, listening.

The woods were silent. Erwin had the uncomfortable feeling that the eyes were still there, watching him.

"Hello? Someone there?"

He felt foolish saying it, and even more foolish when no one answered. Erwin moved the flashlight to and fro, trying to penetrate the trees, but saw nothing. Could someone have survived the wreck? Someone hurt and unable to answer? He glanced again at Josh, saw that he was busy examining the inside of the chopper, and decided to investigate on his own.

The woods became very dark, very fast. The canopy screened out the full moon, and the thin beam of his flashlight worked like a theater spot, illuminating only a small circle and nothing else. Erwin moved slowly, respectful of his environment. In his teenage years he'd disturbed a badger on a late-night hike through the forest, and the bite he'd taken on the knee still ached when it rained. It had been the scariest moment in Erwin's life, and he'd been unable to fight back, his muscles locked with fear.

Since then, Erwin avoided confrontation of any sort. He stopped playing sports. He walked away from fights. Thinking of himself as a coward was much easier to deal with than the horror of being attacked.

Movement, to the left. Erwin got the flashlight there in time to see something black dart behind a large oak. Too tall for a bear. A person?

He opened his mouth to say something but didn't make

a sound. If it was a person hiding behind the tree, why were they hiding?

Erwin took a step closer, feeling his arms go goosepimply and adrenaline tingle in his bowels.

Then a deer came crashing out of the woods.

Erwin reached out his hands to ward off the impact, dropping his flashlight, bracing his legs. The blow came weaker than he'd anticipated. Weaker, and warmer. The deer's head connected with Erwin's chest but didn't push back. It just sort of stopped—as if he'd been tossed a football—and then came a spray of heat that stung Erwin's eyes.

He took two steps backward, the deer collapsing at his feet, kicking out its legs like it was still running. Then it jerked twice and became still.

Erwin rubbed his eyes, realizing the heat was liquid, and the liquid was blood. He found his flashlight in a bush a few feet away and it was also soaked in blood, the smears on the lens making it cast red light. Hand shaking, he pointed it at the deer and saw a three-foot gash in the animal's side, so deep it cut through the ribs.

"Josh!" he yelled, though it came out as more of a croak.

Then he heard something else moving in the woods.

Sal Morton hadn't cried in more than thirty years, but he was crying now. The shapeless, bleeding thing that his wife had become continued to twitch and gasp on the bed beside him, and rather than allow him to end her agony, the intruder forced Sal to answer a series of inane questions.

"I don't know."

"When was it?" The man's foreign accent was heavy, his voice breathy and almost feminine.

"A long time ago. Years."

"Where?"

Sal eyed his wife, watched her undulate. How could she even still be conscious?

"Please. Just kill her. Kill us both."

"Where were you?"

"In town. At the hardware store. Jesus, please, can't you let her die?"

The man did something with his knife, and the thing that was Maggie mewled like a sick kitten.

Sal reached for her, touched her, and this prompted more screams. He pulled back his hands and clenched his fists, shaking so badly he almost fell off the edge of the bed.

The man appeared amused.

"Will killing her help you focus?"

"Yes. Dear God, yes."

"Then go ahead."

The man offered Sal a pillow. Sal stared at it and wondered for the hundredth time if this was really happening, if this was real. Only a few minutes ago he was fishing, pondering the activities for the upcoming holiday weekend. Perhaps they would eat out, then see a scary movie to celebrate Halloween. But life changed when he walked into that bedroom. The whole world changed. He wasn't ever going to a movie with Maggie again. Instead, he was going to murder her. Could he do it? Did he have the strength?

Sal closed his eyes, tried to picture Maggie the first

time he saw her. A blind date. Sal could no longer remember who had set it up, but he remembered every second of their evening together. Maggie had worn a pink dress, her hair all styled up, and she giggled when she met him, obviously as pleased with his appearance as he'd been with hers. They'd gone bowling and had a wonderful time, even though neither of them possessed any skill or even particularly liked the game. Every year since then, on their anniversary, they'd go bowling. November fifteenth. Just a few weeks away.

"I can't." Sal dropped the pillow.

"You love her."

"Yes."

"She's suffering. See?"

The man did something unspeakable to Maggie, and he kept doing it. Sal tried to shove him away, but the intruder had muscles like brick. Maggie made a sound that didn't sound human, a gurgling moan of pure agony.

"Stop it! Please stop it!"

The man didn't stop. He smiled.

"Only you can stop it, Sal."

Crying out, Sal took the pillow and pressed it hard against what was left of Maggie's mouth, putting his weight on it, trying to drown out her screams, her pain, her life.

She twitched under him, an oddly intimate sensation that reminded Sal of lovemaking. He sobbed and sobbed, and the twitching went on and on, and Sal couldn't tell if it was her or him anymore, but he wasn't going to stop, wasn't going to check to see, had to make sure that she was safe, make absolutely sure that she didn't hurt anymore.

"You killed her," the man said. "You can get off her corpse now."

Sal didn't move. He felt a piercing grip on his shoulder and was tugged backward, the bloody pillow still held tight in his old hands.

Maggie's ruined face was still, her remaining eye staring dully at Sal.

Then her chest shuddered and she gasped, sucking in air.

"Well," the intruder said. "She's a tough one."

Sal squeezed his eyes closed, clamped his hands tight over his ears. He couldn't take anymore. This wasn't supposed to be happening. This isn't how their lives together were supposed to end. He'd always pictured a quiet, peaceful death for them. Going to sleep and never waking up. Slipping in the shower and a quick bump on the head. Dying in a hospital bed, the morphine drowning out whatever killer lurked in their elderly bodies. Not like this. Not awful like this.

"Here." The man handed Sal his knife. "Put it in her heart."

Sal held the knife like he'd never seen one before. Maggie's chest rose and fell, accompanied by a wet, rattling sound. He reached out tentatively, gently laying his fingers on her breastbone.

"Right there. Press down hard, so you get through the ribcage."

Sal focused on the spot, trying to block out the reality of the act. This wasn't his wife. He wasn't killing her. This was a normal, routine task, like filleting a fish. A job that needed to get done. Unpleasant, but necessary.

Sal pushed down on the knife, forcing it in to the hilt, making himself stone for her sake. He held it until

Maggie's heart ceased to beat, until the vibrations in the knife's handle stopped.

"That did the trick." The intruder clapped him on the shoulder. "Congratulations, killer."

The moment descended on Sal, pierced him. He cried out, an ineffectual curse at the universe for letting this happen, and then tried to pull the knife from his wife's chest so he could plunge it into the monster who caused this. Sal tugged, but the knife stayed put.

"This knife is meant for more delicate work and has no blood groove," the intruder said. "You have to twist it to break the suction."

He demonstrated. There was a sound like an infant suckling. The man freed the blade and then wiped it clean on the bedsheets.

"Now let's try to concentrate on answering my questions."

Sal's body shook, but he thrust out his chin at his tormentor.

"No. I won't do it."

Darkness seemed to spill out of the intruder's eyes.

"Yes, you will. You think you know pain, old man? You know nothing of pain. You'll answer every question I have and beg me to ask more of them."

"No," Sal said, folding his frail arms, silently swearing on Maggie's head to not give this bastard the satisfaction. "You won't get anything out of me."

It took less than three minutes for the intruder to prove Sal wrong.

• • •

Fran Stauffer dumped the used coffee grounds into the garbage can beneath the cash register and wondered— not for the first time that night—why she had traded shifts with Jessie Lee.

Merv, whose name graced the marquee of the diner, had hired Jessie Lee back at the beginning of summer.

"She's a kid, needs to work to help pay for her wedding," Merv had said, winking in a way he thought was charming but Fran considered condescending. "Besides, it'll give you some time off. You've been running this place solo for seven years."

Fran could have objected, and Merv probably would have listened. But badly as Fran needed the money—and everyone in Safe Haven seemed to need money these days—fewer hours at Merv's meant more time with Duncan. So Merv hired Jessie Lee, but more often than not Fran wound up working her shifts anyway.

Al, one of their regulars, had grown roots on the last counter stool. He held out an empty cup of coffee as if begging for change. Al was sixtyish, fat, and sported a walrus mustache that was waxed to little curls on either side. Nice guy, so-so tipper, a little too talky and a little too flirty.

The diner phone rang. Fran made no move to get it. Dollars to donuts it was a local, wanted to know if he could get a meal in before they closed for the night. Fran opened the top of the coffee machine, put in a cleaning tablet, and pressed the brew button. She took the practically empty carafe of leaded and gave Al another hit of caffeine. After five rings, the phone stopped.

"That was probably a customer," Al said.

Fran smiled a waitress smile. "I'm not in it for the money. I'm in it because I love filling salt shakers."

Al chuckled. "Well, you make a damn good cup of coffee." He twisted the end of his mustache. "And you're easy on the eyes, too."

Fran knew she was tired because—for the briefest instant—she imagined herself romantically involved with Al. She squinted at him, marveling at how desperate she'd become.

While Fran didn't consider herself beautiful, she had a full head of long, curly blond hair, and pale blue eyes, and a body that still fit nicely into a size six. Her late husband had told her, often, that she looked like Melanie Griffith. Fran could see the resemblance, when her makeup was on and she wore something flattering. She certainly didn't lack for male attention. At one point or another, Fran had been propositioned by every eligible bachelor in town, and by countless others during the busy tourist season. But she hadn't been on a date in months.

If she were in her twenties like Jessie Lee, she would have gone out more often. These days, romance came in the form of Lifetime on cable, books on tape borrowed from the library, and late-night baths with plenty of bubbles and a detachable oscillating shower head.

She'd given up hope on men. And though she didn't mention it in therapy, Fran knew she'd also pretty much given up hope for happiness, as well.

A car horn snapped her out of her reverie. Fran glanced out the storefront window, saw a pickup truck motor past. Then a car. Then another car. Something was going on. Perhaps some kind of sports thing. A local team had apparently won, judging by the yells accompanying the horns. Fran didn't follow sports, and she was in no mood for the diner to fill up with fans. She eyed the cat clock on the wall, its yellow eyes synchronized to its pendulum tail. Almost midnight. Merv had left an hour ago, trusting her to cook if any business walked in. None had. And none would. It was time to get home. She walked to the front door and flipped the hanging sign over to CLOSED.

Picking up a tray, Fran did a quick tour of the floor, pulling ketchup from the tables. She took the bottles back to the counter and unscrewed the caps, soaking them in some seltzer water from the soda fountain. Then she pulled a box of ketchup from under the counter and used the spigot to top off each bottle.

"This is kind of embarrassing." Al held the check in his hand and a pained smile stretched across his hairy face. "I only have eight dollars on me."

Fran sighed. Al's bill was $8.32. Some shift. She wondered if she even made enough to cover groceries; she'd planned to stop at the Circle K on her way home.

"Don't worry about it, Al. You'll get me the next—"

Fran's words caught in her throat when the lights went out. The darkness came fast and complete, as if someone had cinched a black bag over Fran's head. She immediately shoved her hands out in front of her, banging her knuckles while reaching for the counter. Her fingers gripped the edge of the counter, tight, as if there were a chance it would be pulled away from her.

Since the accident Fran didn't do well in the dark.

The silence carried weight. Along with the lights, the perpetual whir of the pie cooler had vanished, along with the white-noise buzz of the overhead fluorescent lights and the *whoosh-whoosh* of the dishwasher that Merv ran practically nonstop in the kitchen. Claustrophobia crawled up Fran's shoulders and perched there like a gargoyle, ready to bite.

Something jingled—keys—and then a sliver of light came from where Al sat. He pointed the keychain's beam in Fran's direction. Her heart pounded so hard she could hear it.

"I . . . I guess we blew a fuse," Fran managed, trying to keep the panic at bay.

"I don't think so."

Al directed the light away from Fran, toward the store-front window. The streetlights were out. So was the Schnell's Hardware sign across the street.

A car honked and buzzed past, making Fran almost wet herself.

"Traffic signal's out, too," Al said. "Might be a power line. Might be the generator."

Al's light played across the stools along the counter, casting long, creepy shadows. The darkness smothered Fran. It clogged her nose and pushed into her lungs, making it hard to breathe.

"Can . . . I borrow that?" Fran swallowed what felt like a golf ball in her throat. "I need to find candles."

The beam hit Fran in the eyes. She stood there, clutching the counter, afraid to move.

"Missy, you look scared out of your head. Afraid of the dark? Is—oh . . . I'm sorry . . . I forgot about . . ."

Fran couldn't see Al, but she could guess at the expression of sympathy his face now wore. She tried to make her voice sound stronger.

"I just need it for a minute, Al."

The silence stretched. Fran felt a scream kicking around in her belly, threatening to come up.

"You know what?" Al finally said. "I've been eating here for twenty years, never been in the kitchen. How about I go with you?"

The relief Fran felt was physical. She sighed, filled her lungs, and walked over to him in the darkness.

J osh VanCamp turned in time to see his firefighting partner and close friend, Erwin Luggs, run straight into him.

The tackle was high, off-center. Four years of high school varsity football practice instantly kicked in, muscle memory prompting Josh to roll away from the pouncing body, retaining his footing even as Erwin ate the ground.

Josh felt something warm and wet on his face, stinging his eyes, and he recognized it as blood just as he dropped his flashlight.

"Erwin, what the—"

Erwin rolled onto his back, illuminating Josh's face with the light he still retained. This brought a burst of pain as Josh's pupils constricted, and he held up his hands to shield the glare. Then, behind him, he heard the familiar sound of the fire truck starting. He glanced over his shoulder, saw the blue and red flashing lights pull away, down Gold Star Road.

Josh took two steps toward the truck, then stopped. He wasn't sure he wanted to catch whoever was driving. Closer investigation of the headless men in the cockpit proved that a broken helicopter blade couldn't have been responsible for their injuries. Josh hadn't ever seen a decapitation, but he saw that the cuts were jagged, not clean, and the high seat backs were intact above the shoulder line. A spinning blade would have cut off the seats as well as the heads.

Someone had murdered them. And Josh had no desire to meet that someone.

He went to his flashlight and shone it at Erwin, who hadn't yet gotten off the ground. Blood soaked his friend so completely he looked like a red monster. Josh ran over and knelt next to him, hands and eyes seeking out the spot that was bleeding.

"Deer." Erwin stammered. "Something killed a deer."

"You hurt? You okay?"

"I'm okay."

Josh offered a hand, helped the larger man to his feet. Then he dug out the cell phone in his front pocket. No signal. He walked ten feet left, and ten feet back, the phone before him like a talisman. Nothing.

He stared back at the helicopter, wondering what to do next. In the bay of the chopper were four empty seats and a large gurney with thick leather straps that looked like something out of a Frankenstein movie. The distance from the neck restraint to the ankle restraint had to be near seven feet, and the chest strap was long enough to encircle a rain barrel. What could have possibly been strapped there?

"We need to call the state troopers," Josh said.

Erwin was trying to find a clean patch on his shirt to wipe his face, but there were no clean patches and he only succeeded in smearing the blood around.

"What about Sheriff Streng?"

Josh knew that this was beyond Streng's capabilities.

He was a nice old guy, probably competent in his day, but whatever was happening was too big for him.

"You wait here for the sheriff, I'll head over to Sal and Maggie's place and use their phone."

"Josh . . . that deer . . . it was almost cut it in half. Whatever killed it . . ."

Josh finished the sentence in his mind: *Is out there in those woods.* He took another look at the Frankenstein gurney, set his jaw, and headed into the trees.

J ust before the electricity went out, the phones throughout Safe Haven began to ring. First one. Then five. Then twenty. Then several hundred, all within a five-minute period. Late-night phone calls usually didn't mean good news, but every resident who received this one immediately shrugged off any sleepiness and began dialing other residents, per instructions.

Land lines and cells, from old-fashioned rotary ding-a-lings to the modern rock ringtones programmed in by teenagers, echoed out through the night, through the woods, carrying across Big Lake and Little Lake McDonald, fading out and finally mingling with the crickets and owls.

An exodus soon followed, whoops and hollers and horns accompanying vehicles as they headed into town. At long last, prosperity had found its way to Safe Haven, filling the heads of every man, woman, and child with dollar signs.

The celebration would be short-lived.

• • •

Sheriff Ace Streng pulled onto Gold Star Road, the Jeep's four-wheel drive biting into the sand and gravel surface and leaving tire marks in its wake. His brights were on. So were his undercarriage beams and the hunting spots on the overhead roll bar. All of that wattage, and the light still couldn't penetrate more than two feet into the forest. These trees were ancient, thick, and they lined the sides of the road, their tops bending over and obscuring the night sky. It was like traveling down a winding, high-arched tunnel.

Streng drove by a house almost entirely hidden by foliage, tried to recall the name of the owners. His mind gave up the answer a mile after he passed. The Kinsels. Snowbirds, gone someplace that didn't have minus-thirty-degree winters and four feet of snow by January.

"Where are you hiding?" Streng asked himself, scanning ahead for the swirling red lights of Josh's fire truck. Streng could imagine a whole fleet of helicopters lost in these woods. If daylight never came, they'd never be found. The forest liked to hide things. A plane went missing ten years back—one of those experimental one-seaters flown by some rich moron who hadn't bothered filing a flight plan—and it had taken a week of continuous searching before they found the wreck, less than two hundred yards from Big Lake McDonald's east shore. By that time, a family of raccoons had already moved into the cockpit, and an egret had built its nest on the tail section. The coyotes took care of the pilot.

He reached down and rubbed his right calf, then his left

one. Shin splints. The pain sometimes acted up when he drove. Every so often he toyed with the notion of seeing a doctor about it but always dismissed that as weakness. As his late father liked to say, "It's better to have two bad legs than a single healthy one." And Dad knew that from experience.

His cell rang, and Streng peered down his nose at the number. Mayor Durlock, from Safe Haven. In a town of less than a thousand, a helicopter crash was headline news, and the mayor never missed an opportunity to speak to the press.

"Sheriff? Something wonderful has happened."

"Not for the people in the helicopter."

"Helicopter? What? Oh." Durlock sounded sleepy. Or maybe he'd been drinking. "This is about the lottery."

"Lottery?" Streng asked. But he was talking to a dead line. No signal. He tried redial, it didn't work, and he tucked the phone away and concentrated on driving.

Still no sign of Josh, and the road dead-ended in maybe a thousand feet. Streng passed Sal's property and was reaching for his cell to call the firefighter when he heard the sound.

Having grown up in the Northwoods, Streng knew animal calls. The warning hoot of owls. The howl of timber wolves. The crazy piccolo chorus of the loons. This didn't sound like anything Streng had ever heard before. It was loud and shrill, but with a gurgling quality to it. Like a woman screaming underwater.

Streng brought the Jeep to a stop and rolled down the windows, his ear facing the forest.

"OOOOHOOOOOHOOOOHOOOOOGGGGGGGG HHH . . ."

This time it sounded less animalistic, more human. But what could cause a person to make a sound like that? Was it Josh and Erwin, screwing around? And where was it even coming from?

He pulled onto the grass alongside Sal's house, put the Jeep in park, dug the flashlight out of the glove compartment, and stepped onto the scrub grass. The night was unusually quiet, as if the woods were collectively holding their breath. Streng adjusted the beam for maximum distance, unbuttoned the strap on his Kimber Compact Stainless .45, and walked in the direction of the sound.

"AAAAAAAAHHHHHHH NOOOOOOOOO . . ."

That was someone in agony, and you couldn't fake agony like that. The fire truck was still nowhere to be found. All that lay ahead was Sal's place.

Reflexively, Streng pulled his sidearm from his holster and thumbed off the safety. He'd been carrying it cocked and locked. Now it was ready to fire.

He moved at a brisk pace, minding his footing but intent on helping the screamer. Streng was old-school, military trained. He kept the flashlight at his hip in a sword grip and his gun before him at chest level. He'd been shown, years ago, a method of locking wrists so both flashlight and pistol were aiming at the same thing, a move favored by cops in the movies. What the movies didn't show you was the sympathetic limb contractions and hand confusion that occurred while under fire, where combatants would often shine their gun and try to shoot their flashlight. The new moves weren't always the best moves.

Another scream. Definitely coming from the house. Every light was off, making Sal's two-story cabin look like the silhouette of a mountain among the trees. Streng directed his beam at the front door, and from a dozen yards away he saw the pry marks on the jamb, the splinters sticking out like witch's fingers.

Streng tucked the flashlight under his armpit and touched the knob cautiously, as if it were hot. The door opened with a faint creak, and Streng again gripped the flashlight and moved in a crouch as low as his shin splints would allow. The air in the house radiated warmth, and it tingled against his cool skin. The acrid smell of burned popcorn filled his nostrils. The silence seemed total, complete. Not even the click of the furnace or the hum of the refrigerator.

"JEEEEEESUS CHRIIIIIIIIIIIIIIST!"

The scream brought Streng back in time, twenty years earlier, to a traffic accident scene. A pedestrian pinned under a trailer truck, his face pressed against the burning hot muffler. They couldn't move the semi, couldn't lift the semi, couldn't do a damn thing until the tow truck came, and as the victim's face cooked away the screaming became so intense that Streng had actually pulled his gun and considered shooting the poor bastard.

This scream conveyed the same thing; unimaginable pain.

He took the stairs two at a time, calves crying out, jaw set hard, gun steady and leading the charge. The top ended at a hallway. Streng went left, toward the scream, knowing he should announce himself as a police officer, but some instinct, some voice in his subconscious, told him it would be better to use the element of surprise.

Streng stuck his head though the bedroom door, shining his light, gripping his weapon, and he turned out to be the surprised one.

"Hello, Sheriff Streng."

The intruder's voice was high, breathy, with a foreign lisp. Streng's beam spotlighted him, standing next to the bed with a gun to Sal's head. Sal sat on the edge with his legs over the side, his chin and chest bobbing up and down as if he had an accelerated case of the hiccups. Streng glimpsed something on the mattress next to Sal, something bloody and naked and sprawled out—*Jesus, is that Maggie?*—and then Sal screamed again, the force of a foghorn, as the intruder twisted some sort of pink-handled knife into Sal's arm.

No, not a knife. The intruder was manipulating Sal's bone—either the radius or the ulna—which protruded through the split flesh.

Streng aimed his .45, centering it on the intruder's face.

"Drop your weapon!" he yelled.

The intruder offered a humorless smile, continuing to jerk the bone back and forth. Sal's entire body vibrated, his back arched in a scream that Streng felt in his fillings. It went on and on, briefly stopping for Sal to refill his lungs. Streng felt his stomach quiver and clench, the acid burning the back of his throat.

"Your hands are shaking, Sheriff. Are you sure you can hit me? I hope you don't miss, for Sal's sake."

"Drop the weapon!"

In a blur the intruder switched aim from Sal to Streng.

"You drop yours first, Sheriff. I'm sure we can talk this out, like civilized men."

Streng knew if he pulled the trigger it was likely he would die. This man was too fast, too cold. A pro. The best chance for survival was to diffuse the immediacy of the situation by retreating, calling for backup, even though his soul cried out to shoot this creature.

In an eye blink he made his choice: get help. Streng stumbled away, out the door, Sal's screams sticking to him like a shadow. His radio and cell phone were in the car. He had to get down there, call the staties, get a hostage negotiation team here.

Noise. Behind him.

Streng spun, only to see something impossibly huge coming up the stairs.

D r. Ralph Stubin scratched his dry, bald scalp, squinted at the algorithm on his computer screen, and reached for his cup of coffee. It was empty, and had been the last three times he'd picked it up. On this occasion, he actually raised it to his lips before he noticed.

"Mathison! How about some coffee?"

Alan Mathison Turing sat next to the coffee machine, his tail testing the warmth of the carafe by poking it. Mathison screeched. Stubin recognized it as capuchin monkey language for *not done*.

"If I don't have caffeine in my mug in the next ten seconds, no beer for you tonight."

Mathison screeched again, and Stubin knew he was being called the monkey equivalent of *assface*. But rather than pout, Mathison leapt over to the laboratory cabinets, grabbed a 60-cc bulb syringe, and stuck the pointy end into the still-percolating coffeepot. He extracted 30 ccs, walked on two legs over to Stubin, and injected it into the doctor's cup.

"Thank you, Mathison."

Mathison dropped the syringe and hopped up onto Stubin's shoulder, his tail curling gently around his neck. He weighed less than five pounds and sat there so often Stubin barely felt him. The doctor kept his eyes on the computer but reached up to scratch Mathison on the belly. He missed, his fingers tracing the surgery scar along Mathison's scalp.

The monkey screeched, tiny paws pushing him away. Mathison retained his sensitivity about the scar. Not the feel of it—it had healed over a year ago. But its appearance. Stubin had been to four plastic surgeons, but none were willing to work on a monkey for purely cosmetic reasons. They didn't believe a primate could be vain.

Mathison was more than vain. Mathison was a grandiose narcissist. And even though he had a stellar success rate with the females and was universally loved by all who encountered him, both human and primate, the circular scar remained an issue for him.

"You're too self-conscious," Stubin said.

Mathison climbed off the doctor's shoulder and pointed at the Lakers hat Stubin always wore when out in public to hide his baldness. Stubin had been losing hair since the sixties.

"Fair enough. I could get a hat for you, if you like."

Mathison put the baseball cap on his own head. It was so big it covered him to the chest.

"Yours would be smaller, Mathison. I'd have it custom-made. It would be the same as mine but would fit you."

Mathison used the *assface* screech again.

"It doesn't have to be the Lakers. It could be whatever you'd like."

Mathison picked an empty Budweiser can from the garbage and hooted, a sound not unlike a howling ghost. He used that hoot only for things he really liked, such as females and beer. Stubin wrote down *Bud cap for Mathison* on a dry erase board, since there wasn't a scrap of paper in the lab.

Stubin's cell phone rang.

"Can you grab that for me?"

Mathison held the can over his head and howled again. Stubin sighed, swiveled his chair over to the table, and picked up the cell.

"This is Dr. Stubin."

"USAVOIP 6735," said the computer voice in its usual soothing manner.

Unlike General Tope, Stubin immediately knew what the code meant. When he hung up the phone he whispered, "It's happening, Mathison."

Fran knew every inch of the kitchen at Merv's and probably could have found the candles with her eyes closed. But Al and his keychain flashlight provided great comfort to her as they made their way to the storage area.

"Kind of snug back here." Al pointed the tiny light down the aisle, showing the scant distance between the grill and the fryers. "I'm surprised Merv can fit."

The kitchen was laid out like a long hallway, to allow for maximum customer space in the dining area. Oven, cooler, sink, storage, and finally a tiny desk at the end. Above the desk was a filthy window that they never opened; it led to the alley and their Dumpster, along with its accompanying smells.

Besides being the owner, Merv was the cook, and he didn't put anything on the menu that he didn't personally enjoy. As a result, Merv weighed well over three hundred pounds. It was a pretty tight squeeze. The darkness made the space seem even smaller, and Fran fought to keep her breathing under control. Thinking about her breathing made it worse, and she felt her palms go clammy and her chest tighten up.

Panic attack. Since the accident Fran had been having them on a weekly basis. The symptoms—hyperventilating, increased heartbeat, sweating, shaking—were trivial on their own but contributed to an overwhelming psychological response. During an episode, Fran felt as if she were dying.

She'd tried psychotherapy, medications, relaxation techniques, but nothing helped. When the attack came, it took over no matter what she was doing. Yet another reason she didn't date. How awkward would it be during sex if she suddenly froze up and began to cry in terror?

Fran forced herself to talk, but it came out croaky. "The candles should be on one of the racks here."

She took the last six steps to the storage area at a jog, her hands reaching out for the wire shelving. Fran looked past the large cans of tomato paste, past the containers of pasta, and shifted a box of paper napkins to reach for the candles.

Then the flashlight went out.

The darkness hit her like a slap. She uttered a small

yelp, then gripped the steel support bars on the shelving unit and waited for Al to put the light back on.

Five seconds passed. Ten.

"Al?"

Fran's voice was so faint she could barely hear it herself. She cleared her throat and tried again.

"Al? Did you drop the flashlight?"

A shuffling sound, from Al's direction. Was he teasing her? If so, it wasn't funny. The whole town knew about her tragedy. Al couldn't possibly be that cruel.

The silence stretched. Fran heard scratching, like claws on the tile floor.

"Al?"

The power in her voice was surprising, considering how scared she was. But Al didn't answer.

Fran went over some scenarios. Maybe he just dropped his keys. The keychain light probably worked by keeping pressure on the button. But Fran hadn't heard the jingle of keys hitting the floor. The batteries? If they'd died, why wasn't Al answering? Had he suddenly gone deaf?

Perhaps he'd fallen. Or had a heart attack. Or a stroke. That made more sense than Al playing games. Fran probably needed to get to him, to help him. He might be dying.

Fran tried to let go of the shelf, but her hands wouldn't open. The bones in her legs turned into rubber, and she had a hard time keeping her balance.

Then the flashlight came back on.

A sound escaped Fran's mouth that was halfway between a laugh and a sob. She squinted at the light, roughly ten feet away from her, and it brought her more pure joy than she'd felt as a child on Christmas morning.

"Al, what—"

The light went off again. Fran waited for an explanation, an apology.

None came.

"Al?" she squeaked.

He didn't answer. And once again the darkness pressed down on Fran, suffocating her, making her feel trapped and alone and without any hope. Her breath came faster, shallower, and she felt the blood leaching out of her head, the edges of unconsciousness closing in.

And then the flashlight was on.

Then off.

Then on.

Off.

On.

What the hell was Al doing? The light hovered at chest level, so he hadn't fallen. But he wasn't making any attempt to come closer, wasn't speaking, wasn't doing anything but pointing the beam at her face.

Then the light began to move.

Off of her face. To the freezer. To the sink. To the dish rack. Slow, like a spotlight following an actor.

Then to the oven. Over to the fryer, lingering there.

And finally down to the floor, where Al lay on his stomach, one hand clutching the spurting slash in his neck, the other clawing at the tiles, trying to crawl through the growing puddle of his own blood.

The light went out again.

It was never a good time to have a panic attack. But in an actual situation that called for panic, or required immediate action, it was deadly. Fran had gone from hyperventilating to being unable to draw a breath. Her head pounded, and her lungs screamed, and her entire body became jelly except for her death grip on the shelving.

Fran knew about fear. She knew its power to incapacitate. She knew it affected a person physically, mentally, and emotionally and that it became so overwhelming it pushed away all thoughts other than survival. But in some cases fear didn't precipitate fight or flight. Instead it induced the deer-in-the-headlights response. True fear could be an out-of-body experience, watching what was happening to you, yet unable to do anything about it.

Fran could picture herself in the darkness. She saw the terrified expression on her face, eyes wide, mouth hanging open. She saw her knees quiver and her shoulders shake. She saw the tears welling up, tears she couldn't blink away because she was too afraid to even blink.

Then she heard a footstep on the tile floor.

Then another.

Whoever did that to Al was coming for her.

Fran gasped, managing to get some air into her lungs.

The light went on, focusing on Al. A black boot stepped on his neck, pinning his face to the floor, making the blood squirt from the wound in his throat. Then a hand in a black glove reached down to him—a hand holding a knife.

Fran couldn't close her eyes, couldn't turn away, as the knife went to work on Al.

When Al finally stopped moving, the light went off again.

The silence that followed was the loudest thing Fran had ever heard. Louder than the three hours she spent upside down in the car, her husband Charles dead in the driver's seat beside her, hanging by his seat belt, his blood dripping onto her face—*plop, plop, plop* . . .

Something hit Fran in the chest, bringing her back to the present, making her flinch. It clung to her shirt. Warm and wet, like a towel. What was it? What had he thrown at her?

She shook her shoulders, but it didn't move. Fran needed to let go of the shelf, needed to release her hands so she could knock off whatever—

The flashlight came on, pointing at her. Fran looked at her chest and saw something red and rubbery and shredded hanging there. Something wearing Al's walrus mustache.

And then the light went off.

Fran screamed. She screamed and screamed and then her paralysis broke and her hands opened up and she batted Al's face off herself, arms flailing out as if she were being attacked by a swarm of bees.

After five seconds of pure, explosive panic, Fran froze, the cry dying in her throat, her hands stretched out into the darkness surrounding her.

Another footstep.

Then a low chuckle.

Strangely, Fran no longer thought of herself or the horror of what was happening. Instead, she thought of Duncan. Her son was a miniature version of Charles, except he had Fran's pale blue eyes—so pale they looked like ice. He had just turned ten, an age when it really wasn't cool to hang out with Mom anymore. But Duncan still tolerated her attempts at playing catch and her lame efforts at video games. He even allowed her to pick the movies they saw together, occasionally sitting through something more serious than a Jim Carrey comedy.

She thought of the walks they took when he was younger, and the family vacations they'd gone on when Duncan's father was still alive, and the day he was born, after sixteen grueling hours of labor, and how holding him for the first time made her cry with unrestrained joy. She thought of his teenage years, just around the corner, which he'd have to face without any parents if she died.

Fran couldn't let that happen.

Reaching behind her, Fran felt along the shelves, her hands clasping around a five-pound can of tomato paste. She raised it over her head and waited.

The flashlight came on again, less than five feet away from her.

Fran threw the can as hard as she could. She didn't wait to find out if she'd hit the killer or see what damage she'd done. She was already running away from him, climbing on the desk, seeking the window to the alley.

Her fingers met cool glass, covered in a film of grease and dirt and cobwebs. She found the latch, tried to turn it.

Painted over. Wouldn't budge.

Frantic, she reached around on the desktop, found the phone, and cracked it hard against the window.

Glass shattered, letting in cool night air and the pungent smell of garbage. The window was small, and shards still jutted from the pane, but Fran forced her upper body into the hole. Her hair snagged, but she pushed forward, scooting her chest through the opening as glass cut at her palms and elbows. Then her hands touched the brick on the outside of the building, and she was dragging her hips out, thinking that she'd actually made it, thinking she'd actually gotten away, and her fear transformed into a crazy, almost hysterical sense of relief.

That's when the killer grabbed her ankle.

• • •

Sheriff Ace Streng fired twice at the figure coming up the stairs, the muzzle flashes illuminating something black and enormous. The bullets didn't slow it down, so Streng ran left, to the door on the other side of the hall.

A spare bedroom, unlit, with a musty odor that indicated it hadn't been used in a while. Streng found the window, hurried to it, and fumbled for the lock.

He chanced a look behind him, saw the figure filling the doorway. A sharp, unpleasant smell filled the room, like cigarettes and body odor. Streng aimed and squeezed off three more shots. The thing didn't fall. He turned his attention back to the window, jerked it open, and went face-first out onto the roof. It was steeper than he guessed, and he slipped onto his back and began to skid, the flashlight slipping from his hand and clattering down the incline, winking out when it went over the edge.

Streng spread out his arms, tried to keep from falling. His knuckles scraped against the cold, rough shingles, the skin tearing. He reflexively opened his hand, letting go of the .45, hearing it skitter to a stop above him while he kept sliding down, his momentum picking up.

The trees obscured the moon and stars, and Streng's eyes couldn't penetrate the inky night. But he knew there wasn't much roof left, and if he went over at this speed he'd break his leg. Or his neck.

The sheriff turned onto his side as he slid, and then onto his belly, arms and legs outstretched, toes fighting for purchase. He began to slow down, and then his feet hit the gutter, dug into it, abruptly stopping his descent.

Streng didn't have time to be relieved. He strained his eyes against the darkness, trying to see the ground beneath him.

All he saw was black. How far could it be? Ten feet? Fifteen? The ground would be hard from the cool weather, and there was the chance he'd land on a rock, or worse.

A cracking sound, then a crash. Streng was peppered with glass and bits of wood, and he could feel the whole house thump. Whatever was chasing him was on the roof.

Streng now had no choice. He guessed the man in Sal's room was already making his way down the stairs, gun ready, and the steady *thump thump thump* of that thing's footsteps was closing in fast. Streng swung his legs out over the edge, letting them dangle in the darkness. He gripped the gutter, not expecting it to support his weight, but maybe it would slow him down a bit as it broke.

Without dwelling on it, Streng scooted off the rooftop, ankles tight together, knees bent. The gutter held for a second, then the aluminum split. Streng lost his grip and fell.

He hit faster than expected, and then the ground slipped out from under him in an unnerving way, causing him to pitch forward and fall again, his hands unable to stop his chin from cracking against the dirt.

Streng's vision lit up, sparkling motes swirling before him, and his jaw ached like he'd been hit with a bat. He reached around, felt the loose pieces of wood surrounding him, and realized he'd landed on Sal's firewood cord, stacked up against the house for winter burning.

Streng forced himself to his hands and knees, spat out the blood that was filling his mouth, and tried to get his bearings. He was in the back of the house. The Jeep was parked on the side.

Streng ran for the car.

Aging, Streng often mused while lying in bed at night unable to sleep, *is the body's deliberate and systematic betrayal of the soul.* First the appearance withered, gray hair replacing brown in every place hair grew and even a few where it had never grown before. Wrinkles began at the eyes and mouth, then sent out tributaries to the forehead, cheeks, neck, hands. Everything sagged, including memory. And then when self-esteem was something you could find only in old pictures, the aches and pains ensued. Eye strain. Arthritis. Insomnia. Constipation. Shin splints. Bad back. Receding gums. Poor appetite. Impotence. The heart and lungs and kidneys and prostate and liver and colon and bladder all sputtered like a car low on gas. And then the indignity of disrobing before a doctor one-third your age, only to be told that this is the just the aging process, completely natural, nothing can be done.

Streng fought getting old. He fought it by exercising, and eating right, and supplementing with so many morning vitamins that his stomach rattled for two hours after breakfast. But as he ran for his car, half as quickly as he could run just fifteen years ago, he once again cursed his failing body and the laws of nature that allowed this to happen.

He cursed again when the man in black fell into step beside him.

"Where are you going?" the man said with his foreign lisp, his breath as easy as Streng's was ragged.

Streng couldn't outrun him. He slowed, stopped, and then faced the man, raising his fists. Though he was hardly the 195-pound slab of muscle he had been in his youth, a few of those muscles still functioned.

"So you want to fight?" the man asked.

The sheriff threw a roundhouse punch, aiming for the stranger's neck. The man sidestepped it and in a single fluid motion grabbed Streng's hand and began to squeeze it.

The pain was instant and excruciating. It felt like getting caught in a door, the bones grinding against each other. Streng yelped.

Then combat training kicked in. Streng grabbed the man's shirt, swiveled his right hip behind the man's right leg, and flipped him.

The move was executed perfectly. Too perfectly, and halfway into it Streng knew what was happening. The man didn't let go of Streng and used the momentum of his fall to catapult Streng legs over head, slamming the sheriff onto his back.

Streng stared up at the black sky, his wind gone. He noticed many things at once: the cool grass tickling the back of his neck, the pain in his coccyx that shot down both legs, the spasm in his diaphragm that wouldn't let him draw a breath, and the soft, effeminate laugh of the person about to kill him.

"You've had some training," said the man. "So have I."

Streng felt a hand clamp under his armpit. It squeezed. Fire exploded behind Streng's eyes, and he screamed for perhaps the first time in his sixty-six years. It was like being pinched with pliers, and even though Streng tried to roll away, tried to push back the hand, the pressure went on and on, driving out every thought other than *make it stop*.

"That's the brachial nerve," the man whispered in Streng's ear. "It's one of many nerves in the body."

The man released his grip, and Streng wept. And as he

did, he hated himself for the tears, hated himself for being a frail old man that this psychopath could manhandle like a toy.

"I have some questions for you, Sheriff. Do you think you'll be able to answer them for me?"

Streng wanted to be defiant, wanted to give this man nothing. But his lips formed the word before he could stop it: "Yes."

"That's good. That's very good." The man's breath was warm, moist, on Streng's ear. "But I think I'll still loosen you up a bit first."

The man grabbed Streng's left side and squeezed, fingers digging hard into his kidney, prompting such intense, jaw-dropping pain that Streng passed out midscream.

Duncan Stauffer awoke to the sound of Woof barking. Woof was supposed to be a beagle, but Duncan had a lot of dog books and decided that Woof looked more like a basset hound. Woof was pudgy, with stubby legs and floppy ears and sad red eyes. It was funny because even though his eyes were sad, Woof played all the time. *All* the time. Duncan wondered how he could be so fat, since he ran around all day.

Woof barked again, and Duncan sat up. The dog normally slept on Duncan's bed, sprawled out on his back with his legs in the air. He left only to get a drink of water, let himself out through the doggy door to poop (Mom called it "doing his dirty business"), or greet Mom when she came home from the diner.

Duncan looked over at his SpongeBob digital clock next to the bed, but it wasn't on for some reason. Instead he checked his dad's watch, which he wore all the time since Mom had the links removed so it could fit.

The watch told him it was twelve forty-three.

Woof barked once more, a deep, loud bark that sounded exactly like his name, which was the reason Duncan named him Woof. But this wasn't the welcome-home bark that Woof used when Mom came home. This was Woof's warning bark, the one he used for his fiercest enemies, like the squirrel who had a nest in the maple tree out front, or the Johnsons' gray cat, who liked to hiss at Woof and scare him.

"Woof! Come here, boy!"

Duncan waited. Normally, Woof came running when Duncan called, jumping on him and bathing his face with a tongue that was longer than Duncan's foot.

But Woof didn't come.

"Mom!" Duncan called. "You home?"

No one answered.

Duncan didn't mind being by himself while Mom worked late. He was ten years old, which was practically an adult. His mom used to insist that he have a babysitter, and the one she usually got was Mrs. Teller, who was all bent over because she was so old, and sometimes she smelled like pee. Duncan liked her okay, but she made him go to bed early and wouldn't let him watch his favorite shows on TV, like *South Park,* because they said bad words, and she always wanted to talk about her husband, who died years ago.

Duncan didn't like to talk about death.

After a long session with Dr. Walker, the therapist

convinced Mom that Duncan was mature enough to stay home alone, if that's what Duncan wanted. Which he did. Duncan knew what to do in the case of any emergency. He'd taken the Stranger Danger class in school. He had three planned escape routes if there was a fire. He knew not to let anyone in the house, and how to call 911, and to never cook on the stove or use the fireplace or take a bath while home alone. He thought Mom was being a little crazy about the bath thing, like Duncan would fall asleep in the tub and drown. But he listened to Mom anyway, and she trusted him, and for the three months he'd been without a babysitter it had worked out fine. Duncan hadn't gotten scared once.

Until now.

"Woof!" Duncan yelled again.

Woof didn't come.

It was possible his dog had gone outside, to do his dirty business. Or maybe he saw the Johnsons' cat and went to chase him, even though the cat scared Woof a lot.

Or maybe something got him.

Duncan would never admit it to anyone, not even his best friend Jerry Halprin, but he sometimes believed monsters were real. He wasn't scared of monsters, exactly. He loved watching monster movies, and reading R. L. Stine books with monsters in them, but deep down he thought maybe monsters really did exist.

He didn't tell this to Dr. Walker, but when they had the car accident, and Mom thought Duncan was unconscious in the back seat, he wasn't really unconscious. He saw what happened to Dad, how bloody he was. For weeks afterward, Duncan had horrible nightmares about monsters, biting and clawing and ripping up him and Mom, making them bleed and die. Since he got Woof, most of the nightmares had gone away.

But sitting in his bed, holding his breath and waiting for his dog to come, Duncan wondered if maybe a monster got Woof.

Then he heard it—the jingle of metal tags from Woof's dog collar, just down the hallway.

"Woof!" he yelled happily. He tucked his legs under his butt so when Woof hopped on the bed he wouldn't step on them, and he waited in the dark for his dog to come.

But Woof didn't come.

Duncan listened hard, then called Woof's name again. He heard jingling, in the hall.

"Come on, Woof," Duncan urged.

The jingling got a little closer, then stopped. What was wrong with that dog?

"Speak, Woof!"

Woof, who didn't really need to be told to speak because he spoke all the time, still loved to follow that command, because he usually got a treat afterward. But Woof stayed quiet. Duncan wondered if he was maybe hurt, which is why he stopped barking.

Duncan reached over to the light switch on the wall behind him. He flipped it up. It didn't do anything. He tried flicking it up and down a few times, but his bedroom light didn't come on. *The electricity must be out,* Duncan thought.

Or maybe a monster stole the light bulb.

"Woof!" Duncan said it hard, the way Mom did when Woof did his dirty business on the kitchen floor.

Woof's collar jingled, and Duncan heard him pant. But the dog stayed in the hallway. Did Woof want him to come there for some reason? Or was he afraid of something in the bedroom?

Duncan peeled back the covers and climbed out of bed. The house was warm, but he shivered anyway. Mom made him wear pajamas when she was home, but on the nights she worked, Duncan liked to sleep in his underwear. He wished he had his pajamas on now. Being almost naked made him feel small and alone.

The room was too dark to see, and Duncan walked by memory, heading for the doorway to the hall, hands out in front of him like a zombie to stop him from bumping into walls. After some groping he found the door and stopped before walking through.

Woof's collar jingled, only a few feet in front of him. The panting got louder.

"What's the matter, boy?"

Duncan knelt down and held out his hands, waiting for the dog to approach. When Woof didn't, Duncan felt goosebumps break out all over. He knew something was wrong, really wrong. Maybe Mom was right about leaving him home all alone. Maybe something bad happened to Woof, and Duncan wouldn't be able to help him because he was just a kid.

Duncan stood up and reached for the hall light switch, but it didn't go on. So he pressed the button on his dad's watch and the blue bezel light came on, which was bright enough for him to see the man standing in the hallway, jingling Woof's collar and panting.

• • •

J osh VanCamp moved through the woods at a quick pace, sweeping the flashlight before him like a blind man's walking stick, navigating fallen trees and overhanging branches. He had no explanation for the events so far, but deep in his bones he knew something was terribly wrong.

The underbrush grabbed an ankle, and Josh pulled his foot free and paused, trying to get his bearings. There was less than a hundred yards between the crash spot and the Mortons' house, but it was extremely easy to get lost in the forest, especially at night. He reached into the pocket of his khakis and took out a bubble compass on a leather swatch. Reorienting himself, he headed east, toward Gold Star Road.

Safe Haven didn't have many emergencies. Even when the population tripled during the tourist season, Josh responded to only a handful of calls a week, and they usually amounted to overzealous campers with fire pits that exceeded safety standards or search-and-rescue operations for teenagers who snuck off into the woods to have a quickie. Though Josh became a firefighter because of a strong need to saves lives, he had never actually saved anyone.

Josh navigated through a copse of wrist-thin birch trees, and found his mind drifting to Annie, as it often did. He didn't need grief therapy to realize she was the real reason for his vocation. Soon he would leave Safe Haven and move to Madison, or the Twin Cities, where firefighters actually did risk their lives and do real good for the world.

On his days off he took EMT classes in nearby Shell Lake, and he planned to take his National Registry Paramedic exam next year. Josh didn't know if there was a statute of limitations on mourning, but if there were, his ran out at four years, three months, and eleven days. He had made a promise to Annie, but it was time to move on.

Josh set foot on the sand road and began walking south when he heard the scream. The Mortons were the only folks out here this time of year, and it came from the direction of their house. Josh sprinted toward the sound. Though the night had gone from cool to cold, sweat broke out on his forehead, neck, and underarms. The sand sucked at his shoes, and he almost lost his footing hurdling over a pile of scrap wood next to Sal Morton's mailbox.

Josh jogged to the edge of Sal's property just as the screaming stopped. Josh took a few gulps of air and then cupped his hands around his mouth.

"Hello!"

No one answered.

Josh wondered who was shrieking, and why. He had no doubt it had been a cry of pain. Had the person passed out? Died?

He looked to the house and saw the front door hanging open. That wasn't right. Josh hurried to it and stuck his head in. Darkness and silence greeted him.

"Hello? It's Josh VanCamp, from the firehouse! Does someone need help?"

The wall switch didn't work. Josh went inside, his flashlight sweeping the living room. Empty. He'd been in the Mortons' home before, for Sal's sixtieth birthday, and could vaguely remember the layout. He navigated over to the laundry room, found the circuit-breaker panel open, and noticed the main had been tripped. He pressed it. Nothing happened. Not unusual; in northern Wisconsin, the power went out frequently.

Silence followed him into the kitchen, and then up the stairs. He knew Sal hunted, which meant he had at least one gun, so Josh again announced his presence.

"Sal! Maggie! It's Josh from the fire department!"

He stopped at the top of the stairs and waited. Where were they? Why was the door open? Who had been screaming?

Josh felt wind on his cheek and turned the flashlight to see what could be causing it. A bedroom, the window shattered, white drapes dancing like specters. Then, from the room on the other side of the hallway, a cough.

Josh hurried over but couldn't quite understand what he saw. The bed was soaked in blood. And sitting in the middle was Sal Morton, slack-jawed, staring into space, cradling a right arm that boasted the most horrible compound fracture Josh could have ever imagined. The bone jutted out five or six inches from the flesh.

"Mr. Morton, I'm here! We're going to get you some help."

Josh tried to recall his EMT training. He checked for a pulse in Sal's carotid and found it to be strong, which surprised him considering the amount of blood on the bed. Sal's skin was cool, clammy, and his eyes fixed on a point beyond Josh. Shock. Josh needed to get him to a doctor, which would be quite the trick since his tanker truck was stolen. Sal probably had a car. And Sheriff Streng should be here any minute. Josh pulled out his cell and hit redial, then looked for the upstairs bathroom.

Awful as the fracture appeared, it didn't seem to be

bleeding much. The immediate concern was for infection. Josh found a rag and soaked it with some hydrogen peroxide he found in the cabinet under the sink. He placed it over Sal's mangled arm just as the line picked up.

"Hello?" came a strange voice. Whoever answered the sheriff's phone wasn't the sheriff.

"Can I speak to Sheriff Streng?"

"He's indisposed at the moment."

"Who is this?"

"My name is Santiago." The man had a lisp and sounded Spanish, and Josh had the impression that he was smiling as he spoke.

"Are you with the sheriff?" Josh said.

"Yes. But you can't speak to him."

Josh didn't have time for games like this. Why was Streng even lending out his cell phone? Didn't cops have rules about that sort of thing?

"I need to speak with the sheriff. It's an emergency."

"I don't think he can speak. I believe I just ruptured his kidney."

"What?" *What the hell is going on?*

"Is this the man who just went into the Morton house? How's Sal holding up? Still grieving for his dear, dead wife?"

"His wife? Where's Maggie?"

"She's not on the bed? Hmm. Interesting. I suppose Ajax has her, then."

Josh stared at the huge bloodstain on the bed, and then his eyes climbed up Sal, who continued to stare, mouth agape, across the hall to the adjoining bedroom. Josh followed Sal's stare with the flashlight.

It came to rest on the huge man standing next to the

window, quietly slow dancing with the naked, mutilated corpse of Maggie Morton.

Fran's upper body hung out of the diner's broken kitchen window, Al's murderer clutching the ankle of her right foot, preventing her from getting away. Glass shards dug into her chest, and the smell of rotten food from the alley Dumpster to her left made her eyes water. Fran kicked out with her free foot, connecting with the killer several times, but her rubber-soled shoes bounced off without apparent effect.

Her hands frantically sought something to grab on to, something to hold so she could pull herself out. The Dumpster, a foot away, might as well have been a mile. Her palms couldn't get any kind of purchase on the brick wall. All Fran could do was lean forward, hooking her armpits around the window frame, and try to resist the inevitable yank back into the kitchen.

The yank didn't come. In fact, the killer didn't tug on her at all. He simply held her ankle—hard enough that she couldn't twist away—but without pulling. Fran remembered being a child, getting a booster shot at the doctor's office, and how waiting for it was just as bad as getting it. She wondered how being stabbed with a knife compared to an inoculation needle. Or would he prefer slicing to stabbing?

But seconds ticked away, and still he did nothing but hold her. The anticipation was torture.

Then his other hand touched her bare calf and began to knead it, rubbing up and down.

Fran screamed, this intimate gesture somehow ratcheting up her terror. A moment later, her shoe was pulled off. Then she felt her sock peeling down. What the hell was this guy doing?

She found out when something warm and wet enveloped her toes.

He was sucking them.

Fran squirmed and kicked, but she had no leverage, no way to bend her legs while she was on her stomach. She planted her free foot on the attacker's forehead and pushed, trying to keep his face away. It had no effect. As his tongue squirmed between her toes, his free hand traveled up her leg and rubbed the inside of her thigh under her skirt.

If both hands were holding her, that meant he wasn't holding the knife.

Fran tried to figure out how she could use this to her advantage. Had he dropped the knife? Set it down? Put it in a sheath?

His teeth scraped the knuckle of her little toe, then locked around it.

Oh, Jesus, no . . .

First pressure. Then pain. The killer sawed his teeth back and forth and shook his head like a dog, but apparently the toe didn't want to come off no matter how violent the movement. The agony spiked to unbearable levels, going on and on and on, and Fran kicked his face and pushed against the outside brick wall and then suddenly she slipped free, spilling face-first onto the asphalt, hands out to break her fall.

Fran rolled onto her butt, her back against the wall,

hands seeking out the unrelenting throb that now occupied her entire body and soul. She'd stubbed her toes many times in her life, once while she had an ingrown nail. That pain was a joke compared to this. She probed the wound, trying to judge the severity of the damage in the darkness, sobbing at what she discovered. Her toe was completely gone, a tiny sharp nub of bone sticking out where it used to be.

Fran howled, and then howled even louder when a hand reached through the window and snagged her hair, yanking back her head.

She managed to grab on to the side of the Dumpster, and a tug-of-war ensued. Her neck wrenched backward, but she fought it, felt some hair rip free, and then she was on her feet and hobbling down the alley as quickly as her injury allowed.

When she reached the street she turned left. The darkness covered town like a black blanket. There wasn't a single light anywhere up and down Main Street. The hunter's moon, full and orange, was partially obscured by clouds. No cars. No people. Just a long line of empty stores: Hutch's Bakery, the Fudge Shoppe, York's Books and Cards, Red Cross Pharmacy, Safe Haven Liquor. With their power off, the buildings looked abandoned, dead.

Fran limped to the parking lot, squinting to make out the silhouette of her Jetta, and five steps away from it she let out a cry of anguish.

Her keys were in her purse. Her purse was in the diner.

Fran tried the car door anyway, knowing it was locked, knowing that even if she got inside she couldn't drive without keys. When the door didn't open, she glanced over her shoulder to see if the killer was following her.

He stood directly behind her, and his hand reached out and grabbed her by the neck.

"Hello, Fran," he said. "I'm Taylor. We need to talk."

General Alton Tope didn't believe in luck. Victories and defeats were decided by intelligence, firepower, and strategy. But he had to admit it was a fortuitous circumstance to have the Twenty-sixth Special Forces Group already in Wisconsin, training here at Fort McCoy. They had been putting a prototype tank armor through the paces—it was electrically charged and virtually impervious to rocket-propelled grenades—and were set to return to Fort Bragg tomorrow. Operation Angel Rescue changed their status.

The twelve Green Berets standing at attention in the war room were dressed for combat but hadn't yet been issued weapons. Though they were called after only an hour of sleep, each man appeared alert and determined.

"Parade, rest," Tope commanded, and his men put their hands behind their backs. "Operation Angel Rescue is classified top secret and shall not be discussed ever with anyone in possession of less than two stars. Understood?"

"Yes, General." Unison, strong and loud.

Tope continued. "The town of Safe Haven, Wisconsin, two hundred and seventy clicks northwest, population nine hundred and seven, is under siege. Your job is to capture the insurgents. Dr. Ralph Stubin, a civvie, will be accompanying you on this mission and providing intel."

Tope hit the power button on the remote control, and a

TV in the corner of the room came on. The screen filled with a fish-eye close-up of Dr. Stubin, colored green due to the night-vision camera. The background was indistinct, but the sound was unmistakable; Stubin was in a chopper.

"Am I on? I am? Okay."

The doctor focused on the camera, looking grim.

"My name is Ralph Stubin. I'm a brain surgeon. My specialty is behavior modification, specifically transhumanistic neuropathology. By stimulating portions of the brain electrically, it can be prompted to function more like a computer, with sequential input rather than parallel. In layman's terms, you can download information directly into a person's mind, and programs will automatically execute when certain conditions are met."

Stubin looked right in response to someone speaking to him—probably a soldier telling him to stay on track. He nodded and again stared into the camera.

"Many nations, friend and foe, have experimented with behavior modification. The code name for units composed of modified soldiers is *Red-ops*. A Red-ops unit is a strike force, meant to be dropped behind enemy lines. Their goals are threefold: isolate, overpower, annihilate. They're inserted into small towns, and they torture, rape, and murder everyone they encounter. Red-ops exist to demoralize, intimidate, and frighten the enemy. Basically, they're government-sponsored terrorists. Unfortunately, because of some colossal mistake that we still don't understand, a Red-ops unit is now operating on U.S. soil, and it seems they were accidentally sent by one of our allies."

Stubin looked ready to throw up. Tope couldn't tell if it was from the whirlybird or the situation.

The brain surgeon wiped the back of his hand across his mouth before going on. "The unit has infiltrated the small Wisconsin town of Safe Haven. We don't know where they are or what they're doing. Because of their transhuman behavior modification, we have to assume they're following protocol. They're treating Safe Haven like an enemy territory. If we don't stop them, they'll wipe out the entire town."

Then Stubin bent over and commenced with the vomiting. Tope switched off the TV.

"The briefing will continue on the Huey. Keep in mind that the Red-ops unit will view us as enemy combatants, even though our countries are buddy-buddy at the United Nations. We want to take them alive, with minimal civilian casualties. This is going to be easier said than done. Red-ops commandos have all had the equivalent of Special Forces training. They're experts in hand-to-hand and armed combat, munitions, stealth, tactics, interrogation, and communications. Plus, they're cold-blooded bastards. I've seen what these men can do, and it isn't pretty. Questions?"

The SF-A team captain raised his hand.

"Captain Haines."

"Which country are they from, General?"

"Need-to-know basis, Captain. But they speak our language."

"How about our weapons, General?"

"Nonlethal ordnance includes Blake impact shells, sponge grenades, electric net entanglers, lacrimators, Splatt-Thixotropic rounds, and iotechnical-injector batons. We need them alive."

"And the enemy, General?"

"Bladed weapons and sidearms only."

"Numbers, General?"

"This Red-ops unit has five team members."

This provoked a smile from Captain Haines.

"Permission to speak freely, General?"

"Go ahead, Captain."

"Five men, no rifles? Are you sure you need us? Can't we just send a Girl Scout troop out after these jokers?"

Some chuckles. General Tope betrayed nothing. He certainly didn't say he had two other Special Forces teams, as well as a Navy SEAL team and a Marine recon team, being flown in to assist.

Instead, he cleared his throat and said, "I want you on the landing strip at oh one thirty. Heavy gear, rations for four days, bivouacs. Dismissed."

The team dispersed, double-time. As he watched them go, General Tope had a strong feeling he'd never see any of them alive again. But he couldn't dwell on that, not with so many other things to do.

Tope picked up the scramble phone and contacted the Pentagon to set up the quarantine.

Erwin Luggs heard the screams in the woods and wondered how everything had gone so bad so fast. The fallen helicopter, spread out around him like a giant broken egg, was damn near the creepiest thing he'd ever seen. The situation wasn't helped by the fact that he was soaked, head to toe, with deer blood. It exuded a gamey, metallic stench, and it had cooled and coagulated, clinging to him like jelly.

Another scream came from the trees. Erwin shivered, mostly from the cold, but partly from fear. The night had begun on a promising note. Just two hours ago he was in a hot shower, ready to slip into bed with Jessie Lee Sloan for snuggling and possible nookie. Jessie Lee had been spending too much money on the wedding preparations, and Erwin had been reaping the benefits of guilt sex. Guilt sex almost made up for the overtime hours he had to work to pay for all the extras Jessie Lee was planning, like the custom-made husband and wife figurines for the cake, and a stretch limo that could seat all sixteen members of the wedding party and provide each with champagne.

But it didn't look like there would be any sex tonight, guilt-induced or otherwise. Erwin reeked of clammy animal blood, Sheriff Streng still hadn't arrived, and something evil stalked the forest—something that made Erwin want to run and hide.

A third scream, the loudest of all, and then a punishing silence. Erwin turned away from the chopper and faced the tree line. He knew the sheriff wasn't going to come. He knew because he was pretty certain that last scream came *from* the sheriff. Though distorted, the voice was semirecognizable. What could possibly be happening to him to make the man—a tough man who had seen combat in Vietnam—cry out like that?

Erwin took out his cell phone. He tried Josh. He tried the sheriff. He tried 911. He even tried his fiancée. Each time, he got the same *unable to place your call* recording.

Though a firefighter, Erwin knew he wasn't a particularly brave man. Unlike his friend Josh, who wanted to leave Safe Haven for a bigger town with more danger, Erwin was perfectly fine here. He hadn't risked his life once in six years on the job, and that suited him. But he knew that it was only a matter of time until he'd be forced to do something heroic.

Unfortunately, it looked like the time had come. Erwin took a deep, steadying breath and then headed into the woods, toward the screaming. He figured that Josh must have heard it, too. Maybe he was already there, taking control of the situation. Maybe Sheriff Streng had broken his leg and the screams were from Josh splinting it. Maybe the deer that had bled all over Erwin simply caught its fur on a sharp branch. Maybe those helicopter pilots got their heads cut off in a freak accident.

The maybes didn't last long. As Erwin ventured deeper into the woods, his imagination ate away at his rationalization. Someone, or something, had killed those pilots, and the deer, and probably Josh, and was now killing the sheriff in some horrifying way.

Erwin slowed his pace. Each shadow became a monster. Each twig snap became a pursuit by demons. Jess popped into his mind, with that disapproving look she gave him when he said something stupid around her friends, and Erwin knew how pissed off she'd be if he died. She'd be upset at losing him, of course, but also because her story-book wedding would be canceled and she'd already sent out the invitations.

That settled it for him. Erwin decided he should just head in the other direction, back to the main road. Forget the sheriff. Forget Josh. Forget any possible acts of heroism. He might regret his cowardice for the rest of his life, but at least he'd be alive to regret it.

Erwin turned, then stopped. Which way was the road? He wasn't sure. He took two steps forward, then five more to the right, then seven more in his original direction, and he realized he had no idea where he was.

The cardinal rule when a person got lost in the woods was simple: hug a tree. Staying put meant the search party could find you, rather than chase you in circles. But that rule didn't apply when there was something in the woods trying to cut your head off.

Erwin picked up the pace. He might have been going deeper into the forest, but at least it distanced him from all the creepy stuff. Maybe he'd reach a road. Maybe he wouldn't. At the very least, he could walk until sunrise and then figure out which direction to go.

This is for Jessie Lee, he told himself. *She needs me.*

Erwin focused so intently on escape that when he reached the Mortons' yard he dropped his jaw in surprise. His flashlight beam landed upon Sheriff Streng and some-one else—a man in a black outfit who wore a gun.

Erwin froze. He had known Mr. Streng since he was a kid. His dad was friends with the man, and Streng often stopped by the Luggs household. Erwin could remember throwing the baseball around with him on more than one occasion, and for a while Streng could be counted on to buy him birthday and Christmas gifts.

And now he was being attacked. The man straddled Streng, pinning him down, doing something with his hands. Erwin was about thirty yards away, and he knew he couldn't cross that distance before the man drew his gun, especially since the light had alerted him to Erwin's presence. If he tried to help, he might die.

It took Erwin all of a second to switch off his light and head back into the woods. The act shamed him, but the risk was too high. Erwin liked Mr. Streng, but he didn't want to get shot for him. He hid behind a large pine tree and held his breath, listening for sounds that he was being followed.

"Hey!"

The voice made Erwin flinch. It wasn't Mr. Streng calling him.

"Come out of the woods!"

That didn't seem like a wise idea. Erwin chewed the inside of his cheek and closed his eyes.

"Come out of the woods, or I'll kill the sheriff!"

A scream so raw, so filled with pure pain, shot through the trees, and Erwin wanted to stick his fingers in his ears to make it stop. If the man hoped to lure Erwin from hiding by hurting Mr. Streng, he had another think coming. All it made Erwin want to do was get as far away as possible.

Afraid to switch the flashlight back on, Erwin made his way through the woods by feel, each step taking him farther from the horrible sound that just wouldn't stop.

Up to that point, the worst pain Sheriff Ace Streng had ever experienced was a kidney stone. He'd woken in the middle of the night from a nightmare of someone stabbing him in the side with a hot poker. Once he was awake, the pain didn't abate. After two hours of side-clutching agony, he called 911. His ER nurse had been sympathetic.

"I've had three children, Sheriff. I've also had kidney stones. I'd rather have three more children than another stone."

Having his kidney mauled by the psychopath straddling him felt like a kidney stone times ten. Streng bellowed until his throat burned. He had seen Erwin at the tree line and didn't blame the boy for running off. Hell, Streng would have run away, too, had he known the pain this man was capable of causing.

Finally the terrible fingers quit squeezing, and Streng managed to catch his breath.

"I think you scared him off," the man whispered. Streng had heard part of the phone call, knew he called himself Santiago. "Now, how about we get to those questions I promised, yes?"

"Yes."

"Good. Very good. First question. Where's Warren?"

At first, Streng wasn't sure he heard correctly. Warren? Did he mean Wiley? What could he possibly want with him?

A kidney pinch made him focus.

"I haven't seen him in years," he answered, sobbing.

"I'm not asking when you saw him. I'm asking where he is. Do you know?"

"Yes."

Santiago leaned in close enough to kiss him. The intimacy of the gesture made Streng want to gag.

"Tell me. Where's Warren?"

Streng opened his mouth to tell him, but nothing came out. This surprised Streng. He would have chewed off his own arm to get away from this lunatic, but he couldn't say the address. Even though he knew it meant more torture.

Streng clenched his teeth. He didn't know why he was keeping mum. Certainly Wiley could take care of himself. Hell, Wiley even deserved this hell to rain upon him. But Streng knew that he'd hold out as long as possible.

Perhaps, if he got lucky, his kidneys would fail and he'd die before the pain went on too long.

"Go to hell," Streng said.

And that's when Josh came running out of the Morton house, straight at them.

Santiago moved fast, incredibly fast. In one blurred motion he gained his footing and reached for his sidearm. Streng had anticipated the move and still almost missed it, but he managed to grab the killer's wrist, preventing him from drawing the pistol. That one-second distraction was enough for Josh to catch Santiago in the neck with his forearm, toppling him over.

Josh was big, solid, formidable. But he didn't have training. Streng had seen enough of Santiago to know he'd been taught by the military, probably an elite force. Josh didn't have a chance going toe-to-toe with him. At least, not without help.

Even though movement brought a wave of nausea, Streng rolled onto his side and crawled onto Santiago, wrestling for his gun. The killer jabbed at Streng's eyes, but Streng turned his head away. He chopped at Streng's neck, but Streng tucked his chin into his chest. A blow to the side of his head made Streng see stars, but he refused to let go of that wrist.

And then Josh was behind Santiago, putting him in a

choke hold. The killer reached around, grabbing Josh's hair with both hands. Streng tugged at the holster, freed the pistol, and thumbed off the safety in the dark.

The man flipped Josh over his hip and raised a combat boot to bring down on his head. Streng aimed for the center body mass and fired three times.

The muzzle flashes hurt his eyes, a strobe effect producing snapshots of Santiago recoiling from the impact of the bullets and falling backward.

"Behind you," Josh croaked.

Streng spun and saw the silhouette of an incredibly huge man—someone at least seven feet tall with the chunky body of a professional wrestler—only a few yards away.

The thing that had chased him out onto the roof.

Streng fired four shots, all four hitting home. The large man didn't break stride. Streng fired two more in the direction of his head, and then Josh pulled him to his feet and they were rushing for the trees.

Streng had no idea how far they ran before they finally stopped to rest. Two hundred, perhaps three hundred yards. Streng's breath came in ragged gasps, his hand pressed tight against his injured kidney. Josh clapped a hand on Streng's shoulder, leaned in close to whisper.

"What the hell is going on, Sheriff?"

"I have no idea, son."

But Streng did have an idea. And the idea scared him so badly his knees began to knock.

• • •

Duncan Stauffer stood in the hallway and watched the man in black play with a lighter. It was the biggest lighter Duncan had ever seen—about the size of a Coke can—and the flame shot out of the top like a torch.

At first, Duncan recoiled in terror and even cried a little. He knew about Stranger Danger and the awful things some men did to little boys. He couldn't stop thinking that Mom was right, that he was too young to stay home alone, and it was his fault a bad man got in the house.

After a few minutes of crying, the man began to flick his lighter. That was scary, but it calmed Duncan down somehow, gave him something to focus on. The man hadn't hurt him, hadn't touched him, hadn't said a single word. He just stood there, switching the flame on and off.

"Who are you?" Duncan finally asked.

"I'm—hehehe—Bernie."

Bernie's giggle sounded like a little girl's.

"Where's my dog?"

In the flickering orange, Duncan watched Bernie smile. He touched the flame to the dog collar he still held in his other hand. The nylon collar began to melt.

"Acrylic. This black black dark black smoke contains chlorine, chlorine, dioxins, and furans. Very very very bad to inhale. But I can't help taking a little sniff, a little tiny sniff, because I really—hehehe—*like it*."

Bernie stuffed his nose in a plume of oily smoke and made sniffing sounds.

"Did you . . . burn Woof?" Duncan asked, voice cracking.

"Smell it? Do you smell your dog, Duncan?" Duncan had no idea how the man knew his name. "When fur burns, it smells like hair. Have you—hehehe—smelled burning hair?"

Duncan shook his head. Bernie dropped the collar onto the hardwood floor, where it quickly went out, and reached for Duncan. The boy tried to duck away, but Bernie clamped a large hand around his neck.

"Smell this. Smell it."

He giggled and touched the jumping flame to the side of Duncan's head, above his right ear. Duncan heard a sizzling, snapping sound, like bacon frying, and then smelled the awful odor of his hair melting.

Just as he began to feel the heat, Bernie turned off the lighter. He slapped Duncan's head, smothering the flame but almost knocking him over.

"Smell it. Smell. Bad smell. Did you smell your dog? Answer me! Answer—hehehe—answer me."

"No, I didn't smell that." Duncan touched the side of his head. His hair there felt sticky and hard, like he had gum caught in it.

"After the fur burns, smells pretty good. Like hamburgers. Dogburgers. Hehehe. People smell like barbecue ribs when they burn. Hehe—and they taste like ribs. Smoky. Smoky and good. Have you ever been burned?"

Duncan was very close to wetting his underwear. He couldn't answer but managed to shake his head.

"Pain. Lots of pain. See?"

Bernie lifted up his black shirt and showed his chest. His whole body was covered with shiny pink scars, and it looked a lot like the spiced ham Mom bought at the deli for his school lunch.

"Bad burn. Dead nerves. See?"

Bernie touched the fire to the scar tissue and held it there.

"Can't feel it. But smell—hehehe—smells good. Good smell."

A sickly sweet odor invaded Duncan's head, pushing away the stench of burning hair. The fact that it smelled tasty made it even more disgusting.

Bernie pulled his shirt back down. "Hungry, hungry, makes me hungry. Hehehe. Give me your hand."

Duncan put both of his hands behind him and backed away.

"You won't die. I want to show you. First-degree burns, first degree, only affects the epidermis—the outer layer of skin. Causes redness, swelling. Hurts. Like a sunburn."

Bernie walked after Duncan, trapping him in the corner of the bedroom. Duncan didn't know if he could stand up anymore. His legs wanted to quit. He sobbed, and the sobs turned into hiccups. Where was Mom? How could this be happening?

"Second degree," Bernie continued, "causes blisters. Very painful. They fill with fluid. Can be a few skin layers, layers deep. Papillary and reticular dermis affected—hehehe. These are the burns I use when I'm asking someone questions. Going too deep makes them third degree. Tissue damage. Skin and nerves burned away, so the pain isn't as bad."

Bernie reached around and grabbed Duncan's arm. Duncan tried to pull away, but Bernie was too strong.

"Fourth fourth, fourth-degree burns are when the skin is completely gone, can't ever heal. Fifth degree, the muscle is gone. Sixth degree, bone is charred. That takes a lot of heat. Fourteen hundred degrees. I can't get that hot with my lighter. I need this."

Bernie tucked his lighter into his belt and took out a tiny silver cylinder. He pressed a button and a blue flame shot out.

"A butane torch. Isn't that pretty? See how thin the flame can get? I can use this to write. See?"

Bernie released Duncan and began to roll up his sleeve. Duncan tried to scoot around Bernie, but the man nudged his hip and pinned the boy against the wall.

"Isn't this cool?" Bernie said, showing Duncan his forearm. The raised scar tissue formed the word *BERNIE.* "Maybe cool is wrong, the wrong word. This is *hot.* Very hot. You want your name on your arm, Duncan? Hehe. You want to be hot like Bernie?"

Bernie stretched Duncan's arm over his head, and Duncan bawled. Then there was a buzzing sound. Bernie tugged something out of his pocket, something small with a screen that lit up. He peered at it, reading something. Then he pressed a button and spoke.

"Understood. Tell me when I can get rid of the kid."

Bernie put the device away and smiled.

"My friend Taylor has your mother. We may not, may not need you—hehehe."

At the mention of his mother, Duncan found his voice.

"Why . . . why do you have Mom?"

"We need to ask her some things, some questions. Taylor is good at asking. He doesn't use fire. He bites. Taylor likes to bite. He's killed over seventy people. Good at it. So when your mom tells Taylor what she knows, I won't need you anymore."

"You'll let us go?"

"Hehehe—of course not. I'm going to build a really big fire, then cook you and eat you."

The thought that this man wanted to eat him brought Duncan back from hysteria. He recalled from Stranger Danger class what to do if someone grabbed him. Bernie's shoes were thick, so grinding his heel on the top of his foot probably wouldn't work. And since Bernie dressed like a soldier, he probably wore one of those sports cups on his privates. But Bernie's eyes—they were unprotected.

Duncan stuck out his pointer finger and jammed it, hard as he could, into Bernie's eye.

Bernie flinched, crying out, and briefly backed away from Duncan. The boy slipped out of the man's grasp and ran for the stairs fast as he could. He jumped down the last several, landing hard on his bare feet and almost tripping over something furry.

Woof!

Duncan knelt down, felt the rising and falling of his dog's chest. He shook him, trying to get Woof to wake up.

"You little bastard!" Bernie, at the top of the stairs. "I'm going to burn your eyes out!"

Duncan knew he should run, but he couldn't leave Woof. He shook the beagle even harder and felt a lump on the dog's head. Bernie must have hit him or kicked him.

"Woof! Come on, boy! You have to get up!"

A growl, deep in Woof's throat. He twitched, then rolled onto all fours.

"Thatta boy, Woof!"

Duncan felt Woof's warm tongue on his face, and he wrapped his arms around the animal's neck. Then Woof went rigid and began to bark.

"I'll burn you, too, dog," Bernie said, just before Woof lunged and dug his teeth into the man's calf.

Bernie howled, falling onto his butt, and Duncan ran for the front door with Woof on his heels. The night was cold and dark. Duncan knew to go to his neighbor, Mrs. Teller, for help when Mom wasn't home, but Mrs. Teller's lights weren't on. In fact, no one on the block had their lights on. Duncan figured the electricity was out all over. He and Woof ran to Mrs. Teller's front door and he banged on it with both hands.

Something glowed behind him. Duncan turned around and saw orange fire flickering through the windows of his house. Bernie appeared in the doorway, lighter raised above his head, and spotted Duncan. He began to limp after him.

"Mrs. Teller!" Duncan banged harder on the door. "It's Duncan!"

Woof began to bark like crazy. Bernie got closer, close enough for Duncan to hear his manic giggling. Behind Bernie, the fire had spread throughout Duncan's house. He could now see flames in all four front windows, and smoke rose from the roof.

Bernie's face stretched out in a grotesque smile. He came closer, and closer, and got within fifteen feet when Mrs. Teller's door finally opened.

"Stop!" she commanded. Duncan looked at her. Mrs. Teller was close to eighty years old, and her back bent in the shape of a question mark, and Duncan had to help her open jars. But she looked totally scary standing there with Mr. Teller's old shotgun.

Bernie must have thought so, too, because he didn't come any closer.

"Shoot him!" Duncan cried. "He broke into my house and burned it down and hurt Woof and wants to kill me!"

Bernie giggled. "I saw the house on fire and tried to help."

"He's lying, Mrs. Teller!"

"The boy, the boy is obviously upset and confused. I saved his life."

"You're not from around here," Mrs. Teller said.

"I was passing through. Good thing, good thing I did, or else he'd—the boy—would be dead."

"Where's your car?"

Bernie's grin faltered. "What? Oh, there, on the street."

"That's the Chavezes' car," Mrs. Teller said and then aimed and pulled the trigger.

Santiago probed his chest and winced. The liquid body armor—Kevlar fibers soaked in a sheer thickening fluid suspension of nano-silica particles in polyethylene glycol—had done its job and stopped all four rounds. It not only repelled penetration, but the energy of the impacts had been diffused, preventing blunt force trauma. But it still hurt like a bitch. Santiago promised himself he would pay back in kind when he caught up with the sheriff again.

He sat up and stared at Ajax, who was palpating his own body armor, the usual blank expression on his face. Ajax never had any expression, even while he was ripping off a man's arms.

Santiago turned to face the woods and squinted. The

Red-ops team all had enhanced night vision. Santiago vaguely recalled it having something to do with increased rhodopsin stores in his rods, yet another benefit of the Chip. A quick survey of the area failed to reveal the sheriff or the firefighter who had saved him.

A brief swatch of memory clouded his mind, and Santiago thought back to an earlier time, to his home in Bolivia. He remembered the room where prisoners were taken to be broken. Sometimes for interrogation. Sometimes to use as examples. Santiago always had a talent for causing pain.

When he was fifteen years old his family had a small farm, eating some of the goats, cattle, and chickens they raised, selling the surplus at the marketplace in town. But something began killing their livestock, mutilating the animals in grotesque ways. The eyes and genitals were gouged out. The entrails removed and tied into knots and braids. So many bones broken they no longer had any form.

The villagers spoke in hushed tones of a chupacabra on the loose, an evil creature of legend.

Santiago knew better. He was the one who led the animals, with food and gentle coaxing, to a cave in the woods where he would tie them down and torture them for hours.

After several years of butchery, he made the easy transition from the village's livestock to the villagers themselves. Abducting a particularly loud young girl led to his capture and imprisonment. But rather than rot in jail, he was recruited by the secret police, getting paid to indulge in his appetites.

He plied his trade for many years. Santiago grinned, recalling a particularly enjoyable interrogation involving a vise and a cheese grater. He could vividly see the man's face, hear his screams . . .

The Chip sensed the increased electrical function in the amygdala and hippocampus prodded by the memory and instantly ordered a reboot.

"Charge," he said.

Without thinking, Santiago reached into his pants and pulled out a capsule of Charge, breaking it under his nose. The fumes took away the pain, stepped up his heart rate, and dissipated the extraneous thoughts and memories, leaving only the next mission objective: *Find Sheriff Streng.* Santiago didn't question his orders, any more than he questioned the fact that this was obviously American soil. The mission was the only thing that mattered.

Santiago stood up and faced Ajax. The giant was also sniffing a Charge capsule, his eyes rolled back into his skull. A moment later the two of them were sprinting through the woods with the speed and agility of pro athletes, Santiago ducking and dodging foliage, and Ajax knocking it out of the way. They didn't become tired or winded, and their pulses remained under seventy beats per minute—resting heart rates for normal people. Ajax stopped once, to pick up the trail, and within fifty paces the sheriff and his friend were within their sights.

The Red-ops members switched to stealth mode, blending into the woods, silently flowing through the environment like liquid. The sheriff wouldn't get away again.

• • •

Fran Stauffer, lying in the parking lot, her arms tied behind her with a plastic zip line, had never felt such hatred. Fran was a member of Amnesty International. She protested against capital punishment. She even forgave the unknown driver who caused the death of her husband.

But this man, Taylor, had completely shattered her faith in humanity. He did it with one short sentence: "We have Duncan, and we're going to hurt him."

Suddenly human rights no longer mattered. Neither did the sanctity of life. If Fran's hands were free, she would have ripped Taylor's throat out without a bit of guilt or regret.

"You seem angry," Taylor said. He smiled. Taylor didn't look like a monster. He had a strong, angular face that could be regarded as handsome. And his smile was deceptively charming. But Fran had seen what he'd done to Al, and had no doubt he'd do the same, or worse, to her. And to Duncan.

"Leave Duncan alone. He's just a child."

"I believe Bernie wants to eat him. I've seen him do it. In Bosnia he roasted a man's leg and ate it while the fellow was still alive. Personally, I prefer mine raw."

Taylor grinned again and snapped his teeth. Fran fought the revulsion and tried to keep her voice steady, even though it felt like her heart might explode from beating so fast.

"What do you want?"

"I want to know where Warren is."

"Who's Warren?"

Taylor smiled, as if he liked that answer, and lifted Fran's injured foot up to his mouth. Fran tried to kick away, but the man had fingers like steel cables.

"This little piggy went to market," Taylor sang, running his teeth over her big toe. "And this little piggy stayed home."

Fran anticipated even more pain, and she wanted to vomit.

"Please, I don't know anyone named Warren."

"This little piggy had roast beef . . ."

"I really don't know."

"This little piggy had none . . ."

"You have to give me more information! I can't tell you what you want to know unless you tell me what you want!"

Taylor's tongue probed her injury, making her gasp.

"I said before," his teeth knocked against her exposed bone, "I want Warren."

"Who the fuck is Warren!"

"Warren Streng."

"The sheriff's brother? Why the hell would I know where—*Jesus Christ!*"

Taylor bit down just as Fran succumbed to another panic attack. But this time it was a blessing; she hyperventilated, became oxygen deprived, and blacked out.

The blessing didn't last. The sharp odor of ammonia shot up Fran's nostrils, making her eyes burn. She shook her head to escape the smelling salts, realized what was happening, and began to yell for help. As she screamed, Taylor stroked her hair and ran his fingertips over her lips, tracing the O of her mouth.

Then, like an answered prayer, red and blue flashing

lights appeared. They became brighter, and Fran watched the emergency vehicle pull into the lot. A fire truck.

Josh!

Since her husband's death, Josh had been the only man Fran had seen more than once, and she had actually developed feelings for him. Unfortunately, the feelings weren't mutual, and after four terrific dates Josh had stopped calling. Fran had assumed it was because of Duncan—not too many men had the desire to become instant fathers. A shame, too, because Duncan seemed to like him as much as Fran had.

"Josh!" Fran bellowed, extending his name out into three syllables. "Help me!"

Taylor patted Fran on the cheek, then walked casually over to the tanker truck. Fran's vision was blocked by her car, so she scooted up onto her butt. Taylor stood next to the driver's door, speaking casually through the open window. She couldn't see into the truck or hear any words.

"Josh!" Fran cried.

Taylor waved at her and smiled. Then the fire truck began to pull away.

A sob escaped Fran. This couldn't be happening. Why would Josh leave her there? Didn't he hear her?

Fran pushed back against her car door, got her legs under her, and stood up. Then she ran. Behind her she heard Taylor chide, "Don't make me chase you." She ignored him, focusing on catching Josh. If he saw her, he'd help. He had to help.

The truck didn't seem to be in any hurry, cruising down Main Street at a languid pace. Fran's injured foot seemed to catch fire every time it slapped against the pavement, and her balance was seriously threatened by the binding on her wrists. But slowly, agonizingly, she reached the rear of the tanker.

"Josh! Stop!"

Rather than stop, the truck picked up speed. Only a few miles per hour faster, but Fran couldn't match it. She scraped her toe bone against the tarmac, and the spike of agony made her slow down. Miraculously, Josh also slowed down. Did he see her?

Energized, Fran pushed on. The truck was within twenty yards. Ten yards. Five. She made it!

Heaving, bleeding, Fran stumbled up to the passenger side as the door opened.

Sitting up in the passenger seat was Martin Durlock, the mayor of Safe Haven. He was naked, gray duct tape wrapped around his face and wrists slick with blood.

The mayor screamed behind his gag, his whole body shaking. He stretched his bound hands out to Fran, eyes wide and imploring, and then the truck sped up and continued down Main Street, turning left onto Conway, the blue and red strobe lights fading into darkness.

Already light-headed from the running, Fran began to hyperventilate. She cast a dizzy eye back at Taylor, who was shining the flashlight on his own face. He frowned in an exaggerated way, his free hand miming tears running down his cheeks.

Fran closed her eyes and bent over, putting her head between her knees, not allowing herself to pass out. A cool breeze blew across her with a faint whistle, and the river sounds helped her to calm down, to focus.

The river sounds.

Fran lifted her head, realizing she stood on an overpass. Beneath her was a choppy section of the Chippewa River.

A summer day didn't go by without her seeing at least one lonely fisherman propped up along the railing, line dragging the water.

She went to the edge and leaned over the short iron railing, smelling the water below. Fran couldn't see in the dark, but she knew from memory the drop from overpass to water was about fifteen feet. But was it deep enough? If she jumped, would she break her legs? And if she survived the fall, could she stay afloat with her hands tied behind her back?

The flashlight hit her in the eyes.

"I bet that water is really cold." Taylor would be on her in a few more steps. "And I've heard drowning is an awful way to go."

Not as awful as being tortured to death by a madman, Fran thought. But even more important than that was getting to Duncan, making sure he was safe. She held her breath, closed her eyes, and flipped herself over the railing.

The fall lasted only seconds but seemed to take much longer. As she spun through the air she imagined rocks below, jagged steel, broken glass, or perhaps an island in the middle of the river—something other than water that would crack her bones and split her flesh.

But water, and only water, was what she hit, and that was shock enough. Fran entered the river face-first, a strong slap that made her ears ring, then her body plunged down, deeper and deeper, until Fran wondered if the river even had a bottom. The cold assaulted her from every angle, invading every pore and crevice of her body.

Fran twisted around, but disorientation and darkness prevented her from knowing where the surface was. A strong underwater current pulled her sideways, flipped her over. Fran stopped moving, letting the river control her, until the undertow passed and she felt herself being buoyed upward from the air in her lungs. She scissor-kicked in that direction, kicked until her head pounded, her shoulders and neck straining.

And then Fran breached the surface, coughing and sputtering and surprised to still be alive. She floated onto her back and continued to kick, going with the flow, unable to see anything but knowing that she distanced herself from Taylor with each passing second.

Just as Fran got her breathing under control and settled into a steady rhythm, she heard a sound like distant applause. The noise continued to build, and by the time it had grown into a dull roar she realized where it was coming from and what it was.

Fran turned to face forward, the full moon illuminating the rapidly approaching waterfall.

J osh pointed his light into the trees. He couldn't see their attackers, but he knew they were there.

"Who are they?" Josh asked Streng.

The sheriff had both hands pressed to his side, the gun tucked into his holster. "I have no idea. Their uniforms are bulletproof, look military, but don't have insignias. The smaller one had an accent, sounded Spanish."

"What do they want?"

"He kept asking me about Wiley."

Josh turned the beam in the other direction. He could

feel their eyes on him, but he saw and heard nothing. "Who's Wiley?"

"He said *Warren*. That's his given name, but he only goes by Wiley. He's my brother."

Josh looked at Streng. The older man leaned against a tree and winced.

"Does your brother still live in the area?"

"Probably. I don't know. We don't talk." Streng pushed off from the tree, hitched up his pants, and stared into the woods. "We have to go back for Sal."

Josh felt the bile rise.

"We . . . uh . . . don't have to go back for Sal. I tried. I'm sorry, Sheriff. There was nothing I could do."

Josh's mind took him back to the Mortons' house, that huge man holding Sal's dead wife. Josh tried to grab Sal, to get him to run away. Sal refused to move. Then the giant walked over, calmly put his hands on Sal's neck. Josh threw himself at the larger man, but it had no more effect than wrestling a tree. What happened next was something so horrible, so terrifying . . .

"You're sure he's dead?" Streng asked.

"Yeah." Josh would never be able to erase the image, or the sound. "He's dead. Where's your car?"

"Gold Star." Streng pointed in the direction they just came from. "Maybe we could sneak past them."

"No way."

"How about the fire truck?"

"Someone stole it."

"We're batting a thousand, aren't we?" Streng said it without smiling.

Josh pulled out his compass, found east.

"County Road H shouldn't be too far. We have to get moving. Can you run?"

"I'll manage."

Streng didn't look like he could take another step, but they didn't have a choice. Josh headed east as fast as he could push himself, setting the pace, willing the sheriff to keep up with him.

After twenty yards, Streng fell behind.

Josh stopped, flashed the woods, saw a blur of movement in the distance. The killers were almost upon them. And when they caught up, Josh wouldn't be able to protect the sheriff any more than he had protected Sal. Or Annie.

When Anne was diagnosed with leukemia, he promised he would take care of her. He promised she'd get better. He promised they would get married and have kids and live out their lives just as they'd planned.

Fate made him break all of those promises. After she died, Josh vowed he would help others. So he became a volunteer firefighter, then a full-time firefighter, and soon a paramedic. Josh didn't want to let anyone else down.

He motioned for Streng to hurry. Streng lumbered over, breathing heavy.

"Go on without me, son."

"That's not going to happen."

"They don't want you. Just me. Go on."

Josh put Streng's arm over his shoulders and grabbed him on the side, by the belt. They shuffled through the forest for another hundred yards, until Josh's breath was as ragged as the sheriff's.

"Leave me," Streng said between gasps. "We both don't have to die."

"Stop talking. Run faster."

Streng grunted with effort, but the old guy didn't have anything left in the tank. After a dozen more paces, Josh was practically carrying him. They stopped, panting and wobbly, next to a fallen pine tree, and Josh whipped out his compass.

"Do you have any weapons on you?" Streng rasped.

"Just a pocketknife."

"Take it out and be ready to use it. Flash the light over here."

Josh pointed the beam at Streng's trembling hands. The sheriff ejected the clip, counted bullets.

"Four, plus one in the pipe. They're going to come at us from two different directions. The big one, Ajax, will draw the fire, fast and loud. Santiago will come in sideways, sneaky. I need you to get hid, jump Santiago when he comes out. Know where a man's jugular is?"

Josh nodded, automatically picturing it in his anatomy book.

"Go in at an angle, to get under his clothing. Stab deep and twist."

"What about Ajax?"

"I'll keep the big guy busy."

Josh put his hands on Streng's shoulders, looked deep into his eyes.

"You can't handle him. What he did to Sal . . . it was inhuman."

"Sal wasn't armed. I don't care how tall a man is, he takes a few hits to the oil pan, he leaks. Lemme see your knife."

Josh handed him the slim Swiss Army Explorer, the blade extended.

"*That's* your knife? You win that in Cub Scouts?"

Josh didn't find Streng's lame attempt at humor amusing. "Fighting isn't going to work," Josh said. "We should run. The road is less than a mile away."

"You go."

"We'll both go."

"Son . . . I'm all runned out."

"You can make it."

"I can't make it."

Streng gripped the flashlight, directed it downward. The front of his pants was soaked pink.

"That Santiago, he busted up something inside. The only thing keeping me on my feet is adrenaline, and that's wearing off."

Josh felt sick.

"I couldn't save Sal. I hit Ajax with a chair, and he tossed me aside like I was a stuffed toy."

"Not your fault, son."

"I could have done something else."

"We don't have time for a breakdown now, Josh. Head for the road or hide in the bushes, but make your decision quick."

Josh closed his eyes, let the words come out.

"He twisted off Sal's head, Sheriff. Like a bottle cap."

Josh felt the sting of the slap a millisecond after he heard it. Then Sheriff Streng grabbed Josh's collar.

"That Ajax guy stands damn near over seven feet and has to weigh close to four hundred pounds. God only knows what kind of steroids he's on. You couldn't have stopped him if you had a bazooka. Now forgive yourself and move your ass, or we're both going to die here."

The heat rose on Josh's cheek where Streng had hit him, and he nodded and lumbered into the woods to look for a hiding spot, his Swiss Army Explorer clenched tightly in his fist.

T he phone lines are having some trouble," Mrs. Teller told Duncan. "I can call people in town, but anything outside of Safe Haven gets a busy signal. The same for 911. Maybe it has something to do with the electricity being out."

"What's going on?" Duncan asked.

The old woman racked another shell into the shotgun. "Mr. Teller used to talk about this when he was still alive. Help me with these locks."

Duncan helped her twist the three deadbolts on the front door, but his eyes were on the window.

"Don't worry none about the windows. That glass is shatterproof. Mr. Teller redid them a few years ago, when he was getting nutty from the dementia. There's plastic sandwiched between the two panes. You could hit it with a bat, still can't break through."

Duncan aimed Mrs. Teller's flashlight through the window. He watched Bernie sit up, sniff something he held under his nose, and then pick up his big lighter. He attached a piece of metal to it, and the lighter could shoot like a flamethrower.

"Mrs. Teller. I don't think he's trying to break in."

Mrs. Teller peered out the window and frowned.

"That buckshot didn't seem to slow him down much. Next time I'll aim higher."

"Who is he?"

"I dunno, Duncan. Mr. Teller used to rant on about being invaded by the communists, but he went funny in the head before he died. Ain't no communists left, 'cept for the Chinese. And this fella don't look Oriental."

"He wants to kill me and Woof."

Mrs. Teller put her hand on Duncan's head.

"Child, that ain't gonna happen."

Duncan saw what Bernie was doing and shrank away from the window.

"He's starting the house on fire."

"Looks like that's what he's aiming to do."

Woof nudged up against Duncan, and he knelt down and hugged his dog, tight. He didn't want Woof to be as scared as he was.

The room became orange, as the flames leapt from one window to the next. Duncan smelled smoke.

"I think," Mrs. Teller said, "we had better get into the basement."

The waterfall wasn't any taller than five or six feet, but Fran felt like she'd been dropped from an airplane onto concrete. Though she'd tried to go over feetfirst, she'd gotten turned around and landed full force onto her chest. Every particle of oxygen in her lungs got expelled, and then the current pulled her under, dragging her this way and that way, and her diaphragm refused to follow orders and took in a big gulp of water.

Real panic trumped any psychosomatic panic attack she'd ever experienced. Fran had no time to contemplate her health, or her safety, or if she'd live or die. She didn't think about Duncan or her husband. Her life didn't flash before her eyes. She didn't mourn the future she'd never have.

Her whole body and soul, every nerve, every pore, wanted only one thing—*air*. Fran became a primal animal, not thinking, just existing, and to keep existing she had to breathe.

She thrashed and kicked and strained and coughed, the blackness of unconsciousness mingling with the darkness of the surrounding night, and when she broke the surface gagging and coughing and vomiting water, her throat felt like it had been scoured with steel wool, and she was no longer cold and, strangely, no longer afraid.

The current slowed, and Fran floated on her back, taking in air, letting the burn in her lungs recede. She began to plan.

First she needed to get out of the river. The raw panic of almost drowning had kicked up her body temperature a few degrees, but it was falling again. Fran needed to warm up or she'd die.

Freeing her hands was also important. She tried to flex her fists but didn't feel anything. The cold, and the loss of circulation, had made her arms numb.

Then she needed to find Duncan. She had no idea if Taylor was telling the truth, if they had Duncan, or if it was just something he said to hurt her. But she felt in her heart that Duncan was okay. And she intended to keep it that way.

Fran kicked slowly to shore. When she made it close enough, she stood on the river bottom, the sand sucking at her feet, and half walked/half slithered onto land.

Ahead, a small retaining hill paralleled the riverbank, protecting the road from floods. Fran began to climb. Her dripping body made the earth muddy, slippery. Dirt dug into her wounded foot, and rocks and branches tore at her knees as she crawled up the embankment, but she soldiered on, inch by inch, until she finally reached the top, her heart practically stopping when she saw the large man in the dark uniform standing on the road, staring at her.

Sheriff Streng liked Josh, and for a brief moment he considered eating the gun, which would give the younger man a chance to run, to get away, without the burden of dragging Streng along.

Streng dismissed the notion almost as quickly as it entered his head. While he didn't consider himself beyond heroism or self-sacrifice, Streng knew that Josh had no knowledge of combat, no survival skills. As sad a shape as Streng was in, it would be better for both of them if he stayed alive a while longer. At least until they could find help.

Josh's flashlight winked out five yards east. Streng held his breath, listened to the firefighter climb a tree. Good. Even well-trained soldiers sometimes forgot to look up, especially when facing an inferior enemy. Santiago and Ajax were incredibly well trained, but they also seemed cocky.

Who were they? Streng knew they must be connected to the helicopter crash. He needed to ask Josh about it, see if they could figure out where these guys came from. They wanted Wiley, and Streng knew there could be only one reason someone would bother tracking down that old bastard.

They knew. Somehow they knew.

On one hand, Streng shouldn't have had any problem giving Wiley up. He owed him nothing. And Wiley could take care of himself.

But even though he hadn't spoken to him in thirty years, blood was blood. Streng couldn't forgive Wiley. But he couldn't let anything happen to him, either.

Streng held the pistol in a two-handed grip, pointing at the ground, and waited for the bad men to come.

It didn't take long. As predicted, Ajax came into the clearing with the subtlety of a rampaging bull. He paused, stared directly at Streng, and then ran straight at him.

Streng held his ground, trying to listen for the sneak attack, checking his peripheral vision. There. On the left. Santiago, crouched next to a bush. Unfortunately, Josh's tree was in the opposite direction. Streng would have to lure them over.

Streng ran right, yelling, "Leave me alone, you bastards!" so Josh would know it was him. Then he stopped, turned, and fired twice at Ajax.

The muzzle flash showed Santiago was closer than he'd guessed, practically on top of him. Josh must have seen it, too, because he dropped on Santiago like an avalanche, smashing the man into the ground.

Streng went to him, grabbing at clothing and flailing limbs, trying to put a bullet into Santiago's head.

And then, suddenly, he was no longer on his feet.

Ajax had grabbed Streng's gun arm, his massive fingers encircling his entire biceps. He lifted him up like he was a child. Streng's legs kicked feebly, and he lashed out with his left hand, trying to scratch out the giant's eyes. His fingers met flesh, and two of them disappeared inside a massive nostril. Streng pulled, and something tore.

Ajax bellowed, and then Streng was airborne, branches and leaves whipping at his face.

He blacked out when he hit the tree.

Josh stretched his arm back and brought it down like he was throwing a punch, jabbing the knife into Santiago's neck with everything he had.

The dark, and Santiago struggling against him, made Josh miss. Instead, the knife blade connected with the man's breastbone. It felt like stabbing cement. Josh's wrist twisted, and the blade snapped off.

Santiago grabbed the back of Josh's head, wrapped his fingers in his hair, and yanked him to the side. Josh rolled, and then the monster was on top of him.

"I am going to hurt you," Santiago said. Though Josh's heart hammered like an Olympic sprinter's, Santiago didn't even seem out of breath.

Josh tried to bring up a leg, but Santiago pinned them down with his own. He placed his left hand on Santiago's chest, pushing against it, but he might have been pushing against a wall. The man didn't budge.

Josh felt Santiago's hand travel down his side, over his belly, creeping lower and lower until he cupped Josh's testicles.

Josh tried to jackknife into a sitting position, but Santiago held him immobile. Though they seemed to be the same body weight, the soldier was disproportionably strong.

Santiago brought his face to within an inch of Josh's. "I'll pop them like grapes."

If asked which was worse, a tooth drilled without anesthetic or getting kicked in the balls, any man would choose the former. Knowing that the pain was coming terrified Josh to a degree he didn't know was possible. He put even more effort into his shove, bucked and turned, and then remembered that he still held the Swiss Army Explorer in his right hand. Streng had been right; Josh had owned it since Boy Scouts. He'd used it so many times it had become like an extra appendage. Working by feel, Josh flicked open the corkscrew and held the knife in his fist, so the pointed end protruded up through his clenched fingers.

Santiago squeezed. Josh screamed in pain and horror and then punched Santiago in the side of the head. The corkscrew embedded itself in Santiago's ear, but the man didn't budge, didn't release Josh.

The pain in Josh's groin became so bad his vision actually went red. Hand still on the knife, he began to twist the corkscrew. He punctured something—probably the eardrum—and Santiago howled. He released Josh's balls and brought both hands up to his neck. His thumbs quickly found Josh's carotid arteries and pressed down. Josh's vision went from red to black, but before losing consciousness he brought his hand back and slapped at the side of Santiago's head, forcing the knife in deeper.

Santiago went rigid, then collapsed onto Josh, dead weight.

Josh coughed, disentangling himself from the stronger man, pushing him off. He began to crawl, trying to put as much distance between him and Santiago as possible. His testicles glowed with pain, and like most testicular pain it lingered like a gong being struck, refusing to fade away even though the damage had already been done. Josh felt his stomach flutter, and then he threw up between his hands onto a bed of fallen leaves.

He paused for a moment, trembling, and then felt something large on his back.

Ajax.

Josh's jacket bunched up around his shoulders and chest as the giant clenched a handful of material and lifted Josh into the air. Josh's arms and legs untangled beneath him, and he kicked out but found only air.

Josh felt his head become wrapped in something, and he realized it was the huge man's fist, his enormous fingers encircling it like a baseball.

He knew what came next. The twisting. The popping. The pulling. Josh clenched his teeth and made his neck stiff. When the wrenching began, he fought it with his whole body, refusing to let this happen.

His efforts weren't enough. Ajax's strength was inhuman, and slowly, inexorably, Josh's head began to turn. He strained against it, so hard it felt like his temples would explode, straining even as his chin touched his shoulder and the hyperextension began. Josh couldn't imagine a sound more terrifying than hearing his own spine cracking. He screamed in his throat. He shut his eyes, and tears squeezed out of their ducts.

"Ajax!" Sheriff Streng's voice. "That pressure you feel in the back of your neck is a .45. Even someone as big as you wouldn't be able to handle a few slugs in the vertebrae. Put him down, or I'll fire."

Ajax continued to hold Josh, but the twisting stopped.

"The only thing stopping me from killing you is that I have some questions I want to ask. Now stop fucking around and put down the firefighter!"

Ajax's hands opened and Josh fell onto all fours. He took in a gulp of air, let it out as a brief cry of relief.

"Now get down on your knees, big boy. I'm getting a neck strain staring up at you."

Ajax complied. Josh scrambled around behind him, next to Streng. It was difficult to make out in the dark, but Josh saw the sheriff raise a hand up, then bring it down hard against the side of Ajax's head. Ajax flopped over.

"Shoot them," Josh said, a sob still caught in his throat. "Shoot them both."

"I lost the gun. All I've got is a rock and a tree branch, and I just dropped the rock."

Josh considered their options. Their best chance would be to kill them while they were incapacitated. They could grope around in the dark for the gun. Or maybe find his knife. Josh didn't know if he could stomach the actual killing, but he could leave that up to the sheriff.

"We need to run," Streng said.

"But—"

"I know what you're thinking. But what if one of them wakes up before we find a weapon? Then we're both dead. These guys are too skilled, too strong."

"Maybe Ajax has a gun or a knife on him."

"You want to frisk him?"

"We have to try."

Josh's spirit was willing, but his feet did *not* want to go anywhere near Ajax. Santiago scared him in a bullying, sadistic way, but Josh considered him still human. Ajax was like a creature from a bad dream, a monstrous force of nature. He didn't seem to be the same species, or even to belong on the same planet.

But the only way to stop being afraid was to kill him, and the only way to do that was to search him for weapons.

Josh quickly dismissed using his flashlight, as it might wake his tormentors up. He put his hands out before him and walked cautiously through the darkness, trying not to smack into any trees. His knees bumped into Ajax and he drew in a sharp breath. He reached down, amazed that he could touch his chest without bending over. This guy was freakishly huge. Time became measured in heartbeats, only a finite number remaining before the creature woke up.

Josh screwed up his courage and felt around for the giant's belt. He found a Velcro pouch, ripped it open. It held a smooth metal container, and some kind of electronic gizmo, but no weapons. Josh pocketed the box and continued around the perimeter of his hips. A canteen. Josh took it, attached it to his own belt.

Ajax moved, shifting away. Josh stood absolutely still, fighting the impulse to flee. He needed to finish this up fast.

He patted down the rest of Ajax's waistline but found nothing else. Josh wondered why Ajax didn't have a gun and then realized that the man's enormous fingers probably would be too big to squeeze a trigger. Then why not a knife, or some other weapon? Maybe in his vest.

Josh reached up, fingers exploring. The material was soft, pliable. It amazed Josh that it was actually bulletproof. He found an empty pocket, and then a zipper that was stuck. Ajax's chest rose and fell beneath his hands, so huge that Josh felt like he was frisking a fallen horse.

"I found matches, and some capsules." The sheriff's voice startled Josh. He must have been searching Santiago. "You?"

"A container, some sort of electric thing, and water."

Josh reached up higher, touched Ajax's throat. Any thought of breaking the man's spine while he slept vanished when Josh realized how large it was. It would be easier to snap a log in half.

"My knife should be in his ear," Josh told Streng.

"Not there. Maybe he pulled it . . . *umph*."

A gentle rustling sound. Then the forest went quiet.

"Sheriff?"

Streng didn't answer. Josh strained to hear but heard only the steady rasp of Ajax's breathing.

"Sheriff Streng? You okay?"

He felt foolish the instant it left his lips. Of course he wasn't okay. Santiago must have woken up. Maybe Streng was already dead. Why hadn't they run away like the sheriff suggested?

Ajax shifted, emitting a low growl. Josh jumped back. He considered taking off, finding County Road H, following that into town. Maybe he'd be able to flag down a car. Once he got to Safe Haven he could call the state cops. He faced the woods, his legs itching to bolt.

Not without the sheriff, he told himself.

Then he turned, clenched his fists, and headed toward Santiago.

• • •

Fran had never been so cold. Her whole body—not just her bound hands—felt numb, and her teeth chattered. But when she saw the large uniformed figure standing on the dark road, Fran turned and started down the embankment, back into the river.

"Hey! You okay?"

Fran didn't stop. The voice didn't belong to Taylor, but she didn't trust anyone walking alone at night. She tried to keep her balance, to plant her feet firmly after every step, but the slope was steep and she was still dripping. Her damp heel slid on a patch of weeds and she fell onto her back. Before she could move again a flashlight beam hit her face, prompting a wince.

"Fran? Is that you?"

Fran squinted into the light, couldn't make out anyone behind it. But the voice didn't seem threatening, and it was oddly familiar.

She managed to swallow the lump in her throat and said, "Who's there?"

"Erwin Luggs. You work with my fiancée, Jessie Lee, at Merv's Diner. I also teach Duncan."

Erwin. He was one of Safe Haven's firemen, and he taught gym at the junior high. Her son liked him. Jessie Lee complained about him all the time, to the point where Fran wondered why she had agreed to marry him.

Before Fran answered, Erwin had his big hands on her arm and helped her up.

"Jesus, Fran, what happened?"

Fran's eyes widened in fear when she realized Erwin was covered in blood. Erwin seemed to read her reaction.

"It's from a deer," he said.

Fran recovered from the shock. "My hands. Do you have a knife or something that cuts?"

"I've got some fingernail clippers."

"See if they work on this plastic."

Erwin disappeared behind her, and Fran could barely feel his touch as he manipulated her hands and arms.

And then, agony.

Her hands fell at her sides, and the blood rushing back in burned like acid. Her arms, and especially her fingers, were being stabbed with thousands of pins while simultaneously being dunked in lava.

Fran began to cry, and Erwin took his bloody jacket off to drape over her shoulders. It smelled rank, but she welcomed the warmth. Fran opened and closed her fists, trying to make it stop, and Erwin must have mistaken her pain for distress because he put his arms around her in a protective, brotherly way.

"What happened, Fran? Who did this to you?"

Fran sniffled, then went rigid, as if someone had stuck a pole up her spine.

"Duncan. We need to get to my son. Do you have a phone?"

"I've been trying for half an hour. No signal."

"Let me borrow it."

Erwin fished it out of his pocket, handed it over.

"Where's your car?"

"Back at the station."

Fran dialed, but her fingers hit the wrong buttons.

She kept trying, getting the same results. Frustrated, she handed the phone back to Erwin.

"Dial for me."

"There are no bars. We're in the middle of the woods."

"Dial!"

Fran stated her phone number, and Erwin dutifully punched in the digits. Then he held the phone up so she could hear the *we're sorry* recording.

"We need to get to my house, Erwin. Right now."

"I need to get to town. Something's happened to Josh and Sheriff Streng."

"Josh?"

"There was a helicopter crash in the woods, and someone stole our truck. Then I saw the sheriff get attacked by some guy in a black uniform."

Taylor wore a black uniform. And though Fran hadn't seen his face, whoever was driving the fire truck with the mayor also wore black.

"Something's going on," Fran said. "Something bad. Which way is town?"

"About two miles south. This is Harris Street."

Fran knew Harris Street. She hadn't recognized it in the dark. Her neighborhood was less than a mile away.

"Duncan might be in trouble, Erwin. I think one of those men in the black uniforms has him."

Erwin stepped away from her, spreading his hands. "I need to get to town, Fran. I need to—"

She grabbed Erwin by his shirt, the motion bringing fresh tears to her eyes.

"I need your help, dammit! Help me get my son!"

"These men—we need some help. We can't do this alone . . ."

Fran pushed Erwin away, then began to run down the road. Away from town. Toward home.

"Fran!"

Fran ignored him, ignored the pain in her arms, ignored the throb in her injured foot that ignited every time it hit the pavement. Nothing would stop her from getting to her son. Nothing.

Mathison let out a screech of displeasure and hung on to the back of Dr. Stubin's collar. That was how he hid. Stubin also felt like hiding. The helmet and fatigues made him feel like a child playing dress-up, and the fact he hadn't been given a gun hammered home the point; he wasn't a soldier.

Of course he wasn't. Stubin was a scientist. Perhaps the premier brain specialist on the planet, a fact he would someday prove. Traipsing around through the forest playing commando wasn't the best use of his time and skills. But he had to be here, much as he loathed it.

The helicopter had dropped him and Mathison off at the crash site. A sergeant and two privates were also deposited there—for babysitting duty—until the Green Berets arrived. His minders were humorless, no-nonsense, and though they weren't openly hostile Stubin could feel their disdain for his presence.

The three didn't approach the wreck of the chopper; they were probably under orders not to. But Stubin had no such orders, and he spent a few minutes examining the site, with a monkey literally on his back.

The decapitations in the cockpit were a surprise, but Stubin wasn't shocked. Being a brain surgeon, he'd witnessed more than his fair share of gore. He looked closer, the flares and field lighting set up around the perimeter allowing him to do so without needing a flashlight.

The cuts were clean, almost surgically so. Cutting off a human head wasn't easy, and Stubin felt strangely impressed.

Next he poked around in the back of the wreckage and found a large footlocker. It couldn't be opened without a key, but next to it was an electronic panel with buttons and switches.

In the distance, Stubin heard another helicopter. He took it to be the Special Forces team. Stubin checked his watch, did a quick equation in his head, and estimated they'd be here within two minutes.

A moment later Mathison abandoned his hiding place on Stubin's back and leapt out the side door, bounding off into the woods.

"Mathison! Dammit, come back!"

Stubin bounded after him, tripping over some debris on the ground. The soldiers didn't laugh. Nor did they try to stop him when he picked himself up and headed into the woods after his monkey.

The light seemed to reduce by half every five steps, and after walking for less than a minute Stubin was surrounded by the dark. He stared at the helicopter coming in low overhead, holding on to his helmet as it passed. Stubin made an OK sign with his thumb and index, then stuck it into his mouth and blew. The shrill whistle could be heard above the din of the Huey, and Mathison came running out of the trees and stopped to stare at him.

"Don't be afraid, Mathison. It's just another helicopter. Come on."

Stubin crouched down, smiling. He patted his thighs, and then a tremendous explosion shocked his ears, causing the ground to shake and momentarily turning night into day.

The fingers that locked around Streng's throat were cutting off his air, preventing him from answering Josh. The darkness of the woods, and his inability to make a sound, meant he was going to die less than five feet away from his young friend.

Streng knelt next to the killer's prostrate body and struggled against the grip, his efforts no more effective than when Santiago had been on top of him, mauling his kidney. The man had preternatural strength, and Streng felt like he had a noose around his neck rather than flesh and bone.

He reached down, trying to find Santiago's face. The killer's arms were longer, keeping Streng away. But they weren't longer than Streng's legs. Though on his knees, Streng managed to tilt left and get one of his feet in front of him. He kicked Santiago in the side, fiercely. Again. And again.

The killer held on. Streng's balance faltered and he fell onto his side. Still, Santiago squeezed his neck, hands tightening, Streng's vision blurring and going black.

Streng planted both feet under Santiago's chin, using it as a fulcrum. Then he pulled back as hard as he could, using the muscles in his legs and his back, straining and pushing until the claws released him, allowing in sweet, sweet oxygen.

"Josh . . ." he croaked.

The flashlight came on, and then Josh hooked a hand around his belt and bullied him through the woods as fast as they both could move. Streng didn't have a chance to catch his breath, and he kept tripping over things, but Josh never let him fall, never let the pace slacken.

The road appeared suddenly, rising out of the trees like a fever dream, and as the sheriff doubled over and sucked in air he barely noticed Josh yelling. A screeching sound cut the silence of the night, accompanied by the smell of rubber, and then Streng had a hand over his eyes, protecting them from the blinding light coming from—

"Sheriff? Josh? What in the high hell are you doing out here?"

—Olen Porrell's Honey Wagon, a large tanker truck with a cartoon skunk painted on the side. The skunk wore big smile on its face and a clothespin on its nose, and the cartoon balloon next to its head said "Septic and Plumbing!"

Olen climbed out of his truck and hurried over to them. He wore the typical Olen outfit of stained bib overalls, stained T-shirt, and the world's filthiest Brewers baseball cap. In the headlights Streng could see Olen's face clearly but still couldn't make out where the beard ended and the grime began.

Josh clasped the plumber on the shoulder. "We need to get to a hospital, Olen."

Streng righted himself and shook his head. "First I need to get to my office outside of town."

"You need a doctor."

"I need a gun, a telephone, and a new pair of pants. The doctor can wait."

"Someone want to tell me what's going . . . Jesus H. Christmas, what the hell is that?"

Fifty yards ahead of them Ajax stepped onto the road.

"We have to go," Streng said. "Now."

He pulled Olen and Josh back to the Honey Wagon, which was every bit as filthy as Olen. It smelled like the sewage Olen spent his days pumping.

"Who is that guy? What's going on, Sheriff?"

Streng jerked open the cab door and climbed up.

"Olen, where do you stash that twenty-two Long Rifle you use to hunt white-tail out of season?"

"Sheriff, deer season don't start until November seventeenth, and—"

"Give me the damn gun, Olen, or we're all going to die."

Olen reached behind the driver's seat and handed Streng a lever-action Marlin.

"Get in," Streng told Josh and Olen. Then he cranked open the passenger-side window, chambered a round, and aimed at Ajax, who sprinted at them with astonishing speed.

Streng fired five times, fast as he could work the action. Then he checked the rearview. As expected, Santiago was coming up fast.

"Drive! There's another one behind us!"

Olen didn't need any more prodding. He stomped on the gas and the Honey Wagon lurched forward. Ajax hadn't been stopped by Streng's shots and continued to come at them, a charging rhino. Streng switched his grip on the rifle.

"Pull up to him, on my side!"

Olen complied. Streng leaned out the window, feeling Josh's hand on his belt. As the truck passed Ajax, he swung the rifle like a baseball bat. The impact sent a shock of pain through Streng's palms, vibrations traveling up both arms and shaking his shoulders. The walnut stock split in half on Ajax's head, cracking along the pistol grip. But Streng managed to keep hold of the gun, and Josh yanked him back inside. Olen cruised into second gear and Streng dared to hope that they might actually live for a bit longer.

"Olen, you just saved our bacon."

"Happy to oblige, Sheriff. Now one of you wanna tell me what just happened?"

"A helicopter crashed near the big lake," Josh said. "I think it was hauling some kind of military prisoners. They escaped, killed Sal and Maggie Porter, and almost killed us."

"I'll be damned. Never saw a man that big before. Your shots hit him in the chest—I was watching. He didn't even flinch. Think they know about the lottery?"

"Lottery?"

"Mayor called a town meeting, half hour ago. Safe Haven won the Powerball. Everyone is meeting at the junior high, because we all get a share. The phone lines have been burning up with folks sharing the news. I called ten people myself. Didn't anyone call you?"

Streng remembered the mayor's phone call earlier. He wondered if this was connected to the soldiers somehow.

"Turn on Harris, Olen."

"But the junior high is—"

"It can wait. I need to get to my office first."

Then the horizon lit up, accompanied by the *BOOM* of a massive explosion.

S antiago watched the truck speed off, then turned to see the mushroom cloud rising in the distance. It blended into the black sky as the fire died down.

The Special Forces have arrived, he thought and reached for a Charge capsule on his utility belt. His pack wasn't there.

Santiago's upper lip twitched, and a small jolt of panic worked its way through his central nervous system. He jogged over to Ajax, who seemed unaffected by the long gash spilling blood down the side of his head.

"They took my Charge."

Ajax felt around his own belt, then wailed like a sick cow. He was out, too.

"*Putas,*" Santiago said. He touched his wounded ear and snapped his fingers. He didn't hear it. Ruptured eardrum. Then he pulled the communicator out of his front pocket, slid back the cover, and held it to his mouth. "This is Santiago. The bird has flown. What's your position?"

The reply came on the text screen, backlit by a faint green glow.

Gymnasium at the junior high. Running the winner's circle.

"We'll meet you there."

Negative. Remain on target.

"We're . . ."—the words seemed to stick in Santiago's throat—". . . out of Charge."

You're on your own. We're not sharing. Out.

Santiago clicked off, teeth grinding teeth. The mission remained a top priority, but without Charge how long could they keep on track?

Ajax poked stupidly at the wound in his forehead, making it worse.

"I'll fix it," Santiago said, unclipping a propane torch from his belt.

He flicked the flame on. Ajax didn't flinch, didn't moan, as Santiago cauterized the gash. The sizzling sounded a lot like bacon frying.

Santiago kept the flame on for several seconds longer than needed, then touched it to the giant's ripped nostril. He watch, fascinated, as the hairs glowed orange and burned away, and then turned his attention to the new set of headlights coming up the road.

"Hide," he ordered Ajax.

The giant lumbered into the woods, and Santiago stood in the center of the street, waving his hands above his head. The car, a boxy SUV, slowed down and stopped a few yards in front of him. Santiago fixed a placid smile on his face and approached.

"Help you?" the driver asked.

Santiago reached in through the open window, seizing the driver by the throat.

"Yes, you can. But before I take your vehicle, I have a question. Do you know anyone named Warren Streng?"

Duncan's dog glowed green. So did Mrs. Teller. She and Duncan had opened a box of bend-and-shake light sticks and placed them around the room like candles. They weren't very bright but lit up enough of the basement for Duncan to see around him.

Mrs. Teller had called this room a *shelter* and said Mr. Teller built it during one of his paranoid delusions. Shelves lined all four walls, each stocked with canned food, bottles of water, and other supplies like batteries, toilet paper, and boxes of foil-wrapped glow sticks. Duncan loved glow sticks on Halloween and at the state fair. But in this little room the lights were creepy. Mrs. Teller had given him a white undershirt that was too big on him, hanging past his knees. It also glowed green.

Pounding, on the door at the top of the stairs. Bernie had gotten in the house. Though the basement door looked very strong and had a big lock on it, Duncan worried that he'd be able to get in.

"We're safe," Mrs. Teller said. "That's a steel door. Mr. Teller bought only the best. It will hold."

The pounding continued. It sounded like Bernie was hitting the door with something big. Duncan could feel his bones shake with every impact. Woof barked, and Duncan wrapped his arms around the dog's neck, burying his face in his fur.

BAAAAAAAAAM!

BAAAAAAAAAM!

"Oh, dear. It sounds like he's found Mr. Teller's tools."

BAAAAAAAAAM!

"Don't be scared, Woof," Duncan whispered. The dog trembled.

BAAAAAAAAAM!

"We're going to be okay."

BAAAAAAAAAM!

The last sound was followed by a creaking noise, like wood splitting.

"It will hold," Mrs. Teller said again. But this time she didn't sound so sure.

The pain in her arms faded as her circulation returned, and Fran concentrated on the road ahead—left foot right foot left foot right foot. She used to love running, and years ago her tracks graced every trail, road, and highway in Ashburn County. Since the accident Fran had restricted her jogging to the treadmill in the basement. She told herself it was because she didn't want to leave Duncan alone any longer than necessary, but deep down she knew the real truth: running alone scared her. Fran remembered what it was like when something happened and there was no one around to help. She wouldn't put herself in that situation again.

And yet, she'd put Duncan in that situation.

Their therapist, Dr. Walker, had told Fran that it would be good for Duncan to be left alone at night. It would help build his self-esteem. Fran had resisted, and Walker had broken her down her with jargon like *enabling* and *transference*. The next time she saw Dr. Walker he was going to learn some of her jargon, like *broken nose*.

Sound, behind her, and Fran glanced back and saw a figure pounding the pavement in her wake. Erwin. He seemed to have located his spine. Not that she could blame him. Less than an hour ago, Fran had been paralyzed with fear, unable to move. People handled crisis situations in different ways. Hopefully Erwin wouldn't panic; she needed him.

The Pine Village sign at the entrance to her subdivision—framed in pine logs and set into a grass knoll surrounded by decorative stones and violets—was strangely dark. Ground lights normally illuminated it, but along with the streetlamps, they were out.

Fran veered onto Montrose Street, and every house on the block, every house in the development, lacked electricity. Except for the moon, the only light in the area came from over the hill, a disturbing orange flicker that made Fran push herself even harder.

When she reached the crest, her fears were confirmed. Her house, and Mrs. Teller's, burned big and bright.

"Oh, no, oh, God, no . . ."

Fran sprinted down the hill, pain, exhaustion, and fear all pushed aside by the overwhelming need to find Duncan. She ran up to her house, but she couldn't get close. The heat that came off it was like opening a five-hundred-degree oven, and a wave of hot air wicked away the water from her clothes and hair and sucked the moisture from her panting mouth. She tried to take another step closer, the temperature making her skin hurt, and Erwin held her back.

"It's gone!" he yelled, Fran barely able hear him over the crackling, spitting blaze. She watched, horrified, as the roof collapsed, the flames reaching into the sky and doubling the height of her home. A plume of smoke billowed out through the front door, covering them with hot soot.

The front door. It was open. Duncan and Woof must have gotten out.

Fran spun, looking at Mrs. Teller's house. Hers was in much better shape, fire on the porch and climbing up the west wall, but the house still intact. Duncan knew to go there if something happened. That's where he had to be.

Fran rushed across the expanse of lawn, saw Mrs. Teller's front door yawning open through the wreath of flame. She faintly heard Erwin yelling in protest as she dashed through the doorway and into the smoke-filled foyer, running directly into the man dressed in black who pounded on the basement door with a sledgehammer.

Erwin Luggs watched Fran dash into the burning building and knew he should go in after her, but his feet didn't want to move.

Do it! You're a firefighter, for chrissakes.

But Josh wasn't here, he didn't have any of his equipment, and he had a strong feeling that there was someone in that house, someone bad.

He felt something vibrate in his pocket and almost slapped at it in surprise before he remembered his cell phone.

His cell phone. He was getting a signal. Erwin dug it out and put it to his face.

"Erwin? It's Jessie Lee. Where the heck have you been?"

"Jessie Lee! Baby, it's great to hear your voice!"

"Erwin, I'm at the junior high and I put your name down on the lottery list. They're going to call us any minute. You have to get over here."

Erwin wasn't sure what his fiancée was talking about, and normally when Jessie Lee told him to do something he was on it immediately, but while he had a cell phone signal he needed to call someone about this fire.

"Look, honey, I'll call you right back." He hit disconnect and then speed dial for Josh. Though the fire made it hard to hear, his effort was rewarded with a ringing sound. When Josh answered he almost whooped for joy.

"Josh! It's Erwin! I'm at Fran Stauffer's house in Pine Village! Her house is burning down and I need your help!"

"Erwin? I'm with Sheriff Streng. We'll be there soon."

This time, Erwin did whoop. Streng was still alive. Erwin's chest swelled. His cowardice hadn't killed anyone, and this information, along with the reassurance that Josh would be here soon, spurred him to action.

Erwin ran to the side of Mrs. Teller's house and turned on the faucet for the garden hose. He dragged the hose to the front porch and aimed at the foot of the fire. The water vaporized on contact, hissing and steaming, but the flames began to slowly recede. Erwin waved away some smoke and called to Fran.

She screamed in reply.

Josh will be here soon, he thought. Josh always knew what to do.

Fran screamed again. Through the haze, Erwin saw her fighting with a man dressed in black.

Erwin's bowels churned, and he felt like his legs

wouldn't support him. This was just like what happened with Sheriff Streng. He wanted to make this all go away, to turn back time and not pick up the phone when Josh called and told him about the helicopter crash. Everything would work out better if he wasn't a part of it.

The man in black hit Fran across the face, and she fell to the floor. Erwin watched him lift something—it looked like a sledgehammer—and hold it over Fran's head.

I shouldn't be here, Erwin thought.

Then he surprised himself by running into the burning house.

J essie Lee Sloan tried to dial Erwin again and got that annoying message about the cell phone customer not being available. She threw the phone in her purse, annoyed. Why did anyone in Safe Haven even bother with cell phones? They were a cruel joke.

"Is Erwin coming?"

Mrs. Melody Montague, whom Jessie Lee had as a second-grade teacher and who still taught second grade all these years later, leaned into Jessie Lee's personal space. Her breath smelled like mentholated cough drops, and Jessie Lee didn't like her any more now than she did at age seven when Mrs. Montague taught them how to draw Thanksgiving turkeys by tracing their hands. The drawings didn't look like birds—they looked like palm prints—and when Jessie Lee said so she was given a time-out in the corner.

"He's coming," Jessie Lee answered without facing the elderly woman.

"Isn't this exciting? I suppose we should all be mad at Mayor Durlock for using the Safe Haven coffers to buy Powerball tickets, but what a treat that he's sharing it with the whole town. What are you going to do with your forty-thousand dollars?"

"Eighty thousand," Jessie Lee corrected. "After the wedding."

"Of course. I'm sure it will make the wedding even more spectacular."

Indeed it would. Sometimes it seemed to Jessie Lee that she'd been dreaming of her wedding day since her birth. Though Erwin wasn't rich, he'd been working tirelessly to give her all that she wanted, which was one of the reasons she loved him. She had diamond earrings, and a thick gold Omega necklace with matching anklet, and was the only woman in Safe Haven with a Gucci handbag. Erwin treated her like a princess.

Even so, budgetary constraints had forced her to cut back on some of the more extravagant expenditures. But with this money the whole storybook fairy tale could come true. There would be ice sculptures, and a full orchestra, and a gourmet seven-course banquet, and a designer dress rather than one she found at the outlet mall. Her ceremony would be the talk of Safe Haven for years to come.

"Will the next person please come up for their check," the lottery commissioner announced into the gymnasium's PA system. He was a tall, roguishly handsome man who wore a strange black uniform. Mayor Durlock sat next to him, looking oddly depressed considering all of the excitement. Jessie Lee could guess that he was annoyed, having to share the money with the whole town. She certainly would be.

"Melody Montague."

Mrs. Montague squealed and clapped her hands together. As with everyone else, the late hour and long line hadn't depressed her in the least. She scurried up to the podium, shook the lottery commissioner's hand, and he escorted her out of the gym, into the boys' locker room.

A few seconds passed, and another, louder, squeal came from Mrs. Montague. The crowd on the bleachers chuckled, then resumed their conversations.

Jessie Lee looked at her watch, then surveyed the gym. Most of Safe Haven had shown up for this impromptu town meeting. In small towns, bad news traveled fast, but good news spread like lightning. The mayor's initial phone call to his staff had ballooned into everyone calling everyone within fifteen minutes. And people still kept coming. As they entered the gym, the town treasurer, a wisp of a man named Rick Hortach, explained that they'd be cut a check and then added their name to the list. No one seemed bothered by the fact that it was almost one in the morning. Everywhere she looked, Jessie Lee saw big smiles and laughter.

So where the heck is Erwin?

Jessie Lee located her boss, Merv Johnson, in the crowd, spotting the glare of his bald head in the overhead lights. The entire town—Jessie's apartment included—had been without electricity for the past hour, but the junior high boasted two huge gas-powered generators. Jessie Lee stood up and bleacher-walked down two flights, putting her hand on his large shoulder.

"Merv, you came in just before me, right?"

Merv shrugged, all three of his chins jiggling. "I dunno. Wasn't paying attention. You think Corvettes are sexy?"

"Very sexy. Look, I saw the list, and you were one ahead of me. I need to run outside, have a smoke. If you get called next, tell them I'll be right back."

"Sure. What's sexier, black or red?"

"Red, Merv. You'll tell the commissioner?"

"No problem, Jessie Lee. Automatic or manual?"

"Automatic. That leaves your hand free for other things."

Merv slapped his massive thigh and laughed. "Good call, Jessie Lee. I'll make sure you don't get skipped."

Jessie Lee gave him a decidedly unsexy pat on the head, then made her way down the bleachers to the gym floor. A few people waved at her, giddy as children on Christmas morning. She waved back, grinning. Free money brought out the best in people.

Jessie Lee headed for the side door to access the parking lot. Locked. She sighed and walked to the next door down. Also locked. Odd. These were emergency doors, with the long bar across the middle that you pushed on. They weren't supposed to be locked. She had to walk back the way she came in. Rick Hortach eyed her as she walked to the entrance and pushed at the door lever. It didn't budge.

"Rick, what's up with the doors?"

His voice matched his appearance, thin and reedy. "The mayor wants them locked. If anyone leaves, there won't be an accurate head count."

"Next up is John Kramer," the PA system boomed. John gave a hoot, then made his way down the bleachers.

"It's a fire hazard, Rick."

"The mayor said—"

"Does the mayor want me to smoke inside?"

"There's no smoking in—"

"Look, Rick." Jessie Lee leaned in close. "If I don't get my nicotine fix I'm going to bite someone's head off. Now open the door before I start screaming that you touched me inappropriately."

Rick blinked with sad basset hound eyes and then fished around for his keychain and opened the door. Jessie Lee smiled sweetly before leaving the gym and stepping out into the cool, dark night. It took a lot of fumbling through her purse to locate her cigarettes and lighter. She lit up, and the hot smoke saturating her lungs was a gift from God.

After a few puffs she began to get chilly—it was much cooler outside than in the gym. The sleeveless top she wore didn't provide much in the way of coverage. Neither did the denim mini. But the outfit showed off her figure, and it was damn cute.

She rubbed her arms and took a brisk walk across the parking lot to kick-start her circulation. When she reached the end, she spotted the distinct shape of a Ford Fairlane. Seamus Dailey's car. A 1955 Skyliner Crown Victoria, completely restored. Seamus had taken just about everyone in town for a ride at one time or another. Jessie Lee didn't understand why the car was still here, because Seamus had been one of the first people on the list and must have gotten his check a while ago.

Jessie Lee sucked in more smoke and continued to walk. An aisle over was another car she recognized, Mary Porter's beat-up Pontiac. Mary had been driving on the undersized temporary spare for over two years. This also seemed strange. Jessie Lee could have sworn she heard

Mary's name called by the lottery commissioner a half an hour ago at least.

Maybe they're together, Jessie Lee thought. She smirked, imagining Mrs. Porter and Mr. Dailey, both well into their sixties, having a quickie somewhere. Jessie Lee leaned closer to the Pontiac, checking to see if the windows were foggy or the chassis was rocking. The car looked empty.

She finished the smoke, ground it out under the toe of her pumps, and tried Erwin again on the cell. No signal. When she turned to head back in she bumped into a man.

Jessie Lee let out a cry of surprise and stepped backward. It was the lottery commissioner.

"Why aren't you inside?" he asked.

"I stepped out for a smoke. One of my many bad habits."

Jessie Lee smiled brightly. He didn't smile back. Up close, he didn't look as handsome as she originally thought. And something about him struck a chord.

"If you want to get what's coming to you, you need to get back inside."

He flashed a humorless grin, and Jessie Lee realized why he looked familiar. She was a Court TV junkie, and this guy was the spitting image of Marshal Otis Taylor. Taylor was a serial killer and murdered more than twenty women back in the 1990s. He did some really twisted things to them, too, like bite off their fingers and toes.

Jessie Lee didn't like biters. She had a terrible experience with one once.

This guy certainly had the Taylor cold stare down pat. If memory served, Taylor had died by lethal injection about five years ago, so there was no way he could be the real deal. Still, it was kind of creepy. Jessie Lee wondered if she should tell him who he resembled. She decided there wasn't any point—who would like knowing they looked like one of the world's most notorious psychos? Besides, it wasn't a wise idea to annoy the guy cutting forty-grand checks.

"Let's get back, then," Jessie Lee said, offering the commissioner her arm. He took it, roughly, and walked her back to the gym. Once the door closed behind them he headed back to the locker room. Jessie Lee decided he was kind of a dick. Maybe he was pissed off at having to work so late.

She rubbed her arms again and felt something sticky on her shoulder. There, where the commissioner had touched her, was a smear of blood.

Fran's eye fixed on the sledgehammer poised above her head, but rather than fear she felt rage.

"Where's Duncan?" she yelled.

The man in black paused. Smoke swirled up around his shoulders, but Fran could still make out his smile. He bent down, his free hand squeezing her right breast.

"Are you, are you his, Duncan's, mother?"

Fran recoiled from his revolting touch and she tried to push away his hand, but for a thin man he possessed unbelievable strength. The harder she shoved, the harder he squeezed, until Fran could almost feel his fingers touch each other.

"Leave us alone!"

"Yes, yes, you're the mother. Fran. The pictures match. Tell me where—"

And then the man was off her, rolling to the side, the sledgehammer thrown up into the air. Fran watched it arc upward—so clear and detailed it seemed like slow motion—and then crash into the floor just a few inches from her head, cracking the tile and peppering her with broken bits.

She twisted to the side and saw the stranger roll across the foyer with . . . *Erwin!* He'd come through, after all.

Fran turned her attention back to the basement door. She scrambled to it on all fours, staying under the hovering cloud of smoke, and banged on it with her open palm.

"Duncan! It's Mom! Open the door!"

A grunt, to her left. The stranger, though smaller, had managed to get on top of Erwin and straddle him. Fran continued to pound.

"Mrs. Teller! It's Fran Stauffer! Are you in there!"

"Mom!"

Hearing Duncan's voice made Fran want to sing.

"Duncan! Open up! Hurry!"

She put her ear to the door, listening to deadbolts turning and mechanisms engaging. But the door didn't budge.

"Mom! It's stuck!"

Fran coughed—hot, viscous, black smoke hovered at chest level—and reached for the knob. It wouldn't turn. The stranger must have damaged it with the sledgehammer.

A scream, raw and high-pitched. Fran looked. The stranger had some sort of miniature flamethrower. He held it to Erwin's face.

She needed to protect Duncan, but if Erwin were killed she wouldn't be able to fight the stranger herself.

Erwin's howl cut into her, forcing her decision. Fran launched herself at the man in black.

J osh handed his cell over to Streng and listened to the sheriff's conversation with the state police.

"Safe Haven is under attack by an unknown military force . . . armed and very dangerous, they've already killed two that I know of, and there have been several fires and an explosion . . . as many men as you can spare . . . I'll be at my office outside of town . . . reception is spotty, try me on my land line there . . . dammit!"

The sheriff squinted at the phone, which had apparently disconnected. Josh took the phone back, tried to redial. No signal. He put the phone in his pocket and felt the container he'd taken from Ajax. He pulled it out. It looked like a cigarette case, but rounder, and the finish was blackened like gun metal. A latch on the side opened it. Inside, nestled in the felt lining, were rows of amber capsules.

"What are these? Pills?"

Streng opened a matching case and squinted. "Kind of big for pills." He took one out and rolled it between his fingers. "They look like poppers. Who the hell knows? Probably shouldn't mess with them."

Josh considered throwing the case out the window but wound up pocketing it again. Then he studied the electronic device he'd found on Ajax. Like the case, it was made of smooth black metal. But it was solid rather than hollow and had a USB port on the bottom. It also had a large dent in the face, possibly from one of Streng's bullets. Josh played with it for a few seconds, trying to get it to do something. He failed. Then he gave it to Streng, who had similar results.

"Maybe it's a tracking device, like a GPS. Lemme have that canteen."

Josh handed it over. Streng unscrewed the cap and sniffed. He must have judged it safe, because he took a long pull and passed it to Josh. The firefighter drank greedily, surprised at how thirsty he was. They each took another sip, and then the canteen was empty.

"Here's Pine Village."

Olen swung the Honey Wagon onto Montrose Street at a sharp angle, and Josh heard the liquid contents in the tank behind him slosh in protest. He could see the fire behind the hill ahead. Josh's thoughts shifted to Fran: smart, funny, sexy, a great mother, and great all-around person. He really messed up a good thing with her.

Josh willed her to be okay. For her sake, and for Duncan's, but also for selfish reasons. Josh was surprised how much the thought of her being in trouble made him angry.

The Honey Wagon crested the hill, and Josh set his jaw against the inferno before them. Fran's house looked like a palace in hell, every window and doorway belching flame, not a square inch untouched by fire. A lost cause. Anyone trapped inside would be dead by now.

Olen slowed down and uttered, "Wow."

Across from it, another home, burning but in better shape. Josh saw an unattended garden hose, pumping water onto the porch. That had to be where Erwin was. And, hopefully, Fran and Duncan.

"Park by that house," Josh instructed Olen. "What's in your tank right now?"

"Sump water."

"How do you pump it out?"

"Way ahead of you, boss. It's gonna smell to high heaven."

"Smelly is better than burned to the ground."

Before Olen came to a full stop Josh swung open the passenger door, hopped out, and sprinted for the entrance. His groin still ached, and his neck felt like he'd been whip-lashed, but neither slowed him down. He heard Sheriff Streng bark something behind him, the words getting lost in the roar of burning house. Josh pulled his shirt up over his nose and hunched low under the cloud of smoke hugging the ceiling. Small fires dotted the walls and furniture, and the inside temp had to be over a hundred degrees.

Josh scanned the foyer and spotted three people rolling around on the floor. Erwin, Fran, and—Josh couldn't believe it—Santiago. No . . . not Santiago. But someone just as creepy, all dressed in black and sporting a rapturous expression as he tried to hold a flame to Erwin's face.

Josh rushed over, helping Fran pull the intruder off of Erwin. Even with four arms against the intruder's one, it was a battle. But then Erwin became aware of Josh's presence, and he added his weight and strength to the cause. They peeled the intruder off of Erwin, pinning the hand that held the large lighter to the floor.

When Erwin got back to his feet he touched the raw burn on his cheek, grimaced, and made a fist the size of a small ham. He dropped onto the intruder, bellowed out in pain and rage, and began to smash him in the face. As Josh watched, Erwin split the man's nose, cracked his teeth, and bloodied both eyes. The intruder kept a sick grin on his face the entire time, a grin that stayed on even after he lost consciousness.

Josh pried the lighter out of the man's hand and locked eyes with Fran. She looked like she'd been in a war. Her hair was a rat's nest, her clothes were torn, and her skin was a mosaic of soot, mud, and blood. Josh reached out for her hand, but she had already spun away, heading deeper into the house.

"Watch him!" Josh yelled at Erwin. Then he went after Fran.

She knelt next to a closed door, tugging at the knob. He bent down next to her.

"Duncan and Mrs. Teller are in there! It's a bomb shelter!"

Josh's hands joined hers on the knob and they both tugged. The door didn't budge. Josh knocked on it, surprised by how warm it felt. Metal. All firemen hated metal doors. Even worse, the frame also seemed to be reinforced.

"Duncan! It's Josh VanCamp! Can you hear me!"

"Yeah!" The boy's voice was muffled and filled with fear.

"We're going to get you out!" Josh yelled. Then he pulled Fran close and said into her ear, "I have to go to the truck."

Fran grabbed his arm and dug her fingers in. Her eyes got wide.

"Don't leave."

"I'm not leaving. I'll be right back."

Fran nodded and released him. The smoke had built up on the ceiling and floated at chest level. Josh moved in a crouch to stay under it. He squinted at Erwin, who had been joined by Sheriff Streng. They had tied up the intruder and were tugging him out of the building.

Josh beat them outside. He coughed, spat out black, and took a big gulp of cool night air. Olen had a filthy hose clutched in his gloved hands, spraying the side of the house with human waste. Josh could smell it through the smoke. He wrinkled his nose and hopped in the cab of the truck, grabbing the rifle. The stock had a split in it, but it looked able to fire. He didn't think a .22 would do much against a steel door, but he had no other ideas.

"Keep it low, at the foot of the flame," Josh told Olen.

"I am. It's not working."

The fire had reached the second floor. Josh realized that with the equipment they had the house was a goner.

"Keep going. There are people trapped inside."

Olen nodded at him, and Josh went back into the building. Smoke and soot stung his eyes, and the temperature had gone up a dozen degrees. Fran was still next to the door, hitting it with a sledgehammer. Josh touched her shoulder, tugged her away.

"Duncan! Stand away from the door!"

The boy yelled okay.

Josh aimed at the knob, black tears stinging his eyes, and fired. The bullet pinged off the knob, making a shallow dent and nothing more. Josh swore.

"Josh!" Duncan banged on the door. "You have to hurry! The smoke is getting bad!"

• • •

Duncan's eyes stung like someone poked dirty fingers in them, and his nose was running like he had a cold. The smoke was getting really thick at the top of the stairs. Every time he breathed, he coughed.

"Duncan!" Mrs. Teller called. "Come here!"

Duncan didn't want to leave the top of the stairs, even though the walls on either side of him were on fire. He was really scared, but his mom was behind the door, trying to get in. He wanted to be there when she did.

He crouched down, trying to get under the smoke, but it was just as bad by his feet. Duncan pulled his shirt up over his mouth, shrunk back against the heat of the flames, and closed his eyes, hoping Mom would hurry.

A hand grabbed his shoulder, startling him. Mrs. Teller.

"We need to get downstairs, child."

Duncan shrugged away.

"I want to wait for Mom and Josh!"

The old woman coughed. "We'll wait for them downstairs. Come on."

She reached for Duncan's hand, and he fought it, pulling away.

"No!"

"Please, Duncan. Smoke rises. We have to get lower, or we'll die from the smoke."

Duncan sucked in more bad air, filling his lungs with scratchy heat, and coughed it out. It hurt. When Mrs. Teller grabbed his hand again he didn't struggle, reluctantly following her back into the shelter. It had gotten brighter, the soft green light of the glow sticks replaced by flickering orange. Duncan looked up, saw patches of fire on the ceiling, spreading out like an upside-down spill.

It was so hot.

Mrs. Teller took him to the middle of the room, and they crouched on the floor. Woof came over, whimpering. He was scared, too.

Mrs. Teller put her arm around Duncan.

"Remember all the cookies we used to bake together?" she asked.

Duncan coughed, nodded. Sometimes they made different shapes, like squares and triangles. Or giant cookies, as big as the pan.

"You always liked to lick the bowl. Mr. Teller liked that, too. We'll bake cookies again, when we get out of here. Would you like that?"

"Yes," Duncan answered.

But his mind wasn't on cookies. It was on the flames, rapidly spreading to the walls and the supplies on the shelves.

Revulsion coursed through Jessie Lee. The lottery commissioner had gotten blood on her arm. Blood had *tons* of diseases in it. She could practically feel the viruses soaking into her pores. Who knew where he'd been, who he'd slept with?

She dug around in her purse and found a pack of tissue and some moist towelettes that she liberated regularly from the diner. As she wiped her arm and hands, her thoughts of getting sick were replaced by other, more sinister thoughts.

What if the blood isn't his?

She hadn't noticed him bleeding. And this was more than just a few drops.

The scenario popped into her head fully formed. They weren't there to get lottery money. They were there to be killed, one by one. That's why the electricity was out. That's why the doors were locked. That's why the cars from the first people on the list were still in the parking lot. That's why they were taken into the locker room one at a time. That's why, once in the locker room, people would scream. That's why the lottery commissioner looked like that serial killer Marshal Otis Taylor. He actually *was* Taylor. Somehow he escaped the death penalty, and now he was here in Safe Haven, wiping out the entire town one by one.

"That's ridiculous," Jessie Lee said out loud.

She wadded up the dirty tissue and tossed it into the nearest trash can.

"Merv Johnson," the commissioner said into the PA system. Merv stood up and waddled over to Jessie Lee. He winked as he passed her.

Jessie Lee came after Merv on the lottery commissioner's list. She frowned. As ridiculous as her theory was, the thought of going by herself into that locker room suddenly seemed like a really bad idea. She hurried after Merv, reaching out and grabbing his arm.

"Merv—"

"Can't talk now, Jessie Lee. I'm going to grab my check, then hop on the Internet and search for Vettes."

"What if," she felt stupid saying it, but she couldn't get it out of her head, "what if there is no lottery?"

Merv stopped walking. His fat face scrunched up, making him look like a bulldog.

"What do you mean?"

"Did anyone show any credentials? And it's past one a.m., isn't that a strange time to be passing out checks? And why is the lottery commissioner guy wearing a black army outfit? And where's the media? Winning Powerball is a big story."

"Well, why are we all here, then?"

Jessie Lee chewed her lower lip. This all felt foolish, which meant that it probably *was* foolish. Still . . .

"I want to go in with you," she told her boss.

Merv shook his head. "The mayor said one at a time."

"Take a good look at the mayor, Merv. He looks positively freaked out."

They both glanced at Mayor Durlock, who wore an expression that could easily be interpreted as fear.

Merv shrugged. "I'll ask the commissioner. But if he says no, don't push it. I don't want to get on his bad side."

Or he'll eat your toes, Jessie Lee thought. But she agreed, and they approached the boys' locker room together. The lottery commissioner met them at the entrance.

"Only one at a time." He stared at Jessie Lee when he said it.

She wound her arm around Merv's. "We want to go in together."

The commissioner smiled without warmth.

"Your turn will come."

"You know who you look like?" Jessie Lee blurted it

out before her internal censor could stop her. "That serial killer. Marshal Otis Taylor."

Merv's expression became pained. "Jessie Lee!"

The commissioner narrowed his eyes and Jessie Lee suddenly felt cold. She realized that her far-fetched fantasy was right. This *was* Taylor, and if she went in that locker room she was going to die.

"I . . . uh . . . changed my mind." Jessie took a step backward. "I don't want the money."

Taylor grabbed Jessie Lee's arm, his fingers digging in.

"We'll make an exception this time. You can go in together."

"I don't want to." Jessie Lee tried to pull away, but he gripped her too tightly.

"Nonsense," Taylor said. "Let's go."

"No!"

Her shout brought silence to the gymnasium. It stretched on for a few seconds, until someone in the bleachers yelled, "I'll take her share!" which prompted everyone to laugh.

Jessie Lee continued to tug against Taylor's grasp, and Merv put his hand on the man's shoulder and said, "Maybe you should let go."

Taylor glared at Merv, then at the crowd, and finally at Jessie Lee. His eyes were black, expressionless. Like a shark. He opened his hand and she stumbled backward, landing on her ass.

"I'll see you later," he said.

Merv didn't appear scared in the least, but he did ask Jessie Lee, "Are you okay?"

"Don't go in there, Merv."

"You're acting silly. And you're causing a scene."

He lowered his voice to a stage whisper. "Are you on something?"

Jessie Lee felt her face get hot. She was trying to save Merv's life, and he was treating her as if she was stoned, or crazy.

"Merv, you'll die if you go in there."

Merv shook his head, like she was a disappointment, and then Taylor escorted him into the locker room. Jessie Lee stood up, noticing that everyone in the room had their eyes glued to her. Several were snickering. *Morons*. Didn't they see how crazy all of this was? Were they so blinded by greed? They were all going to die, and they just sat around waiting for it, like sheep.

Maybe if she had proof of what was really happening, she could convince the crowd what was going on. At the very least, she could convince herself she wasn't crazy. Jessie Lee held her chin up and marched into the girls' locker room, located next to the boys'.

Back when she attended school here the peephole rumors were legendary. Supposedly there was a loose brick in the boys' shower, and when it was removed you could see into the girls'. Jessie Lee, and every other girl in school, used that excuse as the reason they never took showers, rather than admit to body-image issues and the general all-around embarrassment of public nudity.

Jessie Lee remembered looking for the loose brick on more than one occasion. Not because she feared boys peeping at her, but because she wanted to peep at them. At thirteen, she'd never seen a boy's dick—back then she called them *wieners*—so she and her best friend Mandy Sprinkle went into the girls' locker room during a basketball game and climbed up onto the lockers and into the ceiling panels. They crawled over to the boys' locker room, through pink insulation and mouse droppings, and waited above the showers for the game to end. Then they took turns peering through a small crack, giggling so badly that they thought for sure they'd be caught and expelled.

They didn't get caught. And they saw a variety of wieners. But ultimately the whole episode left Jessie Lee unimpressed. She remained that way for two more years until she made out with her first boyfriend and saw his dick, which looked much more impressive up close and erect.

The memory returned to her as she climbed the last locker and pushed the ceiling tile up and to the side. Her breathing became quick, and her heart rate increased, just as it had the last time she'd done this years before. Only this time she was alone. And this time she wasn't giggling.

She grabbed on to a board—Jessie Lee couldn't remember if they were called rafters or joists—and peered through the opening. Though petite, she weighed more than she did in junior high, and the space above the ceiling tiles felt even more cramped. The pink insulation had been replaced with yellow stuff, and she tugged her shirt up over her nose so she wouldn't breathe in any fiberglass particles.

The ceiling tiles were made of that brittle fire-retardant material and hung below the joists on wires. She reached above the tiles, to the boards, and pulled herself up. The joists were about eighteen inches apart, and she kept her bare knees on one and her hands on another and inch-wormed toward the boys' locker room.

It became very dark, and very hot. Sweat dripped down her forehead and stung her eyes. Dust clung to her, making her skin itch. Heat and dust seemed to clog her nostrils, and after only a few breaths her mouth went dry.

Jessie Lee couldn't remember how far she had to go and couldn't see anything ahead of her. She began to count boards. Six should get her out of the girls' area, and four more would probably take her above the boys' room, though she didn't know where.

The boards were easy to climb across but not comfortable at all. No more than an inch or two thick, they put creases into her knees and palms and made it impossible for her to stretch out and rest.

After crossing four boards her shoulder muscles began to cramp up. She paused, trying to relax her neck, rolling it around in the hot, claustrophobic air. Then she arched her back and reached for the next board.

Her hand found something else. Something furry and bony.

A dead mouse in a trap.

Jessie Lee screamed. She couldn't help herself. Mice freaked her out. She pulled her hand away so fast that her elbow banged into some overhanging support beam. This brought fresh tears to her eyes and a tingling sensation that felt like she'd licked her fingers and stuck them in an electrical outlet.

She froze, squeezing her eyes shut, holding her breath, waiting to see if her outburst had been heard.

Ten seconds passed.

Twenty.

She was met with only silence.

The tingling passed, and Jessie Lee brought the mouse hand back and wiped it on her jeans. She could smell the rot on her fingers—or perhaps she only imagined it—and her tongue curled in her mouth and she gagged. She maneuvered two feet sideways so she'd avoid the mouse trap and then continued forward.

After three more boards she heard something. A man's voice, faint, coming from below. She thought it said, *"Were waring."*

Jessie Lee eased her body down, resting her chest on a joist. It hurt her boobs and made it hard to breathe, but the board took her weight and she lowered her hands to pull back a ceiling tile below her. She lifted it a centimeter, pushed it to the side, and stared. Her view revealed nothing but tile floor and empty lockers.

"I don't know."

Merv's voice, and it sounded like he was crying.

Jessie Lee finessed the tile back into place, did a push-up to get onto all fours, and crawled two more boards forward.

Beneath her, Merv screamed.

The sweat made Jessie Lee's long blond hair cling to her face in spaghetti strands, and she was having a hard time keeping her arms from shaking. Partly from exertion. Mostly from fear. Again she dropped down to chest level and peered through a crack.

This time she saw Merv, sitting in a chair. His chest was covered with blood, and blood drenched the floor around his feet. Behind him, she saw a pair of legs walk past. Legs dressed in black. The face was out of view, but she guessed it was Taylor.

"Where's Warren Streng?" Taylor said.

Merv whimpered. The strong, self-assured man she'd seen only a few minutes ago was gone. Merv had become a frightened shell of himself.

Taylor touched Merv with a small black object, which made a cracking sound. A stun gun. Merv convulsed, moaning.

Jessie Lee knew she had to reach her cell phone and take a picture of this. She could show it to the town, and they'd do something. But she trembled so badly she feared losing her balance and falling through the tiles. She couldn't take her hands off the joist.

Below her, Taylor pulled Merv's head back, exposing his throat. His other hand held a knife.

The motion Taylor used wasn't slitting. It was gouging. Like digging into a peach to remove the pit.

Jessie Lee sucked in both of her lips and bit down to keep from crying out. She watched Merv shake and twitch and bleed an ungodly amount, eventually falling out of his chair and flopping around on the floor like a fish. His palms slapped at the bloody tile, sending droplets skyward, misting Jessie Lee's face. Slowly, eventually, his horrible gyrations slowed down, and he rolled onto his back, the hole in his throat making gagging sounds. He stared upward, locking eyes with Jessie Lee. Then his mouth opened as if to say something.

No words came, though a low gurgle came through the hole in his throat. Then Taylor grabbed his ankles and began to tug him away. Jessie Lee needed to take the picture before he went out of view. Shaking, she reached a hand behind her, seeking the purse strapped to her shoulder, and her hand brushed something sitting on the joist.

Jessie Lee heard a loud *SNAP* accompanied by blinding pain—

She had stuck her fingers in a mouse trap.

Without being able to stop it, she screamed. And as the

sound left her lips, Jessie Lee Sloan realized she was as good as dead.

Fran watched, impotent, as Josh fired twice more at the door between her and her son. The bullets pinged off without even making a dent in the steel.

The smoke had gotten so thick that every breath provoked coughing. The door was too hot to touch, and the temperature around them had risen to the point where the air shimmered at their feet. It seemed as if every bit of moisture in Fran's body had been baked away. But she still picked up the sledgehammer, still pushed Josh aside, and still swung at the doorknob with everything she had.

The door didn't open.

Josh said something to her, but she couldn't understand him above the roar of the flames surrounding them. He pried the sledge out of her grasp, eased her back, and swung it. But not at the door; Josh aimed for the door frame, next to the deadbolt.

The wood gave, and the head of the sledgehammer made a chip in the wall. Josh repeated the process. Fran had to get down on her knees to breathe—the last of the good air formed a pocket below waist level. Josh continued to stand, continued to hammer. Fran kept her eyes glued to the doorjamb, saw it splinter away, and then the dull thud of striking wood was replaced by the clang of metal on metal.

Josh fell to his knees next to her, coughing.

". . . forced," he croaked.

"What?"

"The doorway . . . it's reinforced. We can't get in this way."

Movement, behind them. Erwin knelt next to Fran, put a hand on her shoulder.

"We have to get out of here! The structure is giving out!"

"I'm not leaving my son!"

Erwin and Josh exchanged a glance. Then they each grabbed an arm and dragged Fran out of the house.

Fran kicked. She screamed. She locked her mouth onto Josh's arm and bit him. But they manhandled her out the front door and onto the lawn, through puddles of raw sewage. Fran felt like she was made of glass and about to shatter.

"DUNCAN!" She continued to fight, but they wouldn't let her go. "Please! I have to get—"

And that's when the house collapsed.

Sweat soaked Duncan's hair and ran down his face. The oversized T-shirt stuck to him like he'd worn it swimming. He'd never been this hot before. Hot and thirsty. His tongue felt really big.

"I want something to drink," he said to Mrs. Teller.

"I'm sorry, Duncan. I don't think there's anything left."

Two of the four walls of shelves were burning, along with the supplies on the shelves. The brightness of the flames could be seen through the thick smoke, which had almost filled the room.

Duncan coughed, patted Woof on the head.

"It's going to be okay, boy," he said.

But Duncan knew it wasn't going to be okay. The stairs were on fire. Mom and Josh probably couldn't get to them. He still hoped that they would. Maybe Josh had a fireproof suit. Maybe he had a fire truck with a big hose that would put out the flames really fast.

Duncan wiped his face. The heat was so bad that it was starting to hurt his skin, like sunburn. His head felt funny, too, like he just woke up and was still groggy.

"We're not going to burn," Mrs. Teller said.

Duncan looked at her, squinting through his red-rimmed eyes. Did she know how to escape? He recalled Bernie's lecture, about how bad it hurt to get burned. He didn't want to burn to death. He didn't want to get burned at all, not even a little bit.

"Terrible way to go," Mrs. Teller said. "Terrible way. Burning in a fire."

She had her eyes closed. Duncan didn't think she was talking to him.

"It will be okay," she said. "It will be okay. I can do this. We won't burn. The Lord is my shepherd and He'll give me the strength."

Duncan coughed, then asked, "Strength for what?"

Mrs. Teller stared at Duncan. She was sobbing, so bad it shook her whole body.

"I won't let you suffer like that, child. I won't let you burn to death. I promise."

Duncan didn't like seeing Mrs. Teller like this. She was

an adult. She was supposed to be strong. It made him even more scared.

"What are you going to do?" he asked.

"When the time comes, I'll be strong," Mrs. Teller answered. "I'll take care of us both."

Then she racked her shotgun.

D r. Stubin combed through the wreckage site, looking for something that might help him. The three soldiers who'd been babysitting him were mostly intact, though the explosion had thrown one of them almost fifty yards from where Stubin had last seen him. Another, the sergeant, had actually lived long enough to ask Stubin for help. He died less than a minute later.

The Green Berets had fared even worse. Stubin had found bits and pieces of them, but nothing larger than an arm.

The Huey they'd arrived in no longer resembled anything other than junk. It, and the previous wreck, and been reduced to smoking scrap iron and burning bits of rubber and plastic. The whole area looked like a scene from Dante's Inferno.

Stubin knew General Tope wasn't foolish. He'd counter the loss of his team with firepower, and a lot of it. It was only a question of waiting and the cavalry would come.

The problem was Mathison. After the explosion, he'd fled into the forest. Stubin had called to him, and whistled for him, but the monkey was apparently too spooked to come back. And Mathison was important to Stubin. Very important.

Stubin wasn't sure how much monkey instinct Mathison retained after all of the brain tinkering he'd undergone, but the doctor doubted his capuchin friend could survive in the wild on his own. He'd seek out humans. And it might be the wrong group of humans. Stubin had to find him. But first, he had to salvage what he could from the wreck.

Stubin walked to the epicenter of the disaster, then began a 360-degree spiral outward, watching where he stepped, eyes peeled for anything useful. A radio would be nice.

After five minutes, he hadn't found anything except some broken night-vision goggles and a boot containing three-quarters of a foot. Hadn't they been carrying supplies? Food? Guns? Didn't they know the danger they were facing?

Apparently not, any more than they expected to be blown up.

Moving to the perimeter of the crash site, Stubin poked at a smoking bush with a stick and pried away something that looked like a shotgun, but with a much bigger barrel. It appeared unscathed. He touched it quickly, ascertained it was cool enough to hold, and picked it up. Stubin took a few seconds to locate the lock on the breech, and the barrel swiveled down, revealing a grenade—probably nonlethal if they were following instructions. He pulled the large canister out, judged it in working condition, and let it drop back in.

The grenade launcher had a sling, and Stubin wrapped it around his shoulder and continued hunting. He found two MRE rations, considered leaving them, but realized he didn't know how long he'd be in the woods. They went into his jacket, along with some compact binoculars with one cracked lens. The binocs also had a compass on the top, and amazingly it still worked.

Stubin found north, tried to picture the map of the area he'd seen briefly while riding in the chopper, and deduced he was east of town. He whistled again for Mathison, got no response, and then headed west, toward Safe Haven.

The instant Taylor looked up, Jessie Lee scrambled forward. Her knees banged into the joists, and the mousetrap still pinched her fingers, but she moved as fast as possible while still maintaining her balance. After getting two body lengths away from where she'd been, Jessie Lee held her breath and tried to listen, straining to hear anything other than the hammering of her heart.

She heard nothing.

He won't shoot me, she thought. *Too loud.* He wouldn't want to arouse the suspicions of the mob in the gym. Besides, Taylor hadn't been holding a gun. He *did* have a stun gun, and Jessie Lee was a cornered target. She had to get out of there, fast.

Noise, directly beneath her. The unmistakable clang of a metal locker opening.

She gingerly pulled off the mousetrap and tried to move forward, but there wasn't anyplace further to go—she hit the wall. Turning around while balancing on one-inch sections of board would take more time than she had. She could hear Taylor climbing up the locker, and any second he'd be pushing up a ceiling tile, reaching out with the stun gun.

Jessie Lee chose to move backward. She couldn't see behind her in the dark, but the joists were spaced evenly apart and she could sense where they were. Fast as she dared she began to crab backward, heading for the girls' locker room.

Ahead of her light surged in from where a ceiling tile used to be. She squinted at Taylor, less than three feet away, poking his head through. Could he see her in the dark?

Apparently he could. The killer stared directly at her and offered one of his cold smiles.

"I like the feisty ones. Maura Talbott was feisty. She was my sixth girl, in Madison. I tied her down with baling wire and bit off all of her fingers."

Jessie Lee remembered the TV special, which showed the autopsy photos after the obligatory *parental discretion advised* warning. The victim's fingers weren't all he'd chewed off.

She moved even faster, feet missing the boards and sometimes slipping between them and hitting ceiling tile. She banged her elbow—the same one—and then the thick gold Omega anklet that Erwin bought her became caught on something. One of the wires, holding up the tiles. She tried to pull free, without success. It held her like a claw.

Ahead of her, Taylor crawled up onto the joists. He still had the smile on, and he pressed the button on the stun gun to show her what was in store. A burst of white light crackled across the two probes.

Jessie Lee pushed with her free foot. No good. She crawled back, bending the knee of her trapped leg as she got closer, and then her handhold slipped and her butt fell directly between two boards, breaking through the ceiling tile. Her upper body followed.

She cried out, hands grasping at the air, and for a crazy moment Jessie Lee was free falling to the floor of the boys' locker room, headfirst. But her leg stayed stuck. So instead of falling through, she hung there by her knees, upside down like a child on a jungle gym.

She swung back and forth, the bright lights in the room and the blood rushing to her head adding to her disorientation. It took a moment for the world to stop spinning, for things to come back into focus. When they did, she freaked out.

Bodies. Dead bodies. Stacked ten high, like cordwood, in the showers directly beneath her. At least fifty people. Neighbors. Friends. Jesus—her cousin Rachel. Seamus Dailey. Mary Porter. John Kramer. Sarah Richardson, the head teller from the town bank.

A sob tore loose from Jessie Lee's throat. On top of the pile, close enough to reach out and touch, was her best friend and maid of honor, Mandy Sprinkle.

Blood coated every inch of the showers like paint, so thick Jessie Lee could taste copper. It brought back a long-ago trip to a turkey-rendering plant, to placate a boyfriend who worked there. The blood inside the slaughterhouse flowed knee deep—a swirling river filled with bits of tissue and swarming with flies.

Creaking, above. Taylor.

Jessie Lee tried to pull herself up, to free her leg, but she couldn't get any handholds through the hole she made. She reached ahead of her, sticking her fingers around a square of ceiling tile, and it tore away without supporting her weight.

She lifted her other leg—the one that wasn't caught—but that put too much weight on her trapped knee, causing instant pain.

The creaking got closer and all she could do was hang there, like a piñata waiting for the stick. She tried to scream, but her breath came in shallow pants and all she managed were squeaks.

Control yourself, she thought. *Stop panicking. If you scream, you can save yourself. Someone in the gym will come and investigate. Just fill your lungs with air.*

She tried. She tried harder than anything she'd ever attempted in her twenty-eight years of life. But every time she sucked in a bit of air she saw someone else in the mound of death, someone else she recognized, and the oxygen whooshed out of her.

If she couldn't pull herself up, and couldn't scream, there was one more possibility for escape.

Not wanting to, but not having any choice, Jessie Lee reached out for her best friend, Mandy, atop the pile. She didn't look at her friend's face, frozen in wild-eyed terror. She didn't look at her throat, which had a cut so deep you could see inside of it. Jessie Lee concentrated on Mandy's hand. The same hand she held when they spied on the boys taking showers so long ago, giggling madly.

Mandy's fingers splayed out, as if expecting to be given something. Jessie Lee stretched, but she was inches away from touching them. She tried to swing by her knees, remembering the school-yard trick known as the penny drop. The first pass, she barely touched Mandy's finger. The second time, she grasped her hand but couldn't hold on.

Third time was the charm. Jessie Lee entangled her fingers in Mandy's, then she brought her other hand around and locked on to her friend's wrist.

Dear God, she's still warm.

Jessie Lee reflexively let go, panicked to the point of hysterics. This couldn't be happening. Less than an hour ago she'd been planning her wedding, thinking about the extra things she could do with the lottery money. And now she hung upside down over a stack of her dead friends and neighbors while a psycho tried to kill her.

She made fists and pounded her thighs several times, trying to focus, trying to force courage. Then she began to rock back and forth again. This time when she caught Mandy's hand she held on and pulled. She pulled for all she was worth.

But instead of freeing herself, all Jessie Lee did was drag Mandy off of her roost. Her friend slid across the corpse beneath her and then headed face-first down the pile. Jessie Lee tried to hold on, but the strain on her knees became too great, and then Mandy tumbled to the floor. She landed in the pool of blood, arms and legs akimbo, her eyes staring up at Jessie Lee accusingly.

Jessie Lee again tried to scream, but her lungs wouldn't cooperate.

Not even when Taylor began to bite her knee.

Fran kicked Erwin in the stomach and he released her arm, which allowed her to also twist away from Josh and run back to the blazing house.

The second floor had collapsed onto the first, blockading the doorway with smoking debris. But Duncan was still alive. She felt it. All she had to do was get to him.

Fran ran through grass wet with sewage, around the side of the house, eyes scanning for window wells. She found one and hurried over. It had been filled in with concrete.

Damn Mr. Teller, the paranoid lunatic. Toward the end of his life he'd lapsed into dementia, thinking people were out to get him. Mrs. Teller had mentioned the bomb shelter he'd built in the basement, but Fran had never asked for a tour. She should have. What if there wasn't any other way in?

She ran to the back of the house, saw another concrete plug, and swore. Maybe they could dig, break through the walls . . .

There! A few feet away from the filled-in window well. A metal grating, about half the size of a manhole cover, set into the foundation at ground level. Smoke billowed out. Fran slid across the grass on her knees and banged on it. The square duct was covered with wire mesh, bolted to the concrete.

"DUNCAN! DUNCAN, CAN YOU HEAR ME!"

Josh came up next to her, then Erwin.

"Must be the ventilation for the shelter," Josh said. "Stand back."

He carried the sledgehammer Fran had dropped. Fran leaned away, and Josh made easy work of the grating with two big swings. Fran pried it away, then stuck her head into the opening.

"DUNCAN!"

Smoke poked at her eyes, but the heat was bearable. She could crawl down. Fran shoved one arm in, alongside her head. But she couldn't get her second shoulder through no matter how hard she pushed. The hole just wasn't big enough.

"Mom!" Duncan called, faint but frantic.

"Duncan!" Fran stretched, splaying out her fingers as if she could touch his voice.

"Mom! There's something wrong with Mrs. Teller!"

The smoke, Fran thought. *Oh, God, no, the smoke.*

Then came the thundering *BOOM* of a gunshot.

Duncan jumped to the side just before Mrs. Teller fired the shotgun at him. It was the loudest noise Duncan had ever heard in his whole life, making his ears hum. The pellets hit the concrete floor, and one of them bounced off and hit Duncan in his leg. It stung, like someone had slapped him hard. He looked and saw some blood on his calf.

Then Duncan heard the sound of another shell being racked. Mrs. Teller walked through the smoke, looking very calm except for her eyes, where black soot clung to the tears on her face. She pointed the gun at his head.

"Mrs. Teller! No!"

"I'm so, so sorry, Duncan. It's time."

Duncan's voice cracked. "Time for what?"

"Time for us to go to heaven, Duncan. It will be okay. I promise. It won't hurt at all. And we'll see Mr. Teller there, and we'll all bake cookies."

Duncan's hand darted up and knocked the gun to the side, then he crawled away from her as fast as he could, hiding in the smoke.

The shotgun BOOMED.

"I won't let us burn, Duncan."

Duncan couldn't see her through the smoke, and her voice seemed to be coming from everywhere at once. He hugged his knees and tried to make himself smaller. Why were all of these bad things happening? Where were Mom and Josh?

"Please, Duncan," Mrs. Teller said. "It's better this way."

The shotgun fired, to his left. A large box of toilet paper fell off the shelf and onto the floor, spilling its contents. Woof continued to bark, then growled deep.

"Woof, come!" Duncan yelled, as scared for Woof as he was for himself.

His dog kept snarling. It was too smoky to see what was going on. Duncan thought he heard Mom calling him again, but he couldn't tell. The flames were crackling really loud, and Woof was barking at the fire like it was the neighbor's cat. Three of the four shelves were burning, and the smoke was so bad that every breath hurt.

Then the shotgun BOOMED again, and Woof was silent.

Duncan's heart ached, but he didn't cry—maybe he was finally all out of tears. More than ever he wanted Mom, wanted to give her a huge hug. She'd protect him. She'd make it better.

But Mom wasn't here.

That man, Bernie, had scared Duncan. But he was even more scared now, of Mrs. Teller. She was supposed to be looking after him. How could she do this? Duncan buried his face in his hands, his whole body shaking, wishing none of this was happening, wishing it was a dream.

Then Woof barked.

He's alive!

"Woof!" he called. "Woof, come!"

Woof whimpered. Duncan had heard him whimper only once before, when he got a rabies shot at the vet.

"Woof?"

"I've got your dog, Duncan."

Woof whined again. What was she doing to him? He couldn't see.

"Please, Mrs. Teller. Josh and Mom are going to save us."

Mrs. Teller coughed. "I know they are. Come over to me and your doggie. We'll all wait for them together."

Duncan wanted to believe her. He wanted so bad to believe her. Mrs. Teller never lied to him before.

But then she never tried to shoot him before, either.

"Come over here, Duncan. Your little doggie wants you."

Another cry from Woof.

"Give me the gun." Duncan's voice was tiny, almost a whisper.

"Come here, Duncan. Hurry."

"First you have to give me the gun," he said, louder.

"I've been watching you for years, Duncan. I'm telling you the truth. I want what's best for you. For all of us. I'm your babysitter. And I'm an adult. You need to listen to adults, Duncan. Isn't that what your mother told you?"

Mom did tell him that, all the time. And Duncan ached to hold his dog. He began to crawl toward Mrs. Teller's voice. But the pain in his leg reminded him that he shouldn't believe her.

"Let Woof go, and give me the gun, and I'll come over."

"Duncan—"

"Let Woof go!" Duncan was almost yelling now. He'd never yelled at an adult before. It felt strange, wrong, but he needed her to know how serious he was. "And let me have the gun, Mrs. Teller!"

"You little brat!"

His dog snarled, and Mrs. Teller cried out. Then—so fast it startled him—hot breath bathed Duncan's face. He recoiled, surprised, and Woof licked his cheeks and nuzzled his neck. Duncan hugged the beagle to his chest, wiping his runny nose in Woof's fur. The beagle looked fine—he wasn't hurt at all.

"Duncan . . ."

Mrs. Teller's voice made Duncan tremble. He crawled backward, behind the fallen box.

"Duncan . . . your dog bit me . . . I need your help . . ."

Duncan stayed put. The smoke hung low in the air, thick as storm clouds, and it was getting hard to breathe without coughing.

"I'm bleeding pretty bad, Duncan . . . I need . . . the first-aid kit . . ."

Woof growled at Mrs. Teller. Duncan wrapped a hand in his collar, holding him back. He wanted to shrink and disappear. Why wasn't Mom here yet?

"I wouldn't hurt you, Duncan . . . I need your help . . . please, boy . . . the first-aid kit . . ."

Duncan remembered all the times Mrs. Teller watched him. The cookies they baked together. The twenty dollars she gave him every year for his birthday. She was a nice old lady. She shouldn't die.

But what if she was lying? She was talking slow, but she might be faking. What if she just wanted him to come close so she could shoot him and Woof?

"The . . . first aid . . . it's near the box of canned peas . . ."

Duncan found himself looking around for it, even though he didn't want to, even though it might be a bad idea. It wasn't on the shelf behind him, and that was the only shelf he could see.

"Help me . . . Duncan . . . be a good boy . . ."

Could he trust her? Should he trust her?

"Duncan . . . please . . ."

"Woof," Duncan whispered to his dog, "stay."

And then he crawled off to look for the first-aid kit.

Fran struck the concrete foundation with the sledge-hammer, the wooden handle stinging her palms like she'd pressed them next to a belt sander. She struck again. And again. And again. Chips of stone flaked away, the ten-pound head digging divots into the cement.

"Fran, we have to find another way."

She ignored Josh, ignored all the pain, ignored everything except the task at hand. Swing. Smash. Swing. Smash. If she had to pound a hole all the way to hell to get her son, she would.

Josh put a hand on her shoulder, but she shrugged him off and raised the sledge again. He tried to wrestle it from her, but she refused to let go.

"It's a steel vent." His eyes were glassy but firm. "Even

if you break up the foundation around it, we can't make the vent wider."

"You heard Duncan! You heard that gunshot! That crazy old woman is trying to kill him!"

"We need to find a rope or something, pull him up. But trying to dig through ten feet of dirt, rock, and rebar is just wasting our time."

Fran nodded quickly, letting Josh take the hammer. A rope. If they had a rope, they could snake it down the vent, Duncan could tie it around his waist . . .

Another gunshot echoed out through the grating.

Fran dropped to her knees and screamed her son's name.

Duncan found the first-aid kit next to the peas, right where Mrs. Teller said it would be. It was a large white box, made out of metal, with buckle clasps on the front and a big red cross painted on the lid. He clutched it to his chest, unsure of what to do next.

"Duncan . . . please help me . . . the blood . . ."

"I'll throw it to you," he said, then darted to the right in case Mrs. Teller tried to shoot where she heard his voice.

"I can't see . . . in this smoke . . . you need to bring it to me."

Woof barked at Mrs. Teller. Duncan shushed him. He knew the dog was just protecting him, but he was giving their position away. Duncan went farther right, until he was against a wall. He had to get down to Woof's level to breathe because the smoke was so thick, but even near the floor the air was getting bad.

"Throw me the gun," Duncan said. "Then I'll come to you."

"What? Duncan . . . I can't hear you . . ."

Duncan filled his lungs and yelled, "Throw me—!"

The sonic BOOM blew a hole in the smoke, and bird-shot chewed into the metal first-aid kit Duncan held out in front of him. The kit jumped from his hands like it was alive, and Duncan's hands stung. Just as bad were Duncan's ears—it felt like someone had punched him on both sides of his head, and the ringing was so bad he actually looked for bells. He also realized he'd peed his underwear a little.

He pulled Woof away from the wall, toward the shelves, and then put his hands in front of his face. They hurt like crazy, but there wasn't any blood. Duncan's lower lip trembled, but he didn't cry—maybe he was finally all out of tears. More than ever he wanted Mom, wanted to give her a huge hug. She'd protect him. She'd make it better.

But Mom wasn't here. Only Mrs. Teller. And she was going to kill him unless he did something about it.

The room had gotten brighter, and the green light from the glow sticks was replaced by orange. A shelf had caught on fire. Duncan recalled Bernie's lecture, about how bad it hurt to get burned. He didn't want to burn to death. He didn't want to get burned at all, not even a little bit. He'd rather get shot.

"Duncan? Did I get you? If you're hurt let me know. I can end your pain, child. I'll take all your pain away."

Duncan watched the shelf burn and hugged his dog

tighter. He had to do something. Anything. Or else he and Woof were going to die.

I have to get the gun, Duncan thought. Then Mrs. Teller couldn't hurt him, and he could keep her away until Mom and Josh rescued them.

Duncan knew he had to crawl to her, pull the gun away. She was an adult, but she was always talking about how her bones were old and brittle, how her muscles were getting shriveled up. Duncan always had to open jars for her, and he even beat her at arm wrestling once last year.

But he couldn't move. His legs and arms felt stuck to the floor.

Get the gun! he thought. *Go get the gun!*

His muscles didn't obey.

Then, like a slap, he heard the sound of the shotgun being racked.

Duncan squeezed his eyes shut, as tight as they could be squeezed, and waited. He didn't want to see it coming.

"DUNCAN! CAN YOU HEAR ME!"

Mom!

Mom sounded close, almost like she was in the room. Magically, he could move again. Duncan got to his feet. Mom's voice seemed to be coming from the left, but the only thing there was a shelf stacked with supplies, and many of those supplies were on fire.

"DUNCAN!"

Duncan picked up the big box of toilet paper that had fallen down, and used that to knock the burning supplies off the shelf. There, on the wall, was some sort of vent.

"MOM!"

Duncan yelled with everything he had. Then he climbed

up onto the metal shelf and stuck his hands in the vent grating.

"Duncan! Are you okay!"

"You have to get me and Woof out of here, Mom!" He lowered his voice. "Mrs. Teller is trying to kill us."

Mom didn't answer right away, but he thought he heard her sob.

"Duncan? It's Josh. Are you small enough to fit into the duct?"

Duncan squinted through the grating. Inside it was square, and not very large. But he could probably squeeze in there.

"I think so! But there's a metal vent in the way!"

"Can you pull the vent off?"

Duncan locked his fingers and tugged. The vent didn't move.

"It's on too tight."

"DUNCAN!" Mrs. Teller yelled.

He turned and looked behind him. She stood there, holding the shotgun. Fire stretched to the ceiling behind her. Duncan couldn't see the expression on her face, but she looked very angry. He tore his eyes away and searched the floor, looking for . . .

"Woof!"

The beagle went straight for Mrs. Teller's calf, biting hard and causing her to fall over. The shotgun fell from her hands, and she tried to push and kick the dog away. Woof dodged her blows and kept up the attack.

This time Duncan didn't hesitate. He hopped off the shelf and hurried to the shotgun. It lay there like a rattlesnake. Duncan forced himself to pick it up, surprised by its weight—it was heavier than it looked.

"Duncan!" Josh's voice, through the vent.

Duncan walked back to the shelf. He put his finger on the trigger and tried to hold the gun like Mrs. Teller did, with the butt against his shoulder. He couldn't; the gun was too long. So he held the gun at his side, at waist level, with the stock extended out behind his armpit. Then he aimed at the vent.

The BOOM shook his whole body, and the shotgun jumped out of his hands and went skidding backward across the floor. Duncan didn't look to see where it went. He focused on the duct.

The grating was gone. He'd shot it off.

Duncan ran to the shelf, climbed up, stuck his head into the hole. Yes, he'd be able to fit. Barely. But the duct went up on a slant that was too steep—he couldn't crawl up.

"Duncan!"

"I'm here, Josh! I shot the cover off." He felt absurdly proud of himself when he said that.

"Can you get inside?"

"Yeah. But I don't think I can crawl up. It's too high."

"I'll look for some rope! Hang in there, Duncan!"

Duncan wiped the sweat off of his forehead. It had gotten even hotter. The wall on either side of him was burning, the flames coming closer.

Mom said, "What's Mrs. Teller doing?"

Duncan turned and squinted at her. She was on the floor, still fighting with his dog.

"Woof's attacking her, Mom! Woof! Come!"

Woof barked to Duncan and then trotted over, his tongue hanging out. He looked pleased.

"Up, Woof! Up!"

Woof leapt up onto the shelf, and Duncan hugged his

dog tight. The beagle licked his face, then slobbered all over his ear.

"Mom's going to save us, Woof. We have to go in that vent. Don't be scared."

Woof wasn't scared at all. Upon noticing the duct, he stuck his head inside and barked. Duncan petted Woof's butt and told him he was a good boy. Then he chanced another look over his shoulder.

Mrs. Teller was gone.

"Duncan!" Josh talking. "We're sending down a hose. Wrap it under your arms and tie it around your chest."

The hose made a lot of noise coming down, banging against the aluminum walls of the duct. Woof barked and bit the end when it appeared. Duncan told the dog to sit and tugged the hose out until there was enough to make a knot. Then he paused. If he went up the hole, how would Woof get out?

"You gotta go first, buddy."

Duncan patted the dog's head, then wrapped the hose around Woof's body. He tied it tight enough to make the beagle yip.

"Mom! Josh! Pull Woof up!"

"No! Duncan, you come up right now!"

"Woof's going first!"

Duncan listened to Mom and Josh argue, and then Woof got tugged into the hole. He tried to spread out his paws and pull back, ears flat against his skull, but he was jerked right up the vent.

"Duncan . . ."

It was Mrs. Teller. She was right behind him.

Duncan didn't waste time. He scrambled into the duct after his dog, forcing himself up as far as he could go. The fit was tight. Really tight. And the smoke rose up beneath him, making it a lot harder to breathe, because there were no pockets of good air.

Overhead, the duct clanged, and the hose came down again.

"Wrap it around you, Duncan!"

Duncan's arms were up over his head, so he could grab the hose but had no way to pull it around his waist; he couldn't lower his hands. Instead he held it tight.

"Okay!" he yelled.

Josh pulled so hard on the hose it got ripped from his grasp.

"Duncan!"

"I can't tie it on!" Duncan coughed. "Pull slower!"

Again the hose came down. Duncan became aware of how hot it was getting in the vent. He felt sleepy. He wanted to close his eyes, even though he knew that was a bad idea.

"Duncan!" Mom, yelling. "Grab the hose!"

Duncan managed to get a hand on it. Josh lifted slower this time, and Duncan held on. But after going up only a little ways he felt like he was being stretched in half.

"Hold it!" Duncan croaked. "I'm stuck!"

The oversized undershirt he wore had become caught on something in the vent, and the material was pulling at his neck, choking him.

Duncan tried to shake his head to release the tension. It didn't work, the fabric continuing to cut into his throat. Because he couldn't lower his arms, he couldn't get the shirt off.

I have to let go of the hose, drop down, and take off the shirt, Duncan thought.

And that's when Mrs. Teller grabbed his foot.

Duncan screamed. He didn't want to let go now, even if he got strangled. He tried kicking but didn't have any room. Mrs. Teller's hands grabbed his thighs, hard, her fingers squeezing.

Duncan knew this was the end. He wasn't going to get away. He felt bad for his mom. First she lost Dad, and now him. Smoke filled his lungs, but he tried to talk. He wanted to tell Mom that he loved her, one last time, before Mrs. Teller pulled him down.

But Mrs. Teller didn't pull. She pushed.

Duncan heard the sound of fabric tearing, and then the pressure on his neck eased up. Josh yanked the hose, and Mrs. Teller continued to shove Duncan up the vent, lifting his legs, his ankles, and finally his feet, until he no longer felt her touch.

A moment later Mom and Josh were tugging on his arms, hauling him out of the duct.

"Duncan! Oh, my God, you're bleeding!"

"I got shot, but only a little."

Mom hugged him, and he hugged her, and it turned out he had some tears left, after all, because he started to cry. Woof, not wanting to be left out, stood up on his hind legs and put his front paws on him, joining the hug. Duncan wanted it to go on forever.

Then, from the vent, the sound of screaming.

Duncan pressed away from his mother.

"Mrs. Teller! She's still in there, Mom!" He looked at Josh. "We have to get her out! The fire is going to get her!"

Another scream, and then the sound of a shotgun firing.

Silence followed.

Josh put one hand on Duncan's shoulder and his other on Mom's. He steered them, gently but firmly, away from the house.

"We need to get you both to a hospital."

Even though Mom and Josh didn't say anything, Duncan knew what happened to Mrs. Teller. And it was okay. She was finally with Mr. Teller again. He imagined them both, in heaven, baking cookies.

"I fired a shotgun," Duncan said to Josh, beaming.

Josh tousled his hair.

"You did good, sport. Now let's go make sure your mom is okay."

Duncan saw Josh take Mom's hand, their fingers interlocking, and he smiled.

S heriff Streng sat in the back seat of Mrs. Teller's 1992 Buick Roadmaster station wagon, a vehicle that boasted faux wood side panels and less than ten thousand miles on the odometer. Mrs. Teller had kept it in the garage and was kind enough to leave the keys in the ignition.

Streng had pulled it onto the lawn before the house collapsed, doing so out of necessity. There were too many people to cram into Olen's Honey Wagon, and one of them was dangerous.

The captive had his hands tied behind him, Streng's belt cinched around his legs, and a face that resembled a Picasso painting because Erwin had hit it so many times.

He was no longer an immediate threat, but the sheriff still didn't like being this close.

Streng had frisked him quickly, finding the plastic zip lines they'd used to bind his wrists, assorted matches and lighters, a container filled with more of those odd capsules, a Ka-Bar Warthog knife, and another one of those high-tech electronic devices that he couldn't figure out how to turn on. He put everything, except the knife, in an empty McDonald's bag he'd gotten from Olen's truck. Then he turned his attention back to the pyro.

Like Ajax and Santiago, this man wore a black military-style outfit. And like Ajax and Santiago, he scared the crap out of Streng.

When he began to wake up, Streng Mirandized him, and then he and Erwin put the stranger into the back seat of the Roadmaster. Streng sat next to him. He pressed the thick-bladed combat knife up against the man's throat, but he still kept an arm's length away.

"Wake up. I have questions."

The man peeked at Streng though peach-puffy eyes. He grinned. The missing teeth and swollen face made him look like a jack-o'-lantern.

"Hello, Sheriff Streng. I'd be happy, very happy, to answer any questions you have, as long, as long as you tell me where Warren is."

Wiley again. What kind of horror had his brother brought upon this little town?

"What's your name?"

"Bernie."

"Full name."

"Just Bernie is fine."

"How many people in your unit?"

Bernie stuck his tongue through the gaps in his teeth and made sucking sounds. He seemed to be counting them. When he finished, he said, "Enough to get the job done."

"What's the job?"

"Find Warren. Finding Warren. Warren, Warren, Warren."

"Why do you want to find him?" Streng thought he knew the answer but wanted confirmation.

A line of bloody saliva leaked out the corner of Bernie's mouth.

"Did you take my lighters, Sheriff?"

"Answer my question. Why are you looking for Warren?"

Bernie clenched his jaw. Streng heard a cracking sound. Without flinching or taking his eyes away from Streng, Bernie produced a broken tooth between his grinning, distended lips. His tongue pushed it out, and it slid down his chin on a wave of gory spit.

"Why don't you burn me?" Bernie asked. "Maybe that will make me talk."

Centuries ago Streng served in Vietnam, during the war. He'd seen firsthand the types of things the Cong did to extract information. It had sickened him and remained a subject of nightmares for decades afterward.

When he mustered out and became a rookie cop in Milwaukee, criminal interrogations had been a bit . . . *looser* . . . than they were now. Streng witnessed his fellow officers beat a confession out of a killer using phone books. He'd also watched his squad take turns kicking a known child molester in the groin until he revealed the location of a child he'd abducted. Both times the suspects broke quickly. And both times Streng felt disgusted with himself afterward, even though he hadn't participated in the beatings.

Bernie expected torture. Hell, he probably *deserved* torture. But the willful infliction of pain on a fellow human being just wasn't in Streng's constitution. He decided to try another approach.

"I saw your friends earlier. Ajax and Santiago. Did you all train together?"

Bernie stared malevolently.

"I bet you boys had a lot of training. You think they trained harder than you, or are just better at this stuff?"

Now Bernie shifted in his seat.

"That Santiago, I bet he'd never allow himself to be captured." Streng moved closer to Bernie. "I bet he'd die first."

Bernie took a deep breath, then exhaled hard through his broken nose. A clot blew out of his right nostril, and dark blood oozed out. Bernie extended his tongue and let the blood run over it.

"I smell piss." Bernie licked his bloody lips and grinned. "Did Santiago make you wet yourself, Sheriff? Or— hehehe—is that just old age?"

Streng didn't take the bait. Instead he removed a disposable lighter from his pocket and flicked it on. Bernie focused on it like a cat watches a mouse. Streng let it burn for about ten seconds, then allowed the flame to die.

"Well, you'd know a thing or two about wetting yourself, wouldn't you, Bernie? Pyromania and bed-wetting go hand in hand."

Bernie continued to stare at the lighter.

"Was that what your childhood was like, Bernie? Setting fires? Pissing yourself? Killing little animals? I bet you did a lot of that. Let me guess—did Daddy make special visits to your bedroom at night, when Mommy was asleep?"

Bernie's eyes got big, and his jaw began to quiver.

"Daddy, my daddy, Daddy *burned* me. All over. Mommy would help, would hold me down. Because I was bad. They knew, they knew I was bad, they tried to cleanse me with fire, burn the evil out. But they went away before they could save me. Mommy and Daddy loved me."

Streng fought revulsion, stayed strong.

"Why are you after Warren? Is it money?"

"Money?" Bernie grinned. "Want to see me light my pee-pee on fire? I'll do it for a dollar. A dollar a dollar a dollar. Everyone, all the kids, everyone at the orphanage, they save their money to watch me do it." He locked eyes with Streng. "Got a dollar, Sheriff?"

"I've got a dollar, and I want to see that, Bernie. But first tell me how many are in your unit."

"They love me, love me like Mommy and Daddy. I'm important, so important, to them. Their star pupil. They found me years ago, saved me from the institution. I—"

Bernie's smile died, and then his eyes rolled up into his head. His head began to twitch, and Streng wondered if the man was still trying to frighten him. Truth told, Streng *was* frightened. This man, even tied up, exuded menace like radiators exuded heat. But the spasm went on for several seconds, and Bernie definitely didn't seem in control. Some sort of seizure?

Then, abruptly, it stopped. When Bernie opened his eyes he was no longer grinning.

"Charge," he said.

Streng had no idea what that meant, but Bernie stared straight ahead and didn't say anything else.

"Charge what?" Streng asked.

"Charge."

"I don't understand."

Bernie's mouth began to move. But he wasn't talking. He was chewing.

When the blood began to leak out, Streng realized Bernie was chewing his own tongue.

Someone knocked on Streng's window, startling the hell out of him. He turned and saw Erwin standing there. Streng sought the handle and rolled down the window.

"Josh and Fran—that's the woman from the diner—they saved the boy."

"And Mrs. Teller?"

Erwin shook his head. Streng pursed his lips. While he'd been screwing around with the car, the old woman had died. Could he have done anything to prevent it? How many people had died so far on his shift?

Streng pushed the thoughts away. Guilt later. Right now he had things to take care of.

"Is he okay?" Streng asked.

"Josh wants to take the boy and Fran to the doctor. But I want to go to the junior high and find Jessie Lee. Olen wants to go, too, because of the lottery."

Streng considered his next step. He needed to see a doctor, as well. The throb in his kidney hadn't abated, and the sweat on his forehead spoke of a fever. The nearest hospital was in Shell Lake, a forty-minute drive from here. But that lottery business smelled funny, especially with everything else going on. Could it be connected somehow? Then there was the matter of what to do with Bernie.

"Help me put him in the Honey Wagon," he told Erwin.

Erwin studied his shoes. Streng understood.

"This is a very bad man, son. One who tried to burn your face off. I would have messed him up, too, given the chance."

Erwin nodded, but he didn't seem in any hurry to touch Bernie again and made an extra effort not to look at him. Streng had a squeamish moment, removing his belt from Bernie's legs, but the killer just sat there, silently chewing his tongue. He remained compliant as they walked him to Olen's truck, allowing himself to be buckled into the back seat.

Streng called for Olen, who stopped spraying the burning house with sewage and set upon rolling up his hose. Josh, Fran, and young Duncan came around the side of the house, huddling close together. They were followed by a surprisingly fat dog, possibly a beagle. Streng approached Josh.

"Head to the ER in Shell Lake. Take the Roadmaster. And tell as many people as you can about what's happening here. The staties should be here soon, but I wouldn't mind if the whole army showed up."

He handed Josh the keys.

"How about you, Sheriff? You need a doctor."

"First I need to drop off this one." He jerked his thumb at the cab. "I'm going to have Olen take me to Sal's to get my Jeep and find my gun. Then our friend will go into the Safe Haven lockup."

Safe Haven didn't have an official police station, but Streng kept an office in the Water Department building, and it had a small cell, mostly used for the occasional drunk and disorderly.

"Could they still be at Sal's?"

"Don't see why they would be. They've got other fish to fry."

Josh nodded, then extended a hand. "Be careful."

"You, too."

Streng shook it. The boy also held out his hand. Streng shook that, as well.

"Thanks for coming to get us, Sheriff," Duncan said. There were tear streaks on his dirty face, but his eyes shone clear and blue.

"It's my job, Duncan. You take care of Josh and your mother, okay?"

"Yes, sir."

Streng didn't know Fran well—he'd eaten at the diner only once and the meatloaf had given him fierce indigestion, making a return visit unlikely. But he knew what had happened to her and her husband. The whole county knew. The fact that she was able to get on with her life spoke volumes.

Standing next to her, Streng sensed that inner strength, though he didn't know how long it would last. Both Fran and her boy were black with soot, but she looked like she'd been shoveling coal in hell. As pressed for time as they all were, a quick debriefing still seemed necessary.

"Fran, this might not be an appropriate question considering all that's just happened, but are you okay?"

"The man, the one who attacked Duncan, he dresses like a man who attacked me at the diner. His name is Taylor. He . . . killed Al and then tried to kill me. Over an hour ago."

"You came from the diner?" Streng asked. "Is your car around here?"

"I didn't drive here. I . . . swam. The river. That's where Erwin found me. I had to get to my son."

Streng raised an eyebrow. The river was over a mile away, and the diner was several miles farther.

"How did you know Duncan was in danger?"

"Taylor told me." She narrowed her ice blue eyes. "He wanted to know where your brother Warren was."

Streng flinched. More people hurt, because of Wiley. But why were these commandos going after Fran and her son?

The sheriff stared at Fran, then at Duncan, and he made the connection. A connection that Fran obviously wasn't aware of. Suddenly some things made sense.

"And you've never seen either of these men before? You don't know why they're looking for Warren?"

Fran shook her head.

"Or why they went after you?"

"I only met your brother once, Sheriff. At my wedding. He crashed it, got drunk, and started a fight with my stepfather."

Streng frowned. One more reason to hold a grudge against Wiley.

"You're safe now. Josh will take you to the hospital. I'm . . . sorry this happened to you."

Fran hugged Duncan closer.

"We're survivors," she said.

Streng had no doubt of it.

"When you get out of town the cell reception should improve. I'll call you from a land line. I need to take your statement, Fran. Yours, too, Duncan."

"And Woof's?" Duncan asked.

At hearing his name, the dog cocked his head to the side.

Streng bent down to pat the dog on the head, and the motion brought blinding pain. He still managed to say, "And Woof's."

Josh herded them toward the car, but Fran stopped and turned back.

"Sheriff, do you know what happened to the mayor?"

Streng shook his head.

"I saw him in the fire truck. He was naked and tied up."

"Alive?"

"Yes."

"Did you see who was driving?"

"No. I thought it was Josh at first, but obviously . . ." Her voice trailed off.

"Get to the ER," Streng said. "I'll call later."

They have the mayor, too? Streng said to himself. *What's his link to Wiley?*

Streng had no idea, but he sure as hell was going to find out. Right after he took care of Bernie, he was going to have a long-overdue talk with brother Warren.

But first, he needed a gun.

It wouldn't be wise to visit Wiley unarmed.

When Jessie Lee Sloan was six years old, there was a boy in her first-grade class named Lester Paks. Lester was a textbook full of emotional and mental problems. He laughed and cried for no reason at all. He poked himself with tacks and bit at his fingernails until they bled. He ate markers, and crayons, and glue, and even whole schoolbooks, tearing out a page at a time and wadding it into his mouth while their teacher wasn't looking.

Jessie Lee sat next to him in class. She used to watch him, equally fascinated and repulsed, as he did these odd things. And she always left him alone, until the day Lester reached into his desk and took out Mr. Smiley, the classroom hamster. He put half of Mr. Smiley in his mouth and had already begun to chew when Jessie Lee screamed for the teacher.

Lester got in trouble. Big trouble. They took him out of school, and rumors were he went to a hospital for crazy people. But he came back after a few weeks, and when he sat down at his desk and stared at Jessie Lee he looked meaner than anyone she'd ever seen.

It happened at recess. Jessie Lee was playing four-square with her friends and Lester ran over, dropped to his knees, and bit her on the leg. Bit her and wouldn't let go.

She kicked. She yelled. Her friends, two teachers, and the principal all tried to pull Lester off. But he clamped down like a pit bull, grinding her calf between his teeth, his cheeks puffing out with her blood.

They finally got him off by holding his nose until he passed out.

He never came back to school.

Jessie Lee needed one surgery to stop the bleeding, and two more to fix the scarring. She still retained the mark, a dimpled patch that never tanned.

She didn't have any deep psychological problems after the attack, other than not being able to watch vampire movies. There were occasional nightmares, and a heightened sense of caution around strange dogs, but overall she recovered well. After that experience, Jessie Lee felt like she could handle anything. After all, what could be worse?

Now, hanging upside down by her knees over a stack of corpses in the boys' locker room, she realized that there *were* things worse. That point hit home when she felt Taylor's teeth on her knee.

Jessie Lee hadn't been able to scream because of hyperventilating. Now she couldn't get in any air at all. The psycho's hands kneaded her bare thighs, and she felt his lips and tongue suck hard on her flesh, making hickies. Jessie Lee struggled to shake free, but her foot remained caught by her gold Omega anklet.

Hot breath, on her calf.

Then a nip; something a lover might do.

Every synapse in her brain seemed to fire at once, and Jessie Lee felt as if she would actually go insane with panic.

It got worse. The mouth moved higher, teeth and stubble brushing against her skin. Settling on the knee, opening wide to engulf the entire kneecap.

She knew what being bitten was like. How the skin broke and tore. How veins got pinched and severed. How muscle fiber felt while being gnawed.

And that's when Jessie Lee Sloan began to thrash. Violently. Her body clenched and folded like a switchblade, her head and shoulders twisted back and forth, and a massive surge of adrenaline allowed her to flex her legs. The wire broke, and her foot finally came loose.

There was a millisecond of relief—Taylor's mouth off

her knee, her legs stretching out above her—and then she fell.

Jessie Lee landed, face-first, in a pile of her dead friends and neighbors. But she didn't stay on top, nor did she roll off the side. The corpses shifted to accommodate her weight, parted, and she began to sink into the middle.

She flailed out her arms, trying to climb up, but struggling slicked her in blood and slippery fluids, making her slide down farther. Gory, lukewarm limbs poked her. Pale faces with rictus grins kissed her. More shifting, and a cadaver fell on top of Jessie Lee, sealing her in a decomposing human tomb. This fueled her hysteria, prompting more wiggling, advancing her descent. By the time she exerted enough self-control to stop squirming, Jessie Lee had burrowed halfway into the pile.

It was dark, but unfortunately not dark enough that she couldn't see. The dead were stacked all around, smooshing Jessie Lee on all sides. Her face pressed against someone's lacerated chest. Her right hand became stuck deep in a fatal neck wound. And the stench . . . death smelled like rotten carnations, an odor so powerful she tasted it on her tongue.

Jessie Lee tried to twist around and force her head into open air. She shoved the body above her—a man she recognized from church. His midsection bent upward and his head tilted down. Blood dripped from his mouth onto Jessie Lee's face. She craned her neck, turning away, and it trickled into her ear.

The weight on her chest made it hard to breathe. Being bitten was horrible. Suffocating to death in a pile of corpses was even worse. Jessie Lee kicked out and the pile shifted again, pushing her face into someone's urine-soaked crotch. Then, abruptly, bodies began to topple, and Jessie Lee rolled toward the back wall of the showers, smacking her head against the porcelain tile.

A moment passed, the dead settling into new positions. Jessie Lee's legs burned now that the circulation had returned, and the bump on her head brought fresh tears. She moved her hand up to rub it but stopped when she heard footsteps.

Someone was in the shower.

She stayed still, eyes peering through bent elbows and twisted legs, straining to see the entrance. No good; her view was blocked.

Do I call for help? she thought. It might be someone from the gym, someone who could save her.

Or it might be Taylor.

Lowering her eyes, Jessie Lee examined her clothing and found herself drenched in gore. If she didn't move she would look like just another corpse. He probably wouldn't even notice her. She held her breath, waiting for Taylor to leave.

". . . help me . . ."

The voice, coming from directly beneath her, made Jessie Lee gasp. She tilted her head and saw she was lying on top of Melody Montague, her elderly second-grade teacher. Less than an hour ago they'd been talking about the wedding.

Jessie Lee stared as the slash in Mrs. Montague's neck oozed blood. But the wound hadn't affected her voice, because again the woman said, "Help."

And she said it louder this time.

Jessie Lee glanced back at the entrance to the shower, then to Mrs. Montague.

"Shh." She touched her finger to Mrs. Montague's lips. The old woman didn't seem to notice.

"Please someone help me."

Footsteps. Closer. Taylor, or whoever was in the shower room.

". . . help . . ."

"I'll help," Jessie Lee whispered, "but you have to be quiet."

Mrs. Montague's eyes stared out into space, wide and unfocused. Her chin trembled. She began to shake her head.

Jessie Lee didn't know what to do. Mrs. Montague was going to draw Taylor's attention, and then he'd find them and kill them both. She willed her old teacher to stay still, to be quiet.

". . . help me . . ."

The footsteps stopped on the other side of the pile. Through the tangle of bodies, Jessie Lee could see someone standing there.

". . . please . . ."

Squeezing her eyes closed, Jessie Lee placed a hand over Mrs. Montague's mouth. Mrs. Montague fought against her touch, so Jessie Lee pressed harder.

She needs to be quiet, Jessie Lee said to herself. *She needs to hush, or we'll both die. Please hush, Mrs. Montague.*

Mrs. Montague moaned. Jessie Lee adjusted her hand to also cover Mrs. Montague's nose.

Please be quiet, please be quiet, please be quiet . . .

In the shower, noise echoed. Jessie Lee held her own breath, held it along with Mrs. Montague, willing the footsteps to go away and leave them alone.

The moment stretched until it was spider-web thin.

Just a little longer, just a little longer, just . . .

Mrs. Montague stopped struggling.

Jessie Lee shook with effort not to breathe. Bright motes appeared before her eyes even though they were closed.

The footsteps receded, out the shower entrance, back into the boys' locker room.

Jessie Lee sucked in a breath, then removed her hand from Mrs. Montague.

Her teacher's lifeless eyes stared, accusing.

I . . . killed her.

Jessie Lee told herself she didn't have a choice. They both would have died if they'd been found. Plus, Mrs. Montague was practically dead anyway.

Right?

A sob erupted from Jessie Lee, a long, hard sob that gained in volume until it became a scream.

She continued to scream until the footsteps came rushing back. And it turned out they didn't belong to Taylor, after all.

"Hello, missy."

"Oh, please . . . please help me . . ."

Jessie Lee reached for the figure over the wall of the dead.

The figure reached back—with a stun gun.

J osh pushed the Roadmaster to 50 mph, which was as fast as he dared on County Road JJ, the only road in and out of Safe Haven. Like many northern Wisconsin roads it boasted knots of turns and hills, all penned in by the woods. Deer leapt out of the tree line on a regular basis, and hitting one bigger than a hundred pounds could prove fatal to more than just the animal.

Josh snatched a look sideways. Duncan and Fran sat in the front seat with him. Fran now wore jeans and a sweater, both too large for her, and her thick blond hair had been tied back with a bright red scrunchie. Duncan's attire fit better—jeans and a T-shirt from a boy his age. The clothes were loaners from a neighbor down the street. They hadn't been home, but Fran watched their house when they went on vacation and knew they kept a spare key under the doormat. She was sure they'd understand.

Prior to dressing, Josh had bandaged Duncan's leg wound. A pellet had stung him, leaving a bleeding welt. Josh didn't think there were any lodged inside, but an x-ray would show for sure.

Fran's injuries were harder to dress, especially without anesthetic. That psychopath Taylor had bitten off one of her toes and chewed much of the skin off another. Josh cleaned the wounds, taped gauze around them, and recommended Fran leave her foot shoeless. Fran met him halfway; she wore borrowed open-toe sandals.

Josh tried his cell again. Still no signal. He should be getting one soon, as he got closer to Shell Lake. They'd attempted to use the neighbor's phone to call 911, but repeated attempts resulted only in a busy signal. It didn't matter. Josh estimated they were ten minutes away from the hospital.

Though the evening had dished up countless horrors for all of them, the mood in the car was upbeat. As if they were heading for a carnival, or on vacation, rather than to a hospital and the authorities. Josh guessed their spirits were high because each of them felt ridiculously lucky to be alive.

"There's Mystery Lake," Duncan said, pointing as they passed. "Dad and I used to go there to catch bass. Do you know why it's called Mystery Lake?"

Josh shook his head. "Tell me."

"Because when they first named it, they couldn't tell how deep it was. This was before depth finders. It's deeper than Big Lake McDonald, even though it's only thirty acres big."

"How deep is it?"

"Over eighty feet. I bet there are some really big walleye and bass in there. Do you fish?"

"Only every single day I can."

"Baitcast or spincast?"

Josh smiled. The kid knew his stuff. "Spincast, mostly. I use baitcast for muskie."

"How big was your biggest muskie?"

"Thirty-two pounds, twelve ounces."

"Wow! You use a spinner? Bucktail?"

"Muskie Jitterbug, frog color. The old wooden one. I think muskies like wood instead of plastic because it isn't as hard to chomp down on. That gives you an extra fraction of a second to set the hook before they spit it out."

Duncan leaned closer to Josh, pulling out of his mother's protective hug.

"Will you take me muskie fishing?"

"Sure. I'll take you and your mom."

Duncan made a face. "Mom doesn't like to fish."

"Mom *does* like to fish." Fran tousled Duncan's hair.

"She likes sitting on a boat, casting into the water. Mom just doesn't like to *catch* fish."

"It freaks her out," Duncan explained. "Whenever she gets a bite she screams and hands me or Dad the pole. But we haven't gone fishing since Dad died. When will you take us?"

"We can talk about that later." Fran suddenly became cool. "Josh is a busy man. Very busy."

Josh winced. Fran was giving him a dig because he never called her for another date. They'd gone out only a few times, but Josh had fled from the casual relationship before it developed into something deeper.

"Fran, about that. I owe you an explanation."

He waited for Fran to say, *"No, you don't."* She didn't. He went on.

"I told you about Annie before."

"Who's Annie?" Duncan had shuffled even closer to Josh, their legs now touching.

"She was the woman I was going to marry, but she got really sick. Before she died, she made me promise something."

"What was it?"

"She made me promise that I'd live a long life."

Josh pictured the hospital scene in his mind, holding Annie's hand, her last wish that he wouldn't die young like she had. He felt his eyes well up.

"That sounds like a big promise," Duncan said.

Josh cleared his throat. "It was. And I took it very seriously. But then I became a fireman and planned on becoming a paramedic. I wanted to move to Madison, or Milwaukee. Someplace where I could make a difference."

"But you make a difference here in Safe Haven," Duncan said.

"How many fires have there been in Safe Haven? Well, before tonight?"

"None."

"Exactly, none. So I wanted to go to a bigger city, where I could really help people. Save some lives. But because I made that promise, I decided I would stay here."

"When was this?"

"About a year before I met you and your mom. And I kept my promise to Annie, I didn't go to the big city. But I realized that was wrong. I wasn't happy. I needed to go someplace else, someplace where I could do some good. So I started taking paramedic classes, and as soon as I finish I'm going to move out of Safe Haven."

"Is that why you stopped dating Mom? Because you were leaving?"

"That's why."

"Mom said it was because you didn't know a good thing when you saw it."

Josh glanced at Fran, who was trying to control a smirk. He said, "Sometimes we know good things, Duncan, but we run away from them anyway."

"I think—JOSH!"

Josh reacted instantly, slamming on the brakes, his hand shooting out in front of Duncan so the child didn't pitch forward. The Roadmaster fishtailed, tires screeching, and then skidded to a stop on the gravel shoulder. Josh stared at the road, wondering what animal he'd almost hit. A possum? Raccoon?

Whatever it was, it hopped onto the hood and screeched,

making all three of the car's occupants jump in their seats.

"It's . . . a monkey!" Duncan said.

A small, cinnamon-colored monkey, no more than a few pounds. It walked up to the windshield, knocked on it, and waved.

Duncan clapped his hands together. "That is so cool!"

Woof stuck his head over the back of Josh's seat and woofed at the monkey. The monkey began to hoot, sounding a lot like an owl. Woof's ears went up, and he began to howl, low-pitched and earnest. The animals continued this off-tune duet until Fran told Woof to sit down. The dog licked her face and complied, curling up into a ball on the back seat. The monkey clapped its hands, apparently pleased with the performance.

Duncan scooted forward, putting his hands on the dashboard. "We need to catch him."

"That's not a good idea, Duncan." Fran rolled up her side window, even though it was barely open a crack. "Monkeys bite. And they carry diseases."

"But look, Mom! He's got a collar! He belongs to someone. I bet he's lost."

The monkey nodded his head, like he was agreeing with the boy. Duncan poked Josh on the shoulder.

"What do you think, Josh? Should we help him?"

Josh didn't know of anyone in town who kept a monkey or any place in the area that sold them. Perhaps some tourist had lost him during summer vacation. Ultimately, it didn't matter where the monkey came from. They had more pressing things to do than chase someone's missing pet.

"I think we should leave him here, Duncan. Maybe his owner is nearby, looking for him."

"But you said you wanted to help people. He needs our help. He's all alone out here."

Josh looked at Duncan and felt his will bend.

"Okay, we'll help. I'll check to see if he's tame. Wait in the car."

If the evening hadn't been surreal enough, chasing a monkey put a nice capper on everything. Josh exited the vehicle and closed the door behind him, gently to avoid the loud noise. He smiled at the monkey and slowly held out his hand, feeling more than a little ridiculous.

"Hey, little fella. My name is Josh. I'm not going to hurt you."

The monkey walked up to Josh, stuck out his own hand, and gripped Josh's finger.

He wants to shake hands, Josh thought, amazed. He complied, keeping the motion easy and deliberate. The monkey then hopped onto Josh's arm.

Josh stiffened. His first inclination was to shake the creature off, as he would any strange animal that latched on to him. But this monkey didn't appear hostile. If anything, it seemed completely at ease. Josh kept still while it climbed up to his shoulder. Then it sat there, tiny hands running through Josh's hair.

"I think he's tame!" Josh heard Duncan yell through the car door.

Josh stood there for a moment. The monkey made no attempt to bite his ear off and didn't seem sick or lethargic. Josh glanced at Duncan's face, which had lit up to 120 watts.

"He seems safe," Josh said to Fran. "But I won't bring him in the car unless you say it's okay."

Duncan spun on Fran and began hitting her with mile-a-minute begging. Josh watched Fran sigh.

"Okay. But only until we locate his owner. And if he gets uppity, he goes."

Fran received a big hug from her son, and then Duncan was opening up Josh's door.

Josh sat down carefully, trying not to jostle the primate. Before he'd gotten halfway into the car, the monkey had leapt off his shoulder and into Duncan's lap.

"Easy, Duncan," Josh warned. "Don't try to grab him. Let him get comfortable with you."

The monkey held out a hand, just as he had with Josh. Duncan took it.

"Pleased to meet you. I'm Duncan."

After a customary shake the monkey reached out for Fran. She grasped his tiny monkey paw with two fingers and introduced herself. He pumped her hand up and down. Fran's laughter filled the car, sweet and musical. Josh grinned.

"He's got a tag on his collar," Duncan said. "His name is Mathison."

Upon hearing his name, Mathison chattered in an obviously social manner. It sounded like a bird chirping. This prompted Woof to stick his nose over the seat for a sniff.

"Be good, Woof," Duncan commanded. "He's our friend."

Mathison extended a hand to the dog. When it wasn't shaken, he patted Woof on the head. Woof apparently decided the proceedings weren't that interesting, because he withdrew and went back to sleep.

"Mathison is a New World monkey," Duncan said. "We studied them in school. They come from South America. You can tell because he has a tail. I think he's a cappuccino."

"That's capuchin," Fran gently corrected. "And it looks like he's got a scar on his head."

Fran moved to touch it, and Mathison screeched at her, batting her hand away.

"Sensitive little guy."

"I bet he's hungry," Duncan said. "Capuchin monkeys eat fruit and bugs. We should stop someplace."

Josh marveled at Duncan's resilience. Earlier he'd been shot at by his babysitter and almost burned alive. Children were remarkable. Josh and Annie had talked about having kids. If things had turned out differently, he would have wanted one like Duncan.

Josh started the car, checked his rearview, and then pulled back onto JJ. The turnoff onto the main highway was in a mile or two. Then, on to the ER. Josh wondered what would be open this late where he could get some monkey food. A gas station, probably. Pick up some peanuts, or raisins, or maybe fresh fruit. There was a Farm and Fleet that sold livestock feed. Maybe they would have—

"Thank God."

Fran pointed to the road ahead. Josh saw the blinking red and blue lights in the distance. Lots of them. He cut his speed, waiting for them to approach.

Oddly, they stayed still.

"Why aren't they coming?" Duncan asked.

Josh didn't know, and he didn't like it. He slowed down even further, then had to brake. Both lanes were blocked off with orange traffic cones and neon-yellow barrels. Josh pulled up to them and noticed two rows of steel stinger spikes on the asphalt, extending out into the woods on either side of the road. Josh had watched enough TV to know that police used the spikes to blow tires during high-speed chases.

Josh gazed beyond the roadblock. Parked fifty yards ahead were four police cars, several army Humvees, and an honest-to-God tank.

"DO NOT GET OUT OF YOUR VEHICLE! TURN AROUND AND HEAD BACK IN THE DIRECTION YOU CAME FROM!"

"Why do they want us to go back?" Duncan asked. He scooted closer to Josh again.

"I have no idea, Duncan."

Josh reached for the door handle. Fran grabbed his arm.

"Maybe you shouldn't do that, Josh."

"What are they going to do? Shoot me?"

He opened the door and three shots punched through his driver's-side window. The megaphone boomed again.

"STAY IN YOUR VEHICLE AND TURN AROUND!"

Josh's pants were peppered with tiny square bits of glass. He noticed his hands were shaking. Next to him Fran and Duncan were ducking down, covering their heads. Mathison had jumped into the back seat, where he and Woof huddled together on the car floor.

What the hell were these people doing, shooting at civilians?

"I'm driving a woman and child!" He yelled through the open door but decided to keep his head inside the car. "They need medical attention!"

"TURN YOUR VEHICLE AROUND!"

"Damn it, we need help! We've been attacked! We need to get to a hospital!"

"YOU HAVE TEN SECONDS TO TURN AROUND, THEN WE'LL OPEN FIRE."

Josh stared impotently at Fran, not knowing what they should do.

"We have to go," Fran said.

"Where?"

"Maybe we can park someplace and walk to the road."

"There are at least thirty army guys out there. They have a tank."

"I thought the army was supposed to help us," Duncan said.

"YOU NOW HAVE FIVE SECONDS!"

Josh had no choice. He backed up and continued driving backward until he felt safe enough to close his door and make a three-point turn.

"Now what?" he asked Fran. "This is the only road in and out of Safe Haven."

"We could go back to my neighbor's house. There's obviously something going on. It looks like the authorities are aware of the situation. Maybe we should lie low, wait it out."

Josh wasn't convinced. He tried to come up with a scenario where the military would put up roadblocks. A quarantine of some kind? Were Bernie, Taylor, Santiago, and Ajax here to spread some sort of germ or poison? Or was this a media blackout, ensuring news didn't spread? That could explain the phone problems they'd been having—someone might be jamming the signals and blocking the land lines.

"You need to see a doctor." Josh stared at Fran so she

could see how serious he was. "As soon as possible. Duncan does, too. And I'm not sure going back to Safe Haven is a smart idea."

"How about Doc Wainwright?" Duncan asked. "He gives me my shots every year."

Doc Wainwright had a clinic in town, open Tuesday and Thursday. The other days of the week he divided his time between Shell Lake and Eau Claire.

"He won't be open now, Duncan," Fran said.

"Can't we go to his house? He told me he lives on the lake."

Josh considered it. Wainwright had a house on Big Lake McDonald, on the shore opposite the Mortons'. But Fran needed more than a few stitches and some antibiotics. She needed surgery.

Still, Wainwright was better than not doing anything.

"Doc Wainwright it is," Josh said. He hit the gas and then had to slam on the brakes once again to avoid hitting the man standing in the middle of the road.

Streng and Erwin walked the still-docile Bernie over to the sheriff's Jeep. Streng locked him in the back and tossed the McDonald's bag full of Bernie's things onto the floor of the front seat. Then Streng turned his attention to Sal Morton's house.

"He twisted off Sal's head, Sheriff. Like a bottle cap."

Streng had no reason to doubt Josh. And he really didn't want to go back into that house and see what his cousin had seen. But he'd dropped his .45 on the roof, and he'd feel much safer riding with Bernie if he had it back.

"Erwin, you and Olen come with me, help find my gun."

Erwin's face pinched. "I really need to get to the junior high, Sheriff. If those soldier guys have the mayor, then that whole lottery story could be BS. My fiancée is there."

From what Streng understood, much of the town had gone to that lottery thing. Surely there was safety in numbers. But Streng wasn't going to prevent Erwin from looking after his own.

"Okay. I'll meet you there after I drop off Bernie at my office. If anything strange is going on, grab your girl and run."

"You don't need to tell me twice. See you later, Sheriff."

"Good luck, Erwin."

The men clasped hands, but it felt forced. Or perhaps final. Then Erwin headed back to the Honey Wagon, and Streng again focused on the house. His recent bad experience prompted memory flashes of fear and panic. He pushed those memories aside, shined Olen's dirty flashlight at the front door, and made himself walk toward it.

Darkness and silence greeted Streng as he entered. Though the commonly accepted veteran stereotype spoke otherwise, Streng never had posttraumatic stress disorder, never had any kind of flashbacks. He'd seen some horrible things in the war and still had occasional bad dreams, but he managed to escape Vietnam with both his mind and his body intact.

Stepping into Sal's house, though, brought back a feeling he hadn't experienced in more than thirty years. The hell that was patrol.

Streng hated patrol. You had an equal chance of dying no matter how quiet you were, how careful you were. During those nighttime missions Streng felt like he had a hundred bull's-eyes on his body, each one with rifle crosshairs zeroing in on a different body part. Nowhere to hide, and running was useless. The Cong were part of the jungle, and every tree, every rock, every shadow had deadly potential. All you could do was stay low and hope.

That same feeling enveloped Streng as he crept into Sal's house for the second time that night. The feeling of being watched, hunted. Except this time he didn't have a gun, just a Ka-Bar knife. Not that it mattered much. If Santiago was waiting in the shadows, Streng doubted anything less than a rocket launcher would keep him at bay.

He took the stairs slowly, shining the light on each step so he didn't trip, pausing every three steps to listen. Streng's injured kidney throbbed in time with his heartbeat. Halfway up the staircase the odor of death hit, and hit hard. Streng switched to breathing through his mouth, which didn't help much. He pressed his hand hard against his aching side and ascended to Sal's bedroom.

A snatch of childhood skipped across Streng's mind, him and Wiley and cousin Sal, climbing the fence to the Safe Haven cemetery on Halloween night to prove their preteen bravery. Streng, the youngest of the trio, had been terrified, and before they took more than a dozen steps on hallowed ground he froze, refusing to move.

"There's nothing to be afraid of," Sal had told him. "Everyone here is dead."

"I'm not afraid of the dead," Streng remembered saying. "I'm afraid of what made them dead."

Streng thought he'd come a long way since those childhood years, a long way from being a grunt, from being a rookie cop. But much as a man matured, he stayed the same man. With the same fears.

The sheriff of Ashburn County steeled himself as best he could, pure will forcing emotional detachment, refusing to be swayed by the horrors that he would witness. Then he went into the bedroom.

There was blood. A lot of blood. Painted in black Jackson Pollock madness, thrown across the bedspread, the walls, the carpet.

But there were no bodies.

Streng's shoes made squishing sounds as he walked to the closet, its sliding door closed. He opened it fast, stepping back, pointing the flashlight inside. The beam exposed some hanging shirts and a laundry hamper.

Where were they? Who could have taken them? Santiago and Ajax didn't have time to dispose of the bodies—they'd been right behind Streng and Josh. Unless . . .

Unless they came back for them.

The gray hairs on Streng's arms pricked out like a porcupine, and he had that tingle/surge in his belly that brought instant flop sweat. He could feel the sniper rifles aimed at him, ready to fire, and knew he had to get out of there as fast as possible.

Streng spun and saw Santiago standing in the doorway.

"I guessed you'd come back for your car," he said.

I'm going to die, Streng thought. *Horribly.*

He wanted to ask what happened to Sal and Maggie,

but his throat closed up. That was good—it prevented him from weeping. From begging.

"I'm going to enjoy making you scream," Santiago whispered.

Somewhere, within the old body, the young man's training kicked in, and Streng moved. He feinted left with the knife, then tried to get around Santiago, driving his shoulder into him, hoping momentum would take him to the stairs.

Santiago took the hit and grasped Streng by the shoulder, yanking the sheriff off of his feet. Streng got shoved to the floor, Santiago pouring onto him like liquid. The knife was pried from his grip and tossed aside. Streng reared back the flashlight and lashed out, catching the soldier in the chin. There was a delicious, revolting cracking sound, and Santiago's head snapped back. But he stayed on Streng, his hands pinning down the sheriff's arms, squeezing, forcing him to drop the flashlight.

"I think you broke my cheekbone." Santiago's words were slow, slurred.

Streng hoped he broke every bone in his goddamn head. He wanted to say that aloud, to show some defiance. But he knew he was trapped, knew the pain was coming, and he was afraid if he opened his mouth he'd vomit from fear. Blood—his cousin's blood—soaked through the back of his shirt and pants, cold and wet. He smelled death, and staring up into Santiago's dark eyes, he saw it, as well.

"Give me the Charge."

That was the same thing Bernie said. Was it something Streng took from them?

"Give it to me."

Santiago's hand moved down over Streng's body, seek-

ing out his tortured kidney. *Jesus, no.* Streng tried to find
his voice, to tell him there was some Charge in the Jeep,
when he remembered the metal case he'd taken off Santiago earlier.

"My pocket," he managed to say. "I've got some in my
pocket."

He felt the killer's hand pause on his midsection, and
Streng braced for the agony, if bracing for it was even possible. But Santiago's fingers passed, probing lower, patting
down Streng's pants, finding the case. The killer tugged it
out and cradled it in his palms like a junkie with a fix.

Streng's fist shot out, knocking the case across the
room, onto the bed. Incredibly, Santiago leapt off of him,
going after the Charge. Streng didn't bother hunting down
the Ka-Bar. Instead he rolled onto all fours and crawled
like hell out of the bedroom, heading for the hallway. If he
could make it down the stairs, make it to the car—

Ajax filled the staircase.

Streng went right, into the second bedroom. His shins
pleaded with him to stop, but he picked up speed instead,
crawling toward the broken window, the cool breeze promising freedom, his .45 waiting for him on the roof.

He bumped something in the darkness.

Streng couldn't see, but he knew. His hands rested on a
body, cool and still, and even though he didn't want to do
it he reached up the chest . . . up the shoulders . . . until he
found the empty space and the slick, sharp knot of vertebrae where Sal's head used to be.

Revulsion swirled within Streng, rooting him. His
heartbeat thundered in his ears, but he could faintly hear
someone coming into the room behind him, someone who
wanted to kill him or worse. Streng crawled around his

cousin, his leg brushing something that rolled, something that could only have been Sal's severed head, and then his hands were on the shattered windowpane and he was pulling himself up and Ajax grabbed him by the shoulder.

Streng tried to duck under the gigantic hand, but it locked under his armpit and tugged violently, hurling him across the room. His back hit something—a dresser or desk—bringing a rainbow banner of pain before Streng's eyes. Then he fell, face-first, to the floor.

"Bring him," Santiago said, or perhaps Streng imagined it. Ajax grabbed his ankle, pulled him across the carpeting, and Streng cast about frantically anything to grab. He touched something—something cold and sticky that felt like jelly.

But it wasn't jelly.

It was Maggie.

The jelly feeling came from exposed fat and muscle, most of her skin having been peeled off.

Streng wrapped his fingers around her wrist, and for a moment his body stretched between Ajax and his cousin's wife. Then the giant jerked hard, breaking Streng's grip, making his face skip across the rug and causing a friction burn on his cheek. He was hauled into the hallway, past the staircase—so close yet so out of reach—and into Sal's bedroom, where Ajax lifted him by his leg and held him upside down like a little girl's doll.

Santiago had the flashlight tucked under his arm. Between his thumb and index finger, held at mouth level, was one of those capsules. But rather than eat it, Santiago broke it open and sniffed the contents. Streng watched as the killer vibrated like he'd been plugged into an electric socket, and then a mirthless smile creased his face.

Ajax made an awful sound, an inarticulate vowel jumble that sounded like the cries of the deaf.

"You'll get some in a moment." Santiago pointed at Streng. "Bring him here."

Ajax didn't move. He moaned again, deep and cowlike. The blood pooling up in Streng's head made it feel ready to burst.

"Now, Ajax. Then you'll get some Charge."

Ajax moved forward, and Streng's knuckles dragged the floor and bumped something hard and sharp. *The Ka-Bar.* He latched on to it and almost laughed at his luck.

"No playing around this time, Sheriff," Santiago said. "You're going to tell me where your brother is. Ajax, break his knees. He won't be needing them anymore."

The Ka-Bar Warthog had a thick, heavy blade, and Streng swung it at Ajax's knuckles like he was chopping down a sapling—*hack hack hack*—and the huge fingers released him.

Streng landed on his shoulder, rolled to all fours, and then leapt for the doorway. He took the stairs three at a time, moving faster than he had in more than twenty years. Miraculously, he made it outside without anyone grabbing or killing him.

His Jeep was parked less than fifty yards away. Streng sprinted, pushing past the pain in his legs, his side, his whole body. He dared a quick glance behind him and saw Ajax emerge from the doorway at full speed, fast enough to break through a brick wall.

Streng focused on his vehicle. Fifteen steps away.

Ten.

Eight.

Jesus, they're almost on me.

Six.

Two.

He hit the driver's side and reached for the handle, getting out of the door's way as he yanked it open.

"Charge," Bernie said from the back seat.

Streng tossed the Ka-Bar on the passenger seat, dug the car keys from his pocket, wasted two seconds trying to find the ignition, and started the vehicle just as Ajax slammed into it.

The impact jolted Streng, cracking his head against the window, bringing out the stars. With one hand he fumbled for the gear shift, and the other sought out and found the electric door lock. Streng manhandled the car into first and hit the gas.

A massive palm struck the front windshield, making a spiderweb mosaic out of the glass. The car lurched forward as Ajax's hand broke through, reaching for the steering wheel. The giant caught it, holding on and allowing himself to be dragged up the dirt road alongside the Jeep.

Streng sought out, and found, the Ka-Bar. As the Jeep bounced around and Ajax banged on the door, Streng stabbed at the giant's hand, over and over, the knife tip gouging bone. Little fountains of blood erupted, bathing the sheriff's lap. Streng stabbed hard, then twisted the blade. The fingers opened and Ajax released the wheel, his arm flailing out and pulling the shattered windshield from its mounting. Streng checked the rearview and watched the monster roll into the underbrush, and then his image disappeared because Bernie stood up from his seat, mouth open, his broken and bleeding teeth biting at Streng's shoulder.

Streng smashed down the brake pedal. Bernie bounced

forward and flopped next to him in the front seat, legs in the air, combat boots kicking like mad. One of them connected with the Ka-Bar, knocking it from Streng's grasp.

Streng tugged the door handle and fell out of the car before he got his head stoved in. A ways down Gold Star Road, Ajax was getting to his feet, and farther, coming up fast, was Santiago running full tilt.

Streng ran around the front of the Jeep, opened the passenger door, and pulled out Bernie. Then he grabbed the soldier's hair and drove his forehead once, twice, three times into the oversize steel-belted radial. That took the fight right out of him.

Streng risked another glance behind. Ajax had broken into a jog, and Santiago had taken the lead and would be on him in seconds.

Streng wrestled Bernie into the back, climbed across the passenger seat without bothering to close the door, and hit the accelerator. The Jeep's tires bit into the road, kicking up sand and gravel, and then they finally found purchase and the vehicle lurched forward—but not before Santiago made it to the passenger door and tried to climb in.

The steering wheel dripped slick blood, but Streng clenched it tight and swerved hard, away from Santiago, ripping the open door from his grip. Then he popped the Jeep into second gear, punched the gas, and left Ajax and Santiago in the dust.

Wind whipped at the sheriff's face through the empty space where his windshield used to be, irritating the rug burn on his cheek and burning his eyes, and Streng hurt in so many places he couldn't even take inventory, but for the first time since this hellish ordeal began he managed a small grin.

"Not bad, old man," he said to himself.

He headed toward Safe Haven.

J essie Lee opened her eyes and looked around. She was still in the boys' locker room, surrounded by blood and bodies. The chair she sat in was the same chair that she saw Merv, her boss, die in.

She filled her lungs and let out the loudest scream she could.

But all that came out was a gurgling wheeze, accompanied by the worst sore throat she'd ever had.

"I used this," said a voice from behind her. A voice that wasn't Taylor's. Dangling in front of Jessie Lee's eyes was a pair of surgical scissors, long and thin, bits of tissue clinging to their blades.

"Yelling brings unwanted attention. And who wants to bother and fuss with gags? Messy, disgusting things. So I snipped your vocal cords."

Jessie Lee sobbed—a quiet, pitiful sound. She tried to stand up, but firm hands held her down.

"Taylor and I have a question to ask, and we'd like a quick answer. You've already taken up a lot of our time, and other people are anxious for their turn. And don't worry about us hearing you—I can lip-read."

Taylor stood before her, brushing dust and bits of insulation from his uniform. He cupped her chin, making Jessie Lee look at him.

"Where is Warren Streng?"

Jessie Lee shook her head. Warren was Sheriff Streng's

brother, old and eccentric. He had a shack in the woods somewhere. No one ever saw him.

"I don't know," she tried to say. It came out as a wet whisper.

Taylor crouched. His eyes revealed the depths of hell.

"Think hard. Think very hard."

Jessie Lee wondered if she should make something up, wondered if that would buy her more time. But more time for what? A few extra hours with these psychopaths? Dying here, now, was almost certainly preferable to the worst that could happen. She closed her eyes, paging through her memories to come up with a last thought. Her mind settled on Erwin, the night he proposed. Awkward, stuttering, getting down on one knee during the halftime show at the Packers game, the JumboTron asking, "Jessie Lee, will you marry me?" He put a ring on her finger—a much bigger ring than he could afford—and when she hugged and kissed him, twenty thousand fans cheered.

They would have had a wonderful wedding. And a wonderful marriage. Jessie Lee pursed her lips. She could almost hear Erwin's voice.

"I don't care if I'm not allowed. I'm looking anyway."

It *was* Erwin's voice. Outside the locker room.

"You can't go in there, Erwin." Rick Hortach, the town treasurer. *"You'll ruin it for the rest of us."*

"I need to know if she's in there, Rick. Get out of my way."

Taylor stood up, but his partner said, "I'll handle it— I'm dressed for it," and walked around the corner to the locker room entrance.

Jessie Lee flushed with hope. She had to warn Erwin somehow, had to let him know what was happening.

"I'm sorry, sir." Taylor's partner talking. *"You'll have to wait your turn."*

"I'm looking for my fiancée, Jessie Lee Sloan. Is she in here?"

"ERWIN!" Jessie Lee screamed. She screamed with everything she had, until her shoulders quaked and her throat felt like it caught fire. But all that came out was a high-pitched hiss.

"Miss Sloan was here. She left about five minutes ago, with her lottery check."

"HELP ME!" Jessie Lee tried to stand up, but Taylor swung his leg over her and straddled her lap. She twisted and shoved, and he wrapped a hand in her hair and forced her head back. Jessie Lee felt his lips, and then his warm teeth, on her neck.

"Why isn't her name crossed off the list, then?"

"We're getting around to it."

"I'd like to take a look anyway."

"I'm sorry, that's not allowed."

"ERWIN!" she cried out, one last time. The tears came fast but silent, and her chest heaved with sobs.

"You think you have a chance at getting away?" Taylor said, his breath hot on her ear. "No one gets away."

Taylor nipped at her throat, and she shook her head *NO NO NO NO NO . . .*

"I know she's in there," Erwin said. *"Get out of my way."*

Jessie Lee looked toward the entrance and saw Erwin— big, strong, wonderful Erwin—stride around the corner, his hands clenched into fists. He focused on the stack of bodies in the shower room and his mouth hung open.

"HERE!" Jessie Lee yelled. *"I'M HERE!"*

And Erwin's eyes met hers and pierced her with hope, and then he was rushing at Taylor, bellowing in rage, arms open to grab him.

The knife appeared in Taylor's hand so fast it was almost magic, and he leapt up and smoothly punched the blade into Erwin's chest.

Erwin gasped. He fell to his knees, looked longingly at Jessie Lee, and then pitched forward onto his face.

Jessie Lee ran to the man she loved, burying her face into his back, trying to get her hands under him to put pressure on the wound even though his heart had already stopped beating.

She was so preoccupied with her efforts that Jessie Lee didn't even feel it when Taylor came up behind her and slit her throat.

Fran hugged Duncan to her and stared at the man they'd almost run over. He stood in the middle of the road, only a few feet in front of their car. Tall, in camouflage military fatigues and a matching helmet, some sort of weapon strapped to his shoulder. He had his hands over his head and was waving, trying to flag them down.

"Drive!" Fran told Josh.

Mathison had other ideas. He hopped onto the dashboard and pointed at the man, hooting and chirping.

The man smiled and yelled, "Mathison?"

Josh glanced at Fran. "Your call. We can talk to him, or leave."

"Hello?" The man took a step forward. "Do you have a monkey in there?"

Duncan looked up at her. "It's his monkey, Mom. We should give him back."

Fran used her fingertips to brush the bangs from her son's eyes. He hadn't lost his ability to trust people, to look on the good side of things, even after the night he'd endured. Fran didn't think she could ever trust anyone in a uniform again.

"I'm a scientist," the man said. "I'm here to help. Look, I'm putting down this weapon. I'm not even sure what it is."

Fran had a tense moment when he unslung the big shotgun, but he quickly set it down on the road and raised his hands over his head.

"What do you think?" Josh asked.

Her gut told her they should leave. Even if Mathison did belong to this man, it could be sorted out later. Fran's primary concern was Duncan's safety.

"No one helped us, Mom. After the crash."

Fran couldn't believe that came from his lips. Duncan *never* talked about the accident. Not even in therapy. But she often wondered if he thought about it as often as she did.

It had been late, almost midnight. They were driving home from the annual rodeo in Spooner, a neighboring town. Just ten minutes away from home, her husband, Charles, had slowed down to take a sharp turn on the winding country road. Some nameless driver—either drunk or careless—had taken no such precaution, taking up both lanes and forcing Charles to swerve into the woods to avoid a collision.

Their car went down an embankment and hit a tree, rolling them over and trapping them inside. Charles had been horribly injured. But Fran remained hopeful. They had crashed only a few yards off the road. Someone would see them. Someone would stop.

Twenty-three cars passed them up that night. Fran knew, because she counted. As each one approached, she prayed they would see the wreck and help. Each time, her prayers had gone unanswered.

It took two hours for Charles to bleed to death. And another hour before they were finally discovered. She remembered talking to Duncan during that time, soothing him, even as her husband's life spilled out of his wounds and onto her face. Fran assumed Duncan had blocked the memory. Apparently he hadn't. She looked at her son now, so earnest, so strong, so full of hope, and felt such overwhelming pride it made her chest hurt.

"Okay," she told Josh. "Let's talk to him."

Josh opened the car door and craned his head out the opening. But just as he began to speak, Mathison jumped off the dash and galloped to the man, leaping into his arms. Fran let out a long breath as she watched the happy reunion, her apprehension dropping a notch. The monkey hugged the man, the man hugged the monkey, and both parties engaged in some back patting. Then Mathison jumped down to the street and hopped back into the car, sitting on Duncan's lap and prompting a delighted squeal from her son.

"I take it you two know each other," Josh said to the man.

"We go back a long ways. May I approach? I'm guessing some bad things have happened tonight and you're spooked."

Fran nodded at Josh.

"Okay, you can come closer. But please keep your hands where I can see them. We've had one helluva night."

The man walked forward, keeping his arms raised. He stopped next to Josh's door and squatted. Up close Fran saw that he was older, perhaps late fifties, and so thin his Adam's apple looked enormous. His helmet was askew, revealing a bald head dotted with liver spots. He smiled, his front teeth slightly crooked.

"I'm Dr. Ralph Stubin. You've met Mathison, I see."

Woof walked over and gave Stubin a sniff, then began to bark.

"Woof!" Fran used her firm voice. "Shush!"

The dog woofed once more, then turned a circle and sat back down.

"Is Mathison yours?" Duncan asked Stubin.

"Yes and no. I bought him, but he's a sentient being and really only belongs to himself. We're friends more than anything." Stubin stopped grinning, and his face became serious. "You're probably wondering what's going on here, and how I fit in. I'm guessing there's a roadblock ahead?"

Josh nodded. Fran wondered why Josh didn't speak and realized he was waiting for information before he decided to share any. Smart.

Stubin rubbed his pointy chin. "I was afraid of that. Standard operating procedure, I suppose. Have there been any casualties yet?"

"At least four people have died," Josh said evenly.

"But we got away!" Duncan added.

Fran gave Duncan a small pinch on the bottom, a signal to stay quiet.

"You got away?" Stubin raised his thick gray eyebrows. "Extraordinary."

"Do you know what's going on?" Josh asked.

"I have an idea. This is kind of a long story, and I'm guessing you don't want to invite me into your car. And rightfully so. Do you want to talk outside?"

Stubin's eyes flashed to Duncan, then back to Fran. She understood. There were things her son didn't need to hear.

"Duncan, stay in the car with Woof and Mathison."

Duncan opened his mouth, apparently ready to protest, but then Mathison pulled himself onto Josh's shoulder and began picking at his hair.

"He's grooming you," Stubin said. "He only does that with people he likes."

"Can I pet him?" Duncan asked.

"He doesn't like his head being touched, but he likes belly rubs."

Duncan tentatively tickled Mathison's midsection, and the primate cooed. Fran relished the big smile on Duncan's face, then she and Josh got out of the Roadmaster. She met them by the front of the car.

Josh folded his arms and said, "Okay. Tell us what the hell is going on in this town."

"May I ask your names?" Dr. Stubin asked.

Josh offered his first name only, and Fran followed his lead. There was a round of hand shaking, and Fran found Stubin's palm to be hot and moist.

"Where to begin, where to begin?" Stubin laced his fingers together and rocked back on his heels, looking beyond them. "Okay. You're familiar with terrorism, correct? Not the acts of terrorists so much, but the ideology behind terrorism."

Josh answered. "Violence directed against civilians, meant to cause fear."

Stubin nodded. "Excellent. Yes. It should be added that noncombatants are the targets, but the goal is to send a message to those in power. If you scare enough people, the thought is their government will change its policies. We erroneously believe that terrorism is used primarily by fundamentalists, or extremists. But that's BS. All governments, even Western nations, support terrorists. Sometimes it's through discreet funding—remember the Iran Contra scandal? The so-called freedom fighters that our government supported were a group of raping, murdering thugs, who destroyed more than a hundred Nicaraguan villages."

"Is that what we're facing here?" Josh asked. "Government-sponsored terrorism?"

Stubin frowned. "Actually, what you're facing is much worse. In recent years, many countries have begun training their own terrorists rather than clandestinely funding them. These units are code-named Red-ops. Everyone has a Red-ops program. And one of them has accidentally landed in Safe Haven."

Fran thought about Taylor. While he didn't fit her conception of a terrorist, he certainly did his best to instill fear. "Who sent them?"

"I'm not in the Intelligence loop, but we think they're Canadian. It's very likely they got much of their training in the U.S., though."

"But Canada is our ally," Josh said.

"Yes. That's sort of where I come in. I'm a brain surgeon who specializes in transhumanism. It's a catchall phrase for making humans better with the help of technology. I've been working with our own military, experimenting with enhancing soldier performance. Mathison is one of my early successes."

Fran glanced back at the car. Through the windshield she watched Duncan and Mathison playing what looked like patty-cake. "He seems pretty smart."

"He's very smart. It's safe to say he's the smartest animal who ever lived, except for human beings, and he's probably smarter than a great many of those. I named him after Alan Mathison Turing, the grandfather of modern computers. Turing invented machines that run sequentially, figuring out tasks in linear fashion. The human brain, however, is a parallel processor, absorbing and dealing with a lot of information at once. For example, right now you're looking at me, and listening to my words. But at the same time you can feel the cool breeze, see what's going on behind me, plus you're already formulating more questions to ask, and performing dozens of other biological and sensory processes at the same time. A lot of recent research has been done, trying to make computers more human. My research is opposite—implanting neuroprosthetic devices to make human beings act like computers."

"Brainwashing," Josh said. He didn't sound enthused.

"More like programming. The chip allows for the downloading of information directly into the brain, just like running a program on your computer. When the program is initiated, the subject can function with pinpoint efficiency, able to complete tasks that would normally require years of training. For example, here's one of

Mathison's programs, initiated by a simple word command." Stubin snapped his fingers, getting the monkey's attention. "Mathison!" he called to the car. "Dance, please."

Fran watched as Mathison hopped through the side window and onto the hood. The primate stood on two legs and stuck one paw out in front of him. Then the other. He turned up one palm, the other palm, touched his head with one hand, then the other hand . . .

"Is that . . . ?" Josh asked.

Stubin nodded. "Yes. He's doing the Macarena."

Duncan clapped his hands, delighted. Fran was amused at first, but the display quickly became sort of sad. It reminded her of that old movie *A Clockwork Orange*.

"How long will he dance for?"

"Until the song ends. We can't hear it, but it's programmed onto the chip in his head. The technology is really quite revolutionary. I've been able to grow neurons—actual brain cells—on the silicon of integrated circuits. The neurons actually bridge the gaps between transistors, which transmit electrical impulses just like neurotransmitters. Mathison's dance is a computer program, but to him it feels more like an irresistible thought or impulse. All other thoughts are overridden. As such, he can do things no other monkey can do, without ever even having to practice. Very much like savants can play an entire concerto after only hearing it once, or solve complex mathematical problems without a calculator. With this breakthrough it is now possible to bypass education and automatically download professions into people's brains. With the right program, a man can have all of the skills of a surgeon, or a lawyer, or a mechanic."

Josh said, "Or a terrorist."

"I'm afraid it appears my Canadian colleagues have done just that."

Fran folded her arms. "And you haven't?"

Stubin eyed her, and Fran could detect a sliver of distaste. "I haven't worked on humans. The U.S. government won't allow it. But imagine having a group of soldiers who could follow complicated, specific orders, better and faster, without questioning them."

"We don't have to imagine them," Josh said. "They're here in Safe Haven."

Mathison finished his dance, and Duncan applauded. Fran scanned the tree line, suddenly feeling very exposed. Stubin didn't seem worried.

"The army asked me to come here, to lend my expertise. But I'm afraid the Special Forces unit I came with was killed. I'm trying to get into town where I can contact my superiors." He glanced at the broken window, and then up the road. "I'm guessing the people at the roadblock weren't very welcoming."

"So why are the Red-ops here?" Fran asked.

Stubin adjusted his helmet, and it slipped right back into its original position. "As far as I know, this Red-ops unit crashed here accidentally, and they're carrying out their objective and treating your town like an enemy territory."

"What's their objective?"

"Isolate. Terrorize. Annihilate. That's what they do."

"Then why were they asking about Warren?"

Stubin blinked. "Warren?"

"He's the sheriff's brother. If they came here by accident, how do they know about Warren?"

"That's also standard operating procedure. When a

Red-ops unit invades a town, they seek out information—
phone books, directories, and such—and memorize it."

Fran frowned. "Taylor called me by my name. How did
he know it was me? My picture isn't in the phone book."

Stubin shrugged. "They might have accessed the state
driver's license database. Or maybe he looked through
your personal belongings. He attacked you?"

"At the diner where I work."

"The diner? Do you wear a name tag?"

Fran did wear a name tag. She flushed, feeling stupid.
But it still didn't make sense.

"Taylor knew about Duncan."

"Duncan?"

"My son. Bernie had gone after Duncan."

Stubin stared at her for a few seconds before he spoke.
"I have no idea how they knew that. This makes it a lot
worse."

Fran didn't know how this could possibly get any worse,
but she asked anyway.

"Perhaps the Red-ops units didn't crash here accidentally," Stubin said. "Perhaps they're here on purpose."

Taylor looked at the woman bleeding out on the shower
floor and felt remorse. She was a tasty little morsel,
but he hadn't had the opportunity to really enjoy her. He
recalled his past, before death row, and the women he'd
been with. There was one girl, in Chicago, a tiny thing
with fingers like pretzels that went *crunch crunch*—

Taylor experienced something like a flashbulb going

off in his head, and before the memory became too pronounced the Chip sensed the deviation from the program and rebooted. Without thinking he reached for his case and removed a Charge capsule, breaking it under his nostrils. The fumes—a mixture of acetylcholine, trichloroethylene, amyl nitrite, and several other proprietary ingredients—traveled up his nasal passage, entered his lungs, and then permeated his bloodstream. From there the chemicals reached the brain and defragmented the memory center, clearing it of all unnecessary neurotransmitters.

Taylor stopped thinking about the past and once again reverted to Chip protocol. *Interrogate townspeople. Find Warren Streng.*

He looked at his partner, Logan, who wore civilian clothes rather than the black body armor, the result of changing soon after they'd landed. Logan enjoyed bloodshed as much as Taylor did and had been the lucky one chosen to kill their handlers in the helicopter, cutting their throats so deeply their heads were practically severed. Taylor would have liked that duty, but he'd been busy helping Santiago set the charges, blowing up the chopper to make it look like it had crashed. In the unlikely event they were caught, the government could claim it was an accident, rather than intentional.

Though the Chip didn't allow for personal feelings to get in the way of the mission, if Taylor were to pick his favorite team member it would be Logan. They had similar backgrounds. Both were serial killers, with oral fixations. Both equated pain with sexual arousal. Both were behind bars when the Red-ops recruited them. If it wasn't for one vital difference, they might have been identical twins.

Logan was currently dressed as a townie, but it didn't

fool many people, because everyone here knew who everyone else was and could spot strangers instantly. But if everyone knew everyone, why were they having so much trouble locating Warren?

"Erwin? You in there?"

A male voice, coming from around the corner. Taylor nodded at Logan, who quickly intercepted.

"You're not allowed back here, sir."

"My buddy Erwin just went in there."

"He left."

"He didn't leave. I've been standing here the whole time. Look, I've seen some crazy shit tonight and I just want to make sure . . . Jesus Christ."

The man had gotten past Logan and stood in the locker room, taking in the carnage. He was short and bearded and wore filthy overalls and a filthy baseball cap. Taylor could smell the sewage on him from ten feet away.

Logan came up behind the man, placing a knife to his throat. Taylor shuffled over. The name *OLEN* was stitched onto the man's bibs.

"Hello, Olen. Where's Warren Streng?"

Olen's lower lip bounced like it was made of rubber. "Wiley? He lives on Deer Tick Road, on the little lake."

Taylor moved closer, getting in Olen's face. He noted that even the man's teeth were stained gray.

"You actually know where he lives?"

Olen appeared ready to cry. "I . . . I cleaned out his septic tank a while back."

"Do you have his address?"

"Wiley doesn't exactly have an address. He likes to live off the grid, he says. No mail. No utilities. Only comes into town once in a while."

That explained the trouble they'd been having.

"Whether or not you die depends on how you answer my next question. Can you take us there?"

Logan drew a little blood on Olen's neck to drive the point home.

"Yeah . . . yeah, I can . . . no problem."

"Good," soothed Taylor. "Very good."

A thought, or the chemical/electric approximation of a thought, flashed full-blown into Taylor's mind.

Eliminate townspeople.

He guessed it appeared in his partner's head, as well, because Logan was already kneeling by the backpack and removing gas masks. Taylor forced one onto Olen's face and put one on himself. Then he and Logan donned clear plastic ponchos, gloves, and leggings, and each strapped on a bandolier of aerosol canisters.

"If you try to run, I'll pull off your mask," Taylor told Olen. "And you wouldn't like that."

The three of them walked out of the locker room, into the gymnasium. The crowd of over three hundred didn't react immediately. It took a few seconds for them to notice the gas masks and a few more seconds for them to question what was happening.

By that time Taylor had already activated and thrown two cans, Logan three. The hydrogen cyanide gas was colorless but carried the odor of bitter almonds. The canisters hissed as they rolled through the bleachers, and the smell—coupled with the trio's attire—induced panic. Screams popped up here and there, then mingled and joined into a communal wail that sounded as if it came from a single entity.

People tumbled over each other, tripping down the riser

stairs, falling and trampling and stampeding toward the exits, which did no good because they'd been previously locked. A foolish man rushed Logan, who slashed open his trachea before being touched. Taylor kept Olen in his sights but probably didn't need to bother; the sewage man seemed frozen to the spot.

After sixty seconds the panicked screams were replaced by another sound: wheezing. The gas entered their bodies through the lungs and mucus membranes, and it quickly induced runny noses, dilated pupils, and tightening of the chest. This was followed by coughing, panting, throwing up, urinating, and defecating. Then came convulsions and death.

Taylor found it quite enjoyable to watch. He'd been recruited by the Red-ops, secretly saved from death row, because of his appetite for death. For him, killing was like riding a roller coaster or seeing a good movie. His levels of serotonin and dopamine rose, prompting a sense of well-being and pleasure. The Chip enhanced this effect. Taylor licked his lips, and his heart rate increased, but he made no attempt to touch his growing erection. Rape wasn't in the programming today.

The three of them stood there for almost five minutes. Not everyone died, but those that still breathed were comatose or on their way. Taylor was grateful that the gas mask filtered out odors, because the gym was lousy with bodily fluids. He tugged Olen by the arm and followed Logan to the table near the gym entrance, watching his step. The town treasurer still sat at the table, mouth open and eyes bugged out. He'd managed to get the keys out of his pocket but died before being able to use them. Logan tugged them from his hand.

It took a bit of pulling and pushing to move the large pile of bodies away from the door, and when they got to the bottom of the stack Taylor was tickled to see Mayor Durlock still alive, twitching and wheezing. His chest and face were speckled with bloody vomit, and the front of his pants was stained.

Taylor bent down so the mayor could hear him.

"I lied to you about seeing your wife and daughter again. They're already dead. But thanks for helping out."

Mayor Durlock's face contorted into a lovely mix of shock and anguish, which morphed into pure pain when Logan cut out his eyes. Logan tossed one to Taylor.

"I've got an eye on you."

Then Logan's face went blank. The Chip, rebooting. No time for play right now.

Taylor unlocked the door and dragged Olen outside.

"Where's your vehicle?" Taylor asked.

Olen didn't answer, but he did raise his hand and point to a tanker truck with a skunk painted on the side.

"How far is Warren Streng's place from here?"

Olen stayed silent. Logan poked him in the stomach with the knife, slipping the blade in an inch.

Olen flinched violently, letting out a scream.

"How far?"

"Fifteen minutes."

Taylor and Logan exchanged a knowing look.

"You have ten minutes to get us there," Logan said, "or I'll feed you your own liver."

As they got into the truck, the Chip initiated another thought in Taylor's head. *Call the others.* He held open his plastic leggings and tugged the Multichannel Multipoint Distribution Service Communicator out of his front pocket. He slid back the cover on the MMDSC and held it to his head like a cell phone, speaking loudly to overcome the distortions of the gas mask.

"Head bird acquired. Stand by for directions to the nest."

The Honey Wagon pulled out of the parking lot and onto Main Street, and Logan again poked Olen with the knife, for no particular reason. Taylor smiled; he wasn't the only one aroused by the pain of others. He mentally ran through the next few objectives, and he closed his eyes and pictured the last one. The one that missions always ended with. *Have fun.*

All good soldiers got to partake in a little rest and relaxation when combat duties were finished. Sometimes R&R lasted for days before evac was called. He'd be free to indulge in whatever warped fantasies he could dream up. No rules. No laws. No repercussions. He hoped there would be a few survivors left for playtime. Maybe that sexy waitress, Fran. Taylor smiled. Her blood had been deliciously salty.

The Chip sensed the electrochemical changes in Taylor's cerebral cortex and rebooted. Taylor dug out a Charge capsule and slipped it up under his gas mask.

The fumes took away the daydreams. But Taylor's smile stayed.

Streng pulled into the Water Department parking lot and had his choice of spaces. He parked in the handicapped zone because it was closest to the front door.

Bernie had behaved for the remainder of the ride, sitting silently and staring straight ahead. Streng flipped on the interior light and turned around, studying his captive. Bernie's face had swelled up even more, purple and red hues peeking though the dried blood. Streng noted the lump on his forehead where he'd introduced Bernie to his thirty-two-inch tires and didn't feel a shred of pity. Though the killer was beaten, acting docile, and still had his hands tied behind him, Streng wouldn't relax until he was locked in the drunk tank.

The sheriff considered his next move. He kept a spare gun in his office. Streng didn't want to risk moving Bernie without being armed, but if he left him in the Jeep he could climb out the broken front window and run away. Streng decided he'd put Bernie's seat belt on; it'd be impossible for him to escape without using his hands.

Streng kept his eyes on Bernie's eyes and slowly reached for the belt. This required Streng to lean between the seats, exposing his face and neck to Bernie's few remaining teeth. The farther he reached, the closer he got, until they were face to face. He smelled Bernie's breath, metallic and hot. Bernie's eyes were dark brown, almost black, and betrayed nothing. If eyes were the windows to the soul, this man had none.

What turns a person into a monster like this? Training? Some horrible event in his past? Genetics? How does a man lose his humanity?

Streng felt around Bernie's hips for the seat belt but couldn't find it. He'd have to lower his eyes to look. It would take only a second or two. What could happen in a second or two?

"Fuck that," Streng said. He withdrew his hand, grabbed

the Ka-Bar knife, and stepped out of the Jeep. Then he
opened up the rear door and put the blade tight against
Bernie's throat, revealing a gnarled mass of pink scar tissue at his collar line.

"You move, you die," he said.

He located the seat belt, pulled it around the pyro, and
locked it in place.

"He burned me," Bernie said, startling Streng. "Daddy
did it, to make me stop playing with matches."

Streng pulled away from him and said, "I really don't
care."

Bernie went on. "He put my—my arm—on the stove,
and he . . . *held* it there. I had to count, count to ten. I keep
seeing it. I keep feeling it."

Streng walked back to the front seat. He dug the office keys out of his glove compartment and picked up
the McDonald's bag full of Bernie's belongings from the
passenger-seat floor.

Bernie said, "I don't, I really don't, want to remember.
Stop it, Daddy! Stop hurting me!" Bernie's eyes pleaded
with Streng. "Make it stop." Then he began to shake and
moan, tears forming ski trails in the blood on his cheeks.

"We can't control what happens to us," Streng said, recalling something his father used to say. "Only how we
react to what happens."

Dad had been a lumberjack. He'd been deep in the
woods, scouting virgin forest, when a tree fell and pinned
his leg. He had his hunting knife with him and spent two
days drinking rainwater and hacking away at the tree and
the ground. Neither one gave way. So on the third day he
went to work on his leg. Streng remembered his father telling the story, about trying not to scream while he did it,

for fear of attracting coyotes, and how the bone wouldn't cut so he had to use a large rock to break it. He crawled three miles through the woods, during a terrible storm, and when he finally made it to safety the first thing out of his mouth was to ask for a beer.

Dad wasn't bitter about it. In fact, as soon as he was well enough he went back to the tree and cut a section from it, from which he carved a wooden leg. Then he opened a bar in Safe Haven and named it Stumpy's, which thrived until his death years ago.

If life gives you lemons, make lemonade. Another of his father's optimistic expressions. Dad was always quoting those. Streng didn't know if he'd have the guts to do what his old man did, and then the bravery to carry on, but he hoped so. He also hoped he'd never have to find out.

Bernie, however, didn't seem cut from the same cloth.

"CHARGE!" Bernie screamed, straining against the seat belt. "I NEED CHARGE! MAKE THE MEMORY GO AWAY!"

Streng took that as his cue to leave. The Water Department, like every other building he'd passed on the way over, had no electricity and was dark as death. Streng found one of Bernie's lighters in the sack and flipped it on, using it to light his way. He opened the glass front door and limped past the secretary's desk, down a tiled hall, to the unisex washroom. He caught his reflection in the mirror and wasn't surprised to see he looked like hell. The orange light, and the flickering shadows, made Streng think of cavemen for some reason, primeval campfires from long ago.

Streng set the high-tech lighter on the sink with the catch depressed so it stayed on, and he unbuckled his holster and pants. Taking them off brought sparks of pain, sparks that became full-blown forest fires when he made himself urinate. The dark brown color reinforced Streng's conviction that he needed to get to a hospital.

He flushed, then used the sink to splash water on his face and neck. He also washed his groin, ashamed he'd wet himself earlier. Part of him knew that it wasn't his fault—any healthy young buck would have pissed having his kidney mangled. But a louder, meaner part told him to get used to it, because he was an old man who would soon be in diapers.

Streng told that louder, meaner part to shut up.

He picked up the torch and his stained pants and walked in underwear and socks to his office, two doors down. Streng tried the phone on his desk. Everything he dialed resulted in a busy signal. He had similar results with his cell.

The sheriff wasn't surprised. Something big was happening, and if the bad guys didn't kill the phone lines, there was a chance the good guys had done it to make sure no word of what was happening leaked out. Bless our government and their cover-your-ass policy.

In his closet he had an extra pair of slacks. No extra underwear, but he'd live with that. He stripped off his boxer shorts, set the dirty clothes on a shelf, and pulled on the fresh khakis. On his desk was a bottle of Tylenol. He dry-swallowed three. Then he unlocked his desk drawer and removed a .357 Colt Python and a partial box of ammo. Streng knew it was loaded, but decades of being around firearms made him check anyway.

He also hunted for and found his Mini Fry stun gun in the drawer—the same size and shape as a pack of cigarettes, and it delivered 900,000 brain-scrambling volts. Streng flipped the side switch and the battery indicator glowed green.

Back at the closet, Streng strapped on a holster for the Colt and a nylon fanny pack that Sal bought him for his sixtieth birthday. Streng had refused to accept the gift, calling it a "man purse." Sal insisted, saying that since Streng was now an old fart he needed something to carry all of his medication around. They laughed, drank too much, and Streng hung it in this closet and forgot about it. Now he snapped it onto his waist and thought about Sal as he filled it with the ammo, the Ka-Bar, the stun gun, Bernie's lighters, Bernie's container of Charge capsules, some matches, the Tylenol, and the electronic communicator thing, which vibrated just as Streng picked it up.

It reminded Streng of a Zippo, but slightly larger. A shell of black metal, no obvious buttons or switches, with an outlet in the bottom to plug in a cord. It vibrated again. A pager of some kind? Streng squeezed the top, tapped it on his desk, and pressed the sides. Nothing happened. Then he noticed a tiny seam along the back. He held the bottom, pulled the top, and the cover slid open, revealing a text message on a small green phosphorus screen.

Head bird acquired. Stand by for directions to the nest.

Streng felt a surge of anger. They must have found Wiley.

He played with the device for a few seconds, trying to retrieve older messages, but it didn't seem to have that function. It didn't have a keyboard, either, or any way to send text messages. Just a single button and a small speaker to talk into. Streng figured it translated speech into text, then sent it via microwave or some other high frequency. He tucked it into his man purse and zipped it closed.

Time to move Bernie.

He picked up the lighter, palmed the Mini Fry, and headed back to his Jeep. Bernie's fit had ended and he sat quietly, staring straight ahead. Streng got into the back seat with him, wondering how a man so obviously crazy could be recruited by an elite commando unit. Something to do with those Charge capsules? Ultimately he didn't care. Understanding Bernie was much less important than incapacitating him.

Streng didn't fool around. He used the stun gun.

He held the device to Bernie's neck, the two protruding metal prongs connecting with his skin, and pressed the button to discharge the weapon.

A crackling sound accompanied the white spark, and almost a million volts surged into Bernie's body, disrupting the electrical impulses the nervous system sent to the muscles, causing them to rapidly contract.

Streng knew from experience how it worked—when he'd bought the device he tried it out on himself with the help of a coworker. A one-second burst brought blinding pain. A two-second burst brought extreme muscle spasms. Three seconds could knock a person down, rapidly converting blood sugar into lactic acid and causing instant energy loss. Four seconds brought dizziness and disorientation. Five seconds could pacify even the most determined attacker for up to a few minutes.

Streng hit Bernie with a five-second burst. Bernie jerked, shook for a bit, then flopped over. Streng gave him a hard slap on the cheek to see if he reacted. He didn't. Streng kept the Mini Fry pressed to Bernie's side in case he needed another jolt and used his free hand to unbuckle him. Then he half pulled/half coaxed Bernie out of the car and onto his feet. The killer weaved a bit. Streng grabbed on to the back of his collar to steady him.

"Electricity," Bernie mumbled.

"That's right. Keep moving, or you'll get some more."

They came to the front door. Streng held it open and shoved Bernie inside. Since he didn't have three hands, he couldn't also hold the lighter. The office was too dark to lead Bernie to the cell.

Bernie said, "I have a chip in my head."

"Good for you."

Streng needed light, but he wasn't letting go of the pyro, and he wasn't about to put down the stun gun. So he gave the man another jolt. Bernie dropped to his knees. Streng kept his hand on his collar and shoved the Mini Fry into his fanny pack, fishing around for the lighter.

"I think you rebooted it," Bernie said.

Bernie bolted. Streng reached out with both hands to grab him, but Bernie's momentum took him forward and he scurried down the hall, blending in with the darkness.

A millisecond later Streng had cleared leather on his holster and fired his Colt twice, the reports snapping in his ears and the muzzle flash making him blink. He flicked on the lighter and held it up. The hallway was empty. Did the building have a back entrance? Streng couldn't picture it, but chances were it did. Bernie's hands were still tied, so he'd have a tough time unlocking doors. He was probably crouching somewhere, ready to pounce.

Streng cursed himself for being sloppy. He swung out the cylinder—warm to the touch—and yanked the spent brass, feeding in two fresh bullets. Then he moved down the hall, slow and cautious. He led with the Colt but kept his arm bent and tight against his body so the weapon couldn't be knocked away, reminding himself to aim for the head; Bernie's body armor might stop Magnum rounds.

When he reached the first doorway—the comptroller's office—Streng held his breath and paused, an ear turned to listen. Nothing. He brought the lighter forward, saw a desk, file cabinets, a bookcase, the closet door open and empty. Nowhere to hide.

Streng moved on to the washroom, opening the door in a single clean motion, pointing the gun upward. Empty again.

Four offices left, including Streng's, plus a boardroom and the drunk tank. Streng didn't feel nervous. He was a seasoned cop and a seasoned hunter. Scary as Bernie was, the man was cuffed and had no weapons. Streng simply needed to stay calm, cool, and methodical, and he'd get Bernie. Dead or alive.

A smell wafted up from the hallway. Smoke. Not the cordite from the Colt; something chemical and sharp. Streng's nose led him past two doors, to the mayor's temporary office. On the floor, near the desk, the plastic zip line Streng had used to tie Bernie's hands. The ends were melted and still smoking.

Bernie was free.

Adrenaline spiked through Streng's veins. He looked left, then right, not seeing Bernie, wondering how he could have gotten out of the room without Streng seeing it, realizing he couldn't have so he must have thrown the zip tie in there, spinning around to see Bernie charging at him—

The Colt was shoved to the side just as Streng dropped the lighter, which winked out when it hit the ground. Bernie hit him full body, slamming Streng backward into the desk, driving the air from his lungs.

The sheriff held on to the gun, shoved it into Bernie's stomach as the killer pounded him in the sides. He squeezed off a shot, point-blank. Bernie recoiled, slipping off of Streng, hitting the floor. Streng aimed where he guessed Bernie to be and fired three more rounds. He waited, trying to hear above the ringing in his ears. Nothing. He fumbled for his man purse, located another lighter.

Bernie lay on the floor, sprawled out and eyes closed. Streng's kidney burned, and his gun hand shook, and along with the pain and the fear was a bubble of animal rage. One shot to the head and it would be over. Streng had killed before. In Vietnam. In the line of duty, during a liquor store robbery. But he'd never murdered anyone. The distinction was large. In one case, the person was shooting back. In the other, the person was unarmed.

Streng got down to one knee, aimed the barrel at Bernie. The man deserved this, and probably much more. But was it Streng's job to judge? Even more important than the grayness of right and wrong, would Streng be able to live with himself afterward?

He fired.

The bullet hit its mark, not penetrating the body armor, but flattening out Bernie's kneecap like a stepped-on dog turd. Bernie's eyes popped open and he howled, and Streng grabbed his collar and dragged him across the tile floor, to the cell room. Ignoring Bernie's sobs of agony, he located the correct key, swung open the steel-barred door, and pulled him inside.

Streng didn't feel any sort of vindication or swell of pride when the jail door clanged shut. He'd stood by his morals and hadn't murdered a defenseless man, but that might not have been the right decision. Time would tell.

"Stop hurting me, Mommy!" Bernie wailed. "Please stop hurting me!"

Streng left the room.

J osh checked the rearview mirror and glanced at Dr. Stubin sitting in the back seat. Stubin was petting Woof—the dog had fallen asleep with his head on the doctor's lap and was snoring softly.

Between Josh and Fran in the front seat, Duncan and Mathison also slept, each sitting with their heads back and their mouths open. Fran stared out her window as they drove, absently stroking her son's hair.

"So how do we stop them?" Josh asked Stubin.

"The Red-ops?" Stubin rubbed his nose. "Well, we can assume they're enhanced. Besides the chip implants they've probably had other body supplementations. Better vision. Better hearing. Quicker reflexes. Performance-enhancing drugs for bigger muscles and more endurance. I'm guessing they're wearing the latest in body armor. And possibly, their dopamine and serotonin levels have been tweaked, giving them greater resistance to pain."

"But they can die, right?"

Stubin flashed his crooked teeth. "Everything dies, Josh."

Josh wasn't convinced. "One of them, Ajax, is the biggest guy I've ever seen. Has to be seven feet tall."

"Human growth hormone experimentation. I've studied that. Very difficult to pull off. You said there are four of them?"

"Four that we know about. Ajax, Santiago, Taylor, and Bernie."

"A Red-ops unit in Wisconsin. Amazing."

Josh didn't care for the note of admiration in Stubin's voice. "You think terrorism is amazing?"

Stubin shifted, pushing Woof off to the side.

"You have to understand, Josh. Pure research doesn't exist anymore. You need to have funding. There are the pharmaceutical companies, but they only dump money into drugs. Charities and philanthropists are trying to cure cancer and AIDS. The only group willing to pay for cutting-edge research is the military, and only if it is applicable to some aspect of warfare. But this research has farther-reaching applications. Think of a world without learning disabilities. Where brain disorders are things of the past. Where people could be programmed to know right from wrong and criminal impulses could be controlled."

"And what about freedom of choice?" Fran asked.

Stubin leaned forward. "Do you really believe that freedom of choice exists? India still has a caste system. Most of the Middle East treats women as inferiors and those who practice other religions as enemies. China regulates how many children couples can have, genocide abounds in South America and Africa, Malaysia has a booming underage sex trade, and the list goes on and on. All around the world the people in power abuse it and human rights are ignored. But what if we were incapable of hurting our fellow man? What if our core impulse was to help each other rather than control each other? The human race is destructive. This research could fix it. Purify it."

"I remember another historical figure trying to purify the human race," Josh said. "It didn't work out so well."

Stubin sneered. "Hitler was a fool. You can't breed perfection out of an imperfect species. Genetics are the problem, not the answer."

Josh looked at Fran and saw she was thinking the same thing he was: Stubin had a few loose screws. But the army must have brought him here for a reason other than lectures.

"So what's your function in this?" Josh asked.

"I'm here in an advisory capacity. But unless I can contact the military, my role here is pretty much useless. When I tried to get close, they shot at me."

"And why did you bring the monkey?"

"If I leave Mathison home alone, he gets bored, drinks all the beer, and breaks things. Or maybe he does it out of revenge. When I teach him sign language someday, that's the first thing I'll ask him. Where are we going, if you don't mind me asking?"

"The roadblock won't let us get to the hospital, so we're visiting a local doctor to patch up Duncan and Fran."

"Is the doctor nearby? I noticed we just turned onto Old Mason Road."

Josh raised an eyebrow. "He lives off Old Mason, at the end of Duck Bill. Are you familiar with the area?"

"I memorized the maps while taking the helicopter here."

"The helicopter. That was the explosion earlier?"

"Unfortunately. They landed at the Red-ops crash site. Apparently it had been booby-trapped."

Josh had searched the crash site thoroughly but hadn't seen any traps or explosives. He must have gotten lucky and not triggered any.

They drove for another ten minutes. Josh kept glancing over at Fran, checking on her, and twice he caught her looking back at him. If they got through this, *when* they got through this, Josh wanted to see as much of Fran as he could. He hoped she felt the same. They had a lot of lost time to make up for.

He turned off of Old Mason, onto a sand and gravel road surrounded by forest.

"This is Duck Bill?" Stubin asked. "Why hasn't it been paved?"

"That comes up every few years at the town meeting. The residents here say they like their roads rustic and old-fashioned and want to keep them that way. I think it's because they don't like change."

"Change is inevitable," Stubin said. "You can't ignore technology."

"Ignoring it and choosing not to embrace it are two different things, I think," Josh said. "Here we are."

He parked the Roadmaster on the grass next to Doc Wainwright's house and touched Fran's shoulder. "I'm going to see if he's home. Do you and Duncan want to come in with me?"

"Duncan's asleep. I don't want to wake him up."

"Will you be okay?"

Fran met his eyes. "We'll be fine."

"Are you sure?"

"Yes. Thanks."

Josh let his hand linger for longer than necessary, then nodded and exited the vehicle. The general practitioner lived in a ranch, on the west shore of Big Lake McDonald, surrounded by trees. His electricity seemed to be out, just like everyone else's. Josh had visited him once at his office in town to have a large splinter removed from his palm. He found Wainwright's bedside manner excellent and his skill with a scalpel and tweezers adequate at best. The quintessential country doctor.

He approached the front door warily, as if something might pop out at him at any moment. The woods—a source of tranquility for Josh as long as he could remember—no longer seemed safe or familiar. Josh stopped and studied a shadow on the porch, judged it to be a lawn chair, and continued onward. He knocked three times, waited, and knocked again.

"Doc? It's Josh VanCamp, from the fire department. I have some people here that need medical attention."

Josh waited and knocked once more. No sounds of life from inside the house. The doctor was either a heavy sleeper or he'd been lured into town by the promise of lottery riches. On impulse, Josh tried the doorknob. Unlocked, just like most houses in the Northwoods.

"I'm going to check if he's home!" Josh shouted back to Fran.

He wondered whether she and Duncan would be okay with Dr. Stubin and decided to chance it. Even with everything that had happened to her, Fran seemed able to take care of herself just fine. When they were dating, Fran had told him she suffered from panic attacks. He'd even seen it happen once, during a Tilt-a-Whirl ride at a carnival he'd taken her and Duncan to. Fran froze up when the ride ended, and it took Josh and two carnies to pry her hands off the safety bar and remove her from the car. Perhaps she'd since conquered her demons.

Josh entered the house cautiously. He was breaking and entering, and if Wainwright was waiting in the darkness with a shotgun he'd have every right to blow Josh's head off. But Josh was willing to risk it. Even if the doctor wasn't in he probably had medical supplies. God only knew when they'd get Fran to a hospital. At the very least she needed antibiotics.

"Doc! You home? Anyone here?"

No answer.

He tried the light switch on the wall, which didn't work, and made his way into the kitchen by feel. People kept flashlights in easy-to-reach places, like drawers, or atop the refrigerator. The latter is where Josh found a Maglite, one of the models that used half a dozen D batteries, making it a weapon, as well. He spotted Wainwright's phone. A busy signal. Then he searched cabinets, discovering only dishes and canned goods.

Moving on, Josh located Wainwright's office and quickly found a medical cabinet stuffed with equipment. Josh filled a pillowcase with free samples of Cipro, a vial of lidocaine hydrochloride, a can of aerosol antiseptic spray, two sealed syringes, some acetaminophen samples, forceps, hydrogen peroxide, and a sealed suture needle package.

Outside he heard Woof bark.

Not a friendly bark. A warning bark.

Something was happening. Something bad.

Josh rushed out of the office, through the front door, just in time to see the Roadmaster pulling away down Duck Bill Lane.

• • •

Taylor noted that Olen had begun wheezing. While the gas mask protected the man from inhaling hydrogen cyanide, the chemical had soaked into his clothing and subsequently his skin. From there, it bonded with every cell it could, preventing them from getting oxygen. Taylor figured he had perhaps five minutes left to live. Because of this he took over the driving. They were currently on a rarely used dirt road and had to slow down to navigate the sharp turns.

"How far are we?" Logan asked, poking Olen with the knife. Olen was bleeding from a dozen or so previous pokes.

"We're . . . close. Feel . . . sick . . ."

Then he puked in his gas mask and fell forward, banging his head onto the dashboard.

Logan stabbed him again. Olen didn't flinch.

"He's dead," Logan said.

Taylor hit the brakes. He and Logan tugged Olen out of the Honey Wagon and left him on the side of the road. Then they took off their masks and protective plastic garments and tossed them into the trees. Taylor opened the MMDSC and pressed the talk button.

"Location 1.6 kilometers east on Deer Tick Road. Attempting to locate nest."

Logan spat. "Now we have to search for him. You could have given the guy some of your Charge."

"You could have given him some of yours," Taylor snapped back. "This road is a dead end. If Warren Streng lives anywhere on it, we'll find him." Taylor scanned the tree line and saw a rusty sign nailed to a tree that read "Private Property, Trespassers Will Be Shot."

"Besides," he said. "I think we're close."

When the perimeter alarm went off, Warren "Wiley" Streng switched the video monitor feed to his plasma-screen TV and sat in his lounger, watching the Honey Wagon approach. It stopped, and two people in gas masks pulled a third out of the truck.

The camera used night vision technology, so everything glowed green. But even though it cost a fortune, it wasn't high-definition like the monitor, and the figures were blurry. Wiley used the remote to zoom in and, from the dirty clothing, recognized Olen Porrell as the dead man.

The two others moved quickly and efficiently. Soldiers. No. Special Forces. Their black uniforms were somewhat stiff. Body armor, probably that new liquid kind he'd read about on the Net. One of them used some sort of device to call for backup, then stared at the No Trespassing sign for so long that Wiley was sure he spotted the hidden camera. But the moment passed, and they climbed back into the truck and continued up the road.

They found me, Wiley thought. *After more than thirty years, they finally found me.*

He pulled himself out of the chair and began to prepare for the attack.

• • •

It happened so fast Fran didn't have time to react. Woof barked, and then the car doors were open and men were climbing into the Roadmaster. One of them was tall and thin, and the other was enormous. The giant got into the back seat, tossed Woof out of the vehicle, and placed a huge hand on Fran's scalp, his fingers draping down over her face.

"If you move, he'll twist your head off," said the thin man, his accent foreign and heavy. Fran guessed him to be Santiago, and the large one, Ajax. "Then we'll do the same to your boy."

Fran stayed stock-still. Santiago started the car and fishtailed on the lawn, heading back up Duck Bill Lane. Duncan opened his eyes, looking confused, then terrified. He hugged Fran, and she hugged him back.

"You took your time." Stubin removed something small and black from his pocket. "I've had this thing on for ten minutes."

Santiago frowned. "You might have helped us by saying the address."

"I didn't know the address."

Fran watched Santiago check the rearview mirror. He touched his ear, which was crusted with dried blood. "That firefighter *cabrón,* I have to settle something with him."

"It can wait." Stubin squinted at the communicator. "Taylor and Logan have almost located Warren. They're on Deer Tick Road. Take the next left you see."

It was tough for Fran to find her voice with her skull

being palmed like a basketball, but Duncan reached over and grabbed her hand, giving her strength.

"You found Warren. You can let us go."

Stubin scrutinized her as if she were something he'd stepped in. "I suppose people only see what they want to see and ignore everything else. That's why you trusted me. That's why the U.S. military trusted me."

Fran let the implications of that last line run through her head.

"The Red-ops team isn't from Canada," she stated.

"Of course not. They're ours."

The roadblock made a lot more sense now.

"They're U.S., but the military didn't order this," Fran guessed. "They're going to be angry with you."

"They think I died in that helicopter explosion. Besides, they're so busy making sure that no stories leak out that they aren't even looking for us. Wouldn't CNN just eat this up? U.S. terrorist cell destroys Wisconsin town. They'll nuke Safe Haven before they let the word get out."

"Let Duncan go." Fran pursed her lips, keeping her tears at bay. "Please."

Stubin gave an exaggerated sigh. "You don't get it. You're still useful to us."

"Why?"

Santiago laughed. "Doesn't this dumb *puta* know Warren is her father?"

Fran didn't know what to say, how to react. She'd grown up the only child of a single mother who told Fran that her dad died in Vietnam. Mom got married when Fran was seven, and her stepfather adopted her. She hadn't thought about her birth father in over two decades.

"It gets even better." Stubin smiled, obviously enjoying

this. "I've been looking for Warren for a long time. You couldn't imagine the amount of research it took. The paper trail led me to Safe Haven. When we ran your car off the road a few years ago, we were hoping Warren would come out of hiding to visit you at the hospital or attend the funeral. He didn't. Not exactly father-of-the-year material. Maybe he'll show a bit more affection when we're cutting off his grandson's fingers outside his front door."

Fran felt a panic attack coming on. The increased heartbeat. The sweaty palms. The hyperventilating. She thought back to the crash, to being trapped in the car, and flinched at the knowledge that it wasn't an accident at all, that it was intentional. Her life, and Duncan's, and Charles's, shattered because some madman used her family as a tool to find a father she didn't even know she had.

Fran began to shake. She felt a scream welling up, and she was ready to completely lose her grip on reality when Duncan whispered to her, "I'm afraid, Mom."

And Fran knew she couldn't afford to lose control. She had to remain calm, to look for escape opportunities, to be ready to act. For Duncan's sake. So she stared the panic attack square in the eye and ordered it to go away.

Not this time. Not ever again.

The tremors left, and her heartbeat slowed, and her breathing became steady.

"Don't be afraid of these assholes," she told her son. "I'm not."

Then she held Duncan tight to her chest and tried to be strong enough for both of them.

• • •

Sheriff Streng stopped the Jeep before turning onto Deer Tick Road. He opened the fuse box and used the little plastic pair of tweezers inside to pull out fuses for the brake lights, parking lights, headlights, and interior lights. When he got behind the wheel again he drove completely dark, navigating by feel and by the orange hunter's moon.

En route, the communicator vibrated again, and Streng read a rambling message that he figured out was a live transcript of a conversation. A roadblock was mentioned, along with taking Fran and Duncan to see a doctor. It had to be Josh talking. Streng knew Josh took one of these communicators off of Ajax and wondered if he'd learned how it worked. If so, he needed to be careful; he was giving away his position.

Deer Tick was less a road and more a trail. It wound around the southernmost tip of Little Lake McDonald, but rather than hug the shoreline where the prime real estate was, it went the opposite way into the woods. Streng knew of only a few residences on Deer Tick: displaced trailers and shacks made of corrugated steel, long rusted out. Homes for the poor, the hopeless, and the crazy.

Wiley was one of the crazies.

He'd been that way since they were children. If there was a thimbleful of trouble to be found in all of Ashburn County, Wiley found it, and usually compounded it. He started young, breaking windows with slingshots, skipping school, stealing candy bars and comics from local businesses. That led to teen years marked by hot-wiring cars and boats for joy rides, running away from home for weeks at a time, selling drugs.

Streng had done his share of stupid things as a youngster, but he was more of a casual participant. Wiley was an instigator. Nowadays people like him were known as adrenaline junkies, and they BASE jumped and rode their bikes down mountainsides and went snorkeling with sharks. Back then he was simply known as a juvenile delinquent and probably would have spent his life behind bars if it hadn't been for the draft lottery.

It wasn't Wiley that had been drafted. It was Streng. He had his number called in July of 1972. Wiley enlisted to keep an eye on his little brother.

That plan didn't work out for either of them—right after basic training they were sent to different locations. Streng went to the Second Platoon, Company B, First Battalion, Fourteenth Infantry, in the Chu Pa Region. Wiley went to the Kontum Province and the Fifty-second Aviation Battalion, where he became a helicopter door gunner and one of the most successful black-market traders of the region.

Streng scowled. He hadn't spoken to Wiley in over thirty years and felt it was still too soon. But this had to be done, and there was no one else to do it.

The sand road was in such a state of disuse that grass and weeds grew in the center section between the tire treads. Streng heard them scrape against his undercarriage, a soft sound punctuated by an occasional *thump* when he ran over a fallen tree branch. He hit the brakes when he saw a familiar shape lying in the brush.

The sheriff kept the Jeep running and stepped out to investigate, holding one of Bernie's lighters. Olen Porrell, on his back, a gas mask on his face caked with vomit. Streng had no idea why his friend wore the gas mask, but it apparently wasn't enough to protect him. He didn't want to get too close, so he watched to see if Olen moved or breathed. Olen did neither. Streng took a shallow sniff of air, trying to sense any off odors. He smelled the woods and nothing else.

Wiley liked booby traps. He'd liked them as a kid and really learned to like them in Vietnam, picking up many ideas from the Cong. But gas in an open area dissipated too quickly. Streng decided that this wasn't one of his brother's devices. Olen must have been exposed elsewhere, which also accounted for the missing Honey Wagon.

Streng hopped back into his vehicle and motored up the road even more slowly, checking the sides and behind him as well as ahead. He spotted Olen's truck around the next bend, where the road dead-ended, its headlights on. Streng took his Jeep off-road, burying it in the thicket. The brush was so dense Streng had to crawl over the back seat and exit through the rear hatch. He closed it softly, unholstered his Colt, and crept toward the Honey Wagon.

The truck was empty. Streng imagined the scenario. One of the commandos had gotten to Olen, who knew Wiley's address because he cleaned out his septic tank. They poisoned him to get him to talk, and now they were creeping through the woods, looking for Wiley's house.

Good luck finding it, Streng thought.

When Wiley moved back to Safe Haven, flush with ill-gotten gains, he spared no expense building his dream house. And Wiley's idea of a dream house was very close to Batman's. Hidden underground, with secret entrances and exits, away from the searching eyes of the law, the military, and the enemies he'd made in Vietnam.

The last time Streng visited had been during the day, and even then he hadn't been able to find Wiley's place. At night, with eyes that were thirty years older, he didn't even know where to begin looking. A smarter tactic would be to hunt the people who were after Wiley. He could hunker down, cover himself with foliage, and wait for one of them to—

The blade appeared at Streng's throat with incredible stealth and speed.

"Drop the gun and put those hands up, Sheriff. Don't make me ask twice."

J osh was grateful for the heavy rains this fall, which kept the lake level high and made it possible to navigate the tributaries leading from Little Lake McDonald to the Chippewa River.

He drove a bass boat that he borrowed from Doc Wainwright—a seventeen-foot Nitro with a top speed of forty-five miles per hour. Josh figured he could straighten out the grand larceny charges later. He was worried as hell about Fran and Duncan, and he had to get to Safe Haven and find Sheriff Streng.

Josh adjusted the trim when he entered the shallows so the prop didn't hit bottom, shining the Maglite ahead to avoid the dead trees. The wind bit at his cheeks, making his face tingle. Woof stood beside him, his jowls flapping in the wind, obviously not minding the cold at all. The firefighter turned two wide circles in the murky waters until he found the inlet, and then he buzzed through that and into the Chippewa, heading downstream.

That's when the motor died. A quick survey of the dash controls showed the boat had no gas. Doc Wainwright was probably getting ready to store the boat for the winter and hadn't bothered to fill it.

Rather than waste time cursing his luck, Josh hurried to the front of the boat and swung out the electric trolling motor, locking it into place. He sat in the bow chair and used the foot pedal, navigating south at a speed that wasn't much faster than the current.

Five excruciating minutes later Josh beached the boat along the riverbank, two blocks from the Water Department building. He picked up the pillowcase full of medical supplies and scooped up Woof. Then he climbed over the short decorative iron fence that lined the river's edge and set the dog down on the street. Woof sniffed around, peed, and then fell into step alongside the jogging firefighter.

Town was dead. Dark and dead. Josh checked his watch, noted it was past two a.m. Even so, there should have been some kind of activity, someone driving somewhere. It was eerie. He tried his cell, got the recorded message about no service, and resisted the urge to throw it at the ground.

He got to the Water Department breathing heavy and coated with sweat. Josh noticed the parking lot was empty. The sheriff wasn't in. He decided to head to the junior high and borrow Olen's truck, but before he got three steps away he heard a scream coming from the building.

Bernie, Josh thought. Probably not happy about being locked up. Josh's first impulse was to ignore him and press on. But maybe Bernie knew something. He sounded upset. Maybe that would make him more susceptible to talking.

Josh checked the front door, established that it was open, and followed the wailing inside.

Woof wanted to run on ahead and check it out, but Josh ordered the dog to heel. He set the pillowcase down by the door, adjusted the flashlight focus to the widest beam setting, and walked down the familiar hallway to the drunk tank. Bernie sat on the floor of the cell, hugging himself and whimpering. Bleeding and broken, the killer looked like someone had dropped him from a building.

Woof growled at Bernie, his hackles rising and his tail pointing straight up.

"Charge," Bernie mumbled. "I need Charge."

Josh dug into his pocket, removing the container of pills and the electronic gizmo he took from Ajax. At the sight of this, Bernie hopped onto one foot and stretched his hand through the bars.

"CHARGE! GIVE ME THE CHARGE!"

Surprised, Josh stepped backward. He raised the gizmo.

"Is this what you want?"

"NO! THE CHARGE!"

Josh held up the capsules, and Bernie nodded rapidly, blood and drool running down his fat lips.

"Where's Fran and Duncan?" Josh asked.

"GIVE ME THE CHARGE! THE CHARGE!"

"Answer my questions, I'll give you the pills. Where's Fran and Duncan?"

"Don't know."

"Where's Sheriff Streng?"

Bernie clenched the bars and shook them.

"DON'T KNOW DON'T KNOW DON'T KNOW!"

"Then you're no help to me."

Josh turned to leave.

"NOOOOOO!" Bernie cried. "Check the MMDSC!"

Josh paused. "What's that?"

"The communicator! Check the communicator!"

Josh palmed the electronic thing, showing it to Bernie. "This?"

"YESSSSS!"

"How does it work?"

"Hold the bottom, hold the bottom, pull up on the sides to open the cover."

Josh tried, but that accomplished nothing. He rubbed the large dent in the center and figured the cover might be jammed. He needed some tools.

While Bernie screamed after him, Josh returned to the hallway and went to the janitor's closet. The last time he'd been to the Water Department he'd helped the mayor fix a leak in the sink. The toolbox sat on the closet shelf where he'd left it. He set the Maglite on its base and used two pairs of pliers to open the communicator cover.

It exposed a small green screen. Words began to flash across it.

Head bird acquired. Stand by for directions to the nest.

The message disappeared and was replaced by:

Is the doctor nearby? I noticed we just turned onto Old Mason Road.

He lives off of Old Mason, at the end of Duck Bill. Are you familiar with the area?

Josh recognized the new messages as his exchange with Stubin in the car. How did that get on there? Had their car been bugged? Had Josh accidentally recorded it somehow?

Or did Stubin do it?

A few more lines scrolled by, then the monitor blinked and read:

Location 1.6 kilometers east on Deer Tick Road. Attempting to locate nest.

That must be where the sheriff's brother lived. And probably where they took Fran and Duncan.

"CHARGE!" Bernie called from his cell.

Josh pocketed the device and picked up the Maglite, heading back to the drunk tank.

"YOU PROMISED ME, PROMISED!"

"I have more questions," Josh told him. "Then you'll get the Charge."

"Can't think . . . can't think . . . need Charge . . ." Bernie banged his forehead against the bars in cadence to his words. "Can't think . . . can't think . . ."

"How many soldiers are in your Red-ops unit?"

"Need Charge . . . need Charge . . ."

Josh opened up the metal container, showing Bernie the Charge capsules.

"How many soldiers?"

Bernie twitched, then blinked several times. "Five. Five soldiers. There are five."

"Name them."

"Santiago, Taylor, Ajax, Logan, and Bernie."

Josh took a shot. "Is Dr. Stubin the one who put the chip in your head? Is he the reason you're here?"

"Yesssss," Bernie hissed.

That asshole. Josh should have never left Fran and Duncan alone in the car with him.

"What is your mission?"

"Need Charge . . . need Charge . . ."

Josh removed a pill from the container and tossed it out of the room, into the darkness.

"NOOOOOOOOO!"

"What's your mission?"

Bernie shook his head. "I don't know, I don't know."

Josh threw another pill away.

"I DON'T KNOW! I NEED CHARGE! I CAN TELL YOU IF I HAVE CHARGE!"

Josh considered it, then tossed a capsule into the cell. Bernie hobbled after the pill, snatching it from the floor and holding it under his nose. He squeezed and sniffed.

Josh detected a cloying chemical odor. It took him a moment to place it. Freshman year at UW, he had a roommate named Carlos who was gay. Carlos used poppers—butyl nitrite that came in small bottles labeled "Room Deodorizer" and "Video Head Cleaner"—to enhance sex. From his paramedic classes, Josh knew butyl nitrite was a vasodilator, similar chemically to the amyl nitrite used to treat various heart conditions.

Bernie continued to sniff, and his demeanor went from Hyde to Jekyll. One moment frothing at the mouth, the next a picture of serenity.

"What's your mission?" Josh asked again.

Bernie's eyes became slits.

"Your sheriff shot me in the knee. It's shattered. You can't imagine the pain."

"Tell me your mission and I'll help you."

"How?"

"I have lidocaine."

"Show me."

"Tell me first."

Bernie cocked his head to the side, as if considering

it. Then he said, "Our mission. Interrogate townspeople. Find Warren Streng."

"Why do you want Warren Streng?"

Bernie smiled. His missing teeth made Josh wince.

"Let me have the lidocaine."

Josh walked back into the hall, Woof at his heels. He picked up the pillowcase he'd left by the door and found the lidocaine vial. Back in the cell room, Josh filled a syringe with two milliliters of the fluid while Bernie stared. He slid the needle across the floor to Bernie, and it came to a stop outside the bars.

In his eagerness, Bernie went for it too fast and knocked it away. He stuck his hand through the cell bars and strained for the needle.

"Please . . ." Bernie whimpered. "The pain . . ."

Josh walked over and bent down, reaching for it.

Fast as a whip Bernie had him by the wrist and pulled him up against the bars.

Woof went crazy, jumping and growling and barking. Josh pulled with all he had, but Bernie had arms like anacondas, coiled muscle grabbing him everywhere at once. The killer finally settled on a choke hold, forcing Josh's back against the bars, locking a forearm around his neck.

"Let me out of this cage," he whispered in Josh's ear.

Josh struggled to get a breath in.

"Don't . . . have . . . key . . ." he managed.

"That's a shame. Hehehe. Such a shame." Bernie's other hand appeared before Josh's face, inches from his nose.

It held a lighter.

"Then you *buuuuuurn*."

Bernie flicked on the flame.

• • •

Taylor's MMDSC vibrated and he looked at the message from Logan, who was searching to the west.

Lat 45.9790993 long –91.8996811 . . . Negative.

Taylor frowned. They'd been stomping through the woods for half an hour and hadn't found anything. Had that sewer jockey taken them for a ride? No. He'd been broken. So where was—

Taylor froze. He'd been about to take a step forward, but his augmented vision caught a shadow on the ground that shouldn't have been there. He crouched and got a closer look.

A bear trap hidden in the leaves. Three feet long, rusty from years of exposure to the elements. The old chain attached to a concrete plug buried in the ground.

Taylor knelt down, touching the end of the trap. *Interesting.* The rust wasn't rust at all, but a finish painted to look like rust. The trap also had fresh grease on the hinges. Taylor searched around for a fallen tree branch and found one the width of his wrist. He used that to set off the trap. It worked perfectly, snapping the wood in half with ease.

He stood, casting his eyes upward. In the V of a birch tree, under a bird's nest, he found the video camera. The lens automatically focused on him as he got closer. Taylor used his Ka-Bar to pry the camera from its camouflaged housing. It was wireless. That meant batteries, which would have to be regularly replaced.

Warren was close. Very close.

Taylor resumed the hunt, paying extra attention to where he stepped.

• • •

Streng didn't drop the gun, and he didn't put his hands above his head. As much bad blood as there was between him and Wiley, he didn't believe his brother would slit his throat.

"Scare you?" Wiley asked.

Streng turned around, letting the rage build. Wiley wore a ghillie suit, a uniform made of netting with various pieces of real and artificial foliage woven to it. Leaves were stitched across his chest and fake vines hung from his arms. Twigs jutted from the side of his headgear, altering his profile.

"People are looking for you," Streng said in even tones.

"Two so far. Trained. Recon, searching for my house. Determined types."

"They killed Olen Porrell."

Wiley cleared his throat. "I know. Never should have used someone local for the septic service. Should have hired out of town. After hiding out for so long, I got lazy."

Streng kept his voice even. "Other people have died, too."

"Like I said. Determined types."

Streng clenched a fist and leaned slightly forward. Wiley didn't back away.

"Steady, Ace. I know we got unfinished business. But let's get out of the line of fire first."

Streng did a slow burn, then nodded.

"Step where I step," Wiley said. "I've rigged the property."

Streng followed Wiley through the woods, watching his foot placement. After twenty or so yards, his brother stopped at the carcass of a deer. Wiley twisted a hoof and a hatch in the ground opened up.

"It's steep. Wait five seconds for me to get down."

Wiley scooted onto his buttocks and slid down a dark ramp. Streng counted to five and did the same. He'd been down here once before and braced his legs for the abrupt stop. He didn't brace hard enough, and when he reached bottom his knees hit him in the chest, his shin splints flaming.

A mechanical sound from above, then the metallic click of the hatch closing. Black lights came on overhead, illuminating a garage-sized room with a concrete floor. Two motorbikes and a snowmobile were parked along the far wall, in front of a pegboard that held hundreds of hand tools. A fuel pump occupied the far corner. Against the opposite wall sat an electric generator, its exhaust attached to a pipe that snaked into the ceiling. Wiley approached the generator and flipped a switch. It came on, surprisingly quiet.

"The deer is new," Streng said.

"About ten years old. I kept having trouble finding the entrance, so I needed to mark it."

Wiley unsnapped his ghillie suit and hung it on a peg. Underneath he wore jeans and a black flannel shirt.

"What if someone passes through, sees it twice, wonders why it hasn't rotted?"

"I change it every month. Bear. Badger. Dog. Coyote. There's a taxidermist in Montreal, made a mint on me."

Wiley walked to the only door in the room, opened it, and went through. Streng followed. No black lights here. This hallway was lined with fluorescents, so bright they stung Streng's eyes. The walls were matte white, and the floor was a white laminate that didn't quite match. Four doors lined the hall, and Streng remembered them to be the kitchen, the pantry, the washroom, and a storage area. The final door, where the hallway ended, opened up into what Wiley called the great room.

The room was appropriately named. Perfectly round, and large enough to park three buses side by side. Track lighting lined the fifteen-foot ceiling, an overstuffed leather couch and two loungers faced a large plasma TV, wraparound shelves held thousands of books, records, cassettes, CDs, VHS and Beta tapes, and DVDs, and a big wooden desk with a flat-screen monitor on top sat dead center.

Wiley had gotten many new toys since Streng had last visited, more than twenty years ago. He had come after hearing that his brother had moved back into town from one of the contractors hired to build this place. Wiley'd let him in. Streng could recall their short conversation verbatim.

"Mom's sick. You should see her."

"Can't."

"Can't or won't?"

"Does it make a difference? I'm not going."

"The past is the past. Our parents want to see you."

"I'm not going. And don't you tell them I'm back in town."

"Or else what?"

A fight ensued. Streng left with a broken nose, vowing never to return.

"I started stealing the Internet back in '96." Wiley saw Streng staring at the TV. "Not too long after I started stealing cable."

Streng fixed his attention on his brother, shocked by how he looked. The last time Streng saw him Wiley had wide brown sideburns, a ponytail, and shoulders like a linebacker. Now his head was mostly bald, a few gray wisps clinging to the sides. A wrinkled forehead, saggy cheeks, and a drooping neck. His broad shoulders had become slumped, his posture stooped.

Wiley had gotten old. Only his eyes—ice blue and alert—were an indicator of the man he used to be.

"Once a thief, always a thief," Streng said.

Wiley shrugged. "It's not the money. Utilities mean a paper trail, which can be traced. I don't want to be found."

"But you were found," Streng said. "And people have died because of it. Because of what you did."

Wiley cleared his throat again and then sighed. "It's been a long time, Ace. Mom and Dad are long gone. You still want to hold grudges?"

Streng moved closer to Wiley. "You put our parents in jeopardy, the same way you put this town in jeopardy. You're selfish, Wiley. You only care about yourself."

Wiley folded his arms.

"Do you remember why I enlisted, Ace?"

"To make money selling black-market goods?"

Wiley's eyes went mean. "It was to watch over your sorry butt."

"You were too busy selling drugs and weapons to the Cong to watch over anyone's butt."

Wiley walked over, standing toe-to-toe with Streng. He didn't seem so stooped anymore.

"I did some shit in my day, Ace. But I never sold weapons to the enemy."

"Really? That's what the military told me. That's what they told our parents."

"They lied," Wiley said.

"Well, you sure did something to piss the military off. And knowing your history, it probably wasn't legal."

"You don't know the whole story."

"I know the story. You're a bad egg, Wiley. Always have been, always will be. When the MPs showed up at the house, told Mom and Dad about your little moneymaking ventures in Vietnam, it destroyed them."

"I didn't mean for that to happen. I loved our parents."

"Sure you did. That's why you stayed in touch. That's why you attended their funerals."

Wiley got right in his face. "You always loved to judge me, Ace. Point the finger, say *shame shame shame*. You think you're better than me? What have you done with *your* life, Sheriff? What makes you holier-than-thou?"

Streng planted both hands on Wiley's chest and shoved, hard. Wiley staggered back, recovered, and balled up his right fist, pulling back to swing. Streng was faster. The last time they'd tangled, Wiley had beaten him good.

This time was going to be different.

Streng gut-punched Wiley, releasing twenty years of pent-up anger in one blow.

Wiley crumpled, dropping to his knees, then his ass. He wrapped both arms around his belly and breathed through his mouth. Streng reared back to hit him again when something in the room beeped. Wiley turned his attention to the TV.

"They found one of my cameras," he said.

Streng watched. A soldier, glowing green, seemed to stare out of the plasma screen directly at them. A second later the screen went black.

Wiley got off the floor and picked up a large remote control, switching to another camera. Coming up Deer Tick Road was a car Streng recognized: the late Mrs. Teller's Roadmaster. Wiley switched again, and the car slowed and parked next to Olen's Honey Wagon.

Ajax and Santiago got out. When Streng saw that Fran and Duncan were with them, he deflated.

"Do you know who that woman is, Wiley? That child?"

Wiley stared, not answering. But he gave a small nod.

"How long have you known about them?"

Wiley remained silent. Streng felt the anger return. He approached his brother, putting his hand on the back of his neck and squeezing.

"That's your daughter. That's your grandson. They're in this because of you."

Wiley shrugged out of Streng's grasp.

"I'm not a father. It was a fling. A mistake. I contributed the DNA. That's all."

Streng grabbed Wiley's shirt, pulled him in close.

"They brought those folks here because of you," he said through clenched teeth. "They're going to die because of you."

Wiley met Streng's eyes. "It was a one-night stand, dammit! Right before we shipped out to Nam. I gave her money to get rid of it. She decided not to. Then, when I got back, I had to lie low. I couldn't have a kid. People were after me. It was the only way I could live."

"You call this living?" Streng turned his head and spat on the floor. "You cower underground, under a dead deer, hiding from the whole world. No family. No friends. You're a waste, Warren. A selfish waste. And I'm ashamed to call you my brother."

Streng shoved him away, heading for the exit.

"Where are you going?" Wiley called after him.

"To save that woman and her son."

"I booby-trapped the whole area. If those don't get you, the soldiers will."

Streng stopped and looked at his brother one last time.

"Then I'll die. And I'll be waiting for you in hell, Wiley, to kick your sorry ass."

"Don't be a fool," Wiley said.

Streng didn't answer. He walked out the door.

D uncan shivered. He told himself it was from the cold, but deep down he knew the truth. He was afraid. He was very afraid.

He stood next to the car and held Mom's hand, grateful she was acting so brave. Duncan knew it was an act. She had to be scared, too. But she was hiding it, and he loved her even more for being strong.

Duncan didn't know how things went wrong so fast. He fell asleep in the car, and when he woke up, Josh and

Woof were gone. It turned out Dr. Stubin wasn't a nice guy, after all.

The two soldiers with them were dressed like Bernie, and they seemed just as mean. The big one—the one who was going to twist off Mom's head—was even bigger than Kane on WWE. But the other one was even scarier. Duncan didn't like how he kept looking at Mom, kept touching her.

Mathison didn't seem bothered by any of this. He still sat on Duncan's shoulder, picking though his hair. Duncan reached his hand up to rub the monkey's belly. Mathison cooed. Duncan scratched higher, up Mathison's chest. He felt the monkey's collar, surprised at how thick it was.

"Stop touching the monkey."

Duncan spun around, saw Dr. Stubin pointing his big shotgun at him, the one they'd put in the back of the car. Duncan's hand dropped down, and he felt like he was going to pee himself.

Mom stepped between the gun and Duncan, pushing him behind her.

"Mathison!" Stubin barked. "Come!"

Mathison hopped from Duncan's shoulder to Mom's. He screeched, sounding pretty upset.

"Now, Mathison!"

Mathison climbed down Mom, but instead of going to Stubin he took off into the forest.

Stubin said, "Stupid primate," and turned away from them.

Fran knelt down to Duncan's level. She pushed his bangs out of his face. "It's going to be okay, baby."

"Where's Woof?"

"Josh has him."

"Is Josh coming to rescue us?"

Duncan watched his mother's eyes get glassy, and her lower lip trembled. "If he can, I'm sure he'll try."

Another man dressed in black came walking out of the woods. When Mom saw him, she stood up and got very stiff.

"I've found a few antipersonnel devices and two cameras," the new man said to Stubin, "and Logan found an exhaust vent disguised as a tree stump half a click east. He's close. Underground somewhere."

Stubin nodded. The new man looked at Mom and smiled.

"Hello, Fran. I was hoping we'd see each other again." He licked his lips. "I can still taste you. Yum."

Then the man stared at Duncan. Duncan trembled—it felt like he was looking at the devil.

"I bet you're tasty, too," the man said. "My name is Taylor. You must be Duncan. Did you have fun with Uncle Bernie?"

Duncan couldn't help it; he started to cry. His leg was really sore, and he wanted to go home, but he didn't have a home anymore because it burned down, and bad people kept trying to hurt him and Mom.

Between his sobs he heard his mother say, "We killed Uncle Bernie. And we'll kill you, too."

"No," Taylor answered. "You won't. What's going to happen is we'll find your daddy, make him give us what we want, and then we'll all take turns with you and your boy. If you're lucky, really lucky, *we'll* kill *you* after a few days. But I don't think you're going to be that lucky."

Duncan felt his mom squeeze his hand even tighter. He squeezed it back. He didn't understand why she told

Taylor that Bernie was dead. Maybe Sheriff Streng killed him. And maybe Sheriff Streng would come back and kill Taylor, too.

Duncan closed his eyes and hoped with all of his might that he would.

T he flame touched Josh's cheek and made a crackling/ singeing sound as it evaporated the sweat.

Then the pain hit.

Josh had been burned before, but never seriously. Stepping on a sparkler when he was a kid. Grabbing the handle of a cast-iron skillet that had been on the stove for too long. Getting accidentally touched by a cigarette by some idiot at a rock concert. And in each case, his reaction had been the same: to flinch away from the heat.

But Josh couldn't flinch. Bernie had his arm around his throat, and Josh's head was wedged up against the bars of the cell. Bernie held the lighter—just an ordinary disposable Bic—to Josh's face, and Josh couldn't even turn his head. He flailed his arms and kicked his legs and couldn't break the killer's steel grip.

The pain started bad, then quickly went to unbearable. Josh howled, and Woof hopped around, barking like mad, and Bernie held it there and held it there and *held it there* and then finally pulled away.

"Too deep, hehehe, too deep," Bernie said. "Nerves are dead. Have to find a new spot, new spot."

Bernie waved the flame in front of his eyes. Josh tried to blow it out, but the hand danced away.

"Where next, where next, how about . . . here."

Josh tried to blow, missed, and Bernie held the lighter right under Josh's nose.

Then Bernie screamed and Josh was miraculously released. The firefighter fell to his hands and knees and turned to see Woof, his head between the bars of the cell, biting and tugging at the pants of Bernie's bad leg. Bernie went down, his mashed knee bending in a way it shouldn't bend. He beat on the dog's head, but Woof refused to let go.

"Woof! Come!" Josh yelled.

But Woof wasn't finished with Bernie. He shook his head side to side, making Bernie's knee flex like a rubber hose. Bernie yelled louder than Josh though humanly possible, and then the pyro managed to snag Woof's neck with one hand. The other brought up the lighter.

Josh tugged on Woof's leg to pull him away, but Bernie's grip was solid. Josh frantically looked around for something, anything, saw the pillowcase on the floor, reached for it, and yanked out the can of aerosol antiseptic spray.

When Bernie flicked on the lighter, Josh pointed the can and let him have it.

The results were spectacular. A two-foot blast of fire erupted from the can, hitting Bernie squarely in the face. Josh kept it on him, brought it closer, until the killer released Woof.

The dog pounced away and resumed barking. Josh killed the flame, but Bernie's didn't go out. His hair had caught, and Bernie slapped at the sides of his head, which only fanned the fire, making it larger.

Josh ran out of the drunk tank to the janitor's supply closet, grabbed the mop bucket, took it to the bathroom, and scooped up some toilet water, ran back to Bernie's cell to find him on his knees, beating his burning, blistering, broken face against the bars.

He threw the water, and the fire went out, the smoke and steam rising up from Bernie's head smelling like burnt hair and fried sausage patties.

Bernie fell over, onto his side, his breathing shallow and rapid. Josh focused the Maglite on him, saw that his lips were gone and his eyes were dripping goo. Woof came over.

"Aaaaaaaad. Aaaaaaaad. Oooyyyy. Aaaad oooyyy . . ."

Josh listened to the wheezes, and after a minute thought he understood what Bernie was trying to say.

Bad boy.

That's an understatement, Josh thought.

He hugged the dog tight, stroking his fur, and together they watched the killer take a few more pathetic gasps and then die.

Josh found the can of antiseptic and the fallen syringe full of lidocaine. He sprayed the needle and gently stuck it into his cheek, near the burn. The pain ebbed, and then there was no feeling at all. Next, Josh checked Woof for injury. Woof mistook it for affection and wagged his tail, furiously licking Josh's face.

"From now on, every time I see you, I'm bringing you a steak," Josh promised.

Josh put the syringe and antiseptic back into the pillow-case, and he and Woof left the Water Department building, heading for the junior high.

• • •

Ajax hunts. He creeps through the woods, squinting at shadows, ready to rip apart anything that moves. But he finds nothing. Only trees. The trees are familiar. They remind him of something. Something long ago.

He remembers. A house, with trees in the back. Ajax likes to climb the trees. He's safe in the trees. Safe from the man and the woman. They're mean to him. Hate him. Because he's *fucking stupid*. They call him fucking stupid all the time. Yell at him for being fucking stupid. Because he's fucking stupid he has to go to a special school. The other kids pick on him. He's small and can't fight back. They chase him. Hurt him. When he tells the man and the woman, they hurt him, too. Everyone hurts him.

Ajax gets a lot of practice blocking out the hurt. He may be fucking stupid, but he learns how to control the pain. The kids hit him. The woman uses a belt on him. The man breaks his teeth with a beer bottle. But Ajax doesn't cry. This makes everyone afraid.

Ajax likes making people afraid.

Ajax remembers going into the man and woman's bedroom. They drank beer and hit him for a long time, but now they are sleeping. He has a knife, the one that plugs into the wall that the man uses to cut turkey on turkey day. Ajax is never allowed to have turkey, because he's fucking stupid. But he is smart enough to plug the knife in the outlet, and press the big red button, and cut them cut them cut them while they scream scream scream.

Then Ajax met Doctor. Doctor never called him fucking stupid. Doctor helped Ajax. He gave him special shots, to make him big and strong. He put something in Ajax's head to make him smart.

Ajax likes Doctor.

And Ajax still likes making people afraid.

He remembers going somewhere strange where people talked funny. They finished the mission, and it was Fun Time. Taylor and Bernie were cooking someone, eating parts. Logan and Santiago had a man tied to a tree and were cutting off parts and betting which cut would kill him. Ajax was playing with a woman. He would break her leg, then watch her try to crawl away, then bring her back and break her leg in another spot.

She was very afraid.

Then Taylor showed Ajax how to make her even more afraid. He took off her clothes, used his private part.

Ajax tried it, too.

He liked it.

Ajax wants to try it with the woman from the car. He wants to break her arms and legs and make her afraid and then take off all her clothes and . . .

The giant twitches, the Chip in his head reloading the current objective.

Find Warren Streng.

Ajax searches the woods. Hunting. He wants to find Warren Streng. Wants to find him very bad.

Then he can have Fun Time with the woman.

• • •

The junior high was two blocks away. They ran. For a plump dog Woof kept up easily, even going on ahead and marking his territory on assorted curbs and trees. The school parking lot was full, and, surprisingly, the lights were on. Josh turned the Maglite off but kept it in his hand; its weight reassured him.

The front door was locked. He tried the back entrance, by the gym, and froze. His fire truck was parked alongside the building.

Josh hurried to it, looked in the cab for the keys. Gone. He jogged back to the gymnasium entrance. If the Red-ops had been the ones who stole the tanker, they could be inside the school. People might be in danger.

The door was unlocked. When he yanked it open, Josh witnessed a scene from a nightmare.

"Woof, sit," Josh said. He left the dog and the pillow-case outside and went in.

Dead. Hundreds dead. On the bleachers. On the floor. On each other. Josh had to climb over a small mountain of bodies to get through. He checked a pulse. And another. And another. The bodies were cool to the touch, and there were no sounds other than the ones Josh made.

These were people he knew. His friends. He saw Mrs. Simmons, his next-door neighbor, still sitting down, her eyes wide and her mouth caked with dried puke. Adam Pepper, a part-time volunteer at the firehouse, curled up fetal on the floor. Janie Richter, her face bright pink, her arms wrapped protectively around her son, a boy no more than Duncan's age.

Josh kept checking for pulses, kept finding none. A lump in his throat made it hard to swallow. He followed some bloody footprints to the boys' locker room and saw even more atrocities. Corpses piled to the ceiling, recalling ghastly newsreel footage of the death camps from World War II.

Erwin's fiancée, Jessie Lee Sloan, had her neck cut so badly it was almost turned 180 degrees. And under her—

Erwin.

Josh began to cry. Just tears at first, then a few small sounds. Those bastards had killed his town. They'd killed it and mutilated it and discarded it. Josh felt the gorge rising in his stomach. He kept it down, but he had to get out of the locker room, had to get out of the school.

He stumbled back into the gym, knowing he needed a car, hating himself for what he had to do. Josh decided on Adam, because he knew Adam drove a yellow Ford Bronco, which would be easy to find in the parking lot. He patted down his dead friend's pockets, located the keys, and a horrible thought appeared, fully formed, in Josh's head.

The people in the locker room were sliced up. But what killed the people out here?

He surveyed the grisly tableau once again and couldn't believe he didn't put it all together sooner. The bodily fluids. The quick onset of death.

These people were poisoned.

Josh looked at his hands. What had he touched? Had he contaminated himself somehow?

Jesus, is it still in the air?

He stood up, and a wave of dizziness hit him. Josh rushed to the door, kicked something metal. He tracked it down and saw it was a black canister with HCN written on the side.

Hydrogen cyanide.

Josh blinked. The dizziness led to a headache. He tried to remember the EMT class he took last year, the class on poisons. Cyanide was supposed to have an almond odor. Josh took a shallow sniff but smelled only death. Then he recalled that forty percent of people couldn't detect cyanide by scent. He touched the back of his hand to his forehead and had no idea if he was running a temperature or not.

Continuing on to the exit, Josh felt his chest get tight. He was sure of it now; he had cyanide poisoning. It was in his blood, coursing through his circulatory system. Cyanide inhibited an enzyme that allowed cells to produce energy. His tissue would die, and rapidly.

Josh tripped over a body, landed alongside some poor guy whose face indicated he died screaming—a glimpse at Josh's immediate future. He got up and scrambled for the door, wracking his brain for the treatment used in cyanide poisoning. Diazepam and activated charcoal? No, that was strychnine. Naloxone? That was for opioids.

Amyl nitrite. It induced the formation of methemoglobin, which combined with cyanide and made it nontoxic.

There was amyl nitrite in the Charge capsules.

Josh picked himself up and climbed over several corpses to get to the door. Woof tried to jump up and lick him, but Josh kept him back, worried he'd transfer the poison. He rummaged through the pillowcase, found the case of Charge, and put one beneath his nostrils.

Ready or not . . .

The capsule broke between Josh's fingers and he snorted

hard. His sinuses flooded with a hot chemical odor not un-like kerosene, and Josh's face flushed and his eyes stung and his tongue tasted metal. This was accompanied by a massive head rush that felt like his brain liquefied and sloshed out of his ears.

He held the fumes in his lungs, letting them get absorbed. At the same time, euphoria wrapped its friendly arms around Josh and gave him a big hug. Josh took another sniff, closed his eyes, and allowed a billion thoughts to enter his brain at once, swirling in from all directions. Euphoria mixing with sadness mixing with memories mixing with fantasies. Then the swirl coalesced, forming a ball, and the ball became a face.

Annie.

"I'm so sorry," Josh said. Or maybe he only thought he said it.

"It's not your fault," Annie said. "You can't save everyone."

Then Annie's face changed, and she became Fran.

The image was solid, real, pure. Josh knew he'd been born to rescue people. He hadn't been able to rescue Annie. But he still had a chance with Fran and Duncan.

Josh shook his head, clearing it a little. He needed to find Adam's truck, that yellow Bronco. He took one more sniff of the Charge, picked up the pillowcase, and ran into the parking lot, Woof two steps behind him.

• • •

S treng made it up the ramp to the surface, but it had hurt. The steep climb winded him and his shin splints were on fire and his injured kidney felt like someone stood beside him, twisting a knife. He turned the deer hoof, closing the hatch, and then waited for his energy to return.

After a minute of waiting Streng realized his energy wasn't going to return. So he pressed onward.

The Magnum round from his Colt Python hadn't penetrated Bernie's body armor, but it had done some major blunt-force trauma. Still, Streng decided to aim for the head, and only when he had a clear shot. He wasn't the best marksman, but the Colt had a six-inch barrel, and Streng was accurate to about forty feet.

Now he just had to find one of the bastards. Preferably before they found him.

Streng yawned—which must have been an indicator of how exhausted he was, because he certainly wasn't bored. He decided to head for the vehicles, hoping Fran and Duncan hadn't been moved. Painful as it was, Streng moved in a crouch, alternating between eyeing the ground for Wiley's traps and checking all directions for movement. What he lacked in speed he made up for by being careful, avoiding two bear traps and a covered pit that he guessed housed punji sticks or some other painful deterrent. He wondered if Wiley had ever accidentally killed some wayward hunter or hiker with his paranoia and didn't put it past him.

Lights, up ahead. The Roadmaster's headlights. Streng could make out Duncan sitting on the hood, Fran standing next to him. Streng slowed down even further, pausing after every step, listening to the woods around him. When he got within fifty yards, he saw a thin guy in army fatigues, a grenade launcher hanging at his side. It was someone he hadn't encountered before, and he seemed to be guarding Fran and Duncan.

The guy paced back and forth, not moving or acting like a soldier at all, occasionally looking at the green screen of his communicator.

The communicator.

Streng yanked Bernie's communicator out of his pocket and shielded the screen with his palm. He quickly read through several updates on the search for Wiley's home. They hadn't found it yet.

Streng had learned the term *disinformation* in the army. Infantry regularly used locals to broadcast false information on enemy radio frequencies. This seemed like the perfect opportunity to use an oldie but a goodie.

"Target acquired," Streng whispered into the communicator. "Immediate assistance needed. One click directly north of the vehicles."

That would send them a kilometer in the opposite direction of Wiley's hidey-hole.

A message scrolled across the screen.

We heard you were dead.

Streng hit the button again.

"Did the bitch tell you that?" He forced himself to giggle like Bernie. "She'll burn for it."

He waited. No more messages appeared.

Looking back to the vehicles, the thin guy in the fatigues continued to pace. He didn't even stop to check his surroundings. Streng still took his time, watching his footing, keeping behind cover. He crossed the last few yards on all fours and finally dropped to his belly when he got within the thirty-foot kill zone.

Streng extended his arms out in front of him, propping the butt of his gun on the ground, steadying his wrist by holding it with his left hand. The grenade launcher bothered him. If the guy wore body armor—it was hard to tell from this distance, but Streng assumed he did—then a hit anywhere other than the head meant he'd be capable of returning fire. Streng didn't know what kind of rounds were in the launcher, but he'd seen the M79 in action during the war. It could kill by coming within a few yards of the target. Streng didn't want that thing to go off anywhere near him or the people he was trying to rescue.

Streng watched. The guy paced to the left. Stopped. Turned. Paced to the right. Stopped. Turned. Repeated the process. The sheriff focused on the spot where he turned, cocked the Colt, and waited. When the man once again appeared in his sights, Streng fired at his face.

If the man hadn't been wearing a helmet Streng would have killed him. But his shot was a few inches too high, and it pinged off the guy's headgear. Streng fired three more shots as quickly as he could squeeze the trigger, but the Colt had a kick and the guy was sprinting into the woods, so none of them hit. Streng got to his feet and jogged up to Fran and Duncan, who had ducked down behind the Roadmaster.

"Are there keys?" he yelled before getting there. Fran must have recognized his voice, because she opened the driver's door and checked.

"No!" she called back.

"Look in the truck!"

Streng slowed down, chest burning, knees weak, his side ready to burst. Duncan watched him approach, his eyes wide as dinner plates.

"You okay, son?" Streng wheezed.

Duncan nodded.

"No keys in the truck!" Fran yelled.

"Then we have to move. Follow me."

Duncan held out his hand and Streng took it, half running/half hobbling back to the tree line, heading for Wiley's place. Fran met them and took Duncan's other hand, and they awkwardly maneuvered through the forest, Streng slowing them down so he could look for traps.

"Freeze!"

To the right, next to a big tree. The guy in the fatigues, pointing the grenade launcher at them.

Streng stopped. So did Fran and Duncan.

"Drop the gun," the guy said.

It took Streng a nanosecond to make his decision.

"Run!" he yelled at Fran, pushing her and the child out of the way. Then he dropped to one knee and fired his two remaining rounds.

The guy fired the grenade launcher at the same time.

The sheriff saw a flash, then felt a punch in the chest at the same time he heard the *BOOM*. He doubled over, clutching his gut, and before Streng had a chance to wonder how he could still be alive his eyes began to burn.

Sponge grenade, Streng thought. *Soaked in pepper spray.*

He didn't breathe in—which wasn't too hard, because the wind had been knocked out of him—and clenched his eyelids closed while he crawled out of the smoke cloud. The vapors managed to get up his nose anyway, making him choke and then vomit. But he didn't stop crawling. Blind and oxygen-starved, he moved as fast and as hard as someone half his age.

Streng wasn't sure how far he'd gotten—perhaps five or ten yards away. He chanced taking a breath. It was like inhaling hellfire. Streng spat up again, his nose running like a faucet, the capsicum making his tongue swell up and restrict his airway.

Keep calm, he told himself. *It's only pain. It will pass.*

That's what he'd told the half-dozen suspects he'd maced in the line of duty, watching as they spat and swore, silently wondering how they could be such babies.

He mentally apologized to all of them. This was awful.

A few more yards, and he breathed again. He was still sucking in fire and brimstone, but it wasn't as bad.

It will pass. It will pass.

He felt the communicator vibrate in his pocket. They were coming. And they knew where he was. Streng clung to a nearby tree, used it to pull himself up, and realized he no longer held the Colt. No matter. He couldn't hold off four Special Ops soldiers plus the grenade-launcher guy with just one handgun. His only hope was to make it to Wiley's.

He tried to look around, but his eyes had swollen to slits and his vision was out of focus. Streng considered calling to Fran but didn't want her to reveal her position to the enemy. He would have to go it alone.

The sheriff picked the most likely direction to run, then took off at a jog, hands out in front of him so he didn't run into any trees.

He got four steps before hearing the *SNAP!*

At first he thought he'd simply caught his leg on something. Then the sickening realization hit him a second before the pain.

A bear trap.

Streng fell to his knee, hands seeking the trap, finding the terrible jaws slicing through the muscles of his calf, anchoring into bone.

Then came agony.

Streng buried his face in the crook of his arm, muffling his scream. This was worse than the pepper spray. Worse than the kidney mauling. His whole body quaked in anguish, and if he still had his Colt he would have put it in his mouth and pulled the trigger.

He stuck his fingers in the teeth, tried to pull it apart. It gave—an inch, two, three—and then snapped closed again, prompting another horrific scream.

Streng's mind, insane with pain, struggled to form a lucid thought. He needed something to pry the trap open. Maybe a branch. His hands scoured the ground around him, finding nothing.

The Ka-Bar knife? Streng groped for the fanny pack, finding the Warthog, wedging it into the mechanism and trying to force it open.

No good. The handle was too short. No leverage.

Goddamn you, Wiley.

Streng hated his brother then, hated him more than anyone he'd ever known. He was the cause of this entire mess. And now Streng would be captured, and the pain would get even worse. They'd make him talk. Streng was tough, but Santiago would only have to gently nudge the trap with his foot and Streng would be aching to tell him where Wiley lived. Wiley would die. Fran and Duncan would die. And he would die.

Better if it were only him.

Streng sobbed, coughed, spat, and then raised the knife to his own throat, wishing it was Wiley's. *A bear trap.* That son of a bitch. How could he? Especially knowing what their father went through, his leg trapped under that tree . . .

The sheriff paused. Maybe he didn't have to die. Maybe he still could get away.

He tugged off his belt and cinched it under his knee.

Don't think about it, Streng told himself. *Dad did it. You can do it, too. And if you do, the pain will stop. You're an old fart, anyway. Three weeks away from retirement. What do you need two legs for?*

Streng brought the knife down. And he began.

The jaws of the trap had already done most of the work. Streng stuck the blade in where the teeth were already embedded, following an imaginary line around the circumference of the calf.

Almost like carving the meat off a ham hock, Streng thought.

The pain was still there, but he felt a curious detachment from what was happening. *Detachment.* Streng laughed at the double meaning of the word, but it wasn't a laugh at all, it was a tortured sob, but he had to keep quiet, keep so quiet so they didn't find him, and then the knife was through the flesh and the muscle and the tissue and he pulled and then screamed again because the leg was still caught.

The bone.

He recalled Dad's story, how he used a rock to break his leg bone.

Streng didn't have a rock. But the Ka-Bar Warthog was a heavy blade, razor sharp.

He began to chop.

The belt tourniquet wasn't helping much. Streng's fingers were slick with blood, and he'd become so dizzy it was a struggle to stay awake. He alternated knife blows with manually checking to see if the bone had been severed yet; the pain had become so all encompassing he couldn't tell without touching.

Hack.

Feel.

Hack.

Feel.

Hack.

Feel.

Cut! The bone was cut!

Streng let out a strangled grunt of triumph, put his hands behind him, and tried to pull his leg away again—

—and screamed.

He was still caught.

He palpated the area with muddy fingers. The bone was severed. The flesh was severed. Why was he still—

Son of a gun, Streng thought. *Another bone.*

In all of Dad's stories, he'd never mentioned that a leg had two bones in it.

Streng sought out his fanny pack, located the box of Magnum rounds. He broke it open, selected one, and wedged it in the hinge of his mouth, between two molars.

Bite the bullet, old man.

Moaning deep in his throat, Streng raised the Ka-Bar

and hacked as fast as he could, not stopping to feel, not wanting to drag it out any longer.

He knew he had to keep quiet, but he couldn't anymore. The scream came from deep within and went on and on like a foghorn. Streng hacked and hacked and screamed and hacked.

On the eighth hack his leg came free.

Streng didn't pause to celebrate. He dropped the knife, grabbed two handfuls of dirt, and began to drag himself away from the trap. The pain had reached a point where it seemed like it wasn't even happening to him anymore. It had become another entity, a doppelgänger of himself, a creature of pure suffering. He crawled alongside his pain, down on his belly, pushing himself forward with his remaining leg, determined to get away.

Noise, to his right. Streng squinted.

Ajax.

Streng considered his next move, and realized he only had one—release the belt on his leg and bleed to death.

He reached down, seeking the buckle.

"Aren't you a big one?"

The voice came from the left. Streng stared, saw Wiley in his ghillie suit, holding a shotgun.

"Body armor," Streng managed to say.

Wiley aimed at Ajax and squeezed the trigger.

Streng knew he was hallucinating, because it looked and sounded like Wiley fired eight shots within two seconds.

Ajax crumpled like a demoed building, spraying arterial blood so far that some of it hit Streng in the face.

"Body armor my ass," Wiley said. He reached down and Streng felt himself being dragged.

Abruptly—and absurdly, considering the circumstance—everything became clear to Streng. He had always looked up to Wiley. Put his older brother on a pedestal. Through the haze of pain, Streng realized that he wasted thirty years trying to analyze why Wiley didn't measure up to his standards, when he should have simply accepted him. Family shouldn't judge. Family should forgive.

"I'm sorry," Streng mumbled, hoping his brother heard him.

The sheriff was sure he heard Wiley say, "I'm sorry, too, Ace," right before the pain reached a crescendo and he passed out.

Fran huddled close to Duncan and waited in the strange purple room for her father to come back.

My father. Fran still couldn't get her mind around that.

Two minutes earlier she and Duncan had been running through the woods and were stopped by what appeared to be a swamp monster, vines and sticks hanging from its body.

"I'm Warren," it said. "Follow me."

Fran followed. She'd just seen the sheriff get shot, and much as she mistrusted the man in front of her, she had to protect Duncan. Warren Streng led them to a dead deer, pressed some sort of button, and the ground opened up.

"Slide down. I'll be right back."

Fran clutched her son and they went down the ramp on their butts, Fran using the rubber grips on the bottom of her sandals to slow their descent. When they reached bottom they were in a room illuminated by black lights. The decals on her sweatshirt and Duncan's white shoelaces and socks glowed purple.

Above them the hatch closed. Fran startled at the sound. They'd escaped the Red-ops, yet again, but she still felt a long way from safe.

"Is Sheriff Streng okay?" Duncan asked.

"I don't know, baby."

"Is that guy really your dad?"

"I think so."

"So he's my grandpa?"

"Unfortunately."

Duncan pulled away from her, trying to stand.

"Stay close to me, baby."

"I'm not a baby, Mom."

Fran rubbed his back, like she did when he was an infant and wouldn't go to sleep. "You'll always be my baby, Duncan."

"Can I get lights like this? They're cool."

"We'll see."

The seconds ticked by. Fran wondered what they would do if Warren didn't come back. She guessed this place had more rooms. There was probably food, water, weapons. And so far the Red-ops hadn't been able to find it. Maybe they could stay here for a while, wait for them to leave. Maybe—

A clanging sound, coming from the corner of the room. Fran noticed that some tools on the pegboard were wobbling and a wrench had fallen on the floor.

She stood up, forcing Duncan behind her.

"What is it, Mom?" her son whispered.

"I don't know, Duncan. Someone else is in here."

Movement, to their right, followed by a piercing shriek. Fran flinched, putting her hands up to protect her face as something flew at her. It landed on her chest and hugged her neck.

The monkey.

"Mathison!" Mathison jumped from Fran to her son, giving him a hug, as well. "He must have snuck in when Grandpa opened the secret door!"

She didn't like Duncan calling Warren *Grandpa,* but she didn't press the issue.

Instead she walked away from the monkey and child reunion and approached the pegboard, looking for weapons. Fran selected an awl and a hammer with a straight claw.

A clang, from the surface, echoed through the room.

"Mom?" Duncan whispered. "There's someone coming."

"Come here, Duncan. Quick."

Duncan stood at her side, Mathison on his shoulder. Fran held the awl in one hand, the claw hammer in the other, and waited for the person to come down the slide.

There was a noise from above. It got louder. Closer.

"What if it's *them?*" Duncan asked.

Fran had weapons. She would fight to the death. They wouldn't get her son. She held her breath and raised the hammer, watching as two booted feet came down the ramp.

Warren. And he had Sheriff Streng.

"Fran, Duncan, I need some help."

Warren hit a switch on the wall that closed the above hatch, then hauled the sheriff across the floor, leaving a streak of blood. In the black light it looked like motor oil.

"Get the door," Warren ordered.

Duncan opened the only door in the room, which led into a bright hallway.

"First door on the right. Fran, grab the first-aid box."

Fran stepped over Streng and hurried into the room. She found herself in a large storage area, filled with ranks and files of shelves. Food, paper products, boxes of all types, and on the rear wall—racks of guns.

"Second aisle, a white footlocker, bottom shelf."

Fran spied it, a metal box with a suitcase handle on it, so heavy it took both hands to carry.

"Duncan," Warren said, his hands on the sheriff's bleeding leg, "get some jugs of water. Last row, second shelf. Fran, pull this suit off me. And the shotgun."

Warren wore a camouflage holster on his back, which housed a shotgun that nestled against his spine. Fran removed both holster and gun, then located the snaps on the swamp-monster outfit and tugged it off. Warren's eyes met hers, and Fran was stricken by how much they looked like Duncan's. Like her own.

"In the box, get me a scalpel."

Fran opened up the footlocker and shelves folded out like a tackle box. She found a scalpel in a slot and handed it to Warren.

"I got the water, Grandpa."

"Pour it on the sheriff's leg, Duncan."

Warren cut away Streng's pants. Fran glanced down, saw the gory stump where the calf used to be, and had to turn away.

"Duncan," she said. "Leave the room."

"Like hell he's leaving the room," Warren barked.

"He's a child."

"He's got hands. I need those hands. Pour the water, Duncan. And keep pouring until I say quit."

"It's okay, Mom. I can help."

Duncan pulled the cap off a water container and sprinkled some out.

"Faster, son, dump it on there."

Duncan upended the jug, and Fran stared, mortified, as it flushed away the blood, exposing several wormy blood vessels and two pink bones.

"Fran, give me some clamps."

Fran didn't move, paralyzed by the spectacle before her.

"Clamps, Frannie! They look like scissors."

Frannie. Her mom used to call her Frannie.

Fran found a clamp and handed it to Warren.

"Keep pouring, Duncan. Right here, where my fingers are. Good job."

Warren locked the clamp around one of the slimy purple worms.

"Another one, Fran. And give me the big silver syringe, the one with two tubes coming out the sides."

Fran searched the box. Warren clamped off another artery. She heard a chittering sound, saw Mathison sitting on a shelf, watching the proceedings with a worried expression.

"I'm out of water, Grandpa."

"Get more."

"I got it," Fran held the strange-looking syringe out to Warren. The plunger had a loop on the end, and instead of a conventional tip it boasted a valve with two plastic tubes, each ending in a catheter. He took it, rolled up his sleeve, and shoved a needle into his wrist.

"Pull the plunger to take blood from my artery," Warren said.

Fran did as instructed, tugging on the loop and staring as the syringe filled with blood. Warren searched for one of the sheriff's veins. He located one in the crook of Streng's elbow.

"Pour some water on my hands, Duncan. They're too slippery."

Duncan complied. Warren found the vein on the third try, and Fran gently pressed the plunger without being told. Warren's blood flowed into Streng.

"His leg, Duncan, keep going. And more clamps, Fran. And a package of gauze. Hand over the blood tranfuser."

Warren pulled and pushed on the plunger, sucking and pumping faster than Fran had dared to try. Streng moaned, his head shaking.

"There's a glass bottle, Fran, bottom of the box, called *pethidine*. Find it, and fill up one of those small syringes. Duncan, see what I'm doing with this syringe? You do the same."

Duncan took over the blood transfusion. Warren tied off two more blood vessels while Fran found the bottle and syringes.

"Now what?" she asked.

"Shoot him in the leg."

Fran squirted a few drops of liquid from the needle and plunged it into the sheriff's thigh.

"Good. Now I need to see if I got them all. Undo the belt, slowly. Get ready to put it back on if I say so."

Fran scooted closer, kneeling in the widening pool of red. It soaked into her pants, warming her cold legs.

"Ready . . . go!"

She unbuckled the belt and a small stream of blood squirted out of Streng's stump, in time with his heartbeat. Warren pinched the artery closed and applied a clamp.

"Hand me the transfuser, Duncan, and pour more water on him."

The water ran off mostly clear.

"I think we got all the bleeders. Find the vial marked *potassium,* Fran, and fill another syringe. That will help clot his blood. Duncan, go to where you found the water and bring me a white plastic bottle of rubbing alcohol."

While Fran located the vial, Warren dabbed the wound with gauze pads, saturating one after another.

"Good, Duncan. Pour the whole bottle on his leg."

"Mom uses this when I get cuts," Duncan said. "It's going to hurt."

"It would hurt more if he got an infection and died. That's why your mom uses it on you. Now let it flow, son."

Duncan was right. When the liquid hit Streng's leg his eyes popped open and he jackknifed into a sitting position, letting out a cry that made all three of them flinch. Warren gently pushed him back down and applied more gauze. Fran jabbed the second syringe into his leg and depressed the plunger.

"Duncan, give that transfuse a few more pumps. Frannie, squirt one of those tubes of antibiotic ointment on the stump, and then we can close him up."

Fran reached for the ointment, then stopped herself.

"Don't call me Frannie," she said.

Warren waited.

"Mom called me Frannie, when I was growing up. You weren't there. You aren't allowed to call me that."

"Okay. *Fran*, can you put on the ointment?"

Fran squeezed the contents onto Streng's leg, and then Warren stitched a flap of skin closed over the stump, leaving the clamps sticking out. Then he packed on gauze and bandages. She watched him work, weaving the tape through the clamps, moving quickly but efficiently. When he finished he wiped his hands on his jeans and stood up.

"Can you pass me one of those plastic IV bags? The one that says *saline* on it?"

Fran fished around for the bag, while Warren pinched the needle out of his arm. When she located it, he attached the tube to the inlet valve and placed it on a shelf above Streng.

Warren cleared his throat. "There's a bathroom around the corner and a kitchen with a laundry room. Both have sinks if you two want to get cleaned up. There are some extra shirts hanging next to the washing machine."

Fran looked at her hands, her clothes, and found herself completely saturated with blood.

"I need you both back here pronto. We need to plan for when they get in."

"How can they find us?" Duncan asked. "We're hidden."

"They'll find us. They won't stop until they do."

"Why?"

"Because I have something they want."

"What?"

Warren didn't answer.

"It would be nice to know," Fran said, rage bubbling up to the surface, "why these people have been trying to kill us, and why my husband had to die."

Warren let out a slow breath.

"Tell me," she ordered.

"No."

"You owe me that."

"I don't owe anyone a goddamn thing."

"Then why the hell did you let us in? If you don't care about anything, why didn't you just let us die?"

Warren stared at her for a moment and seemed to come to a decision.

"I was reckless when I was younger. Got into a lot of trouble. Raised some hell. I met your mother right before I shipped off to Vietnam. I'm sure she was a wonderful lady, but the truth is I'd only spent a few hours total with her, so I didn't know her too well."

"Stick to the story."

"They say war changes people. It didn't change me. I kept on doing what I always did. I sold drugs, supplies, stolen goods. I smuggled people, too. I had the connections. Wound up being in charge of the black market for the Kontum Province."

Warren coughed. He bent down and grabbed the water jug, taking a long sip before he continued.

"Anything of value went through me. Not just contraband. Information, too. I passed the important stuff on to the higher-ups—I was a criminal, not a traitor. But near the end of my tour I got something unique. Something I couldn't give to the higher-ups."

Warren went to a shelf, opened an old shoe box. He reached inside and removed a blue plastic disk, big as a donut but less than an inch thick.

"A local came to me with this. An eight-millimeter film. Said he found it in a movie camera, near a South Vietnamese village that the enemy had bombed. Told me it was worth a lot. I watched it, realized what it was, and paid him. I was already rich, but this would make me more money than I could ever use."

"So this is all about a stupid roll of film?" Fran couldn't get her mind around it. "What's on it?"

"You don't want to know. It's bad. Real bad."

"Tell me."

"No."

Fran folded her arms. "Why not?"

"It will put you and Duncan in danger."

She snorted. "How could we be in any more danger?"

"You could. Trust me."

Fran tried a different tactic. "So why didn't you sell it?"

"I tried. After the war ended, I shipped my stuff back here. Contacted the potential buyer. I was going to buy a big mansion in Beverly Hills." Wiley shook his head. "I was a fool. Instead of millions, he sent some men over. I wouldn't tell them where I hid the film. They tried to make me talk. They tried hard. I got lucky, managed to get away. I knew they'd come after me again, so I disappeared."

"If they're after the film, let's give it to them," Fran said. "Then they'll leave us alone."

Warren shook his head. "They won't leave us alone. They'll kill us whether they get the film or not."

"How do you know?"

Warren met her gaze. "Because that's what I'd do."

Fran snatched the roll from him. She was tempted to throw it against the wall, as if destroying it would make all of this horror disappear. She raised it over her head, waited for Warren's reaction.

He did nothing.

"Don't you care if I destroy it?" Fran asked.

"No. I stopped caring about things a long time ago."

"But isn't it the reason you live like this?" Fran swept her hand across the room. "Underground, surrounded by traps?"

"I live like this," Warren said in calm, even tones, "because this is what I deserve."

Fran hadn't expected that answer. She asked again, "What's on this film, Warren?"

"We need to get cleaned up." Warren headed for the door. "They'll find us soon."

"I want to see it."

"No."

Fran drilled her eyes into him.

"Show me the film. You can't just tell me half the story."

"Are you sure? If you watch it, you can't unwatch it. I know."

"Show me."

"You don't want to see it. Believe me."

She thrust the film into his chest. "Show me, goddammit."

Warren's face seemed to sag.

Then he said, "Okay."

The projector looked like a small oval suitcase with a metal snap on top. Wiley lifted it by the handle and set it on the hallway floor, then took off the left side of the shell, exposing the inner workings. He plugged it into the wall outlet. Then he opened up the round blue container and removed the film. Seeing it again made Wiley's stomach clench.

"Duncan, why don't you go wash up in the kitchen and get a snack," he said.

"I want to stay here with you and Mom, Grandpa."

"Go on, Duncan," Fran said. "This one is adults only."

Duncan sighed, then plodded down the hall and through the kitchen door.

"I've only seen this three times." Wiley spoke while threading the film through the projector's sprockets. "The first time, back in Vietnam. Then twenty years ago, when I bought a video camera and transferred it to VHS. The last time was just a few months ago, when I made a digital copy on my computer."

"Why don't we watch it on one of those other formats?"

"Because both of those have large screens. This way, I can make the image small."

Wiley frowned. Even small, it still hit like a sucker punch. But at least you didn't see as much detail.

"Can you flick the wall switch?"

Fran pressed it, and the overhead fluorescents winked out. Wiley turned the knob to run and aimed the square of light at a blank spot on the wall. The image was half the size of a sheet of paper.

They watched.

The first shot was inside a helicopter, obviously in flight. The camera jerked and jolted, making a blurry pan across the faces of five men sitting in the bay. They all wore black uniforms, their expressions no-nonsense.

"Does this have sound?" Fran asked above the clackety-clack of the projector.

"It's silent."

"Who are these men?"

"A secret military unit. They aren't wearing any insignia, but you can tell they're U.S. by their boots and weapons. Plus it's one of our choppers. And see there?"

Wiley pointed to a sixth man, standing by the door, looking smug.

"He's got major's stripes. These are our boys, no doubt."

The film cut to the helicopter after it landed, the cameraman following the six others out of the bay and onto the ground. They were in a village, a poor one, surrounded by jungle. A handful of ramshackle buildings stood alongside a dirt road. Clothing hung on drying lines. Livestock roamed freely.

There were people in the village. Vietnamese peasants. They looked at the approaching unit with curiosity, some of them openly smiling. None of them ran away.

You should have, Wiley thought.

Another cut, and the villagers were being rounded up, gathered in the middle of the town. Over fifty in total.

Then the soldiers raised their M16s.

Wiley winced, knowing what was coming.

Villagers panicked but couldn't escape their fate. The men in the black uniforms opened fire. The people began to drop.

"Notice they aren't shooting to kill," Wiley said. "They're aiming for legs, so they can't run away."

When the whole town was on the ground, screaming, panicking, bleeding, the soldiers set down their guns and drew their knives.

The first peasant died by having his belly slit open.

The cameraman got a close-up of his insides being yanked out.

"Oh, Jesus," Fran said.

It got worse. Much worse. Throats were slit. Eyes gouged out. Limbs hacked off. Scalpings. Beheadings. Castrations. Skinnings. When the pregnant woman came onscreen, Wiley had to look away.

The cameraman had a hard time keeping up. He sometimes got in close to see detail work, other times pulled away to catch multiple atrocities happening at once.

Wiley glanced at Fran. She had her hand over her mouth, her eyes wide with horror. He looked back at the flickering image.

They were at the scene where the soldiers began to undress.

"Can I turn it off now?" Wiley asked.

Fran nodded. He reached for the knob and stopped the evil, grateful for the reprieve.

Darkness and silence filled the hallway.

"What happens next?" Fran whispered.

"The soldiers rape many of the people who are still alive. And some who aren't. They don't discriminate with age, sex, or orifice. Sometimes they even make new orifices. Based on the position of the sun in the shots, it went on for at least four or five hours. Then they kill the few who are still alive, dismember the bodies, put everything in a big pile, and set it on fire."

"And then?"

Wiley took a deep breath, let it out through his clenched teeth.

"Then it gets kind of confusing. There's a quick shot of them setting up charges, and then it jumps to a big explosion, and the camera spins away and dies out. I think the cameraman got too close before it blew, and he died. That's how they lost the camera. But before that happens, it reveals the name of the village, on a sign. It was in South Vietnam."

Fran turned on the lights. Wiley squinted against the sudden glare.

"South Vietnam?" she said. "We were fighting to liberate South Vietnam. They were our allies."

"That's why no one ran away when the chopper landed. They probably thought we were there to help them."

Fran was silent for several seconds. Then she spoke a single word.

"Why?"

"When I saw the film the first time, I recognized the major. He was the man I went to after the war ended. I asked him the same thing."

"What did he say?"

"He said the military was creating a new type of soldier. But before they went into the field, they needed to be tested. They picked a town that wouldn't see it coming, wouldn't fight back."

Wiley turned the knob to reverse the film, keeping the bulb off. They both watched it slowly rewind.

"You went to the major to get money from him."

Wiley didn't answer. But he managed a slight nod.

"That unit," Fran said. "Did it have a name?"

"The major called them a Red-ops unit."

Fran stood. "Those fuckers outside. They're a Red-ops unit, too."

"I figured as much."

"Why didn't you expose this? Why didn't you go to the press?"

Wiley had thought about that many, many times. He didn't go at first because he wanted the money he thought he could extort from the major. But instead of paying, the major had sent two of his Red-ops team to visit Wiley, to get him to reveal the location of the film.

They worked on him for less than an hour. But they'd inflicted enough pain in that hour to last a lifetime. Nothing permanent had been done to him. Just squeezing. Hitting. Pulling. Breaking.

Wiley would have talked within the first few minutes, but the film was at his parents' house, shipped back from Vietnam with the rest of his war booty. As selfish as he'd been in the past, as reckless and unconcerned for their feelings, he wasn't going to let these animals get their hands on his parents. Even if it meant dying in agony.

He got lucky. The Red-ops soldiers the major had sent were geniuses at torture but pretty stupid otherwise. They talked slow. Repeated themselves a lot. Wiley convinced them the film was under his bed, and they believed him. When they couldn't find it, they brought Wiley over. He reached into the hidden slit in his mattress, grabbed the gun he kept there, and killed them both. Then he hurried to his parents' house, grabbed all of his stuff, and fled.

That had been the last time he ever saw them.

He could have gone to the press after that. But he was terrified that they'd find him. And they'd hurt him, and his mom, and dad, and brother. So he drifted around for a few years, coming back to Safe Haven after his folks had died, building this bunker where he separated himself from the world.

"You could have stopped them," Fran said. "Even while you were hiding here. All you had to do was mail the damn film to one of the networks."

Wiley told her the truth.

"That film cost me everything. My freedom. My family. I wasn't going to give it away for free, unless I got something in return. I was scared. But mostly, I was greedy."

Fran stood up, her face twisted with contempt.

"I hate you. I hate you so much."

Wiley didn't contradict her. He hated himself, too.

He watched her as she walked away.

M om came into the kitchen, but she didn't say anything. She walked to the sink and went at her fingernails with soap and a scrub brush.

Duncan said, "Mom?"

She didn't answer.

He tugged her shirt.

"Mom? I need to pee."

"I'll be done in a few minutes, baby."

"I can go by myself."

Mom didn't turn around. She kept scrubbing. "No. I don't want you alone with that man."

"He just saved the sheriff's life, Mom. And he's hiding us."

"I don't care. Wait until I've finished."

Mom scrubbed even harder, so hard that Duncan wondered if the blood was coming from her. He took one step backward. Two. Three. Then he sneaked out into the hallway, Mathison hanging on his shoulder. The bathroom door was open, and the sheriff's brother was wiping his hands on a towel.

Duncan stared at him. His dad's parents died before he was born, and his mom's parents when he was just a baby. It was weird to think that he actually had a grandpa.

"Is it okay if I call you Grandpa?" Duncan asked.

"I haven't earned the right for you to call me that."

"Your name is Warren, right?"

He glanced down at Duncan and cleared his throat. "Yep."

"Is that what people call you?"

"They call me Wiley."

"Why?"

"My brother stuck me with that nickname when we were kids. Because I was always sneaking around, trying to be crafty."

"Like the cartoon? Wile E. Coyote?"

He cleared his throat again. "Kinda like that."

"You clear your throat a lot."

"I haven't used my voice in a while. Now how about we stop with the questions and go get some guns."

"Okay, Wiley."

Wiley hung up the towel and Duncan followed him back to the storage room. Wiley stopped by his brother, examined the bandage, and grunted. Then he went on to the back wall, by all the guns. Like the tools in the purple room, all the guns were on a pegboard. Wiley had about thirty of them.

"You ever shoot a gun before, Duncan?"

"Just one. A shotgun. I shot a vent, Wiley."

Duncan liked saying the name Wiley.

His grandpa removed a gun hanging by its trigger guard.

"This should be easier to handle than a shotgun. It's a Hi-Point 380 Polymer. Hi-Point is the maker, 380 is the caliber of the bullet, and it's called a Polymer because some parts are made out of composite plastic, so it's lighter."

He held the gun out to Duncan. Duncan shook his head.

"Mom doesn't want me to touch guns."

"Why not?"

"Because I could die."

"Do you know which end the bullets come out?"

Duncan pointed to the barrel.

"Don't aim that end at your head," Wiley said, "and you won't die."

That seemed sensible to Duncan. He took the gun.

"It feels like a toy."

"It's not a toy. It's a deadly weapon. The first rule when using firearms is to treat the weapon with respect and always assume every gun is loaded."

Duncan nodded. "Did you ever get shot?"

"No."

"I did." Duncan proudly showed off his bandaged leg. "With a shotgun. It hurts, but not too bad. Josh said he doesn't think the pellet is still in there. He's the one who put the bandage on."

"Is Josh your friend?"

"Yeah. He went out with my mom a while ago. I think he's going to go out with her again. They look at each other a lot, you know, like they're going to kiss and stuff. He's going to take us muskie fishing. Do you fish?"

"Not for a long time."

"Maybe you could come with us. I mean, if you want to. Do you want to?"

"I'm not very good company."

"Maybe you're just out of practice."

"I wasn't good company even when I was in practice, Duncan."

"You should come with us anyway. It will be fun. Is that a Desert Eagle?" Duncan pointed at a large handgun near the top of the pegboard.

"Yep. How'd you know that?"

"Grand Theft Auto IV," Duncan said. "Mom won't let me buy it, but I play it over at my friend Jerry's house on his Xbox 360."

Duncan gave Wiley the Hi-Point, and Wiley unhooked the Desert Eagle from the wall and handed it to him, butt-first. The gun was cool-looking but heavy.

"It's too big for my hand," Duncan said.

"You'll grow into it."

Duncan extended his finger, but he couldn't reach the trigger.

"Did you ever kill anyone?" he asked without looking at his grandpa.

Wiley crouched down, so he and Duncan were face-to-face. He didn't look angry, but his face was very serious.

"When you ask a man a question like that, Duncan, you need to look him in the eye."

Wiley's eyes were light blue, just like his. Duncan stared right at them.

"Did you ever kill someone, Wiley?"

"Yes, I have."

"Bad guys?"

"Some were bad."

"Did you ever kill any good guys?"

Wiley cleared his throat. "I have."

"Why?"

"To cover up some bad things I did."

"Couldn't you have just shot him in the leg or something?"

"I could have. But I didn't."

Duncan thought it over.

"I know bad people do bad things," Duncan said. "But maybe sometimes good people do bad things, too."

Wiley appraised the child.

"I go to bed every night hoping you're right, Duncan."

"DUNCAN!"

Mom yelled so loud that Mathison jumped from his shoulder and went running off. She stormed over to him, pointing her finger.

"Put down that gun!"

Duncan set it down on the table. "Mom, I was just—"

"You!" Mom's finger went from him to Wiley. "What kind of man gives a ten-year-old boy a gun?"

Wiley cleared his throat. "Some people are going to break in here, Fran, and try to murder us. Duncan has a right to defend himself same as me and you."

Mom grabbed Duncan's hand, but she kept her eyes on Wiley.

"You're insane! Stay the hell away from my son! Do you get it? We don't need you in our lives! We never did!"

"Fran . . ."

Mom pulled Duncan away from the guns and was leading him out of the room when they both heard a beeping sound. Mom stopped, looking around for the source. Wiley hurried past them both.

"That's the alarm," he said, strapping on his shotgun holster. "They've found the entrance."

J osh broke another capsule under his nose—his fourth— and swung the Bronco onto Deer Tick Road. The Charge no longer gave him a head rush—just a headache. He was also short of breath and queasy, symptoms of both cyanide poisoning and amyl nitrite overdose. Josh didn't know if that meant he needed more Charge or less.

I've got to get to a hospital, Josh thought. He even had a plan on how to get through the roadblock. But first he had to find Fran and Duncan.

He used the back of his hand to wipe sweat off of his forehead, pushing the speedometer to thirty-five. The Bronco ate up the dirt road, easily taking the bumps and turns. When he passed the final bend he saw Mrs. Teller's Roadmaster in the distance, the headlights still on. And next to it, Olen's Honey Wagon.

Josh mashed the brake, causing Woof to lose his balance on the front seat and slip onto the floor.

"Sorry, buddy. We're going to find Duncan. Do you want to find Duncan?"

Woof barked.

"Good boy. We're going to find Duncan. Yes, we are."

Josh jammed the Bronco into park and hunted around the back seat. Adam kept a load of crap back there, and Josh swore he saw a clothesline earlier. He found it and tied an end around Woof's neck. Then he grabbed his Maglite and his pillowcase of supplies and climbed out of the truck. The world seemed a little wobbly, and he felt more than a little woozy, so he leaned against the fender and rested for a minute.

Woof barked again—it was too high for him to jump. Josh helped him to the ground.

"Where's Duncan, Woof? Find Duncan. Go, boy!"

Woof tugged on the makeshift leash, and Josh jogged behind him. Part of Josh—the tiny part that still remained rational through all of the fumes he'd inhaled—knew that wandering around with a flashlight and a barking dog would attract the Red-ops. But he wasn't scared. In fact, he felt in control and powerful. Invincible, even.

The dog sniffed everything: trees, bushes, leaves, sticks, rocks, and the open air. Josh began to wonder if Woof was just out for a good time, but then he strained against the rope and started barking like crazy.

"Duncan?" Josh called, sweeping with the flashlight.

The beam landed on a woman. A woman wearing hiking books and a blue-jean miniskirt. She was in her thirties, attractive. Her face looked like she might have been crying recently.

"Oh, my God!" she shrieked. "You've got to help me!"

Woof snarled at the new arrival, and Josh reined him in so he didn't bite her.

"What are you doing out here?" he asked.

"My friends and I were camping and we got attacked by these guys—oh, my God, it was awful! Do you have a phone or a car?"

She moved closer. Josh noticed she had long blond hair tied back in a ponytail and the sleeveless top she wore was dotted with blood. She was *seriously* built. Her calves above the boots bulged with muscle. So did her bare arms.

She didn't appear to have any makeup on, but she wore several pieces of jewelry, including a thick gold Omega necklace and matching anklet. On her finger was a large diamond engagement ring.

"Can you help me?" she repeated. "Please?"

Josh shook his head—not to say no, but to clear it. Woof kept barking. Something was wrong, but he couldn't pin down what. He was on edge. No, not on edge. *Excited.* He felt a tremendous urge, a *need,* to do something. But he wasn't sure what.

He blinked, his mouth went dry, and suddenly he knew what he needed to do.

You have to kill her.

The thought didn't shock Josh like he felt it should have. Rather, it appealed to him.

That's the drugs talking. It's the Charge.

No, it's not the Charge. She's Red-ops.

"Where's your car?" she pleaded. "What's wrong with you? Are you drunk?"

How could she be Red-ops? She's just some scared girl. It's the Charge. The chemicals are messing with your mind.

Then what is she doing out here, all by herself? She's one of them. You have to kill her.

Josh dropped the rope and Woof charged at her. She kicked the dog in the side and he yelped and rolled into the bushes.

"Your dog just attacked me!"

She was four steps away.

You can't kill her.

Yes, you can. This woman is the enemy. Kill her. Bash her head open.

Three steps away now.

She's just a camper. She needs your help. The drugs are making you aggressive, making you crazy.

It's not the drugs. She's one of them. You need to kill her before she kills you.

"Please. You have to protect me."

Josh held his hands out in front of him.

"You . . . you shouldn't come any closer." But even as the words left his lips, he wanted her closer. Much closer.

"I need your help, mister. Please."

Kill her kill her KILL HER!

Two steps away.

"Stay back. Stay away from me."

The Charge is warping you. Making you violent. But you're in control. You don't have to give in to every little urge. Fight it. Do the right thing.

"I was attacked." Her eyes narrowed. "Don't you care?"

One step away.

"Yes, I care. Look how much I care."

Josh used the Maglite like a club, smashing it across her face, trying to bust her skull open. The woman almost kept her balance but tripped on something in the weeds and kissed the ground.

SNAP!

Blood blossomed upward like a Roman candle.

Yes!

No . . .

"Oh, God, no . . ."

The woman stared at Josh with dead eyes, her head squished in the center like Mr. Peanut, the bear trap dripping crimson.

You killed her.

Woof limped over and Josh backed away, scared he might hurt the dog, too. Jesus Christ, what did he just do? Why did he hit her when she was obviously just looking for help? He killed her. He freaking killed her.

An accident. It was an accident.

No, it wasn't.

You didn't mean to kill her.

That's what all killers say.

Josh looked at his hands. Murderer's hands. They were shaking. How was he supposed to live with himself? He felt his stomach do flip-flops, like he'd swallowed a live carp.

What now? Run away? Hide the body? Turn himself in?

He wanted to save lives. That's all he wanted to do. That was the promise he made to himself. To help others. To make the world a better place.

And now . . .

Over. His life was over. He couldn't live with this.

Could he?

Maybe the Charge contributed, made him paranoid. Maybe it even made him temporarily insane. He didn't mean to kill her. Just stop her. He didn't know she'd fall on a bear trap.

No. He *did* want to kill her. He wanted it so bad he couldn't stop himself.

Could he have stopped himself?

His eyes became glassy. He shook his head again, a litany of "should haves" and "whys" flying at him from all angles.

This is how it feels to be a murderer.

Josh set his jaw, embraced the responsibility.

It was ultimately his decision to hit her. He made the choice. Now he had to deal with the consequences of his actions. That's how a civilized society worked. All criminals could justify their crimes. They all had reasons, excuses. But human beings weren't programmable robots. Following instincts, or orders, or drug-induced impulses, were not excuses.

Everyone had free will. And no one ever had the right to murder another human being.

I belong in jail, Josh thought.

He dropped to his knees, unsure if he should cry for the poor soul he just slaughtered, or for himself.

Look at the jewelry.

He peeked through his tears. He'd seen that anklet and necklace before. And the ring—that was the ring he helped Erwin pick out when he proposed to Jessie Lee.

Josh begged the universe that he was right, that this woman was indeed a soldier and had played a part in butchering his friends. He crawled over to her, not looking at her face, and patted down her skirt. No pockets. The sweater didn't have any, either. Josh almost began to cry. He checked to see if she had some sort of purse or backpack, but she didn't. Then he held her dead hand, looked at the ring and anklet again, and doubted himself.

Maybe those weren't Jessie Lee's. Maybe he just desperately wanted them to be.

"What did I do? What did I—"

There. In her other hand. A knife.

Josh pried it from her fist. A combat blade. Then he heard a soft buzz. He followed it to her hiking books and dug a black communicator out of an ankle holster.

The relief enveloped him. He wasn't a murderer. It was self-defense. The Charge made him aggressive, but it also made him sense something his conscious mind was unaware of. Josh was so happy he almost kissed the communicator. He restrained himself, sliding the cover open instead, reading the last message.

Warren found.

He reasoned it out. The Red-ops had Fran and Duncan. The Red-ops found Warren. So either the Red-ops had brought Fran and Duncan to Warren's place, or—

Or they didn't need Fran and Duncan alive anymore.

Dread slapped euphoria right out of Josh. He whistled for Woof, patting the beagle's head and giving him a scratch under the muzzle and winding his hand around the end of the clothesline.

"Find Duncan, Woof. Find Duncan, boy."

The dog licked Josh's face, then took off running. He sprinted after Woof, but the dog's direction was erratic, zigzagging, and Josh couldn't run full-tilt, periodically shining the Maglite at the ground to make sure he didn't wind up in a bear trap.

Woof got farther and farther away, and Josh let out yard after yard of line until he was holding the very end, the dog disappearing into the undergrowth.

Then, abruptly, Woof stopped. The leash went slack.

Josh halted next to a tree, panting, the whole forest lopsided.

"Woof! Come, boy! Woof!

Josh whistled. He whistled again.

"Woof! *WOOF!*"

No answer.

Josh gathered in the rope, pulled it about a few feet, and

then it went taut. He didn't feel the dog on the end. There was no movement at all. The line must have been caught on something.

He paused, wondering what to do next. His feeling of invincibility had faded, passed. Josh thought about taking another Charge capsule and quickly decided he'd rather die of cyanide poisoning that have *that* shit in his system again.

Instinct told him something had happened to Woof. Something bad. Maybe a trap. Or maybe something even worse.

He thought, fleetingly, of leaving the dog there, going on without him. But Woof saved his life, and if Josh could return the favor he would. No matter how much it scared him.

Josh began to walk, winding the clothesline around his arm as he did. He took five steps. Listened. Heard nothing. Took five more steps. Listened. Called quietly, "Woof." Heard nothing. Took five more steps. Listened.

A whine. Faint. Coming from the bushes ahead. The rope trailed beneath them.

Josh pulled lightly on the rope.

The rope tugged lightly back.

Another whine. Louder. Woof was hurt.

Josh gripped the Maglite tight, trying to control the shaking as he pointed it at the bushes, trying to penetrate inside them.

The bushes shook, then stilled.

If it were any other dog on the planet, Josh would have dropped the rope and run in the opposite direction. But he forced himself forward, one foot in front of the other, crouching down where the rope disappeared in the foliage.

The rope began to pull. Gently. Josh tightened his hand around it and tugged, feeling some resistance. He tugged harder, pulling the rope back.

"Woof," he called, louder.

Woof whined in response.

Relieved, Josh tucked the Maglite under his armpit and began to reel in the clothesline, hand over hand. He wound a yard around his arm. Two yards. Five yards. Knowing he was getting close to the end.

Then, blessedly, Woof bounded out of the trees, running up to Josh, putting his paws on his shoulder.

But Woof wasn't attached to the rope. His collar was off, and he had some clothesline tied around his snout.

So what was . . . ?

Santiago poked his head out of the bushes, scaring Josh so badly he jumped backward. The killer stood up, facing Josh, Woof's collar buckled around his neck.

"I found Logan," Santiago said. "Was that you, did that to her? I'm surprised. She was very good. A woman, yes, but she liked to get her hands dirty."

Josh backed up. Santiago carried no weapons, but his hands were balled into fists.

Woof growled, trying to bark.

"And what of Bernie?" Santiago asked. "We haven't heard from him lately."

Josh's wanted to say something tough, but his voice wasn't working. He nodded his head.

"Bernie, too? Impressive. Especially from someone with no training, no skills at all. You must be a very lucky man." Santiago grinned. "But your luck has just run out."

"Woof," Josh managed. "Go."

Woof whined.

"Go!" Josh yelled.

Woof took off. The killer came at Josh low and fast, so fast that Josh missed when he swung the Maglite. He tackled Josh, lifting him up off the ground, driving him into a tree. It felt like someone had stuck a tube in Josh's mouth and sucked out all of his oxygen. He fell onto all fours, struggling to breathe, but all that came out was a high-pitched wheeze.

Santiago knelt next to him and Josh felt the man's lips touch his ear.

"This is for Bernie."

And then Josh was flat on his face, his right arm pinned behind his back in a hammerlock. Santiago grabbed his little finger.

Bent it.

Kept bending it.

Kept bending it.

Josh actually heard the *crack*.

Tears came, but his wind hadn't returned so he couldn't suck in a breath to scream.

"This is for Logan."

Josh's ring finger bent back, hyperextended, and cracked like a twig. But Santiago didn't let go. He kept manipulating it, kept pulling, until Josh's entire world was a reduced to a white-hot pinpoint of pain.

"And this is for my ear."

Santiago didn't move on to the middle finger. He went back to the pinkie.

The killer twisted it around a full 360 degrees before Josh finally passed out.

* * *

Wiley stared at his plasma-screen TV in the great room. Three men stood around the fake deer at his entrance. One was the soldier who'd found his camera. The other was an older man in fatigues who didn't look like a soldier at all. The third, incredibly, was that big son of a bitch he'd shot.

Wiley used the remote control to zoom in. The giant was bloody, and his right arm hung limp, but he'd miraculously survived eight shotgun slugs. Wiley had hunted bear before and never needed more than four. He was liking their chances less and less.

Fran and her boy also gawked at the TV, motionless.

"If you want to survive," he told them, "you have to do everything I say. Fran, have you ever fired a gun before?"

Fran shook her head. Wiley reached behind him and pulled the shotgun out of his shoulder rig.

"This is a Beretta Extrema2, a semiautomatic shotgun. It will fire as fast as you can pull the trigger, and it has a recoil system so it won't take your arm off. Just point and shoot."

Fran showed no reluctance in taking the gun. "Show me how to reload."

"I have to go back to storage, get more shells." Wiley stared hard at Fran. "Should I bring a gun for Duncan?"

Fran's gaze went from him, to her son, to the Beretta. She managed a small nod.

"I'll be right back. It doesn't look like they've figured out how to open the door yet. When they do, the alarm will sound again. Push that table over, get behind it, and shoot anything that comes through the door that isn't me. It's also possible they'll go after the generator. There are candles around the room, matches on the table. Light them all."

Wiley didn't wait for a response. He jogged back to the storage area and headed for the gun rack. He grabbed another semiauto shotgun, a Benelli Super Black Eagle II. Then he strapped on two more holsters, one for a Glock G17 .45 ACP, the other for his 50-caliber Desert Eagle. He also clipped an A. G. Russell tactical folding knife to his belt. A leather bag sat on the table, and he filled it with ammo for all three weapons, along with some 380 rounds and the Hi-Point for Duncan.

"Wiley."

He glanced back, saw his brother had his eyes open. Wiley went to him.

"How you doing, brother?"

Ace offered a weak grin. "Never been better."

Wiley scooped up the water jug, tilted it so Ace could take a sip.

"Need another shot of Demerol?"

"It depends. Where are the bad guys?"

"Knocking at the front door."

Ace shook his head. "Instead of the drugs, how about something in a Magnum?"

Wiley smiled for the first time that day, which was also his first smile of the decade. It felt strange, unnatural. But also good.

"Got a Taurus in .357, and a Ruger in .44," he said.

"Gimme the Taurus."

"Ruger has more stopping power."

"Too much kick. Throws off the aim."

Wiley patted his brother on the chest. "I miss these little conversations, Ace."

He turned his attention to the open first-aid box and dug out a syringe and a bottle of Prilocaine.

"This won't put you to sleep. Just numb the area."

Ace winced when Wiley gave his stump several injections. Then he went back to the pegboard, added the Taurus and a box of rounds to the ammo bag, and slung it over his shoulder.

"This won't be pleasant," he told Ace.

Ace only cried out twice as Wiley dragged him across the floor to the great room. Once when he first moved him by pulling his arm, and again when his stump accidentally hit the doorway.

"It's me!" Wiley called out to Fran. "Hold fire!"

He tugged Ace over to the sofa and couldn't tell who was breathing harder, him or his brother. Fran had followed directions and overturned the large oak coffee table. She'd set it on an angle to the doorway, so it would be the last thing someone saw when they opened the door and walked into the room. Wiley approved and felt something akin to pride.

It took all three of them to lift Ace up onto the sofa. The sheriff stayed stoic, though his face scrunched up and his forehead beaded with sweat. Wiley propped some pillows behind his back and aimed him at the door, on an angle like Fran had done. Then he spent a minute showing her how to load the Beretta and showing Duncan how to work the slide on the Hi-Point to jack the first round into the chamber.

"The TV," Streng said, pointing. "They've got Josh."

Everyone looked at the plasma screen. Someone held one of Wiley's remote cameras in front of a man's face.

The man was screaming in terrible pain. Wiley was grateful there wasn't audio.

"We have to help him," Fran said.

Wiley shook his head. "No. They want us to open the door so they can get in."

Josh's scream went on and on. Wiley couldn't imagine what horrible thing they were doing to him. He picked up the remote and switched it off.

"Put it back on," Fran said.

"Don't torture yourself by watching it."

"We have to save him." Fran's eyes were glassy, pleading. "He came back for us."

"I know you don't want to risk Duncan's life just to save Josh."

"Please." Fran was crying now. "Please do something."

"We can't. He's dead. Forget him."

Fran walked up to him, met his eyes. "That should be you out there, not Josh. He's a good man. Have you ever done a single good thing in your life?"

"This isn't about me."

"Of course it's about you. Everything has always been about you, you selfish bastard. If you're not going to do anything, I am."

"They'll kill you."

"I'd rather die fighting than live in fear."

"You'll leave Duncan without a mother?"

Duncan appeared at his mother's side. "Mom?"

Fran knelt down, hugged her son. "I'll be back, baby. It's okay."

Wiley shook his head, amazed. "This man means that much to you?"

Fran looked up. "Yes."

Wiley cleared his throat again. When was the last time he'd spoken to someone? Weeks? Months? When was the last time he cared about anyone other than himself?

He looked at Ace. "You and Duncan hold down the fort. I'll need Fran to work the hatch."

Duncan looked up at him, his small face so full of hope.

"Are you going to save Josh, Wiley?"

Wiley stared down at his grandson. What would a grandfather do? He chose to pat the boy on the head and wink at him.

"I sure as hell am going to try."

D r. Stubin had to walk away because Josh's screaming was giving him a headache. While the brain specialist had never broken a bone, he couldn't imagine why a few bent fingers would make a man howl like that. That Special Forces sergeant Stubin killed earlier had his arm blown off and made a lot less noise.

Stubin had set the timer on the explosives in the helicopter footlocker—left there for him by the Red-ops team when they'd landed—and blown up the Special Forces team when they landed. The sergeant babysitting him had barely even whimpered—even when Stubin beat him to death.

Stubin sighed. This operation had taken much longer than necessary. Stubin didn't blame himself. Warren Streng had proven much harder to find than anyone could have guessed. The lottery ruse was a quick and relatively

simple way to gather and interrogate a small group of
people, and it had been used by the Red-ops many times
throughout the world. Greed had no color, race, or politi-
cal affiliation. But it turned out no one knew where the
bastard was hiding. And even now that they'd found him,
they couldn't get him out of the bunker he'd built for himself. Under that fake deer was a steel hatch that couldn't be
forced open, not even by Ajax. If torturing Josh didn't gain
them entrance, they'd have to go back into town and raid
the hardware store to make explosives.

Stubin checked his watch. The military had quaran-
tined the town, as expected. But General Tope would be
sending in more Special Forces units soon. Good as the
Red-ops were, they were only five people, and Ajax was
functioning in a diminished capacity and might not last
the night.

Stubin wanted to get this done as quickly as possible.
Truth told, he hated these monsters that the army had
forced him to create. Ajax cut up his parents at the age
of eleven. Bernie had been given the death penalty for
burning down a nursing home. Taylor—a vicious schiz-
oid serial killer—was another death-row rescue. They'd
gotten Santiago from South America, a sadistic freelance
interrogator who wound up working for the wrong side
and was captured by the CIA. And Logan was another
psycho who'd been plucked from the mental ward, prone
to such violent outbursts that her diet consisted mainly of
thorazine.

Human garbage, each of them. But they were the only
ones he was allowed to perform the implantations on. The
only ones he could experiment on. The military spent
incredible amounts of time and money teaching soldiers

how to kill, and some of them still hesitated at the moment of truth. How much easier it was to take killers and turn them into soldiers.

So now, under his care, he had five Hannibal Lecters with Rambo training and transhuman modifications. The Chip made them programmable, controllable. The Charge rebooted the Chip when it sensed other thoughts interfering with the program. It also fine-tuned their instincts, making them more aggressive, faster, stronger. There were also indications it unlocked powers of the mind known only to monks and mystics. The ability to withstand pain. To function in extreme conditions. To heal faster. Some experiments had shown it could even enhance extrasensory perception.

But who was utilizing this untold power? Who was the subject of his brilliance?

Psychotics and maniacs.

What a waste of my talents, Stubin thought.

Stubin wanted to work on normal people, not crazies. But the government wouldn't allow it, and no private company would dare fund such a project. When he acquired the film, everything would change. After spending decades being a slave of the U.S. government, he'd get out of his indentured servitude and wind up with some serious money, as well. Stubin figured the film was worth at least two hundred million. He'd set up another lab, one with complete freedom, in Mexico. He'd run his experiments on the locals—bribes ensuring the full blessing of the Mexican government.

And what better way to fulfill his dream than to use the very Red-ops unit he'd been forced to create? They were supposed to be in Afghanistan now, wiping out some village where the Taliban was suspected of hiding. But Stubin decided to run his own program instead. Instead of the Middle East, he brought them here, to find Warren Streng.

The military thought they could control Stubin, keep him in line.

They had greatly underestimated him.

A dog whined nearby, and Stubin froze. That stupid mutt the kid doted on. Maybe if breaking Josh's fingers couldn't get them to open the doors, setting the dog on fire would.

"Here, doggy," Stubin said, his voice high-pitched and sounding ridiculous. "Here, Woof. Come to Dr. Stubin."

Woof jumped out from behind a tree, his tail wagging. He had some rope tied around his snout.

"Good boy. Come here. Come here, doggy."

The beagle took a few tentative steps toward Stubin and stopped, looking away.

Then the gunfire began.

J osh had been willing to die to protect Fran and Duncan. He didn't want his suffering to put them in jeopardy and had done his best to not react to the pain. Seeing the hatch open made him feel dirty, as if he hadn't tried hard enough.

Santiago continued to hold him, putting a knife up to his throat. Taylor blended into the woods. Ajax stood there watching.

Two seconds passed.

Then five.

Ajax approached the entrance. Then the hatch closed again.

Before Josh could figure out what was happening he heard half a dozen shots come from behind. He was pushed forward, Santiago falling on top of him.

Josh rolled onto his side and Santiago was already up and stumbling into the woods. Someone ran up to Josh and fired a shotgun in Santiago's direction, then swung it ninety degrees and fired at the retreating Ajax.

"You hit?" Warren Streng asked Josh.

Josh had no idea. It had all happened so fast.

"How did you—?"

"Back entrance. Came at them from behind. Fran worked the hatch as a diversion. You hit?"

"I don't think so."

"Then move your ass."

Josh didn't have to be told twice. They hurried to the entrance and Warren twisted one of the dead deer's hooves. The hatch opened, revealing a metal slide.

"Thanks for—"

"Not over yet. They're watching us, and now they know how to get in. Move." Warren stared down at Josh's mangled right hand. "Can you shoot lefty?" he asked.

"Not very well."

Warren handed Josh a massive handgun. "Now's your chance to learn. Anything that comes down the ramp, kill it."

"What about you?"

"I'm going to put an end to this. How many?"

"Santiago, Taylor, Ajax is the big one. And Dr. Stubin—he's the leader."

"I also saw a girl."

Josh shook his head.

"Are they armed?"

"I only saw knives. But they're experts with them. Also, there's a dog. Woof. He's one of the good guys."

Warren nodded, shoved Josh onto the ramp, and the firefighter fell onto his butt and slid down into the darkness. Josh almost dropped the gun, and his broken fingers banged against the wall, causing him to cry out. He saw purple light below, and when he hit the bottom someone pointed a shotgun at his head.

Fran.

She set the gun on the ground and hugged him, hugged him so hard that it almost hurt. Josh hugged her back, surprised by the depth of emotion he felt. He never wanted to let go.

"Are you okay?" she asked, her cheek on his ear.

"I'll live. Duncan?"

"He's here, with Sheriff Streng."

A clanging sound from the outside. Warren had closed the hatch.

"They're coming," Josh said.

"I know. My father told me what to do."

"Your father?"

"Long story. Come on."

Fran picked up the gun and led Josh to the only doorway in the large room. It opened up to a brightly lit hallway. When Fran saw his hand she lost all color.

"Oh, my God, Josh. And your face . . ."

She touched his chin, which he didn't feel because he was still numb from the lidocaine. The blurry vision had returned. He removed the metal case from his pocket but couldn't open it with only one hand.

"We can deal with that later," he said. "Can you open this and break one of the capsules under my nose? I've got cyanide poisoning."

"Oh, Josh . . ."

Fran didn't ask how it happened, which saved him from telling her that most of the town had been killed. They could compare horror stories when they were safe.

The Charge fumes hit, and it was like being shaken awake. After a minute of deep breaths he felt better.

"So what's the plan?" he asked.

"Warren said this hall was a perfect bottleneck. We're going to catch them in a crossfire, me in the kitchen, you in the storage room."

"Sounds good. Let's—"

Josh stopped midsentence as they both heard the unmistakable sound of the hatch opening.

W iley lifted the night-vision monocular to his eye and surveyed the woods around him. All clear. He hadn't bothered with the ghillie suit because it was bulky and often became tangled on things; Wiley wanted to be able to move as fast as possible. He wasn't sure that at his age, in his condition, he could take out three highly trained soldiers, even though he had the firepower advantage. But that wasn't his goal. You didn't win at chess by killing pawns—you won by checkmating the king.

The night was as cool and crisp as biting into an apple,

something he hadn't done in a while. Wiley ordered supplies and food through the Internet, using a credit card with a false name and a delivery service that drop shipped pallets to his property once a month. Fresh produce didn't make the cut.

Wiley butted up to a pine tree, breathing heavy, and absently wondered if Duncan liked apples. There were a lot of things he wondered about Duncan, and Fran. Maybe, if he cleaned up this mess, he'd have a chance to learn some of those things.

Most men never got a second chance. But this was Wiley's. To make it right. To stop being afraid.

To finally forgive himself.

He peered through the monocular, the lens gathering up the ambient light and focusing it into a green image. There, thirty yards away, a man walking a dog. He saw the outline of the helmet, the different uniform, and watched the man walk through the woods with the grace of a drunk on roller skates. Dr. Stubin.

He came at them from the side, staying low and stopping every four paces to check for other enemy combatants. As he got closer, he noted Stubin wasn't carrying any weapons and the dog wasn't on a leash. The dog would pick up his scent, or hear him, any time now. Wiley decided to speed up the process.

Hiding behind a thick oak, Wiley hooted like an owl. Woof responded by whining.

"It's just an owl, you stupid dog," Wiley heard the man say.

When Woof poked his nose behind the tree, Wiley gave him a pat on the head, stepped out, and pointed the shotgun in the guy's face.

"Hoot hoot," Wiley said.

Stubin called for help. Or at least he began to before Wiley broke his nose with the stock of the Benelli. The man dropped to his knees, sobbing and gushing blood. Wiley kicked him over, put a foot on his chest.

"You're Stubin, right?"

"Yes . . . yes . . ."

"You running the show?"

"You broke my nose . . ."

Wiley touched the shotgun barrel to Stubin's head.

"Are you running the show?"

"I'm . . . I'm a scientist . . ."

"Then you're no use to me."

Wiley unclipped the tactical folder from his belt and flicked open the blade with his thumb.

"I'm the leader," Stubin blubbered.

"You're going to call off your men."

"I . . . can't."

Wiley pressed the blade to Stubin's cheek.

"I can't! They have microchips implanted in their brains . . . they're following an uploaded program . . . they won't stop until their mission is complete, no matter what I tell them. I'd have to reflash their BIOS, and I only have that equipment back at my lab!"

"So the only way to stop them is to kill them?"

"Yes!"

Wiley waited. Stubin lasted three seconds before shaking his head, sprinkling blood and tears.

"No! There's an EPFCG in Mathison's collar. You press the button, it explodes, emitting an electromagnetic pulse. It will fry everything electronic within fifty yards."

"Define *everything*."

"Integrated circuits, vacuum tubes, transistors, inductors. And the chips in their heads."

"This is in the monkey's collar?"

"Yes. Yes! I told you how to do it."

"Then I really don't need you anymore." Wiley raised the knife.

"But you do need me! You do! I can give your life back!"

Wiley waited.

"Do you still have the film?" Stubin asked. "Of the training exercise on the Vietnam village?"

"That wasn't a training exercise. It was butchery."

"They were an early prototype of the Red-ops program. I used organic brain modification back then—surgery. And the drugs weren't as pure. The microchips make them much more controllable."

Wiley didn't get it. "If you had a hand in that, what do you need the film for? It's been sitting in a box for thirty years. I wasn't a threat to you or your program."

"I need it for money. Just like you."

Wiley thought it through.

"You want out," he said.

"Badly."

"Why didn't you just expose this yourself?"

Stubin shook his head. "No proof. Since that film got lost, nothing has been allowed to be documented. There's no paperwork. No photos. No video. No record of anything I've done. You can guess how that's torture to a scientist. Plus I'm like a prisoner. I'm forced to live in my lab, and it's searched twice a day. I have six people watching me at all times, even though they have no clue why. I do my research on an encrypted computer, and I don't even know the code. Only one man in the whole nation has clearance."

"The major," Wiley said. "The one on the film."

"Yes."

Wiley shook his head. "I got news for you, buddy. If you try to blackmail him, he'll come after you, too."

Stubin blinked. "Blackmail him? I'm going to sell the film to our enemies. They'll pay hundreds of millions to embarrass the United States."

"He'll still come after you," Wiley said.

"He'll be kicked out the military and arrested for war crimes. But even if he tries, I'll be on foreign soil, with an army of Red-ops around me. As soon as I get the film, I'm leaving the country with the unit. They can protect you, too. You can come with us. We'll split the money."

Wiley looked around, scanning the trees for unfriendlies.

"Money's not something I need," he said.

"What *do* you need?"

"To correct my mistake."

Wiley raised his knife again. Stubin's eyes got wide.

"I'm a scientist!" he said, talking fast. "I'm doing this for the good of mankind. I'm going to help millions of people. My research is revolutionary. Please."

His eyes were wide and pleading.

"Sometimes good people do bad things," Wiley whispered.

"Exactly! Sometimes you have to do things that aren't ethical for the greater good."

Wiley said, "I agree."

The blade was sharp and went through Stubin's neck without too much trouble. Wiley wiped it off on Stubin's shoulder, clipped it back onto his belt, and pulled the clothesline from Stubin's dead hand. He used the monocular to check the area, found it clear, and jogged with Woof down to the dry creek bed, where his second entrance was hidden behind the exposed root system of a large fir tree hugging the bank.

Unlike the main entrance, this was for emergencies only, and Wiley had to get on his belly to fit inside. He pulled on a fake root and tugged open the door, then called Woof to the small opening, patted his head, and took the rope off his snout. The dog sniffed at the hole, then happily climbed in. Wiley followed, feetfirst so he could close the door behind him. The tunnel was actually a PVC pipe with a four-foot circumference, roughly fifty feet long. It angled into the ground at a slighter incline than his main ramp. Wiley had to pause several times to catch his breath and allow his heart rate slow down.

The tube let out into his kitchen closet. Woof jumped on him and licked his face when Wiley made it through. Wiley patted the dog on the head, opened the closet door, and said, "Don't shoot," when Fran swung her shotgun at him.

The expression on Fran's face when she saw Woof was priceless. The beagle ran right to her, and she rubbed its muzzle and kissed his nose, beaming. It reminded Wiley of Fran's wedding, the last time he'd seen her smile. He hadn't meant to crash the ceremony, hadn't meant to be intrusive. Wiley went out of curiosity, not to cause trouble. But the curiosity turned to regret and self-loathing, which led to drinking too much and getting into a shoving match with Fran's stepfather—a much better man than Wiley ever was.

Wiley watched Fran and Woof, silently jealous of the dog.

"Thank you," Fran said without looking at him. "And thank you for saving Josh."

"He's in the storage room?"

"Yes. The Red-ops, they're inside, too, but haven't gotten through the hallway door."

Wiley figured it would take them a while. It was a steel security door with a brace across the center. Impossible to open without tools. Unfortunately, they had a whole garage full of tools in there with them.

A floor-shaking *BAM!* coming from the hallway confirmed they'd already gotten started.

"I'll send Josh in here with you," Wiley said. "Go give Duncan his dog."

Fran nodded, heading for the door.

Wiley called to her. "Hold on a second."

She stopped. He went to her. "Aim the shotgun at the door."

Fran complied. Her angle was good, but she had the butt tucked under her armpit rather than tight in the shoulder. Wiley got behind her, helped her adjust the stock.

"It's got a recoil buffer, but it will still kick. Lean into it when you start firing. And don't be scared by the noise—it will be the loudest thing you've ever heard."

"Am I aiming right?" Fran asked.

He put his hand on hers, raised the barrel.

"Match up the back sight with the front sight."

"Like this?"

I'm actually holding my daughter, Wiley thought.

"Perfect. You're doing perfect."

Wiley released her, watched her walk away. Then he

went to the storage room, calling out before entering so Josh didn't shoot him.

"Thanks again for saving my ass," Josh said.

"I want you to go into the kitchen with Fran and Duncan. We're going to hold them off as long as we can, then I want you three to go into the closet and escape the back way, up the tube."

"What about you and Sheriff Streng?"

"He can't make it, and I won't leave him. When the soldiers get in they'll have access to my weapons. I want you to be long gone by then. Understand?"

Josh nodded.

"One more thing. When all this is over, you should come back here. In those boxes, next to the bottled water, are a few hundred thousand dollars worth of gold, gems, cash. And take this." He handed Josh a thin black object, made of plastic. It was about the size of his fingernail, and said "8GB" on the top. "A micro SD card. Can be read on computers and cell phones. It holds a digital copy of an old eight-millimeter film."

"Fran told me about it."

"Make sure the press gets it. Tell them what you've seen here, what's been happening."

"I will."

"Where's that monkey? Mathison?"

"I don't know. I've only seen Fran."

"We need to—"

Wiley caught a blur in his peripheral vision—someone running past the doorway. Someone in black.

Dammit! They must have followed me in through the PVC pipe.

Wiley raced into the hall, saw Santiago pulling off the barricade, yanking open the door.

That big son of a bitch, Ajax, rushed in like a charging linebacker.

Wiley shot slug after slug at him, emptying the Benelli, not missing a single one.

The giant staggered, bleeding from the face and neck, his body armor smoking where the shots hit. But the son of a bitch kept coming.

Wiley dropped the gun and pulled his Glock, backpedaling as he squeezed the trigger, Josh racing to the great room ahead of him.

Ajax got within ten yards.

Wiley aimed for the face, but the huge man was enraged, shaking his big head from side to side like a bull, picking up speed.

Eight yards away, coming on fast. He was going to plow right into Wiley, and the force would no doubt cripple or kill the older man.

Wiley took a different approach. Rather than try to follow the swaying of Ajax's head, he kept the Glock rock steady. He forced out a breath, sighted down the barrel of his weapon, waiting for the massive forehead to line up with his sights.

Five yards and closing.

Ajax bellowed.

Wiley kept both eyes open and fired.

The bullet entered Ajax's face just below his right eye, making a small hole. As it left his skull the hole was much larger, blowing out a section of skull big enough to put a fist into.

Ajax dropped to his knees and pitched forward like a felled tree, a mist of red floating to the floor after him.

But it was too late; the other two had gotten into the storage room, and to the guns.

Wiley turned and ran, following Josh into the great room, locking the door behind him.

Duncan went from being very happy to being very scared. Mom brought in Woof, and told him Josh and Wiley were also okay, and just when he started hugging his dog there were gunshots and Josh and Wiley came running in.

"Cover the door," Wiley said. "They're coming, and they're coming armed. Duncan! Where's that monkey?"

Duncan was too surprised to speak. He pointed to the sofa. Mathison sat on the armrest, looking agitated.

"Duncan, you need to grab his collar. It's really a special kind of bomb. It has a button. You press it and it will kill the bad guys."

"How?" Duncan managed.

"They have microchips in their heads. This sends a signal, breaks the chips."

"Mathison has a chip in his head. Will it hurt him, too?"

Wiley stared at him, and Duncan could tell by his expression that it *would* hurt Mathison.

"He's my friend," Duncan said.

"Duncan, we're all going to die if we don't press that button."

Duncan nodded and swallowed. He walked slowly over to Mathison, the tears making it hard to see.

"I'm sorry, little guy," Duncan said. "It's the only way to save everyone."

Mathison put his tiny paws on his scarred head and screeched. Duncan wondered if he understood what Wiley had said. Duncan held out his hand, trying not to cry too much, and the monkey leapt off the sofa and darted across the room.

Shooting, from the hallway. Duncan turned and saw the door begin to shake. He ran after Mathison, but the monkey screeched at him again and tugged at his collar.

He did understand, Duncan thought. *And he doesn't want to die.*

"They're here!" Wiley yelled.

Duncan looked over at the doorway just as everyone began to fire their guns. The room sounded like bombs were going off, so loud that it hurt Duncan's head. He knew he should fire back, try to help, but it was so noisy and he was so scared and he was just a kid and what could he do anyway?

The shooting went on and on, and Duncan crouched down with hands pressed to his ears and started to cry, wishing it would end.

Finally Wiley yelled, "Conserve your ammo!" and everyone stopped.

All the gunfire had made the room smoky, and Duncan waved his palm to clear the air and see. Mathison was gone. Josh and Mom were behind the table. Wiley and Sheriff Streng were behind the sofa. Duncan realized he'd dropped his gun somewhere. He scanned the floor but didn't see it.

"I'm out of bullets!" Josh said. His voice sounded far away. "So is Fran!"

"Where's the ammo bag?" Wiley called.

"I left it in the kitchen," Fran said. "Where's Duncan? Duncan!"

"I'm here, Mom!"

Fran crawled over, hugging him.

"Where's your gun, baby?"

Duncan was sobbing now, full blown. "I . . . I dropped it. I'm sorry, Mom. I don't want us all to die."

"It's not your fault, baby," she was crying, too, and she smoothed his hair and touched his cheek and looked so sad. "It's not your fault."

Josh scooted over, putting his arms around both of them.

More gunshots, from Wiley. Then he yelled, "I can't hold them! They're coming in!"

Duncan closed his eyes. He hoped it wouldn't hurt too bad when they killed him.

And then he heard someone cooing.

Mathison.

The monkey walked up, walked up on two legs just like a little person. He had his collar in his tiny hand and was holding it out for Duncan. He looked so sad.

Duncan took the collar, which was thick and heavy. He ran his fingers over it and found the button under the buckle.

"Thank you," he whispered to Mathison.

He patted the monkey on the head, right on his scar. Instead of flinching away, Mathison closed his eyes and opened his arms to be held. Duncan embraced him, hugging hard.

"Bye-bye, Mathison." Duncan told him, his voice breaking. "I'm so sorry."

Then he pressed the button and threw the collar at the door.

There was a loud crackling sound, a flash, and the lights went off. The room became darker, but not totally black, because of the candles he and Mom had lit earlier.

"They're down!" Josh yelled. "The Red-ops are down!"

Everyone cheered but Duncan. He cried, softly stroking the belly of his friend, Mathison, limp in his lap.

He did it," Wiley said. "Duncan did it." The words came out more like a rasp, and then he fell to his knees and onto his side.

"Josh!" Ace yelled. "Something happened to my brother!"

Wiley heard people walk over, saw them bringing candles. Josh crouched next to him, pressed his fingers to his carotid.

"Talk to me, Warren," Josh said. "What happened? Were you shot?"

"No," Wiley said. It was tough to breathe. And it hurt. He forgot how much it hurt.

"Help me look for wounds. Let's get his shirt off."

Josh and Fran tugged at his clothes and Josh said, "Oh . . . Warren."

"Why didn't you tell me, you old bastard?" Streng asked.

"We weren't . . . we weren't exactly on speaking terms, Ace."

"How long ago?"

Wiley touched the scar on his breastbone. "Ten years. Went to the ER in Madison. They put in the pacemaker." He winked at his brother. "Runs on a microchip."

"Fran told me about the film," Ace said. "That's why you didn't stay in touch."

"People after me. Too dangerous. Didn't want them to go after you or our parents."

Someone grabbed his hand. He stared, saw it was Fran. She squeezed it tight, and he tried to squeeze it back.

"Wiley!" Duncan ran over, knelt next to him. He was still holding the monkey, and he set its dead body down on the sofa. "What's wrong, Wiley?"

Wiley coughed. "Bad heart, son. Couldn't take all the excitement."

"Are you going to be okay?"

Wiley shook his head. "No. I'm sorry, Duncan. I really would have liked to go fishing with you."

Duncan hugged him, and for the second time in far too long, Wiley smiled.

"Do you like apples?" he asked his grandson.

"Yeah, Grandpa. I like apples."

Wiley cleared his throat, and then he felt his heart beat for the last time.

"I like apples, too."

• • •

Streng closed his eyes. An hour ago, he'd wanted to kick Wiley's ass. But now he felt a loss even greater than his missing leg.

Though Streng hadn't followed his brother's footsteps into seclusion, he did live alone. He had a job, yes, and buddies, and even a small circle of lady friends to help keep warm on chilly winter nights. But Streng had never married, never had children. Wiley was the last of his family. And just as they were rebuilding their relationship after half a lifetime apart, he was taken away.

"How are you doing?" Josh placed his hand on Streng's shoulder. "Your leg, I mean."

"I'm managing."

"The front entrance won't open. It runs on electricity. But there's a secret exit. It's going to be hard on you. We'll have to pull you up with rope."

Streng shook his head. "I think I'll stay here a while. I've got food, medicine. Even if you get me out, we can't get to a hospital."

"I've got a plan for that. And we won't leave you behind."

Streng saw the seriousness in Josh's expression and gave in.

"Okay. Wiley's desk chair has wheels on it. Let's roll that bad boy over here and get me mobile."

Streng tucked the Taurus into his belt and allowed Fran and Josh to manhandle him into the chair. It took every speck of effort he had left not to scream when they set him down too fast and three of the clamps knocked against the floor, but he managed to contain it.

"What about Grandpa and Mathison?" Duncan said. "Are we leaving them here?"

"We'll come back for them, Duncan. We have to get the sheriff to a hospital first."

Duncan patted Mathison on the head and reluctantly followed.

"Come, Woof."

Woof sat next to Wiley and didn't move.

"Woof, come!" Duncan said again.

Woof licked Wiley's face, then howled. Then he moved to Mathison and nudged the monkey with his nose.

"Woof!" Fran yelled. "Come, now!"

Woof picked up Mathison in his mouth, ever so gently, and trotted after them.

"Woof! Put that down!"

"It's okay, Fran," Streng said. "Woof just isn't ready to say good-bye yet."

Duncan joined Josh behind Streng's chair, helping him push. They moved slowly, no hurry, no speaking, everyone holding candles. It reminded Streng of a funeral vigil.

They gave a wide berth to the dead bodies of Santiago and Taylor and rolled Streng into the dark hallway, maintaining silence. Streng remembered how angry he'd been with Wiley when he shipped all of his black-market stolen goods to their parents' house after the war, telling their father to hide it all, implicating them in his crimes. Then he remembered a time many years earlier, when he'd twisted an ankle playing in the woods, and Wiley carried him home on his back.

Wiley had known there was a chip in his pacemaker.

He told Duncan to press the EMP anyway, to save their lives. That was the Wiley that Streng swore he would remember.

Their procession moved into the kitchen, quiet and solemn. Streng almost felt it sacrilegious to speak.

"Josh, there should be rope in the storage room. Fran will go up first, then Duncan, then you, and the three of you can pull me up."

"What about Woof?" Duncan asked.

Streng turned to Josh. "Is it too steep for Woof?"

"It's a plastic pipe. His paws will slip."

"Then he can go up before me."

"What if you get stuck?" Fran said. "One of us should go up behind you, if we have to push."

Streng sighed. "Okay, I'll go up third, then Josh."

"Josh can't use his hand," Fran said. "He can't push. I'll go up last."

"Fran—" Streng and Josh said it at the same time.

"It will be okay. Let's find some rope."

Josh went off to the storage room. Streng stared at Fran and Duncan, and the realization hit him. Wiley hadn't been the last of his family. Fran was his niece, and Duncan his great-nephew. The thought warmed him.

"I found rope," Josh said. "And some Demoral, Fran, for your toes."

"How about your fingers?" she said.

"Are you kidding? I'm so numb I could play tennis."

Josh attended to Fran, giving her a shot in the foot. Then Fran tied one end of the rope under Streng's armpits and the other to Josh's belt.

"Be careful," she said to Josh.

"I will."

They looked deep into each other's eyes for so long that Streng finally said, "You going to kiss, or stare at each other all day?"

Josh kissed her. Duncan giggled. Then Josh went into the closet and up the hole.

They waited, listening to Josh's progress, every grunt and wheeze getting farther. After two minutes he yelled down, "I made it!"

"Can you do this, Duncan?" Streng asked.

"No problem. I bet I'm faster than Josh."

"I bet you are, too."

And then something chirped. Streng looked around, wondering where the sound came from. Another chirp, and Streng determined the sound was coming from Woof.

The dog gingerly set Mathison onto the floor.

The monkey chirped again.

"Mathison!" Duncan exclaimed. He scooped the primate up and rubbed his belly. "Josh! Mathison's alive!"

Streng's smile died on his face.

"Fran, you and Duncan up the pipe, now."

"Sheriff—"

"If Mathison didn't die, the others might still be alive, too."

Fran nodded, hurrying Duncan to the hole. He began to climb, Mathison perched on his shoulder. Fran got in after him.

"We'll pull you up as soon as we get to the top."

Streng nodded and said, "Go!" Then he undid the knot on his chest and tied the rope around Woof's chest.

"Take care of them, boy," he said.

Woof licked his face and then yelped as he got jerked off his feet and up the pipe.

Streng took the Taurus out of his pants and looked in the cylinder. No bullets. He checked his man purse and found two left.

One for Santiago. One for Taylor.

He'd be *damned* if he let those creatures touch his family.

Streng set the gun in his lap and waited.

Santiago came in first.

"Hello, Sheriff. You're not looking very well."

Santiago held a large-caliber semiauto in one hand and a knife in the other.

"I can't tell you how sorry I am that the EMP didn't kill you," Streng said.

"Kill me?" Santiago smiled. "It liberated me. I'm a free man now, Sheriff. I don't have to follow orders anymore."

"Good. Then you can leave us alone."

Santiago laughed.

"This isn't about finishing the mission. This is about revenge. Your brother hurt me, Sheriff. The body armor stopped the bullets, but I'm all broken inside. And you broke my cheekbone."

"I hope it's painful," Streng said.

"It's very painful. And the only thing that helps when I'm feeling this way is to take out my pain on someone else. Like you and your friends. Your suffering will go on for days. I'll make you scream so much your throat will go raw. You'll beg me for—"

In one smooth motion Streng picked up the Taurus and shot Santiago above the nose. The Magnum round blew the entire back of his head off, shutting the son of a bitch up for good.

The killer crumpled, and Streng used his remaining

foot to push himself over to the body, anxious to reach the dropped gun.

"Sheriff!" Fran called down from the pipe.

Streng ignored her, concentrating on the semiautomatic. If he got it in time, he might be able to end this once and for—

The first bullet hit Streng in the stomach. The next two punched into his chest.

Streng fell off the chair, onto his back, the Taurus flying across the room. Streng couldn't breathe, and he began to shiver even though it wasn't cold.

Taylor walked over and stared down at Streng. He was smiling. Streng reached up behind him, searching for Santiago's gun. His fingers touched something else instead.

"You . . ." Streng said.

"Yes, Sheriff. It's me."

"You . . . have . . . got . . ."

Taylor leaned down, grabbed Streng by his shirt. It didn't hurt; Streng was past the point of feeling pain. But he knew he had only seconds before he died, and he really needed to get this in.

"You've . . ." Streng whispered, ". . . got . . . something . . ."

"Speak up, old man."

Streng smiled, blood bubbling up from his lips, but he managed to say, "In . . . your . . . eye . . ."

Then he brought up the knife he'd taken from Santiago's hand and stabbed Taylor in the face.

•   •   •

Taylor flinched in time, and the knife missed his eye socket and glanced off his cheekbone. He brought up a hand to feel for damage and found he could touch his teeth through the new hole in his cheek.

Taylor screamed in pain and rage and began to stomp on the sheriff, which did nothing, because the man had already died. He stormed over to the sink, pressed a towel to his face, and began to tremble. Then he set his gun on the countertop and automatically reached for the Charge capsules. Taylor broke one under his nose and—

—nothing. It didn't relieve the pain. Didn't calm his mind. Didn't focus his thoughts. Taylor threw the capsules onto the floor, made a fist, and punched a cabinet, splitting the wooden door in half. His brain was a mess of signals, each one telling him to do something different. It used to get like that sometimes, before Dr. Stubin put the Chip in. He couldn't figure out what to do next, but then the answer appeared in his head and blinked like a beacon.

Kill them. Kill them all.

Taylor picked up the gun and raced for the closet. He shoved his upper body into the PVC pipe and began to crawl. His cheek continued to bleed, making his hands slip on the plastic, and that only fueled his rage. He'd kill that fucker Josh first. Or maybe he'd just break his knees, so he could watch what Taylor did to the woman and the boy. From now on, his only mission objective, for the rest of his life, was *Have Fun*.

The outdoors smell hit Taylor, and he saw he was close

to the exit. He stuck his head out of the hole and looked around, squinting at the darkness, seeking out his prey.

"Hey!"

Taylor craned his neck up and saw Fran standing above the opening, holding a very large rock.

Then everything went black.

Fran followed Josh's directions and made a left, turning the Bronco onto Pine Glen Way. She had never been so tired in her life.

In the back seat, Duncan, Woof, and Mathison all slept in a big pile. To her right, Josh held her hand between turns.

"This is a dumb question," Josh said, "But how are you doing?"

Fran pictured it happening once again—Taylor's head coming out of the hole, her raising up the rock, smashing it onto his face. She hadn't intended to get his attention first, but it seemed proper that he saw it coming. And it had to be her doing it. Not only because Josh couldn't lift anything with his broken fingers, but because killing Taylor herself was the only way she'd ever be able to sleep again.

"I'm okay," she answered.

"Really?"

"Really."

She felt Josh hold her hand a little bit tighter.

"Adam's house is at the next clearing. Right here."

Fran turned and put the truck into park. Josh took the

keys, and Fran carried Duncan around the house, down the pier, to Adam Pepper's pontoon boat. Woof and Mathison tagged along. They boarded the boat, and Josh used the keys to start it while Fran untied the mooring lines.

Big Lake McDonald was still, quiet. A huge orange hunter's moon reflected on the surface, and Fran felt herself get a little sleepy. She snuggled up to Duncan in the back seat while Josh guided them to the inlets, made his way into the river, and took it downstream.

"We have a full tank of gas, and we're making good time," Josh said. "The Chippewa River feeds a tributary right before the waterfall. We can take it to Eau Claire. They have a hospital."

Fran closed her eyes. When she opened them again, they were passing Safe Haven and the section of the river where she'd jumped in. It seemed like a very long time ago.

"You and Duncan can stay with me for a few days," Josh said. "For as long as you need to. When I get my hand patched up, I'm going back to Wiley's. Since he and Sheriff Streng are, um, gone, you're the sole heir. Wiley showed me some money, some gold. That's yours now. He wanted you to have it. Plus, he gave me a digital copy of that film you saw, told me to take it to the press."

Fran liked that idea, going to the press. It sort of reversed the curse her father had brought upon the town. She also liked the idea of living with Josh for a few days.

This time she wasn't going to let him get away.

"I think—" Fran began, stopping when she saw the five military boats speeding their way.

• • •

General Alton Tope pressed *end* on the laptop, signing off the mobile USAVOIP security connection a few seconds after the president hung up. The satellite photos, and early reports from the infiltration team, had been grim. Safe Haven had been annihilated. Almost a thousand people killed. A very impressive display.

Tope had been somewhat curious how the commander in chief of the armed forces would handle the situation but wasn't surprised by his decision. A cover-up and media blackout would save the nation from embarrassment, worldwide disapproval, and a whopper of a lawsuit by the relatives of the slaughtered. The casualties would be blamed on a carbon monoxide leak. The area would be sealed off until the Red-ops team was found and dealt with. End of crisis.

But then they found the survivors. People who had been there.

They were thoroughly searched. So was the boat. Nothing of interest was discovered.

The man, Josh, claimed they didn't know anything. He said he mangled his hand in a boating accident, the same accident that hurt Fran and her son, Duncan. Fran stuck to the same story. The boy started to cry when questioned, and they hadn't been able to get anything out of him.

Their explanation for having Dr. Stubin's monkey was also plausible—they found it on the road. Tope knew that Stubin and the monkey were dropped off at the original crash site. When the second chopper exploded, the monkey could have run off.

But Tope had popped in during their questioning and felt in his bones they were holding back. These people knew something. Something that was a threat to the country.

If it had been up to him he would have dealt with it differently. Tope was very good at covering things up. The secret was to tie up all loose ends. But it wasn't Tope's call. The president's orders in regard to the survivors had to be followed, much as it left a bad taste in Tope's mouth.

The army had taken over an office building outside of Safe Haven, as a base of operations. Tope left his makeshift command post and walked down the hall. Two soldiers guarded the break room where the survivors were housed. They saluted. Tope returned the salute and dismissed them. He unbuckled the strap on his sidearm and walked into the room.

They were sitting together, their arms around each other, looking appropriately scared. But defiant, too. Even the boy. That proved to Tope that they'd lived through something. He'd seen that look before, in combat troops who had witnessed heavy action. The thousand-yard stare.

"I know you're lying," Tope said.

No one answered.

"You may have seen some things," Tope went on. "You might even think you know what's going on. But how important do you think the lives of three people are compared to national security?"

Tope leaned against the wall and folded his arms.

"This situation will be resolved. And not in a way that will be satisfying to you. You'll be tempted to talk to the media, try to explain what happened, set the record straight. You'll have no proof, of course. We're almost done cleaning up everything. But if you try, you'll be found and dealt with. If it were up to me, you'd be dealt with right now. No offense."

"You're an asshole," Josh said. "No offense."

Tope leaned over to Josh, resting his hand on the butt of his .45.

"Your new home is in Hawaii. You'll be taken by helicopter to Dane County Regional Airport, where you're booked on flight 2343 to Honolulu. You'll be met at the airport by a man who will take you to your new house, and he'll give you information to access your new bank account, which contains ten million dollars. You'll quietly live out the rest of your lives there. You also have to cut all ties with friends and relatives and never try to contact them."

"Too late," Fran said. "They're all dead."

"It shouldn't be a problem, then. Are you willing to accept this offer?"

He drilled his eyes into them, hoping they'd refuse.

"Yes," Josh said.

Tope nodded. He knew the president was wrong. These people would talk and cause all sorts of problems. The smart thing to do was take them out back and shoot them.

"Where's Mathison and Woof?" Duncan asked.

Tope squinted at the boy. "Who?"

"The monkey and the dog," Fran said. "We want them."

"The dog goes with you. The monkey is government property."

"We want the monkey, too," Fran said.

Tope blinked, not believing what he was hearing. They were in no position to bargain.

"Give us Mathison," Josh said, "And you'll never have to worry about us blabbing."

The general recalled the president's words. *Give them what they want.* The man was soft, too soft to run the country the way it needed to be run. But Tope was a soldier, and soldiers followed orders. That was the way things worked. That was the way they would always work.

"Fine," he said. "Don't ever try to come back to the upper forty-eight."

Then he turned on his heels and walked out the door.

N o one spoke during the car ride to the airport. They were escorted through security, walked to the plane, and seated in the back, Fran between Josh and a very drowsy Duncan.

"What about the animals?" Fran asked their handlers, two soldiers in full dress uniform.

"You can pick them up at baggage claim," she was told.

They were watched until everyone else had boarded, and then the soldiers left. The plane taxied to the runway, then took off. Fran kissed her sleeping son on the head. Then she looked at Josh.

"We did it," she said.

"I was worried Duncan would say something. He's a great kid."

"When you told him we'd all die unless we lied, he took it to heart."

"It was the truth. They would have killed us."

"I know. That man, the one who knew we were lying. He was the one on the film. He was the major who started the Red-ops program."

"Good," Josh said. "Then we'll bring him down, too."

The captain came over the sound system, informing the passengers that the flight would take a little over thirteen hours. Fran reached up behind her, checked the scrunchie in her hair. The tiny micro SD card was still there, tucked between the fabric and elastic.

"We could do what they said," she said. "Stay quiet. Spend the rest of our lives in Hawaii on their hush money."

"Someone has to be accountable, Fran. Don't you think?"

Fran nodded. That's what she'd hoped Josh would say.

"And what if they come after us?" she asked.

Josh reached over, took her hand with his good one.

"If we survived this night, we can survive anything."

She looked at him. "Together?"

"Together."

Fran closed her eyes, rested her head against Josh's shoulder, and, for the first time since her husband died, allowed herself to hope.

Taylor opened his eyes. He was still in the tube, and his head was killing him. The last thing he remembered was that bitch, Fran, dropping a rock on his face. Taylor reached up to feel the damage.

Except his arm didn't work.

He tried his other arm and had identical results. He

tried to turn around, but his legs, his toes, his ass: everything below his neck refused to move.

She'd paralyzed him. The bitch had paralyzed him.

Rage came first. Then panic. Then rage again. Then depression.

Minutes passed. Hours. The sun came up.

Taylor stared up at the sky, tears streaking down his face, and waited for those military assholes to find him. They'd help. After all, they were all on the same side. Maybe this wasn't a permanent injury. Maybe something was just out of place. They could fix him. They could fix him and he'd track down that bitch and—

The coyote stopped a few yards away. Lean and gray, eyes intent. It stared at Taylor and sniffed the air.

"Get the fuck away from me!" he yelled.

The animal stayed where it was. Watching. Waiting.

A moment later, another one joined it.

Taylor shook his head and snarled. He shouted. He swore.

The two became three. Then four. The one who arrived first, the original one, came closer. So close that Taylor could smell his musky fur, his meaty breath. The coyote paused, then licked Taylor's bloody cheek.

"Get away!"

It bit his shirt and began to pull. Two others joined in, jerking and tugging him out of the tube, dragging him to the dry creek bed.

They started on his fingers.

Taylor screamed and screamed and screamed for help. He screamed until his throat bled.

No help came.

ABOUT THE AUTHOR

Jack Kilborn prefers not to share personal details about his life. He could be living anywhere. Possibly near you. Visit him at www.JackKilborn.com.

More chilling horror from

JACK KILBORN

Please turn this page
for a preview of

TRAPPED

Available Winter 2010

Sara Randhurst felt her stomach roll starboard as the boat yawed port, and she put both hands on the railing and took a big gulp of fresh, lake air. She wasn't anywhere near Cindy's level of discomfort—that poor girl had been heaving nonstop since they left land—but she was a long way from feeling her best.

Sara closed her eyes, bending her knees slightly to absorb some of the pitch and roll. The nausea reminded Sara of her honeymoon. She and Martin had booked a Caribbean cruise, and their first full day as a married couple found both of them vomiting veal piccata and wedding cake into the Pacific. Lake Huron was smaller than the ocean, the wave crests not as high and troughs not as low. But they came faster and choppier, which made it almost as bad.

Sara opened her eyes, searching for Martin. The only one on deck was Cindy Welp, still perched over the railing. Sara approached the teen on wobbly footing, then rubbed her back. Cindy's blond hair looked perpetually greasy, and her eyes were sunken and her skin colorless; more a trait of her addiction to meth than the seasickness.

"How are you doing?" Sara asked.

Cindy wiped her mouth on her sleeve. "Better. I don't think there's anything left in me."

Cindy proved herself a liar a moment later, pulling away and retching once again. Sara gave her one last reassuring pat, then padded her way carefully up to the bow. The charter boat looked deceptively smaller before they'd gotten on. But there was a lot of space onboard; both a foredeck and an aft deck, a raised bow, plus two levels below boasting six rooms. Though they'd been sailing for more than two hours, Sara had only run into four of their eight-person party. Martin wasn't one of them. It was almost like he was hiding.

Which, she supposed, he had reason to do.

A swell slapped the boat sideways, spritzing Sara with water. It tasted clean, just like the air. A gull cried out overhead, a wide white M against the shocking blue of sky. Sara squinted west, toward the sun. It was getting low over the lake, turning the clouds pink and orange, hinting at a spectacular sunset to come. A month ago, when she and Martin had planned this trip, staring at such a sun would have made her feel alive and loved. Watching it now made Sara sad. A final bow before the curtain closes for good.

Sara continued to move forward, her gym shoes slippery, and the warm summer breeze already drying the spray on her face. At the prow, Sara saw Tom Gransee, bending down like he was trying to touch the water rushing beneath them.

"Tom! Back in the boat, please."

Tom spun around, saw Sara, and grinned. Then he took three quick steps and skidded across the wet deck like a skateboarder. Tom's medication didn't quite control his ADHD, and the teenager was constantly in motion. He even twitched when he slept.

"No running!" Sara called after him, but he was already on the other side of the cabin, heading below.

Sara peeked at the sun once more, retied the flapping floral print shirttails across her flat belly, and headed after Tom.

As she descended the tight staircase, the mechanical roar of the engine overtook the calm sound of the waves. The captain was the ninth person on the boat, and Sara hadn't seen him lately either. Her only meeting with him was during their brief but intense negotiation when they arrived at the dock. He was a short, grizzled old man, tanned and wrinkled, and he fought with Martin about their destination, insisting on taking them someplace closer than Rock Island. He only relented after they agreed to bring a radio along, in case of emergencies.

Sara wondered where the captain was now. She assumed he was on the bridge, but didn't know where to find it. Maybe Martin was with him. Sara wasn't sure if her desire to speak with Martin was to console him or persuade him. Perhaps both. Or maybe they could simply spend a few moments together without talking. Sara could remember when silence between them was a healthy thing.

A skinny door flew open, and Meadowlark Purcell burst out. Meadow had a pink scar across the bridge of his flattened nose, a disfigurement from when he was *blooded in* to a Detroit street gang. The boy narrowed his dark brown eyes at Sara, then smiled in recognition.

"Hey, Sara. I be you, I wouldn't go in there for a while." He fanned his palm in front of his nose.

"I'm looking for Martin. Seen him?"

Meadow shook his head. "I be hangin' with Laneesha and Tyrone, playin' cards. We gonna be there soon?"

"Captain said two and a half hours, and we're getting near that point."

"True dat?"

"Yes."

"Cool."

Meadow wandered off. Sara closed the bathroom door and tried the one next to it. In the darkness she made out the shape of a chubby girl asleep on a skinny bed. Georgia. Sara tried the next door. Another cabin, this one empty. After a brief hesitation, Sara went into the room, pulled the folding bed away from the wall, and laid down.

The waves weren't as pronounced down here, and the rocking motion was gentler. Sara again thought of her honeymoon with Martin. How, once they got their sea legs, they spent all of their time on the ship, in their tiny little cabin, skipping exotic ports to instead order room service and make love. After a rough beginning, it turned out to be a perfect trip.

Sara closed her eyes, and wished it could be like that again.

I t was a night exactly like tonight, ten years ago," Martin said. "Late summer. Full moon. Just before midnight. The woods were quiet. Quiet, but not completely silent. It's never completely silent in the woods. It seems like it is, because we're all used to the city. But there are always night sounds. Sounds that only exist when the sun goes down and the dark takes over. Everyone shut your eyes and listen for a moment."

Sara indulged her husband, letting her eyelids close. Gone were the noises so common in Detroit; cars honking, police sirens, arguing drunks and cheering Tigers fans and bursts of live music when bar doors swung open. Instead, here on the island, there were crickets. A breeze whistling through the pines. An owl. The gentle snaps and crackles of the campfire they sat around.

After a few seconds someone belched.

"My bad," Tyrone said, raising his hand.

This prompted laughter from almost everyone, Sara included. Martin kept his expression solemn, not breaking character. Seeing Martin like that made Sara remember why she fell in love with him. Her husband had always been passionate about life, and gave everything his all, whether it was painting the garage, starting a business, or telling silly campfire stories to scare their kids.

Her smile faded. They won't be *their kids* for very much longer.

"It happened on an island," Martin continued. "Just like this one. In fact, now that I think about it, this might actually *be* the island where it all happened."

Tyrone snorted. "This better not be the same island, dog, or my black ass is jumping in that mofo lake 'n' swimming back to civilization."

More laughter, but this time it was clipped. Uneasy. These teenagers had never been this far from an urban environment, and weren't sure how to act.

Sara shivered, zipping her sweatshirt up in front. All the things she wanted to say to Martin earlier were still bottled up inside because she didn't have the chance. Since the boat dropped them off, it had been all about hiking and setting up camp and eating dinner. Sara hadn't been alone with him once. He'd been intentionally avoiding her. But she hadn't really tried that hard to corner him, either. Sara didn't want to have *the talk* any more than he did.

"Was it really this island?" Laneesha asked. Her voice

was condescending, almost defiant. But there was a bit of edge to it, a tiny hint of fear.

"No, it wasn't," Sara said. "Martin, tell her it wasn't."

Martin didn't say anything, but he did give Laneesha a sly wink.

"So where was it?" Georgia asked.

"It wasn't anywhere, Georgia." Sara slapped at a mosquito that had been biting her neck, then wiped the tiny splot of blood onto her jeans. "This is a campfire story. It's made up, to try to scare you."

"It's fake?" Georgia asked. "Pretend?"

Sara nodded. "Yes, it's pretend. Right, Martin?"

Martin shrugged, still not looking at Sara.

"So what pretend-happened?" Laneesha asked.

"Eight people," Martin said. He was sitting on an old tree stump, higher up than everyone else. "Camping just like we are. On a night like tonight. On what might be this very island. They vanished, these eight, never to be seen again. But some folks who live around here claim to know what happened. Some say those unfortunate eight people were subjected to things worse than death."

Meadow folded his arms. "Ain't nothin' worse than death."

Martin stared hard at the teenager. "There are plenty of things worse."

No one spoke for a moment. Sara felt a chill. Maybe it was the cool night breeze, whistling through the woods. Or maybe it was Martin's story, which she had to admit was getting sort of creepy. But Sara knew the chill actually went deeper. As normal as everyone seemed right now, it was only an illusion. Their little family was breaking apart.

But she didn't want to think about that. Now, she wanted to enjoy this final camping trip, to make some good memories.

Sara scooted a tiny bit closer to the campfire and hugged her knees. The night sky was clear, the stars bright against the blackness of space, the hunter's moon huge and tinged red. Beyond the smoke Sara could smell the pine trees from the surrounding woods, and the big water of Huron, a hundred yards to the west. As goodbyes went, this was a lovely setting for one.

She let her eyes wander over the group. Tyrone Morrow, seventeen, abandoned by parents who could no longer control him, running with one of Motor City's worst street gangs for more than two years. Dressed in a hoodie and jeans so baggy he has to walk with one hand holding them up.

Meadow was on Tyrone's right. He was from a rival Detroit club. That they were sitting next to each other was a commitment from each on how much they wanted out of the gangsta life.

On Meadow's side, holding his hand, Laneesha Simms. Her hair was cropped almost as short as the boys', but her make-up and curves didn't allow anyone to mistake her for a man.

Georgia Dailey sat beside Laneesha. Sixteen, white, brunette, pudgy.

Tom Gransee predictably paced around the fire, tugging at his sleeveless tee like it was an extra skin he wanted to shed.

These were kids society had given up on, sentenced into their care by the courts. But Martin—and by extension, Sara—hadn't given up on them. That was why they created the Second Chance Center.

Sara finally rested her gaze on Martin. The fire flickered across his handsome features, glinted in his blue eyes. He had aged remarkably well, looking thirty rather than forty, as athletic as the day she met him in a graduate psych class twelve years ago.

"On this dark night ten years ago," Martin continued, "this group of eight people took a boat onto Lake Huron. The SS Minnow."

Sara smiled, knowing she was the only one old enough to have caught the *Gilligan's Island* reference, the boat the castaways had taken on their three-hour tour.

"They had some beer with them," Martin said. "Some pot . . ."

"Hells yeah." Tyrone and Meadow bumped fists.

". . . and were set to have a big party. But one of the women—there were four men and four women, just like us—got seasick on the lake."

"I hear that." In her oversized jersey and sweatpants, Cindy looked tiny, shapeless. But Sara noted she'd gotten a little bit of her color back.

"So they decided," Martin raised his voice, "to beach the boat on a nearby island, continue the party there. But they didn't know the island's history."

Tom had stopped his pacing and was standing still, rare for him. "What history, Martin?"

Martin smiled. An evil smile, his chin down and his eyes hooded, the shadows drawing out his features and making him look like an angry wolf.

"In 1862, a prison was built on this island to house captured Confederate soldiers. Like many Civil War prisons, the conditions were horrible. But this one was worse than most. It was run by a war profiteer named Mordecai Plincer. He stole the money that was supposed to be used to feed the prisoners, and ordered his guards to beat them so they wouldn't stage an uprising while they starved to death. He didn't issue blankets, even during the winter months, giving them nothing more to wear than sacks with arms and leg holes cut out, even when temperatures dropped to below freezing."

Sara wasn't a history buff, but she was pretty sure there had never been a Civil War prison on an island in Lake Huron. She wondered if Martin was using Camp Douglas as the source of this tall tale. It was located in Chicago near Lake Michigan and considered the northern counterpart to the horrors committed at the Confederate prison, Andersonville. Yes, Martin had to be making this up. Though that name, Plincer, did sound familiar.

Martin tossed one of the logs they'd cut earlier onto the fire. It made a *whump* sound, throwing sparks and cinders.

"But those starving, tortured prisoners staged a rebellion anyway, killing all the guards, driving Plincer from the island. The Union, desperate to cover up their mistake, stopped sending supplies. But the strongest and craziest of the prisoners survived. Even though the food ran out."

"How?" Tom asked. "You said there are no animals on this island."

Martin smiled, wickedly. "They survived . . . *by eating each other.*"

"Oh, snap." Tyrone shook his head. "That shit is sick."

Sara raised an eyebrow at her husband. "Cannibalism, Martin?"

Martin looked at her, in what felt like the first time in hours. She searched for some softness, some love, but he was all wrapped up in his menace act.

"Some were cooked. Some were eaten raw. And during the summer months, when meat would spoil, some were kept alive so they could be eaten piece by piece."

Sara did a quick group check, wondering if this story was getting too intense. Everyone appeared deadly serious, their eyes laser-focused on Martin. No one seemed upset. A little scared, maybe, but these were tough kids. She decided to let Martin keep going.

Martin stood up, spreading out his hands. "Over the last five decades, more than a hundred people have vanished on this part of Lake Huron. Including those four men and women. What happened to them was truly horrible."

The crickets picked that eerie moment to stop chirping.

Cindy eventually broke the silence. "What happened to them?"

"It's said that these prisoners became more animal than human, feeding on each other and on those men unlucky enough to visit the island. Unfortunately for this group of eight partyers, they were all doomed the minute they set foot onto Plincer's Island. When their partying died down, and everyone was drunk and stoned and passing out, the killers built a gridiron."

The word *gridiron* hung in the air like a crooked painting, blending into the forest sounds.

Tyrone whispered, "They built a football field?"

Martin shakes his head. "The term *gridiron* is used for football these days, but it's a much older word. It was a form of execution in ancient Rome. A layer of coals are spread on the ground, stoked until they're red-hot. Then the victim is put in a special iron cage, sort of like a grill, and placed on top of the coals, roasting him or her alive. Unlike being burned at the stake, which is over in a few minutes, it takes hours to die on the gridiron. They say the liquid in your eyes gets so hot, it boils."

"That's enough, Martin." Sara stood up and folded her arms across her chest. "You've succeeded in freaking everyone out. Now who wants to roast some marshmallows?"

"I want to hear what happened to those people," Tom said.

"And I want to be able to sleep tonight," Sara replied.

Sara's eyes met Martin's. She saw intensity there, but also resignation. Eventually his lips curled into a smile.

"But we haven't gotten to the part where I pretend to be dragged off into the woods, kicking and screaming. That's the best part."

Sara placed her hands on her hips. "I'm sure we would have all been terrified."

Martin sat back down. "You're the boss. And if the boss wants to do marshmallows, who am I to argue?"

"I thought you're the one who created the Center," Laneesha asked.

Martin glanced at Sara. There was kindness in his eyes, and maybe some resignation, too.

"Sara and I created it together. We wanted to make a difference. The system takes kids who are basically good but made a few mistakes, sticks them into juvie, and they come out full-blown crooks. The Center is aimed at taking these kids and helping them change." Martin smiled sadly. "Well, that *was* its purpose."

"It's bullshit the man cut your funding, Martin." Meadow tossed a stick onto the fire.

"It sucks," Cindy added.

There were nods of agreement. Martin shrugged. "Things like this happen all the time. I'm sorry I couldn't do more for you kids. Sara and I don't have any children of our own, but you guys are like our—"

Martin screamed in mid-sentence, then fell backward off the log, rolling into the bushes and the darkness.

Sara, like everyone else, jolted at the sound and violent action. Then laughter broke out, followed by a few of the teens clapping.

"That was awesome, Martin!" Tom yelled into the woods. "It think I wet my freakin' pants."

The applause and giggles died down. Sara waited for Martin to lumber out of the woods and take a bow.

But Martin stayed hidden.

"Martin, you can come out now."

Sara listened. The woods, the whole island, was deathly quiet.

"Martin? You okay?"

No answer.

"Come on, Martin. Joke's over."

After a moment the crickets began their song again. But there was no response from Martin.

"Fine," she called out. "We're not saving you any marshmallows."

The forest was silent. Sara picked up the bag of marshmallows and began passing them out, the kids busying themselves with attaching the treats to the sticks they'd picked out earlier. If her husband wanted to screw around in the woods, he was welcome to do so.

"Now what?" Tyrone asked, raising his like a sword.

"You put it in the fire," Tom said. "Duh."

"Ain't never roasted marshmallows before, white boy."

"It's like this, Tyrone." Sara held her stick six inches above the flame. "Like we did with the hot dogs. And keep turning it, so it browns evenly on all sides."

Everyone followed her lead. Sara allowed herself a small, private smile. These were the moments they came out here for. Everyone getting along. No fighting. Criminal pasts momentarily forgotten. Just six kids acting like kids.

"Mine fell off," Cindy said.

"Wouldn't eat it no how. Oughta change yo name to Annie Rekzic."

"Respect," Sara reminded Meadow.

"Sorry. My bad."

There was a comfortable silence. Sara forced herself to stay in the moment, not look over her shoulder for Martin. He'd come back when he was ready.

"I'm on fire." Georgia held her stick and mouth level and blew hard on the burning marshmallow. Then she bit into it carefully. "Mmm. Gooey."

"Like an eyeball on the gridiron." Tom plucked his off the stick and pretended it was oozing out of his eye socket.

"Awful way to die," Cindy said. "Guy I knew, had an ice lab in his basement. He died like that. When he was cooking a batch it blew up in his face. Burned him down to the bone."

"You see it?" Tyrone asked.

"Cops told me about it."

Tyrone frowned, his face looking ten years older. "Saw a brother die, once. Drive-by. Right next door to me. I was eight years old."

"I saw someone die, too," Tom said.

Tyrone sneered. "Man, yo gramma doesn't count."

"Does too. I was there. Does it count, Sara?"

"It counts. And let's try to talk about something other than death for a while."

"Damn." Meadows stuck out his tongue. "My shit is burned. Tastes nasty."

"I like the burned ones." Georgia held out her hand. Meadows passed it over. "Thanks."

Sara bit into hers. The perfect combination of sweet and toasty. She loaded up another one, then felt her neck prickle, like she was being watched. Sara turned around, peering into the trees. She saw only blackness.

"When is Martin coming back?" Cindy was poking her stick into the fire. She still hadn't replaced her lost marshmallow.

"He's probably just beyond the trees," Sara said. "Waiting to jump out and scare us again."

"What if someone grabbed him?"

"Cindy, no one grabbed him. We're the only ones on this island."

"You sure?"

Sara made an exaggerated motion out of crossing her heart. "And hope to die."

"What if he had an accident?" Cindy persisted. "Maybe hit his head on a rock or something?"

Sara pursed her lips. There was a slight chance, but it could have happened.

"Tyrone, can you go check?"

Tyrone sneered. "You want me to go in those woods so he can jump out 'n scare the soul outta brother? No way."

Sara sighed, and just for the sake of argument she let her imagination run unchecked. What if Martin's little stunt really had gone wrong and he'd hurt himself? What if he'd fallen into a hole? What if a bear got him? There wasn't supposed to be any bear on this island—according to Google, there wasn't supposed to be any animal here larger than a raccoon. But what if Google was wrong?

She sighed. Her imagination had won. Even if this was a stupid trick on Martin's part, Sara still had to go check.

"Fine. I'll do it." She got up, handed her stick to Cindy, and dusted off her jeans, staring into the darkness of the woods surrounding them.

And the woods were dark. Very dark.

The confidence Sara normally wore like a lab coat suddenly fell away, and she realized the very last thing in the world she wanted to do was tread into that darkness.

"Tom, can you help me look?"

Tom shook his head. "He can stay out there. I'm not leaving the fire."

"Ain't got no balls, white boy?"

"You go then, Meadow."

"Hells no. At this particular time, Laneesha be holding my balls."

Laneesha rolled her eyes and stood up. "Y'all are cowards. C'mon, Sara. We'll go find him."

Sara blew out the breath she'd been holding, surprised by how grateful she was for the girl's offer. "There's a flashlight in one of the packs. I'll find it."

She walked over to her tent and ducked inside. It was

dim, but the fire provided enough illumination to look around. Sara cast a wistful glance at the double sleeping bag. She tugged her eyes away, then located the backpack. Pawing through the contents, she removed a canteen, a first-aid kit, some wool socks, a bottle of Goniosol medication, a hunting knife, the papers . . .

Sara squinted at them, staring at the bottom of the last page. It was unsigned. Irritated, she shoved them back in. She eventually dug out the Maglite, pressing the button on the handle. The light came on. It was yellowish and weak—which annoyed Sara even more because she told Martin to buy new batteries.

Putting the papers out of her mind for the time being, she left the tent and joined Laneesha, who was staring into the woods where Martin disappeared.

"If you see any cannibals," Tom said to their backs, "don't tell him we're here."

"Y'all are weak," Laneesha said.

Sara eyed her, normally cocky and busting with attitude, and saw uncertainty all over the girl's face.

"The story was fake, Laneesha."

"That Plincer cat ain't real?"

"He might be real. The name is familiar. But the way to make campfire stories sound believable is to mix a little truth with the lies."

"How 'bout all them cannibal soldiers, eating people?"

"Even if that was true, and it wasn't, it happened over a hundred and forty years ago. They'd all be long dead."

"So Martin just joshin'?"

"He's probably just waiting to jump out and scare us," Sara said.

"Prolly. That'd suck, but be better than someone grabbing him."

Sara raised an eyebrow. That possibility was so far out she hadn't even considered it. "Did you see someone grab him?"

"It was dark, 'n' he was right in front of that bush. Thought maybe I seen somethin', but prolly just my mind playing tricks 'n' shit."

Now Sara was *really* reluctant to go into the woods. She knew the Confederate story was BS, but wondered if perhaps someone else was on the island.

That's crazy, Sara thought. *There's no one here but us.*

There were over a hundred of these islands on Lake Huron, from the size of a football field up to thousands of acres. This was one of the big ones, a supposed wildlife refuge. But there was no electricity, and it was too far from the mainland for there to be anyone living here.

Other campers?

Sara reminded herself to be rational. Occam's Razor. The simplest solution was usually the right one. Martin joking around made much more sense than unknown habitants, or coincidental campers, or old Warden Plincer and his imaginary gang of southern maniacs.

Still, they did have that radio the boat captain gave them. Sara wondered if her husband goofing off qualified as an emergency, because she was almost ready to contact the captain and beg him to return.

"Let's do this," Laneesha said.

Sara nodded. Practically hip to hip, the women walked around the bushes and stepped into the thick of the woods.

When they'd hiked to the clearing earlier that afternoon, the woods had been dark. There were so many trees the canopy blocked out most of the sun. Now, at midnight, it was darker than anything Sara had ever experienced. The blackness enveloped them, thick as ink, and the fading Maglite barely pierced it more than a few yards.

"Be easy getting lost out here," Laneesha said.

Sara played the light across the trees, looking for the red ribbon. They'd tied dozens of ribbons around trunks, in a line leading from the campsite to the shore, so anyone who got lost could find their way back. But in this total darkness every tree looked the same, and she couldn't find a single ribbon. Sara had a very real fear that if they traveled too far into the woods, they wouldn't be able to find their way back to the rest of the group. After only a dozen steps she could no longer see the campfire behind them.

"Tyrone, Cindy, can you guys hear me?" she called out.

"We hear you! You find any cannibals yet?"

Neither Sara nor Laneesha shared in the ensuing chuckles. They trekked onward, dead leaves and branches crunching underfoot, an owl hooting somewhere in the distance.

Sara had always been ambivalent about camping, having only gone a few times in her life. But now she realized she hated it. Hated camping, hated the woods, and hated the dark.

But she had hated the dark for a very long time. And with damn good reason.

"Martin," Sara said, projecting into the woods, "this isn't funny. It's stupid, and dangerous."

She waited for a reply.

No reply came.

"I like Martin," Laneesha said, "but fuck 'em. I'm a city girl. I don't do creeping 'round the forest at night. This is a total bad idea."

Sara agreed. There was no hole or trench around here he could have fallen into, and if Martin hit his head he'd be lying nearby.

Still, if this was a prank, it was being taken too far. It wasn't funny anymore. It was just plain mean.

And then Sara understood what was happening, and she felt her face flush.

Her husband was doing this because he was angry.

Is this how it's going to be? Sara thought. *Rather than act like the caring adult she fell in love with, he's going to start behaving like a jerk?*

Well, two could play that game.

"You can stay out there!" she yelled.

Her voice echoed through the trees, fading and dying. Then . . .

"elll . . ."

The sound was faint, coming from far ahead of them.

"Wassat Martin?" Laneesha asked.

Sara squinted, crinkling her nose. "I'm not sure. Could have been an animal."

"Sounded like *help*. Know any animals that call for help?"

"Martin!" Sara shouted into the trees.

There was no answer. Laneesha moved closer to Sara, so close Sara could feel the girl shivering.

"We should go back."

"What if it's Martin? He could need help."

"You the social worker. Y'all good at helping people.

I'm a single mom. I gotta take care of myself for my baby's sake. 'Sides, prolly just an animal."

"*help* . . ." The voice was still faint, but there was no mistaking it.

Martin. And he didn't sound angry. He sounded scared.

Sara began to walk toward the voice. "You go back to camp," she said to Laneesha. "Martin! I'm coming!"

The trees were so thick Sara couldn't walk in a straight line for more than a few steps. Even worse, the Maglite was getting dimmer. How far ahead could he be? Fifty yards? A hundred? The woods seemed to be closing in, swallowing her up. There was no red ribbon anywhere.

She stopped, trying to get her bearings. Sara couldn't even be sure this was the right direction anymore.

A rustling noise, to her left. Sara turned.

"Martin?"

Then something tackled Sara, something strong enough to knock the wind right out of her lungs. Before Sara could see what it was, the flashlight went flying and winked out.

VISIT US ONLINE
@ WWW.HACHETTEBOOKGROUP.COM.

AT THE HACHETTE BOOK GROUP WEB SITE YOU'LL FIND:

CHAPTER EXCERPTS FROM SELECTED NEW RELEASES

•

ORIGINAL AUTHOR AND EDITOR ARTICLES

•

AUDIO EXCERPTS

•

BESTSELLER NEWS

•

ELECTRONIC NEWSLETTERS

•

AUTHOR TOUR INFORMATION

•

CONTESTS, QUIZZES, AND POLLS

•

FUN, QUIRKY RECOMMENDATION CENTER

•

PLUS MUCH MORE!

BOOKMARK HACHETTE BOOK GROUP
@ WWW.HACHETTEBOOKGROUP.COM.